SWALLOW BARN

SWALLOW BARN;

OR,

A SOJOURN IN THE OLD DOMINION

John Pendleton Kennedy

With an Introduction by Lucinda H. MacKethan

Louisiana State University Press
Baton Rouge and London

Library of Congress Cataloging-in-Publication Data

Kennedy, John Pendleton, 1795–1870.
  Swallow barn, or, A sojourn in the Old Dominion.

  (The Library of Southern civilization)
    1. MacKethan, Lucinda Hardwick.   II. Title.
  III. Series.
  PS2162.S93   1986   813'.3   85-23215
  ISBN 0-8071-1322-0 (pbk.)

CONTENTS

ACKNOWLEDGMENT

I would like gratefully to acknowledge the kindness and interest of Edmund Pendleton Dandridge, Professor Emeritus of English at North Carolina State University, for allowing me to study private family papers relating to The Bower and especially for permission to quote from the unpublished memoir by Serena Catherine Dandridge.

INTRODUCTION

John Pendleton Kennedy's *Swallow Barn; or, A Sojourn in the Old Dominion* has been out of print many times since it first appeared in 1832. Yet this light period-piece by a Baltimore lawyer has somehow persistently refused to stay forgotten. Kennedy himself was willing to consign his first novel "to that oblivion which is common to books and men—out of sight, out of mind."[1] Not until 1851 did he bring out the revised edition that his publisher had recommended in 1835. Today, we can note how often the book has returned from oblivion and how varied have been the bases for each renewal of critical interest.

Swallow Barn's durability seems in some measure due to Kennedy's refusal to frame definite purposes for the book. In the preface to the 1851 edition, he said that his work could be described "as variously and interchangeably partaking of the complexion of a book of travels, a diary, a collection of letters, a drama, and a history." His persona Mark Littleton tells the friend to whom he plans to narrate his adventures that "you shall hear from me again presently; but whether in some descriptive pictures of this old dominion, or in dramatic sketches, or in a journal, or in some rambling letters, I cannot yet foretell."

From the first, then, *Swallow Barn* has resisted categorization. It is a novel that is not a novel, an unromantic romance, written by a man who was and was not a southerner, who was and was not even a writer, at least by his own reckoning. Published only a year after the slave Nat Turner led a bloody revolt against whites in tidewater Virginia, *Swallow Barn* was offered as a chronicle of a pleasant, peaceful plantation society located in that same Tidewater area. The 1830s would see the nation embroiled in sectional rivalry, yet *Swallow Barn* blithely sets a traveler from the North on a quest for southern entertainments, in the pursuit of which he manages merrily both to revere and to ridicule almost all of the Old South's icons. A New England reviewer of the first edition was able to take pleasure in *Swal-*

1. Quotations from *Swallow Barn*, including Prefaces, are from the 1851 edition unless otherwise noted.

low Barn because, he said, "the author intended to 'show up' the
Virginians." A reviewer from Kennedy's native Baltimore was just as
pleased, however, because he saw in the book "a portraiture of the
amiable and the natural, the domestic and cheerful."[2] Readers have
continued to find whatever they look for in *Swallow Barn*, a phenomenon that is indicative of the book's strengths as well as its
weaknesses.

Let us consider, first, some biographical information and some of
the cultural and literary forces that operated to make *Swallow Barn*
a unique and a representative product of its period. Then we will
take up questions of Kennedy's design for the novel, the ideological
and artistic choices that governed what is now regarded as the most
important fictional portrayal of plantation society by one intimately
involved in that place and time.

Some of *Swallow Barn*'s unusual degree of flexibility is undoubtedly a reflection of the author's personality and position. John
Pendleton Kennedy had to weigh contrasting values in his familial,
social, economic, and residential loyalties, but he nevertheless managed to act with equal ease in many different contexts. Born in Baltimore on October 25, 1795, he lived most of his life in Maryland, the
border state that looked north in pursuit of trade and manufacture
and south in its agricultural practices. Through his mother, née
Nancy Pendleton, he was allied to a thriving planter clan of old Virginia, aristocratic gentlemen and ladies whose plantations were
spread throughout the Shenandoah Valley–Berkeley County regions
of a state far more southern in its leanings than was Maryland.
Through his father, John Kennedy, he belonged to the Baltimore
merchant class. Although his father had come to America from
Northern Ireland, the Kennedys zealously traced their lineage back
to Scottish kings and earls. John Kennedy's business failures in 1809,
however, caused his family to depend on his wife's Virginia landhold-
ings from that time on. Through his father, then, John Pendleton
Kennedy knew well the nature of economic difficulties.

By his two marriages, Kennedy strengthened his ties to Balti-

2. "Swallow Barn," *New England Magazine*, III (1832), 79; Baltimore
American (1832), quoted in J. V. Ridgely, *John Pendleton Kennedy* (New
York, 1966), 42.

more and to merchant families much more successful than his own. In 1824 he married Mary Tenant, daughter of one of the most prominent men in Baltimore. Nine months later, she died in childbirth, and their infant son died within a year. He married a second time in 1829. His new wife, Elizabeth Gray, was the daughter of a self-made man of fortune, Edward Gray, who succeeded in textile manufacturing and helped to provide financial security for his son-in-law and daughter for the rest of their lives. Gray loved to play the feudal lord at his factory outside Baltimore, but he opposed slavery and distrusted southerners as idlers.

Baltimore became Kennedy's permanent home, and he took Gray's political and economic preferences as his own, but his Virginia relatives and their plantations kept a strong hold on his sympathies and his imagination. A mountain-bound plantation named The Bower, located near Martinsburg, now in West Virginia, provided the setting that helps create the allure of Kennedy's first novel. Owned by his mother's sister and her husband, The Bower became his parents' home in 1825. Although Kennedy was by then committed to his Baltimore career as lawyer-businessman-politician, his earlier visits to The Bower stirred his desire to capture its way of life. Even in 1828 he saw that that existence in Virginia was fading away. "How completely the elegancies of society and the best points of a luxurious mode of living, have been invaded by a stiff, awkward, and *churchly* morality," he complained to Elizabeth Gray.[3]

Kennedy moved between two very different realms, one steeped in agrarian tradition and communal values, the other energetically determined to turn villages into glittering cities, a provincial federation of states into a commercial world power. The attractions each held for him reflect the directions that America itself was choosing during his lifetime. The change in the nation's sense of its destiny was largely accomplished during the 1820s, the decade that saw Kennedy deciding to live in the world of the future but to write about the one area he knew that was still hanging on, however tenuously, to a more gracious past.

In the 1820s the frontier opened beyond the Virginia mountains

3. John Pendleton Kennedy to Elizabeth Gray, August 19, 1828, in Charles Bohner, *John Pendleton Kennedy* (Baltimore, 1961), 76.

that shadowed The Bower; the frontiersman-warrior Andrew Jackson took the reins of government from the traditionally privileged class; and the East turned increasingly to trade and manufacture, so that slavery would find ever fewer supporters north of Maryland. In *Swallow Barn*, Kennedy includes a Fourth of July celebration that shows his nation's as well as his region's confusion over identity. During the course of the festivities, the men of the community gather to discuss new currents in government. They are asking, in essence, how shall a small, rurally oriented community respond to the irreverent Old Hickory and a government that wants "to cut up our orchards and meadows, whether or no"? "What's the use of states," one country philosopher asks, "if they are all to be cut up with canals and railroads and tariffs?"

The American sense of split identity that prevailed in the 1820s is well illustrated by two of Kennedy's important literary friendships— with Washington Irving and Edgar Allan Poe. The cosmopolitan, popular, yet conservative Irving was, with James Fenimore Cooper, the only successful professional writer of fiction in America in 1832. Edgar Allan Poe, however, whose materials were as unique as Irving's were derivative, was without family, fortune, and almost without friends. Yet he became America's first great fiction writer, with no small assistance from Kennedy.

Kennedy would claim kinship with Irving in more than one way (he found that he and Irving were related by blood through Scottish ancestors). More important, Kennedy used in *Swallow Barn* the "sketchbook" design that Irving often employed to pull his tales together in books. In particular, *Bracebridge Hall*, with its sketches of the life and times of an English squire, bears so many similarities to *Swallow Barn* that when Kennedy published his book under the pseudonym Mark Littleton, many reviewers attributed the work to Irving. Kennedy did not meet the acknowledged dean of American literature until 1833, after he had sent Irving a copy of his novel. The two became close friends, and Irving even visited The Bower with Kennedy. To Mrs. Kennedy, Irving once wrote that her husband took pride "in showing the world that a literary man can be a man of business," and he urged Kennedy as late as 1853 to take his writing more seriously, "to write diligently now for a few years on some good work." Like Irving, Kennedy looked to eighteenth-century neoclassical humorists, particularly Addison and Goldsmith, for a narrative voice that was quietly charming, for scenes crowded with picturesque detail, and for a tone gently satirical of the foibles of provincial characters. Like Irving too, Kennedy was an established figure in society, a man conservative in his tastes, a convivial observer of country scenes. In aim, however, Kennedy was far more serious than Irving was, and far less romantic as well. As William S. Osborne has shown, some scenes in *Swallow Barn* constitute a "deliberate burlesque" of Irving's love of remoteness and his preference for romantic lore over the everyday pursuits of real people.[4] Although Irving could announce that the impetus for his writing was a longing "to escape, in short, from the commonplace realities of the present," Kennedy, in his 1832 preface, asserted that he was attempting to catch the mood of "the ordinary actions of men, in their household intercourse." In his 1851 preface, looking back at his achievement and the world he had tried to mirror, Kennedy would sense that *Swallow Barn* was itself "a relic of the past," yet he still claimed that it was "a faithful picture of the people, the modes of life, and the scenery of a region full of attraction, and exhibiting the lights and shades of its society with the truthfulness of a painter who has studied his subject on the spot."

A comparison between Irving and Kennedy reveals some borrowing and debts as well as some inventiveness on Kennedy's part. His other significant literary friendship, with the outcast rebel Poe, shows the limits of his originality but also confirms his sharp insights as a literary critic. Kennedy's acquaintance with Poe began in 1833, when Kennedy served on a panel charged with awarding fifty dollars for the best prose tale submitted to a contest sponsored by a Baltimore weekly, the *Saturday Visiter*. Kennedy's friend and fellow judge John Latrobe read aloud from one entry, a small quarto-bound collection called *Tales of the Folio Club*, and all the judges responded with enthusiasm. "MS. Found in a Bottle" received the prize, and Poe found in Kennedy a mentor whose value to him is

---

4. William S. Osborne, Introduction to *Swallow Barn* (New York, 1962), xxxii.

recorded in a comment by Poe in 1836: "I know that without your timely aid I should have sunk under my trials."[5]

Kennedy was especially impressed with Poe's "classical and scholar-like" virtuosity and recommended him to T. W. White of Richmond, Virginia, the owner of the *Southern Literary Messenger*, as "highly imaginative, and a little given to the *terrific*." Yet in temperament as well as circumstances, no two people could have been more different than Kennedy and Poe. In one particularly despairing letter, Poe asked Kennedy to "console me—for you can. But let it be quickly—or it will be too late." How, we wonder, did he find consolation in Kennedy's prompt, concerned, but sadly mechanical reply: "Rise early, live generously, and make cheerful acquaintances and I have no doubt you will send these misgivings of the heart all to the Devil." The early-rising, generous, cheerful Kennedy could not see that the "brooding and boding inclination" of Poe's mind constituted his genius as well as his curse. Yet when Poe died, Kennedy knew better than most how to rank him: "Poor Poe!" he wrote in his journal. "He was an original and exquisite poet, and one of the best prose critics in this country. His works are among the very best of their kind."

The sunny, placid environs of the Meriwether plantation in *Swallow Barn* are a million miles distant from Poe's haunted, nightmare landscapes. Indeed, it has been suggested that Poe's depiction of Roderick Usher and his decaying mansion represents a tormented inversion of the southern planter's world. Because Kennedy's and Poe's visions were so different, it is all the more intriguing to find one scene in *Swallow Barn* that is similar to material in "MS. Found in a Bottle." Near the end of *Swallow Barn*, tired perhaps of satirizing his hero's half-chivalrous, half-clownish courtship, Kennedy drops Ned Hazard's story and turns to another rather surprising hero—a slave named Abe whose unruly behavior led to his being sent to serve a Chesapeake pilot. Out at sea Abe reforms, becomes a skilled, intrepid pilot, and finally meets a hero's fate when his vessel is lost in the daring attempted rescue of a brig stranded in the bay

5. All quotations concerning Kennedy and Poe are from the excellent discussion by Jay B. Hubbell in his Introduction to *Swallow Barn* (New York, 1929), xvi–xxi.

during a fierce winter storm. Only one member of Abe's crew survives, by binding himself to a spar that carries him to shore. He tells a strange story of how, during the terrifying night, Abe's ship was passed three times by a "spectre" ship, which each time called out an "awful salutation." The third contact with the apparition brought disaster. Abe's ship "parted at every joint, and all, except the relator himself, were supposed to have been ingulfed in the wave."

In "MS. Found in a Bottle," Poe's narrator too sees a phantom ship bearing down across stormy seas upon his own struggling craft; he alone of the crew survives. When the two ships collide, he is thrown aboard the huge ghost vessel. Of course, both Kennedy and Poe were drawing on Coleridge's "The Rime of the Ancient Mariner" and its skeleton ship as well as on the popular Flying Dutchman legend that William Gilmore Simms and other antebellum writers used. In many later tales, Poe would develop intricate functions for gothic elements similar to what we see in "MS. Found in a Bottle," the first story to appear with his signature. Yet for Kennedy, the specter ship represents a rather odd departure, given his satiric treatment of superstition and folklore through Ned Hazard's tongue-in-cheek display of romantic love. When Kennedy incorporates Hafen Blok's ghost story into his book, he self-consciously gives the tale to a local rustic to tell, purely as a kind of digressive exercise in a mode that he himself is rejecting. He once commented to Poe that "you find a hundred *intense* writers for one *natural* one," and his own emphasis on the natural is reflected in his style and his subject matter. The romantic originality that Poe, Hawthorne, and Melville would display in the twenty years following *Swallow Barn*'s publication never tempted Kennedy. His two other novels, *Horse-Shoe Robinson* (1835) and *Rob of the Bowl* (1838), retreated to more traditional ground in their form—they proceeded along lines already well defined in the historical romances of Scott and Cooper.

Except for the long story "A Legend of Maryland" (1860), which James Russell Lowell placed in the *Atlantic Monthly*, Kennedy published no new fiction after 1838, surrendering the territory of the southern historical romance to Simms. We have no reason to believe that Kennedy could not have done at least as well as Simms in a career as a writer. Nonetheless, Simms's own admission that "the

South don't care a d——n for literature or art" helps to explain why Kennedy abandoned an unpredictable future in a field that caused Simms lifelong frustration.[6] By the time the Civil War separated Kennedy the staunch Unionist more or less permanently from the Old South, he had already become a stellar success in politics and law, which, unlike fiction writing, the South revered as professions. Kennedy served as representative and speaker in his state legislature, as U.S. congressman from Maryland, as assistant secretary of state, and as Millard Fillmore's secretary of the navy.

Kennedy's reputation as a writer has been kept alive down to the present time largely because of his first book, *Swallow Barn*. Especially during recent years, when the historical models for the literature of the Southern Renaissance have increasingly been explored, *Swallow Barn* has emerged as "the literary origin of the plantation legend," as William R. Taylor said in *Cavalier and Yankee*. Literary historians such as Francis Pendleton Gaines, Jay B. Hubbell, Alexander Cowie, and Arthur Hobson Quinn have also asserted the prominence of *Swallow Barn* as the antebellum forerunner of the plantation novel that post-Reconstruction writers turned into the South's most effective propaganda weapon. Yet as Richard Beale Davis observes, Kennedy was actually working within a fairly well established tradition. Writing of a subgenre of fiction that he calls "the Virginia novel," Davis shows convincingly that although *Swallow Barn* is commonly assumed to be the first such work, there were "some four or five really significant Virginia novels in the thirty years before Kennedy published his loosely joined series of sketches of Virginia life." Davis offers a cogent description of this genre, for which *Swallow Barn* represents a kind of high-water mark in antebellum times: "This novel was romantic in general tone but often strongly realistic in detail, presenting stereotypes of a particular kind of lady and gentleman and young belle and beau, and including 'originals' and slaves (the last often comic or minstrel-show types). Frequently it was realistic in the same sense that Scott's novels were. . . . Its character stereotypes developed further into symbols

6. William Gilmore Simms to James Henry Hammond, December 24, 1847, in *The Letters of William Gilmore Simms*, ed. Mary S. Oliphant *et al.* (5 vols.; Columbia, S.C., 1953), II, 386.

of Virginia life and southern life. Its heirs in local-color romance, in fictional common-sense realism and ideality, and even in the social-problem novel are to be met with even in our time." Davis notes that the works preceding Kennedy's in this genre were all by native or resident Virginians. Among these, he discusses three books by John Davis, the Englishman who promoted the lore of Captain John Smith that Kennedy also found attractive; the anonymous *Tales of an American Landlord* and George Tucker's *The Valley of Shenandoah*, both published in 1824; and James Ewell Heath's *Edge-Hill*, published in 1828, which in its sentimentality looks forward better than *Swallow Barn* does to post-Reconstruction portrayals of the plantation.[7]

In addition, there are two other writers whose works reinforce *Swallow Barn*'s Virginia connection in its form. Certainly the novel's design owes much to Irving's *Bracebridge Hall*, yet James Kirke Paulding and William Wirt employ non-native, outsider narrators who relate visits to Virginia in the form of letters to nonsouthern audiences. Irving's good friend and a New York resident, Paulding in *Letters from the South* (1817) gave a northerner's impressions of Virginia that were formed during leisurely travels and set down in essaylike letters to a friend back in a northern city. Kennedy's friend and political mentor William Wirt, born in Maryland and later a successful Virginia lawyer and statesman as well as author, compared Kennedy's style in *Swallow Barn* to Paulding's. "Too much like Paulding's conceited style for my taste" was the way Wirt put it. Such criticism seems slightly ungracious when we consider that Kennedy dedicated *Swallow Barn* to Wirt and, in his dedicatory preface, named Wirt's own *The Letters of the British Spy* as a model for his book. Wirt's book was published anonymously in 1803. In a series of ten essaylike letters, an aristocratic Englishman uses his outsider position to comment wittily on several prominent Virginians. Wirt recommended Kennedy for political advancement in the 1820s, and Kennedy in 1849 would bring out a highly complimentary biography of Wirt, who, like himself, had sacrificed literary

7. William R. Taylor, *Cavalier and Yankee* (New York, 1963), 159; see Richard Beale Davis, *Literature and Society in Early Virginia, 1608–1840* (Baton Rouge, 1973), 233–56.

pursuits for work in government. Still, Wirt did not like *Swallow Barn*; he thanked Kennedy gracefully for the dedication, but he wrote another friend that the book had "too much verbage & too little matter."[8] Perhaps Wirt was annoyed to see himself mirrored, with slightly comic exaggeration, in a *Swallow Barn* character named Philly Wart.

The most popular fiction writers of Kennedy's time were Sir Walter Scott and James Fenimore Cooper. Certainly Kennedy, though to a lesser degree than Simms, included in his novels many of the motifs that these leaders in the historical-romance genre had used with such success. The stereotypical heroes and heroines, the trauma of star-crossed love (afforded comic treatment in *Swallow Barn*), the historically based class and cultural divisions, and the pastoral images of threatened rustic simplicity, all appear on Kennedy's stage and actually account for much of the unevenness as well as the charm of his books, and especially the first one. However, in examining Kennedy's literary accomplishments in *Swallow Barn*, we will be looking primarily toward those elements that make this work a unique response to the tensions that Kennedy's own particular time and place engendered.

Kennedy wrote *Swallow Barn* over a period of several years; in fact, some of the material was written as early as 1825. As many as five drafts of one chapter survive among Kennedy's papers, offering proof that in spite of his self-deprecating pose as a casual author, he worked diligently and consciously to produce his novel. And although *Swallow Barn* had several literary sources, it is also evident that Kennedy had much more than mere imitation in mind and that he took great pains to do justice to the world he chose to depict— the very real Virginia of his plantation kinfolk. Frank Meriwether might resemble Squire Bracebridge, but he was also clearly modeled on Kennedy's uncle Philip Clayton Pendleton, a southern gentleman in the classic style whom Kennedy admired tremendously. Bel Tracy, according to some of Kennedy's relatives, was modeled on one of his Dandridge cousins who lived at The Bower. And while the sprawling southern estate named Swallow Barn might,

8. William Wirt to Dabney Carr, May, 1832, in Osborne, Introduction to *Swallow Barn*, xxviii.

as some have argued, have been intended to suggest similarities between feudal English country life and southern plantation society, it
nevertheless had an actual counterpart in The Bower, a place whose
charms were very apparent to Kennedy.

A memoir written in 1893 by Kennedy's cousin Serena Catherine
Dandridge when she was in her fifties attests to the reverence that
family members felt for this ancestral home, which had been built
on land deeded to the first Adam Stephen Dandridge by Lord Fair-
fax. She writes of her family, who made their house a home to the
Kennedys: "In true cavalier spirit, the host and hostess welcomed
not only *their* friends but their *friend's* friends, to what was merrily
nicknamed Liberty Hall. The resources of the house were manifest,
fat cattle in the pastures, poultry in the surrounding hills, many gardens in the rich bottom-lands in front, with fifty servants always at
one's beck and call."[9]

Kennedy changed the location of his Bower from the western part
of Virginia, where the Dandridge estate nestled among forest hills,
to the Tidewater region, placing his fictionalized version on the
south shore of the James River. In an early draft, Mark Littleton
went directly to western Virginia, but Kennedy in his final draft
chose the Tidewater, partly because the traditional planter aristocracy there seemed unchanged or in decline while the area around
Martinsburg was becoming commercialized. Probably Kennedy also
hoped that the switch might make less recognizable some close resemblances between his fiction and the realities of life at The
Bower. In shifting his locale, however, Kennedy did not materially
alter the vision of plantation life that The Bower afforded. And although he had evidently intended, as he later told his publisher, "to
represent an old decayed place with odd and crotchety people in-
habiting it," the picture that emerges from *Swallow Barn*, while satiric, is also fondly loyal in its ultimate evaluation of the quality of
life on the plantation.[10]

Serena Dandridge tells us of The Bower that "the house is a noble

9. Serena Catherine Dandridge, Memoir (MS in possession of Edmund
Pendleton Dandridge, Raleigh, N.C.).
10. Kennedy to George P. Putnam, May 3, 1851, in Bohner, *John Pendleton Kennedy*, 78.

structure, built of brick, & it is in colonial fashion." Of the gardens
she says, "Back of the house lay numerous terraces and plots,
planned by the artistic taste of my grandmother. . . . We gloated on
the Paradisaical beauty of the beloved home & loved to put a wealth
of flowers about it." Her description of The Bower resembles the
plantation settings later created by Thomas Nelson Page for the
stories of *In Ole Virginia* (1887). Kennedy is often credited with
being the first to use the plantation house as an analogue of the Old
South's "Paradisaical" order; certainly his younger cousin, growing
up at The Bower, saw her plantation in that light.[11] Yet when we
read Kennedy's opening description of Swallow Barn, we see that he
meant this manor to be a microcosm of a society at once highly cul-
vated and provincial, narrow-minded and hospitable, formal and
disordered.

Especially in the 1832 edition of *Swallow Barn*, we see an author
looking with clear eyes at incongruities in the southern garden world
that the house itself reflects. Swallow Barn "squats like a brooding
hen" (19) on the southern bank of the James. After describing how
the family over the years added buildings onto the main brick structure, Kennedy in the first edition goes on to say that the additions
seem "ill at ease in that antiquated society" (20). In fact, the whole
"squat and frowning little mansion," he comments, "but for the family pride, would have long since been given over to the guardian
birds of the place" (21). In the 1832 and the 1851 edition, Kennedy
mentions a porch upheld by "massive columns" that have been
"split by the sun" ("sadly" split [I, 21], in 1832; "somewhat" split, in
1851). In the earlier edition, the house is encased in an atmosphere
of decay and melancholy, awkwardness and pretension. When Kennedy revised in 1850, he not surprisingly softened this impression,
leaving out, for instance, an extended description of a decrepit old
nag stabled in the "swallow" barn, "peering through the dark window of the stable, with spectral melancholy, his glassy eye moving
silently across the gloom" (I, 23).

In the 1851 edition, once well-launched into his portrayal of life
on the plantation, Kennedy satirizes the setting less and the charac-

11. Dandridge, Memoir (MS in possession of Edmund Pendleton
Dandridge).

ters more, granting increasing grace and dignity to the house itself. When thinking of this country estate as a kind of pastoral counterpart to the modern city, he begins to stress "the calm and dignified retirement" of its natural haunts. There is a half-serious note in his remark, through Littleton, that a stay at Swallow Barn gives a new sense of what is important. Littleton decides that complete happiness might well be attained with "a thousand acres of good land, an old manor-house, on a pleasant site, a hundred negroes, a large library, a host of friends, and a reserve of a few thousands a year in the stocks." Seen first at twilight, with its lights beckoning hospitably, Swallow Barn looks like a castle.

Yet in a different mood, Kennedy creates as a border to this enchanting kingdom a weed-choked, stagnant swamp, giving the idea of the plantation as pastoral fiefdom a decidedly ironic twist. There is a vaguely ominous note sounded when Kennedy makes this blasted stretch of land the object of a lawsuit between the genial Frank Meriwether, Swallow Barn's proprietor, who would love to give the land away, and his stiff, fractious neighbor Isaac Tracy of The Brakes. Tracy sees the land not as it is, a marshy waste filled with briers and snakes, but as a symbol of an inheritance, a principle attractive just because it can be fought for. The swamp, sadly, provides his only reason for being. Given Kennedy's view that the South's secessionist leanings were folly, Tracy's frivolous suit can be seen as an ironic parable. The land that the old gentleman goes to court to win is a worthless, uninhabitable maze.

As with Kennedy's shifting attitudes in his portrayal of the estate, his creation of characters involves a usually pleasing mixture of strength and weakness. Frank Meriwether is cheerful and generous, considerate of equals and dependents alike, practical and tolerant. Yet he is also full of "magnificent notions"; he is, in other words, very opinionated, especially in matters pertaining to the superiority of all things Virginian. Bel Tracy, Isaac's daughter, is styled after Sheridan's Lydia Languish, with her silly notions of romance and her "freakish" preference for exaggerated refinements. Yet like Scott's Di Vernon, she is also at times more hoyden than lady, galloping across meadows in complete control of a spirited horse or matching wits with her courtiers. Frank's brother-in-law Ned Hazard is in the throes of a courtship that threatens, as Mark Littleton says, to turn his rambling letters into a novel. Ned is for the most part a level-headed, unpretentious young man. But his sense of what southern honor demands can move him to provoke a brawl at a country store, and his acquiescence to Bel's insistence on the hollow forms that she associates with chivalry makes him sometimes as foolish as she is. Around the story's main characters, Frank and Ned of Swallow Barn, Bel and her father of The Brakes, Kennedy sets a group of folk reminiscent of Scott's and Cooper's galleries of country types: the plantation mistress who makes "all things go like clock-work"; the foggy, fussy plantation tutor; the sensible and witty family lawyer, Philpot Wart, who is given a comic foil in the ridiculous figure of Singleton Oglethorpe Swansdown, a pretentious fop. Through Wart and through Swansdown, who represents Isaac Tracy in the swamp lawsuit, Kennedy is able to bring his comic perceptions of his own profession into his story. The subject of law in relation to honor in the Old South is lightly but revealingly touched upon. *Swallow Barn* also exposes the place and problems of women in a patriarchal plantation system. Two idealized young belles of the manor, Lucy and Victorine, provide Kennedy an opportunity to offer a rather serious discourse on the value of educating girls at home. In the old maid Prudence Meriwether, he shows the desperation of a fading belle threatened with her culture's worst fate—spinsterhood.

The foundation of this Virginia squirearchy is not ignored, and indeed, for modern critics, the comments on slavery are the most useful portions of Kennedy's book. Slavery exists at Swallow Barn in the mildest and most congenial of forms. Meriwether, we are told at the start, is held "in most affectionate reverence" by his slaves. Slaves, called only "negroes" throughout, are present in every scene, appearing as washerwomen, grooms, fiddlers, and endless troops of "sundry little besmirched and bow-legged" black children. Black "servants" drive carriages, serve juleps, conduct possum hunts, sing ballads, and deliver lectures on horse training; the young ones dart about the bushes "like untamed monkeys." In one representative scene, meant for comedy but disquieting to anyone who has read the "battle royal" scene in Ralph Ellison's *Invisible Man*, Ned orders a group of scantily clad black children, described as "a pack of antic and careless animals," to have a footrace for the prize of a coin. In the ensuing mad scramble, money is thrown into the air, and one child, a "strange baboon in trowsers," manages finally to pick a small coin out of the dirt with his teeth.

The great majority of sketches that Kennedy's cousin David Strother provided as illustrations for the 1851 edition depict slaves performing various chores in minstrel-show fashion. The first Virginia character met by Mark Littleton is an old free Negro named Scipio. Escorting Littleton to Swallow Barn, Scipio entertains him with descriptions of "the splendors of the old-fashioned style." Certainly any reader of Thomas Nelson Page's "Marse Chan" sees the model for that story's faithful black retainer, narrator Sam—especially in Scipio's pathetic recitation of "how the estates were cut up, and what old people had died off, and how much he felt himself alone in present times." Yet we can also see stirrings of the sentiment that produced Paul Laurence Dunbar's poem "We Wear the Mask" and Ellison's devious grandfather figure in *Invisible Man* when Scipio, "laughing till the tears came into his eyes," says that "people think old Scipio a fool, because he's got sense."

Critics frequently mention "The Quarter," the chapter in which Kennedy gives the narrative to Frank Meriwether so that he can speak, in a voice devoid of humor or sarcasm, as a model slaveholder on the necessary evil of slavery that it is his uncomfortable duty to sustain. Meriwether neither justifies nor excuses his position; he simply explains it and also outlines a plan for mitigating the system's excesses through some startling reforms. Kennedy expanded and rephrased this chapter for the 1851 edition. Never a defender of slavery, Kennedy in this treatment of blacks in *Swallow Barn* shows how ever more deeply even he became entangled in the pastoral mystique of the world he set out to satirize. In the 1851 edition, Meriwether's monologue takes on more pointed political overtones. Yet the 1851 edition also reveals Kennedy's increased sensitivity to some of the degrading remarks about blacks in the first edition. A "flatnosed pigmy" (I, 114) is described, but in the 1851 edition, this same personage becomes a "flat-nosed compeer," and Ned's comment when he dismisses the dignified old servant Carey, "Now old gentleman, you have done your duty, so creep to your kennel" (I,

132), is cut entirely. Charles Bohner reports that in an early draft of
the novel, a slaveholder almost strikes a slave who grins at an inap-
propriate moment. This potentially damaging passage was omitted
before the manuscript went to press in 1832.[12]

In *Swallow Barn* the issue of slavery dominates in ways that Kennedy scarcely intended. The story of Abe, which takes over the last
part of the novel, indicates that Kennedy was quite as trapped by
slavery's contradictions as was his character Frank Meriwether. Kennedy winds up his story of Ned's courtship in a chapter sarcastically
entitled "The Fate of a Hero." Here, Ned, "braving" the possibility
of Bel's refusing his proposal, acts first terrified and then ridiculous
but is never "heroic" in any sense. The chapter ends inconclusively,
yet Littleton announces that he is only too glad to leave the lovers at
this point, whereupon he turns to what Kennedy must have felt was
more pressing unfinished business—he goes on the tour of "the
quarter" with Meriwether. Kennedy's purpose changes from mock-
heroic satire to a romance about two heroes, Abe and Captain John
Smith, who could not belong to the world of Swallow Barn. One was
excluded by an act of rebellion; the other, by time.

The tale of Abe offers a real hero, yet only in actions that take
place after his banishment from the plantation for his "insurrection-
ary" activities. In mentioning Abe's acts of a "lawless character," how
conscious was Kennedy of the recent Nat Turner rebellion? Abe's re-
formation as a seaman and his subsequent heroism might be seen,
in one respect, as Kennedy's attempt in fiction to present the Old
Dominion, and particularly its slaves, in a light quite different from
the glare that Nat Turner and his band had cast upon them. One
feeling motivated Abe in the rescue that was doomed from the start.
He was "impelled," Kennedy says, "by that love of daring which the
romances call chivalry." And although Bel's chivalry is ridiculous,
Abe's is a "gallant thing"; it is "a gallant sight to see such heroism
shining out in an humble slave of the Old Dominion." Gallant, perhaps, but certainly suicidal was Abe's noble enactment of a code that
Kennedy lampoons throughout the novel. At the last, Kennedy
seems to have found satire inadequate as a means for concluding his

12. Bohner, *John Pendleton Kennedy*, 86.

sketchbook of the Old South. Through Abe he retreats into the form of romance, which reveals both the nobility and the futility of heroism in a nonsatiric genre that allows a slave his freedom—but only through the act of choosing to die for one of his master's cherished ideals.

Kennedy's third and final use of the word *hero* is an even further retreat. In the 1832 edition, he had included a forty-five-page essay on Captain John Smith, and it was actually one of the first sections that he had written for his book, as early as 1825. Although much of this section was excised in the 1851 revision, it was still very important to Kennedy to include a vision of the man he called a "True Knight of Virginia." In the 1832 edition, he had said that Smith's whole purpose had been "to rear up his beloved Virginia into a thriving and happy commonwealth" (II, 307). In 1851, he still found it necessary for Mark Littleton to retreat into Meriwether's library, to retreat, thereby, into a more heroic past freed from the problems that Littleton had witnessed in the Virginia of the present.

Looking upon the fading of aristocratic values in his Virginia of the 1820s and witnessing the South's suicidal defense of slavery beginning in the 1830s, Kennedy sought in history the only secure final haven for his fiction of a "happy commonwealth." From Swallow Barn's library, Mark Littleton can look out at the same James River "upon which Smith and his faithful Mosco . . . two hundred years gone by, had sailed." Thus Kennedy allows the present to flow back into the safe harbor of a past shaped by a bold, uncomplicated hero who was "moulded in the richest fashion of ancient chivalry" and "dedicated, in his maturer years, to the useful purposes of life." For Kennedy, as for other writers of the romantic period, the value of history was its providing "facts sufficiently dim by distance" that still possessed an unassailable veracity. John Smith could make a virgin wilderness anything he liked, and Littleton says that the imagination can "make what it pleases" out of history. Kennedy, however, most certainly found at the end of *Swallow Barn* that he could not make what he pleased out of present-day Virginia. Perhaps in 1832, but surely by 1851, Kennedy could see the future more clearly than he could interpret the present. In 1864, Kennedy's brother wrote to tell him of the sad fate of The Bower, which had offered shelter to the cavalry during some fierce battles. At this "once fine estate" and homes like it in the region, one saw "the many firesides deserted, the poverty close bordering on want . . . the ruin and wreck that is everywhere over the land."[13] With some regret but with perhaps more relief, Kennedy must have been content to let Mark Littleton consign his plantation safely to the region of memory. Back home in New York, Littleton reports that he has become famous for his "long stories and rapturous commendations of Swallow Barn." For his part, Kennedy, in his next two novels, used the form of the historical romance; he took no more imaginative travels through Virginia mazes.

Mark Littleton's tour of the quarter turned Kennedy's plantation still life in a direction highly suggestive of a long and distinguished line of more accomplished southern novels. The theoretical, patriarchal defense of slavery in "The Quarter" is followed unaccountably by a legend of a rebellious slave who longs for freedom and whose mother is left to grieve when he dies willingly for his master's cause. Kennedy expends a great deal of time and effort on the image of the grief-crazed old mammy, Lucy. Her mournful visage remains with us much as does the visage of Mollie, who dominates *Go Down, Moses* through Faulkner's concluding portrait of her sorrow for her grandson, returned in death to the society that betrayed him. *Swallow Barn's* stories of Abe and Lucy, in their turn, seem to lead Kennedy on a search deep into history for a positive image of Virginia's heritage with which to close his book. The strategy behind this arrangement, perhaps decided upon·unconsciously for the most part, lifts *Swallow Barn* out of the tradition of plantation novels cemented by Thomas Nelson Page and places it at the beginning of a list of southern works that combine manners and ritual, history and pastoral, realistic insight and romantic obsession, to probe the roots of the South's complex inheritance. This list includes Simms's romances of the Revolution; Twain's *Adventures of Huckleberry Finn, Connecticut Yankee, Pudd'nhead Wilson*, and even *Life on the Mississippi*; George W. Cable's *The Grandissimes*; Robert Penn Warren's *All the King's Men*; Faulkner's *Absalom, Absalom!* and *Go Down, Moses*; and Ralph Ellison's *Invisible Man*.

13. Philip P. Kennedy to John Pendleton Kennedy, January 30, 1864, *ibid.*, 230.

Kennedy's realistic exploration of the social scene makes *Swallow Barn* an early American work that deserves recognition as a prototype of a national novel of manners. In this connection, it is interesting to note how very different Kennedy's slant on American manners was from both Cooper's and Nathaniel Hawthorne's. Cooper in his 1828 *Notions of the Americans* complained of the American novelist's "poverty of materials," particularly in the matter of characterization. The problem was caused, Cooper felt, by a sameness of "deportment" in his native country: "I have never seen a nation so much alike in my life." As late as 1860, Hawthorne in his preface to *The Marble Faun* was to echo Cooper (given the year and the crisis over slavery, his comments are unaccountably obscurantist or heavily ironic): "No author, without a trial, can conceive of the difficulty of writing a Romance about a country where there is no shadow, no antiquity, no mystery, no picturesque and gloomy wrong, nor anything but a common-place prosperity, in broad and simple daylight, as is happily the case with my dear native land."

As early as 1832, on the other hand, Kennedy had felt that "the under-currents of country-life are grotesque, peculiar and amusing, and it only requires an attentive observer to make an agreeable book by describing them." By 1851, he felt that American writers were in danger of losing what, for Cooper and Hawthorne, they had not even developed: the 1851 preface to *Swallow Barn* mourns that "an observer cannot fail to note that the manners of our country have been tending towards a uniformity which is visibly effacing all local differences. . . . What belonged to us as characteristically American, seems already to be dissolving." Kennedy was drawn to a road not taken by his New England contemporaries, who most often created socially isolated individuals caught up in imaginative quests for connection with nature. Kennedy's characters, however, belonged together in a secular society, which, for good or ill, defined their patterns of action and their identities. Thus his commitment to the actualities of the Old South—not just its quaintness but also the sober realities of its politics, economics, and social practices—makes his first novel a work that creates an essentially new American path.

A NOTE ON TEXTS AND SOURCES

Swallow Barn was first published by Carey and Lea of Philadelphia in two volumes in 1832 under the pseudonym Mark Littleton and with a dedicatory letter to William Wirt. In 1851, G. P. Putnam of New York brought out a revised one-volume edition that included twenty illustrations by Kennedy's cousin David Strother. Kennedy also added a new preface entitled "A Word in Advance, from the Author to the Reader." In his revisions for the second edition, Kennedy excluded a long section on the exploits of Captain John Smith. He also rephrased some affected or archaic language. In the early chapters, particularly those describing Swallow Barn and its inhabitants, he softened some of the satire. Two expansions are significant: in Chapter IV, Kennedy added material concerning the proper education of young women, and he redrafted Chapter XLVI to address the intensified attacks on slavery. All later editions of the novel have been based on the 1851 version.

The manuscript of *Swallow Barn* is located, as are all of Kennedy's papers, at the library of the Peabody Institute in Baltimore, Maryland. The holdings in this collection amount to five thousand volumes, Kennedy's entire library. Included are manuscripts of all his books, journals, and some four thousand letters. The *Swallow Barn* materials include a sheaf of unbound notes and passages changed or dropped for the final version, an outline of the order of chapters showing numerous shifts, and a volume of reviews of the book, labeled "Scraps."

Significant modern editions with valuable introductions are J. B. Hubbell's, published by Harcourt, Brace in 1929, and William S. Osborne's, published by Hafner in 1962. Biographies of Kennedy include the "official" one by Henry Tuckerman (New York, 1871), Charles Bohner's *John Pendleton Kennedy: Gentleman from Baltimore* (Baltimore, 1961), and J. V. Ridgely's *John Pendleton Kennedy* (New York, 1966), written for the Twayne Series.

The following articles and books contain useful material:

Bohner, Charles. "Swallow Barn: John P. Kennedy's Chronicle of

Virginia Society." *Virginia Magazine of History and Biography*, LXVIII (July, 1960), 317–30.

Cardwell, Guy. "The Plantation House: An Analogical Image." *Southern Literary Journal*, II (Fall, 1969), 3–21.

Davis, Richard Beale. *Literature and Society in Early Virginia, 1608–1840*. Baton Rouge, 1973.

Foster, Edward Halsey. *The Civilized Wilderness: Backgrounds to American Romantic Literature, 1817–1860*. New York, 1975.

Gaines, Francis Pendleton. *The Southern Plantation: A Study in the Development and the Accuracy of a Tradition*. New York, 1924.

Hubbell, Jay B. *The South in American Literature, 1607–1900*. Durham, 1954.

Parrington, Vernon L. *Main Currents in American Thought*. Vol. II. New York, 1927.

Simpson, Lewis. *The Dispossessed Garden: Pastoral and History in Southern Literature*. Athens, Ga., 1975.

Taylor, William R. *Cavalier and Yankee*. New York, 1963.

Yellin, Jean Fagin. *The Intricate Knot: Black Figures in American Literature, 1776–1863*. New York, 1972.

SWALLOW BARN

DEDICATION OF THE FIRST EDITION OF
SWALLOW BARN
To William Wirt, Esq.

DEAR SIR,

I have two reasons for desiring to inscribe this book to you. The first is, that you are likely to be on a much better footing with posterity than may ever be my fortune; seeing that, some years gone by, you carelessly sat down and wrote a little book, which has, doubtless, surprised yourself by the rapidity with which it has risen to be a classic in our country. I have sat down as carelessly, to a like undertaking, but stand sadly in want of the wings that have borne your name to an enviable eminence. It is natural, therefore, that I should desire your good-will with the next generation.

My second reason is, that I have some claim upon your favour in the attempt to sketch the features of the Old Dominion, to whose soil and hearts your fame and feelings are kindred. In these pages you may recognize, perhaps, some old friends, or, at least, some of their customary haunts; and I hope, on that score, to find grace in your eyes, however I may lack it in the eyes of others.

I might add another reason, but that is almost too personal to be mentioned here: It is concerned with an affectionate regard for the purity and worth of your character, with your genius, your valuable attainments, your many excellent actions, and, above all, with your art of embellishing and endearing the relations of private life. These topics are not to be discussed to your ear,—and not, I hope, (to their full extent,) for a long time, to that of the public.

Accept, therefore, this first-fruit of the labours (I ought rather to say, of the idleness) of your trusty friend,

Mark Littleton

April 21, 1832.

WIRT'S REPLY TO KENNEDY'S DEDICATION
To John P. Kennedy, Esq.

Baltimore. May 23, 1832

MY DEAR SIR,

If you should chance to know a certain Mark Littleton, author of "a righte merrie and conceited work," called Swallow Barn, which is occupying all the public attention that can be spared from politics, I would thank you to make my respects and acknowledgments to him for a handsome copy of this work, and the well-turned dedication with which he has complimented me. He might have chosen a patron more auspicious for himself, but no one with kinder and warmer feelings and wishes for his success. The dedication proves his ability to give interest to trifles. With regard to the Book itself, I have been so engaged as to have been able to make but little progress in it. But as far as I have read, it is full of gaiety & goodness of heart, and the author trips it along, on "light fantastic toe," with all imaginable ease and grace. The characters are well sketched & grouped, and the plan as well as the incidents are new & fresh, so far as I have gone. But I have read too little of it to play the critic with merits. The object of this note is simply to carry my thanks to the author, without delay, for the present of the book and the honor of the dedication—and I trouble you with this agency, because of the *on dit* that the author is in the circle of your acquaintances. Good night—

W[illia]m Wirt

KENNEDY'S PREFACE, 1832 ed.

I have had great difficulty to prevent myself from writing a novel. The reader will perceive that the author of these sketches left his home to pass a few weeks in the Old Dominion, having a purpose to portray the impressions which the scenery and the people of that region made upon him, in detached pictures brought together with no other connexion than that of time and place. He soon found himself, however, engaged in the adventures of domestic history, which wrought so pleasantly upon him, and presented such a variety of persons and characters to his notice, that he could not forbear to describe what he saw. His book therefore, in spite of himself, has ended in a vein altogether different from that in which it set out. There is a rivulet of story wandering through a broad meadow of episode. Or, I might truly say, it is a book of episodes, with an occasional digression into the plot. However repugnant this plan of writing may be to the canons of criticism, yet it may, perhaps, amuse the reader even more than one less exceptionable.

The country and the people are at least truly described; although it will be seen that my book has but little philosophy to recommend it, and much less of depth of observation. In truth, I have only perfunctorily skimmed over the surface of a limited society, which was both rich in the qualities that afford delight, and abundant in the materials to compensate the study of its peculiarities. If my book be too much in the mirthful mood, it is because the ordinary actions of men, in their household intercourse, have naturally a humorous or comic character. The passions that are exhibited in such scenes are moderate and amiable; and a true narrative of what is amiable in personal history is apt to be tinctured with the hue of a lurking and subdued humour. The undercurrents of country-life are grotesque, peculiar and amusing, and it only requires an attentive observer to make an agreeable book by describing them. I do not think any one will say that my pictures are exaggerated or false in their proportions; because I have not striven to produce effect: they will, doubtless, be found insufficient in many respects, and I may be open to the charge of having made them flat and insipid. I confess the incompetency of my hand to do what, perhaps, my reader has a right to require from one who professes a design to amuse him. Still I may have furnished some entertainment, and that is what I chiefly aimed at, although negligently and unskilfully.

As to the events I have recounted, upon what assurance I have given them to the world, how I came to do so, and with what license I have used names to bring them into the public eye, those are matters betwixt me and my friends, concerning which my reader would forget himself if he should be over-curious. His search therein will give him but little content; and if I am driven into straits in that regard, I shelter myself behind the motto[1] on my title-page, the only one I have used in this book. Why should I not have my privilege as well as another?

If this my first venture should do well, my reader shall hear of me anon, and much more, I hope, to his liking: if disaster await it, I am not so bound to its fortunes but that I can still sleep quietly as the best who doze over my pages.

The author of the Seven Champions has forestalled all I have left to say; and I therefore take the freedom to conclude in his words:

"Gentle readers,—in kindness accept of my labours, and

be not like the chattering cranes nor Momus' mates, that
carp at every thing. What the simple say, I care not;
what the spightful speak, I pass not: only the censure of
the conceited I stand unto; that is the mark I aym at,
whose good likings if I obtain, I have won my race."

Mark Littleton

[1] "And, for to pass the time, this book shall be pleasant to read
in. But for to give faith and believe that all is true that is contained therein, ye be at your own liberty.–*Prologue to the Morte
D'Arthur.*"

(*Facsimile of 1853 title page*)

SWALLOW BARN,

OR

A SOJOURN IN THE OLD DOMINION.

BY

J. P. KENNEDY.

REVISED EDITION.

With Twenty Illustrations by Strother.

NEW-YORK:

G. P. PUTNAM & COMPANY, 10 PARK PLACE.

1853.

CONTENTS.

A WORD IN ADVANCE, FROM THE AUTHOR TO THE READER.

———•●•———

SWALLOW BARN was written twenty years ago, and was published in a small edition, which was soon exhausted. From that date it has disappeared from the bookstores, being carelessly consigned by the author to that oblivion which is common to books and men—out of sight, out of mind. Upon a recent reviewal of it, after an interval sufficiently long to obliterate the partialities with which one is apt to regard his own productions, I have thought it was worthy of more attention than I had bestowed upon it, and was, at least, entitled to the benefit of a second edition. In truth, its republication has been so often advised by friends, and its original reception was so prosperous, that I have almost felt it to be a duty once more to set it afloat upon the waters, for the behoof of that good-natured company of idle readers who are always ready to embark on a pleasure excursion in any light craft that offers. I have, therefore, taken these volumes in hand, and given them a somewhat critical revisal. Twenty years work sufficient change upon the mind of an author to render him, perhaps more than others, a fastidious critic of his own book. If the physiologists are right, he is not the same person after that lapse of time ; and all that his present and former self may claim in common, are those properties which belong to his mental consciousness, of which his aspiration after fame is one.   The present self may, therefore, be expected to examine more rigorously the work of that former and younger person, for whom he is held responsible.   This weighty consideration will be sufficient to account for the few differences which may be found between this and the first edition.   Some quaintness of the vocabulary has been got rid of—some dialogue has been stript of its redundancy—some few thoughts have been added—and others retrenched.   I shall be happy to think that the reader will agree with me that these are improvements :—I mean the reader who may happen to belong to that small and choice corps who read these volumes long ago—a little troop of friends of both sexes, to whom I have reason to be grateful for that modicum of good opinion which cheered my first venture in authorship.   Health and joy to them all—as many as are now alive !   I owe them a thanksgiving for their early benevolence.

Swallow Barn exhibits a picture of country life in Virginia, as it existed in the first quarter of the present century.   Between that period and the present day, time and what is called " the progress," have made many innovations there, as they have done every where else.   The Old Dominion is losing somewhat of the raciness of her once peculiar, and—speaking in reference to the locality described in these volumes—insulated cast of manners.   The mellow, bland, and sunny luxuriance of her old-time society—its good fellowship, its hearty and constitutional *companionableness*, the thriftless gayety of the people, their dogged but amiable invincibility of opinion, and that overflowing hospitality which knew no ebb,—these traits, though far from being impaired, are modified at the present day by circumstances which have been gradually attaining a marked influence over social life as well as political relation.   An observer cannot fail to note that the manners of our country have been tending towards a uniformity which is visibly effacing all local differences. The old states, especially, are losing their orignal distinctive habits and modes of life, and in the same degree, I fear, are losing their exclusive American character. A traveller may detect but few sectional or provincial varieties in the general observances and customs of society, in comparison with what were observable in the past generations, and the pride, or rather the vanity, of the present day is leading us into a very notable assimilation with foreign usages The country now apes the city in what is supposed to be the elegancies of life, and the city is inclined to value and adopt the fashions it is able to import across the Atlantic, and thus the whole surface of society is exhibiting the traces of a process by which it is likely to be rubbed down, in time, to one level, and varnished with the same gloss. It may thus finally arrive at a comfortable insipidity of character which may not be willingly reckoned as altogether a due compensation for the loss of that rough but pleasant flavor which belonged to it in its earlier era. There is much good sense in that opinion which ascribes a wholesome influence to those homebred customs, which are said to strengthen local attachments and expand them into a love of country. What belonged to us as characteristically American, seems already to be dissolving into a mixture which affects us unpleasantly as a tame and cosmopolitan substitute for the old warmth and salient vivacity of our ancestors. We no longer present in our pictures of domestic life so much as an earnest lover of our nationality might desire of what abroad is called " the red bird's wing"—something which belongs to us and to no one else. The fruitfulness of modern invention in the arts of life, the general fusion of thought through the medium of an extra-territorial literature, which from its easy domestication ámong us is scarcely regarded as foreign, the convenience and comfort of European customs which have been incorporated into our scheme of living,

—all these, aided and diffused by our extraordinary facilities of travel and circulation, have made sad work, even in the present generation, with those old *nationalisms* that were so agreeable to the contemplation of an admirer of the picturesque in character and manners.

Looking myself somewhat hopelessly upon this onward gliding of the stream, I am not willing to allow these sketches of mine entirely to pass away. They have already begun to assume the tints of a relic of the past, and may, in another generation, become archæological, and sink into the chapter of antiquities. Presenting, as I make bold to say, a faithful picture of the people, the modes of life, and the scenery of a region full of attraction, and exhibiting the lights and shades of its society with the truthfulness of a painter who has studied his subject on the spot, they may reasonably claim their accuracy of delineation to be set off as an extenuation for any want of skill or defect of finish which a fair criticism may charge against the artist. Like some sign-post painters, I profess to make a strong likeness, even if it should be thought to be *hard*,—and what better workmen might call a daub, —as to which I must leave my reader to judge for himself when he has read this book. The outward public award on this point was kind, and bestowed quite as much praise as I could have desired—much more than I expected—when the former edition appeared. But " the progress" has brought out many competitors since that day, and has, perhaps, rendered the public taste more scrupulous. A book then was not so perilous an offering as it is now in the great swarm of authorships. We run more risk, just now, of being let alone,—unread,—untalked of—though not, happily, unpuffed by a few newspapers, who are favorites with the publisher, and owe him some courtesies.

I wish it to be noted that Swallow Barn is not a novel. I confess this in advance, although I may lose by it. It was begun on the plan of a series of detached sketches linked together by the hooks and eyes of a traveller's notes; and although the narrative does run into some by-paths of personal adventure, it has still preserved its desultory, sketchy character to the last. It is, therefore, utterly unartistic in plot and structure, and may be described as variously and interchangeably partaking of the complexion of a book of travels, a diary, a collection of letters, a drama, and a history,—and this, serial or compact, as the reader may choose to compute it. Our old friend Polonius had nearly hit it in his rigmarole of " pastoral-comical, tragical-comical-historical-pastoral"—which, saving " the tragical," may well make up my schedule: and so I leave it to the " censure" of my new reader.

INTRODUCTORY EPISTLE.

TO ZACHARY HUDDLESTONE, ESQ.,

PRESTON RIDGE, NEW-YORK.

DEAR ZACK:

I CAN imagine your surprise upon the receipt of this, when you first discover that I have really reached the Old Dominion. To requite you for my stealing off so quietly, I hold myself bound to an explanation, and, in revenge for your past friendship, to inflict upon you a full, true, and particular account of all my doings, or rather my seeings and thinkings, up to this present writing. You know my cousin Ned Hazard has been often urging it upon me.—so often that he began to grow sick of it,—as a sort of family duty, to come and spend some little fragment of my life amongst my Virginia relations, and I have broken so many promises on that score, that, in truth, I began to grow ashamed of myself.

Upon the first of this month a letter from Ned reached me at Longsides, on the North River, where I then was with my mother and sisters. Ned's usual tone of correspondence is that of easy, confiding intimacy, mixed up, now and then, with a slashing raillery against some imputed foibles, upon which, as they were altogether imaginary, I could afford to take his sarcasm in good part. But in this epistle he assumed a new ground, giving me some home thrusts, chiding me roundly for certain waxing *bachelorisms*, as he called them, and intimating that a crust was evidently hardening upon me. A plague upon the fellow! You know, Zachary, that neither of us is so many years ahead of him. My reckoning takes in but five years, eleven months and fifteen days—and certainly, not so much by my looks. He insinuated that I had arrived at that inveteracy of opinion for which travel was the only cure; and that, in especial, I had fallen into some unseemly prejudices against the Old Dominion which were unbecoming the character of a philosopher, to which, he affirmed, I had set up pretensions; and then came a most hyperbolical innuendo— that he had good reason to know that I was revolving the revival of a stale adventure in the war of Cupid, in which I had been aforetime egregiously baffled, "at Rhodes, at Cyprus, and on other grounds." Any reasonable man would say, that was absurd on his own showing. The letter grew more provoking—it flouted my opinions, laughed at my particularity, caricatured and derided my figure for its leanness, set at nought my complexion, satirized my temper, and gave me over corporeally and spiritually to the great bear-herd, as one predestined to all kinds of ill luck with the women, and to be led for ever as an ape. His epistle, however, wound up like a sermon, in a perfect concord of sweet sounds, beseeching me to forego my idle purpose; (Cupid, forsooth!) to weed out all my prejudicate affections, as well touching the Old Dominion as the other conceits of my vain philosophy, and to hie me, with such speed as my convenience might serve withal, to Swallow Barn, where he made bold to pledge me an entertainment worthy of my labor.

It was a brave offer, and discreetly to be perpended. I balanced the matter, in my usual see-saw fashion, for several days. It does mostly fall out, my dear Zack (to speak philosophically), that this machine of man is pulled in such contrary ways, by inclinations and appetites setting diversely; that it shall go well with him if he be not altogether balanced into a pernicious equilibrium of absolute rest. I had a great account to run up against my resolution. Longsides has so many conveniences; and the servants have fallen so well into my habitudes; and my arm-chair had such an essential adaptation to my felicity; and even my razors were on such a stationary foundation—one for every day of the week—as to render it impossible to embark them on a journey; to say nothing of the letters to write, and the books to read, and all the other little cares that make up the sum of immobility in a man who does not care much about seeing the world; so that, in faith, I had a serious matter of it. And then, after all, I was, in fact, plighted to my sister Louisa to go with her up the river, you know where. This, between you and me, was the very thing that brought down the beam. That futile, nonsensical flirtation! But for this fantastic conceit crossing my mind with the bitterness of its folly, I should indubitably have staid at home.

There are some junctures in love and war both, where your lying is your only game; for as to equivocating, or putting the question upon an *if* or a *but*, it is a downright confession. If I had refused Ned's summons, not a whole legion of devils could have driven it out of his riveted belief, that I had been kept at home by that maggot of the brain which he called a love affair. And then I should never have heard the end of it!

"I'll set that matter right, at least," quoth I, as I folded up his letter. "Ned has reason, too," said I, suddenly struck with the novelty of the proposed journey, which began to show in a pleasant light upon my imagination, as things are apt to do, when a man has once relieved his mind from a state of doubt:—" One ought to travel before he makes up his opinion: there are two sides to every question, and the world is right or wrong; I'm

sure I don't know which.   Your traveller is a man of privileges
and authoritative, and looks well in the multitude : a man of mark,
and authentic as a witness.   And as for the Old Dominion, I'll
warrant me it's a right jolly old place, with a good many years
on its head yet, or I am mistaken.—By cock and pye, I'll go and
see it .—What ho ! my tablets,"———

Behold me now in the full career of my voyage of discovery,
exploring the James River in the steamboat, on a clear, hot fifteenth of June, and looking with a sagacious perspicacity upon
the commonest sights of this terra incognita.   I gazed upon the
receding headlands far sternward, and then upon the sedgy banks
where the cattle were standing leg-deep in the water to get rid of
the flies : and ever and anon, as we followed the sinuosities of the
river, some sweeping eminence came into view, and on the crown
thereof was seen a plain, many-windowed edifice of brick, with low
wings, old, ample and stately, looking over its wide and sun-burnt
domain in solitary silence : and there were the piny promontories, into whose shade we sometimes glided so close that one might
have almost jumped on shore, where the wave struck the beach
with a sullen plash : and there were the decayed fences jutting
beyond the bank into the water, as if they had come down the hill
too fast to stop themselves.   All these things struck my fancy as
peculiar to the region.

It is wonderful to think how much more distinct are the impressions of a man who travels pen in hand, than those of a mere
business voyager.   Even the crows, as we sometimes scared them
from their banquets with our noisy enginery, seemed to have a
more voluble, and, I may say, eloquent caw here in Virginia, than
in the dialectic climates of the North.   You would have laughed
to see into what a state of lady-like rapture I had worked myself,
in my eagerness to get a peep at Jamestown, with all my effer-
vescence of romance kindled up by the renown of the unmatchable

Smith. The steward of the boat pointed it out when we had nearly passed it—and lo! there it was—the buttress of an old steeple, a barren fallow, some melancholy heifers, a blasted pine, and, on its top, a desolate hawk's nest. What a splendid field for the fancy! What a carte blanche for a painter! With how many things might this little spot be filled!

What time bright Phœbus—you see that Jamestown has made me poetical—had thrown the reins upon his horse's neck, and got down from his chafed saddle in the western country, like a tired mail-carrier, our boat was safely moored at Rocket's, and I entered Richmond between hawk and buzzard—the very best hour, I maintain. out of the twenty-four, for a picturesque tourist.

At that hour nature draws her pictures *en silhouette* : every thing jet black against a bright horizon ; nothing to be seen but profiles, with all the shabby fillings-up kept dark. Shockoe Hill was crested with what seemed palaces embowered in groves and gardens of richest shade; the chimneys numberless, like minarets ; and the Parthenon of Virginia, on its appropriate summit, stood in another Acropolis, tracing its broad pediment upon the sky in exaggerated lines. There, too, was the rush of waters tumbling around enchanted islands, and flashing dimly on the sight. The hum of a city fell upon my ear ; the streets looked long and the houses high, and every thing brought upon my mind that misty impression which, Burke says, is an ingredient of the sublime, —and which, I say, every stranger feels on entering a city at twilight.

I was set down at " The Union," where, for the first hour, being intent upon my creature comforts, my time passed well enough. The abrupt transition from long-continued motion to a state of rest makes almost every man sad, exactly as sudden speed makes us joyous; and for this reason, I take it, your traveller in a strange place is, for a space after his halt, a sullen, if not a melancholy animal. The proofs of this were all around me; for here was I—not an unpractised traveller either—at my first resting place after four days of accelerated progression, for the first time in my life in Richmond, in a large hotel, without one cognizable face before me ; full of excellent feelings without a power of utterance. What would I have given for thee, or Jones, or even long Dick Hardesty ! In that ludicrous conflict between the social nature of the man and his outward circumstances, which every light-hearted voyager feels in such a situation as mine, I grew desponding. Talk not to me of the comfort of mine own inn ! I hold it a thing altogether insufficient. A burlesque solitariness sealed up the fountains of speech, of the crowd who were seated at the supper-table; and the same uneasy sensation of pent-up sympathies was to be seen in the groups that peopled the purlieus of the hotel. A square lamp that hung midway over the hall, was just lit up, and a few insulated beings were sauntering backward and forward in its light: some loitered in pairs, in low and reserved conversation; others stalked alone in incommunicable ruminations, with shaded brows, and their hands behind their backs. One or two stood at the door humming familiar catches in unconscious medleys, as they gazed up and down the street, now clamorous with the din of carts and the gossip of serving-maids, discordant apprentice boys and over-contented blacks. Some sat on the pavement, leaning their chairs against the wall, and puffing segars in imperturbable silence: all composing an orderly and disconsolate little republic of humorsome spirits, most pitifully out of tune.

I was glad to take refuge in an idle occupation; so I strolled about the city. The streets, by degrees, grew less frequented. Family parties were gathered about their doors, to take the evening breeze. The moon shone bright upon some bevies of active children, who played at racing games upon the pavements. On one side of the street, a contumacious clarionet screamed a harsh bravado to a thorough-going violin, which, on the opposite side, in an illuminated barber-shop, struggled in the contortions of a Virginia reel. And, at intervals, strutted past a careering, saucy negro, with marvellous lips, whistling to the top of his bent, and throwing into shade halloo of schoolboy, scream of clarionet, and screech of fiddle.

Towards midnight a thunder gust arose, accompanied with sharp lightning, and the morning broke upon me in all the luxuriance of a cool and delicious atmosphere. You must know that when I left home, my purpose was to make my way direct to Swallow Barn. Now, what think you of my skill as a traveller.

when I tell you, that until I woke in Richmond on this enchanting morning, it never once occurred to me to inquire where this
same Swallow Barn was! I knew that it was in Virginia, and
somewhere about the James River, and therefore I instinctively
wandered to Richmond; but now, while making my toilet, my
thoughts being naturally bent upon my next movement, it very
reasonably occurred to me that I must have passed my proper
destination the day before, and, full of this thought, I found myself humming the line from an old song, which runs, " Pray what
the devil brings you here !" The communicative and obliging
bar-keeper of the Union soon put me right. He knew Ned Hazard as a frequent visitor of Richmond, and his advice was, that I
should take the same boat in which I came, and shape my course
back as far as City Point, where he assured me that I might find
some conveyance to Swallow Barn, which lay still farther down
the river, and that, at all events, " go where I would, I could not
go wrong in Virginia." What think you of that ? Now I hold that
to be, upon personal experience, as true a word as ever was set
down in a traveller's breviary. There is not a by-path in Virginia
that will take a gentleman, who has time on his hands, in a wrong
direction. This I say in honest compliment to a state which is
full to the brim of right good fellows.

The boat was not to return for two days, and I therefore
employed the interval in looking about the city. Don't be frightened !—for I neither visited hospitals, nor schools, nor libraries,
and therefore will not play the tourist with you: but if you wish
to see a beautiful little city, built up of rich and tasteful villas, and
embellished with all the varieties of town and country, scattered
with a refined and exquisite skill—come and look at Shockoe Hill
in the month of June.—You may believe, then, I did not regret
my aberration.

At the appointed day I re-embarked, and in due time was put

down at City Point. Here some further delay awaited me
This is not the land of hackney coaches, and I found myself
somewhat embarrassed in procuring an onward conveyance. At
a small house to which I was conducted, I made my wishes known,
and the proprietor kindly volunteered his services to set me forward. It was a matter of some consideration. The day was
well advanced, and it was as much as could be done to reach Swallow Barn that night. An equipage, however, was at last procured
for me, and off I went. You would have laughed "sans intermission" a good hour if you had seen me upon the road. I was set up
n an old sulky, of a dingy hue, without springs, with its body sunk
between a pair of unusually high wheels. It was drawn by an
asthmatic, superannuated racer with a huge Roman nose and a most
sorrowful countenance. His sides were piteously scalded with
the traces, and his harness, partly of rope and partly of leather
thongs, corresponded with the sobriety of his character. He had
fine long legs, however, and got over the ground with surprising
alacrity. At a most respectful distance behind me trotted the
most venerable of outriders—an old free negro, formerly a retainer in some of the feudal establishments of the low countries. His
name was Scipio. His face, which was principally composed of a
pair of protuberant lips, whose luxuriance seemed intended as
an indemnity for a pair of crushed nostrils, was well set off
with a head of silver wool that bespoke a volume of gravity.
He had, from some aristocratic conceit of elegance, indued himself for my service in a ragged regimental coat, still jagged with
some points of tarnished scarlet, and a pair of coarse linen trowsers, barely reaching the ankles, beneath which two bony feet
occupied shoes, each of the superficies and figure of a hoe, and on
one of these was whimsically buckled a rusty spur. His horse
was a short, thick-set pony, with an amazingly rough trot,
which kept Scipio's legs in a state of constant warfare against the

animal's sides, whilst the old fellow bounced up and down in his
saddle with the ambitious ostentation of a groom in the vigor of
manhood, and proud of his horsemanship.

Scipio frequently succeeded, by dint of hard spurring, to get
close enough to me to open a conversation, which he conducted
with such a deferential courtesy and formal politeness, as greatly
to enhance my opinion of his breeding. His face was lighted up
with a lambent smile, and he touched his hat with an antique
grace at every accost; the tone of his voice was mild and subdued,
and in short, Scipio had all the unction of an old gentleman. He
had a great deal to say of the "palmy days" of Virginia, and the
generations which in his time had been broken up, or, what in his
conception was equivalent, had gone "over the mountain."
He expatiated with a wonderful relish upon the splendors of the
old-fashioned style in that part of the country; and told me very
pathetically, how the estates were cut up, and what old people had
died off, and how much he felt himself alone in the present times,
—which particulars he interlarded with sundry sage remarks, importing an affectionate attachment to the old school, of which
he considered himself no unworthy survivor. He concluded
these disquisitions with a reflection that amused me by its pro-
fundity—and which doubtless he had picked up from some popular
orator: "When they change the circumstance, they alter the
case." My expression of assent to this aphorism awoke all his vanity,—for after pondering a moment upon it, he shook his head
archly as he added,—"People think old Scipio a fool, because
he's got sense,"—and, thereupon, the old fellow laughed till the
tears came into his eyes.

In this kind of colloquy we made some twenty miles before the
shades of evening overtook us, and Scipio now informed me that
we might soon expect to reach Swallow Barn. The road was
smooth and canopied with dark foliage, and, as the last blush of

twilight faded away, we swept rapidly round the head of a swamp where a thousand frogs were celebrating their vespers, and soon after reached the gate of the court-yard. Lights were glimmering through different apertures, and several stacks of chimneys were visible above the horizon; the whole mass being magnified into the dimensions of a great castle. Some half-dozen dogs bounding to the gate, brought a host of servants to receive me, as I alighted at the door.

Cousins count in Virginia, and have great privileges. Here was I in the midst of a host of them. Frank Meriwether met me as cordially as if we had spent our whole lives together, and my cousin Lucretia, his wife, came up and kissed me in the genuine country fashion. Of course, I repeated the ceremony towards all the female branches that fell in my way, and, by the by, the girls are pretty enough to make the ceremony interesting, although I think they consider me somewhat oldish. As to Ned Hazard, I need not tell you he is the quintessence of good humor, and received me with that famous hearty honesty of his, which you would have predicted.

At the moment of my arrival, a part of the family were strewed over the steps of a little porch at the front door, basking in the moonlight; and before them a troop of children, white and black, trundled hoops across the court-yard, followed by a pack of companionable curs, who seemed to have a part of the game; whilst a piano within the house served as an orchestra to the players. My arrival produced a sensation that stopped all this, and I was hurried by a kind of tumultuary welcome into the parlor.

If you have the patience to read this long epistle to the end, I would like to give you a picture of the family as it appeared to me that night; but if you are already fatigued with my gossip, as I have good reason to fear, why you may e'en skip this, and go about your more important duties. But it is not often you may meet such scenes, and as they produce some kindly impressions, I think it worth while to note this.

The parlor was one of those specimens of architecture of which there are not many survivors, and in another half century, they will, perhaps, be extinct. The walls were of panelled wood, of a greenish white, with small windows seated in deep embrasures, and the mantel was high, embellished with heavy mouldings that extended up to the cornice of the room, in a figure resembling a square fortified according to Vauban. In one corner stood a tall triangular cupboard, and opposite to it a clock equally tall, with a healthy, saucy-faced full moon peering above the dial-plate. A broad sofa ranged along the wall, and was kept in countenance by a legion of leather-bottomed chairs, which sprawled their bandy legs to a perilous compass, like a high Dutch skater squaring the yard. A huge table occupied the middle of the room, whereon reposed a service of stately china, and a dozen covers flanking some lodgments of sweetmeats, and divers curiously wrought pyramids of butter tottering on pedestals of ice. In the midst of this array, like a lordly fortress, was placed an immense bowl of milk, surrounded by sundry silver goblets, reflecting their images on the polished board, as so many El Dorados in a fairy Archipelago An uncarpeted floor glistened with a dim, but spotless lustre, in token of careful housekeeping, and around the walls were hung, in grotesque frames, some time-worn portraits, protruding their pale faces through thickets of priggish curls.

The sounding of a bell was the signal for our evening repast. My cousin Lucretia had already taken the seat of worship behind a steaming urn and a strutting coffee-pot of chased silver, that had the air of a cock about to crow,—it was so erect. A little rosy gentleman, the reverend Mr. Chub, (a tutor in the family,) said a hasty and half-smothered grace, and then we all arranged ourselves at the table. An aged dame in spectacles, with the mannerly silence of a dependent, placed herself in a post at the board, that enabled her to hold in check some little moppets who were perched on high chairs, with bibs under their chins, and two barefooted boys who had just burst into the room overheated with play. A vacant seat remained, which, after a few moments, was occupied by a tall spinster, with a sentimental mien, who glided into the parlor with some stir. She was another cousin, Zachary, according to the Virginia rule of consanguinity, who was introduced to me as Miss Prudence Meriwether, a sister of Frank's,—and as for her age,—that's neither here nor there.

The evening went off, as you might guess, with abundance of good feeling and unaffected enjoyment. The ladies soon fell into their domestic occupations, and the parson smoked his pipe in silence at the window. The young progeny teased " uncle Ned" with importunate questions, or played at bo-peep at the parlor door, casting sly looks at me, from whence they slipt off, with a laugh, whenever they caught my eye. At last, growing tired, they rushed with one accord upon Hazard, flinging themselves across his knees, pulling his skirts, or clambering over the back of his chair, until, worn out by sport, they dropped successively upon the floor, in such childish slumber, that not even their nurses woke them when they were picked up, like sacks, and carried off to bed upon the shoulders.

It was not long before the rest of us followed, and I found myself luxuriating in a comfortable bed which would have accommodated a platoon. Here, listening to the tree-frog and the owl, I dropped into a profound slumber, and knew nothing more of this under world, until the sun shining through my window, and the voluble note of the mocking-bird, recalled me to the enjoyment of nature and the morning breeze.

So, you have all my adventures up to the moment of my arrival. And as I have set out with a premeditated purpose to register what I see and hear—an inky and therefore a black intent, say you—you shall hear from me again presently; but whether in some descriptive pictures of this old dominion, or in dramatic sketches, or in a journal, or in some rambling letters, I cannot yet foretell. I shall wait upon my occasions. Perhaps I shall give you something compounded of all these. And if a book be the upshot—who's afraid? You may read or let it alone, as you please. " That's the humor of it "—as Nym says.

It may be some time before we meet; till then, I wear you in my heart.

MARK LITTLETON.

Swallow Barn, June 20, 1829.

CHAPTER I.

SWALLOW BARN.

SWALLOW BARN is an aristocratical old edifice which sits, like a brooding hen, on the southern bank of the James River. It looks down upon a shady pocket or nook, formed by an indentation of the shore, from a gentle acclivity thinly sprinkled with oaks whose magnificent branches afford habitation to sundry friendly colonies of squirrels and woodpeckers.

This time-honored mansion was the residence of the family of Hazards. But in the present generation, the spells of love and mortgage have translated the possession to Frank Meriwether, who having married Lucretia, the eldest daughter of my late Uncle Walter Hazard, and lifted some gentlemanlike incumbrances which had been sleeping for years upon the domain, was thus inducted into the proprietary rights. The adjacency of his own estate gave a territorial feature to this alliance, of which the fruits were no less discernible in the multiplication of negroes, cattle, and poultry, than in a flourishing clan of Meriwethers.

The main building is more than a century old. It is built with thick brick walls, but one story in height, and surmounted by a double-faced or hipped roof, which gives the idea of a ship bottom upwards. Later buildings have been added to this, as the wants or ambition of the family have expanded. These are all constructed of wood, and seem to have been built in defiance of all laws of congruity, just as convenience required. But they form altogether an agreeable picture of habitation, suggesting the idea of comfort in the ample space they fill, and in their conspicuous adaptation to domestic uses.

The hall door is an ancient piece of walnut, which has grown too heavy for its hinges, and by its daily travel has furrowed the floor in a quadrant, over which it has an uneasy journey. It is shaded by a narrow porch, with a carved pediment upheld by massive columns of wood, somewhat split by the sun. An ample court-yard, inclosed by a semi-circular paling, extends in front of the whole pile, and is traversed by a gravel road leading from a rather ostentatious iron gate, which is swung between two pillars of brick surmounted by globes of cut stone. Between the gate and the house a large willow spreads its arched and pendent drapery over the grass. A bridle rack stands within the inclosure, and near it a ragged horse-nibbled plum-tree—the current belief being that a plum-tree thrives on ill usage—casts its skeleton shadow on the dust.

Some Lombardy poplars, springing above a mass of shrubbery, partially screen various supernumerary buildings at a short distance in the rear of the mansion. Amongst these is to be seen the gable end of a stable, with the date of its erection stiffly emblazoned in black bricks near the upper angle, in figures set in after the fashion of the work on a girl's sampler. In the same quarter a pigeon-box, reared on a post and resembling a huge tee-totum, is visible, and about its several doors and windows a family of pragmatical pigeons are generally strutting, bridling, and bragging at each other from sunrise until dark.

Appendant to this homestead is an extensive tract of land which stretches some three or four miles along the river, present-ing alternately abrupt promontories mantled with pine and dwarf oak, and small inlets terminating in swamps. Some sparse portions of forest vary the landscape, which, for the most part, exhibits a succession of fields clothed with Indian corn, some small patches of cotton or tobacco plants, with the usual varieties of stubble and fallow grounds. These are inclosed by worm fences of shrunken chestnut, where lizards and ground-squirrels are perpetually running races along the rails.

A few hundred steps from the mansion, a brook glides at a snail's pace towards the river, holding its course through a wilderness of laurel and alder, and creeping around islets covered with green mosses. Across this stream is thrown a rough bridge, which it would delight a painter to see; and not far below it an aged sycamore twists its roots into a grotesque framework to the pure mirror of a spring, which wells up its cool waters from a bed of gravel and runs gurgling to the brook. There it aids in furnishing a cruising ground to a squadron of ducks who, in defiance of all nautical propriety, are incessantly turning up their sterns to the skies. On the grass which skirts the margin of the spring, I observe the family linen is usually spread out by some three or four negro women, who chant shrill music over their wash-tubs, and seem to live in ceaseless warfare with sundry little besmirched and bow-legged blacks, who are never tired of making somersets, and mischievously pushing each other on the clothes laid down to dry.

Beyond the bridge, at some distance, stands a prominent object in the perspective of this picture,—the most venerable appendage to the establishment—a huge barn with an immense roof hanging almost to the ground, and thatched a foot thick with sunburnt straw, which reaches below the eaves in ragged flakes. It has a singularly drowsy and decrepit aspect. The yard around it is strewed knee-deep with litter, from the midst of which arises a long rack resembling a chevaux de frise, which is ordinarily

filled with fodder. This is the customary lounge of half a score
of oxen and as many cows, who sustain an imperturbable companionship with a sickly wagon, whose parched tongue and droop-
ing swingle-trees, as it stands in the sun, give it a most forlorn
and invalid character ; whilst some sociable carts under the sheds,
with their shafts perched against the walls, suggest the idea of a
set of gossiping cronies taking their ease in a tavern porch.
Now and then a clownish hobble-de-hoy colt, with long fetlocks
and disordered mane, and a thousand burs in his tail, stalks
through this company. But as it is forbidden ground to all his
tribe, he is likely very soon to encounter a shower of corn-cobs
from some of the negro men ; upon which contingency he makes
a rapid retreat across the bars which imperfectly guard the entrance to the yard, and with an uncouth display of his heels
bounds away towards the brook, where he stops and looks back
with a saucy defiance ; and after affecting to drink for a noment,
gallops away with a braggart whinny to the fields.

CHAPTER II.

A COUNTRY GENTLEMAN.

THE master of this lordly domain is Frank Meriwether. He is now in the meridian of life—somewhere about forty-five. Good cheer and an easy temper tell well upon him. The first has given him a comfortable, portly figure, and the latter a contemplative turn of mind, which inclines him to be lazy and philosophical.

He has some right to pride himself on his personal appearance, for he has a handsome face, with a dark blue eye and a fine intellectual brow. His head is growing scant of hair on the crown, which induces him to be somewhat particular in the management of his locks in that locality, and these are assuming a decided silvery hue.

It is pleasant to see him when he is going to ride to the Court House on business occasions. He is then apt to make his appearance in a coat of blue broadcloth, astonishingly glossy, and with an unusual amount of plaited ruffle strutting through the folds of a Marseilles waistcoat. A worshipful finish is given to this costume by a large straw hat, lined with green silk. There is a magisterial fulness in his garments which betokens condition in the world, and a heavy bunch of seals, suspended by a chain of gold, jingles as he moves, pronouncing him a man of superfluities.

It is considered rather extraordinary that he has never set up for Congress : but the truth is, he is an unambitious man, and has a great dislike to currying favor—as he calls it. And, besides, he is thoroughly convinced that there will always be men enough in Virginia willing to serve the people, and therefore does not see whỳ he should trouble his head about it. Some years ago, however, there was really an impression that he meant to come out. By some sudden whim, he took it into his head to visit Washington during the session of Congress, and returned, after a fortnight, very seriously distempered with politics. He told curious anecdotes of certain secret intrigues which had been discovered in the affairs of the capital, gave a clear insight into the views of some deep-laid combinations, and became, all at once, painfully florid in his discourse, and dogmatical to a degree that made his wife stare. Fortunately, this orgasm soon subsided, and Frank relapsed into an indolent gentleman of the opposition ; but it had the effect to give a much more decided cast to his studies, for he forthwith discarded the " Richmond Whig " from his newspaper subscription, and took to " The Enquirer," like a man who was not to be disturbed by doubts. And as it was morally impossible to believe all that was written on both sides, to prevent his mind from being abused,·he from this time forward took a stand against the re-election of Mr. Adams to the Presidency, and resolved to give an implicit faith to all alleged facts which set against his administration. The consequence of this straight-forward and confiding deportment was an unexpected complimentary notice of him by the Executive of the State. He was put into the commission of the peace, and having thus become a public man against his will, his opinions were observed to undergo some essential changes. He now thinks that a good citizen ought neither to solicit nor decline office ; that the magistracy of Virginia is the sturdiest pillar which supports the fabric of the Constitution ; and that the people, " though in their opinions they may be mistaken, in their sentiments they are never wrong ;"—with some such other dogmas as, a few years ago, he did not hold in very good repute. In this temper, he has of late embarked on the millpond of county affairs, and nothwithstanding his amiable character and his doctrinary republicanism, I am told he keeps the peace as if he commanded a garrison, and administers justice like a Cadi.

He has some claim to supremacy in this last department; for during three years he smoked segars in a lawyer's office in Richmond, which enabled him to obtain a bird's-eye view of Blackstone and the Revised Code. Besides this, he was a member of a Law Debating Society, which ate oysters once a week in a cellar ; and he wore, in accordance with the usage of the most promising law students of that day, six cravats, one over the other, and yellow-topped boots, by which he was recognized as a blood of the metropolis. Having in this way qualified himself to assert and maintain his rights, he came to his estate, upon his arrival at age, a very model of landed gentlemen. Since that time his avocations have had a certain literary tincture ; for having settled himself down as a married man, and got rid of his superfluous foppery, he rambled with wonderful assiduity through a wilderness of romances, poems, and dissertations, which are now collected in his library, and, with their battered blue covers, present a lively type of an army of continentals at the close of the war, or a hospital of invalids. These have all, at last, given way to the newspapers—a miscellaneous study very attractive and engrossing to country gentlemen. This line of study has rendered Meriwether a most perilous antagonist in the matter of legislative proceedings.

A landed proprietor, with a good house and a host of servants, is naturally a hospitable man. A guest is one of his daily wants

A friendly face is a necessary of life, without which the heart is apt to starve, or a luxury without which it grows parsimonious. Men who are isolated from society by distance, feel these wants by an instinct, and are grateful for the opportunity to relieve them. In Meriwether, the sentiment goes beyond this. It has, besides, something dialectic in it. His house is open to every body, as freely almost as an inn. But to see him when he has had the good fortune to pick up an intelligent, educated gentleman,—and particularly one who listens well!—a respectable, assentatious stranger!—All the better if he has been in the Legislature, or better still, if in Congress. Such a person caught within the purlieus of Swallow Barn, may set down one week's entertainment as certain—inevitable, and as many more as he likes—the more the merrier. He will know something of the quality of Meriwether's rhetoric before he is gone.

Then again, it is very pleasant to see Frank's kind and considerate bearing towards his servants and dependents. His slaves appreciate this, and hold him in most affectionate reverence, and, therefore, are not only contented, but happy under his dominion.

Meriwether is not much of a traveller. He has never been in New England, and very seldom beyond the confines of Virginia. He makes now and then a winter excursion to Richmond, which, I rather think, he considers as the centre of civilization ; and towards autumn, it is his custom to journey over the mountain to the Springs, which he is obliged to do to avoid the unhealthy season in the tide-water region. But the upper country is not much to his taste, and would not be endured by him if it were not for the crowds that resort there for the same reason which operates upon him ; and I may add,—though he would not confess it—for the opportunity this concourse affords him for discussion of opinions.

He thinks lightly of the mercantile interest, and, in fact, undervalues the manners of the large cities generally. He believes that those who live in them are hollow-hearted and insincere, and wanting in that substantial intelligence and virtue, which he affirms to be characteristic of the country. He is an ardent admirer of the genius of Virginia, and is frequent in his commendation of a toast in which the state is compared to the mother of the Gracchi:—indeed, it is a familiar thing with him to speak of the aristocracy of talent as only inferior to that of the landed interest,—the idea of a freeholder inferring to his mind a certain constitutional pre-eminence in all the virtues of citizenship, as a matter of course.

The solitary elevation of a country gentleman, well to do in the world, begets some magnificent notions. He becomes as infallible as the Pope; gradually acquires a habit of making long speeches ; is apt to be impatient of contradiction, and is always very touchy on the point of honor. There is nothing more conclusive than a rich man's logic any where, but in the country, amongst his dependents, it flows with the smooth and unresisted course of a full stream irrigating a meadow, and depositing its mud in fertilizing luxuriance. Meriwether's sayings, about Swallow Barn, import absolute verity. But I have discovered that they are not so current out of his jurisdiction. Indeed, every now and then, we have quite obstinate discussions when some of the neighboring potentates, who stand in the same sphere with Frank, come to the house ; for these worthies have opinions of their own, and nothing can be more dogged than the conflict between them. They sometimes fire away at each other with a most amiable and unconvinceable hardihood for a whole evening, bandying interjections, and making bows, and saying shrewd things with all the courtesy imaginable. But for unextinguishable pertinacity in argument, and utter impregnability of belief, there is

no disputant like your country-gentleman who reads the newspapers. When one of these discussions fairly gets under weigh,
it never comes to an anchor again of its own accord ;—it is either
blown out so far to sea as to be given up for lost, or puts into
port in distress for want of documents,—or is upset by a call for
'the boot-jack and slippers—which is something like the previous
question in Congress.

If my worthy cousin be somewhat over-argumentative as a
politician, he restores the equilibrium of his character by a considerate coolness in religious matters. He piques himself upon
being a high-churchman, but is not the most diligent frequenter
of places of worship, and very seldom permits himself to get into
a dispute upon points of faith. If Mr. Chub, the Presbyterian
tutor in the family, ever succeeds in drawing him into this field,
as he occasionally has the address to do, Meriwether is sure to fly
the course ; he gets puzzled with scripture names, and makes
some odd mistakes between Peter and Paul, and then generally
turns the parson over to his wife, who, he says, has an astonishing
memory.

He is somewhat distinguished as a breeder of blooded horses ;
and, ever since the celebrated race between Eclipse and Henry,
has taken to this occupation with a renewed zeal, as a matter
affecting the reputation of the state. It is delightful to hear him
expatiate upon the value, importance, and patriotic bearing of
this employment, and to listen to all his technical lore touching
the mystery of horse-craft. He has some fine colts in training,
which are committed to the care of a pragmatical old negro, named
Carey, who, in his reverence for the occupation, is the perfect
shadow of his master. He and Frank hold grave and momentous
consultations upon the affairs of the stable, in such a sagacious
strain of equal debate, that it would puzzle a spectator to tell
which was the leading member in the council. Carey thinks he

knows a great deal more upon the subject than his master, and their frequent intercourse has begot a familiarity in the old negro which is almost fatal to Meriwether's supremacy. The old man feels himself authorized to maintain his positions according to the freest parliamentary form, and sometimes with a violence of asseveration that compels his master to abandon his ground, purely out of faint-heartedness. Meriwether gets a little nettled by Carey's doggedness, but generally turns it off in a laugh. I was in the stable with him, a few mornings after my arrival, when he ventured to expostulate with the venerable groom upon a professional point, but the controversy terminated in its customary way. "Who sot you up, Master Frank, to tell me how to fodder that 'ere cretur, when I as good as nursed you on my knee?"

"Well, tie up your tongue, you old mastiff," replied Frank, as he walked out of the stable, "and cease growling, since you will have it your own way;"—and then, as we left the old man's presence, he added, with an affectionate chuckle—"a faithful old cur, too, that snaps at me out of pure honesty; he has not many years left, and it does no harm to humor him!"

CHAPTER III.

WHILST Frank Meriwether amuses himself with his quiddities, and floats through life upon the current of his humor, his dame, my excellent cousin Lucretia, takes charge of the household affairs, as one who has a reputation to stake upon her administration. She has made it a perfect science, and great is her fame in the dispensation thereof!

Those who have visited Swallow Barn will long remember the morning stir, of which the murmurs arose even unto the chambers, and fell upon the ears of the sleepers;—the dry-rubbing of floors, and even the waxing of the same until they were like ice;—and the grinding of coffee-mills;—and the gibber of ducks, and chickens, and turkeys; and all the multitudinous concert of homely sounds. And then, her breakfasts! I do not wish to be counted extravagant, but a small regiment might march in upon her without disappointment; and I would put them for excellence and variety against any thing that ever was served upon platter. Moreover, all things go like clock-work. She rises with the lark, and infuses an early vigor into the whole household. And yet she is a thin woman to look upon, and a feeble; with a sallow complexion, and a pair of animated black eyes which impart a portion of fire to a countenance otherwise demure from the paths

worn across it, in the frequent travel of a low-country ague. But, although her life has been somewhat saddened by such visitations, my cousin is too spirited a woman to give up to them; for she is therapeutical in her constitution, and considers herself a full match for any reasonable tertian in the world. Indeed, I have sometimes thought that she took more pride in her leech craft than becomes a Christian woman : she is even a little vain-glorious. For, to say nothing of her skill in compounding simples, she has occasionally brought down upon her head the sober remonstrances of her husband, by her pertinacious faith in the efficacy of certain spells in cases of intermittent. But there is no reasoning against her experience. She can enumerate the cases—" and men may say what they choose about its being contrary to reason, and all that :—it is their way ! But seeing is believing—nine scoops of water in the hollow of the hand, from the sycamore spring, for three mornings, before sunrise, and a cup of strong coffee with lemon-juice, will break an ague, try it when you will." In short, as Frank says, " Lucretia will die in that creed."

I am occasionally up early enough to be witness to her morning regimen, which, to my mind, is rather tyrannically enforced against the youngsters of her numerous family, both white and black. She is in the habit of preparing some death-routing decoction for them, in a small pitcher, and administering it to the whole squadron in succession, who severally swallow the dose with a most ineffectual effort at repudiation, and gallop off, with faces all rue and wormwood.

Every thing at Swallow Barn, that falls within the superintendence of my cousin Lucretia is a pattern of industry. In fact, I consider her the very priestess of the American system, for, with her, the protection of manufactures is even more of a passion than a principle. Every here and there, over the estate, may be

seen, rising in humble guise above the shrubbery, the rude chim
ney of a log cabin, where all the livelong day the plaintive moaning
of the spinning-wheel rises fitfully upon the breeze, like the fancied notes of a hobgoblin, as they are sometimes imitated in the
stories with which we frighten children. In these laboratories
the negro women are employed in preparing yarn for the loom,
from which is produced not only a comfortable supply of winter
clothing for the working people, but some excellent carpets for
the house.

It is refreshing to behold how affectionately vain our good
hostess is of Frank, and what deference she shows to his judgment
in all matters, except those that belong to the home department ;
—for there she is confessedly and without appeal, the paramount
power. It seems to be a dogma with her, that he is the very
" first man in Virginia," an expression which in this region has
grown into an emphatic provincialism. Frank, in return, is a
devout admirer of her accomplishments, and although he does not
pretend to an ear for music, he is in raptures at her skill on the
harpsichord, when she plays at night for the children to dance ;
and he sometimes sets her to singing ' The Twins of Latona,'
and ' Old Towler,' and ' The Rose-Tree in Full Bearing' (she does
not study the modern music), for the entertainment of his company. On these occasions he stands by the instrument, and
nods his head, as if he comprehended the airs.

She is a fruitful vessel, and seldom fails in her annual tribute
to the honors of the family ; and, sooth to say, Frank is reputed
to be somewhat restiff under these multiplying blessings. They
have two lovely girls, just verging towards womanhood, who
attract a supreme regard in the household, and to whom Frank
is perfectly devoted. Next to these is a boy,—a shrewd, mischievous imp, who curvets about the house, ' a chartered liber-
tine.' He is a little wiry fellow near thirteen, known altogether

by the nick-name of Rip, and has a scapegrace countenance, full
of freckles and devilry; the eyes are somewhat greenish, and
the mouth opens alarmingly wide upon a tumultuous array of
discolored teeth. His whole air is that of an untrimmed colt,
torn down and disorderly; and I most usually find him with the
bosom of his shirt bagged out, so as to form a great pocket,
where he carries apples or green walnuts, and sometimes pebbles, with which he is famous for pelting the fowls.

I must digress, to say a word about Rip's head-gear. He
wears a nondescript skull-cap, which, I conjecture from some
equivocal signs, had once been a fur hat, but which must have
taken a degree in fifty other callings; for I see it daily employed
in the most foreign services. Sometimes it is a drinking-vessel,
and then Rip pinches it up like a cocked hat; sometimes it is
devoted to push-pin, and then it is cuffed cruelly on both sides;
and sometimes it is turned into a basket, to carry eggs from the
hen-roosts. It finds hard service at hat-ball, where, like a plas-
tic statesman, it is popular for its pliability. It is tossed in the
air on all occasions of rejoicing; and now and then serves for a
gauntlet—and is flung with energy upon the ground, on the eve
of a battle; and it is kicked occasionally through the school-
yard, after the fashion of a bladder. It wears a singular exterior, having a row of holes cut below the crown, or rather the
apex, (for it is pyramidal in shape,) to make it cool, as Rip explains it, in hot weather. The only rest that it enjoys through
the day, as far as I have been able to perceive, is during school-
hours, and then it is thrust between a desk and a bulkhead,
three inches apart, where it generally envelopes in its folds a
handful of hickory-nuts or marbles. This covering falls down—
for it has no lining—like an extinguisher over Rip's head. To
prevent the recurrence of this accident, he has tied it up with a
hat-band of twine.

From Rip the rest of the progeny descend on the scale, in regular gradations, like the keys of a Pandean pipe, and with the same variety of intonations, until the series is terminated in a chubby, dough-faced infant, not above three months old. This little infantry is under the care of mistress Barbara Winkle, an antique retainer of the family, who attends them at bed and board,—and every morning, I am told, plunges the whole bevy, one by one, into a tub of cold water, at which they make terrible wry faces.

This mistress Barbara is a functionary of high rank in the family, and of great privileges, from having exercised her office through a preceding generation at Swallow Barn. She is quite remarkable at that time of day when festive preparations are in progress. A dinner-party calls forth all her energy, and exhibits her to great advantage as an effective woman. She glides up and down stairs like a phantom, and you are aware of her coming by a low jingle of keys. One moment she is whipping cream, and the next threatening the same operation on some unlucky youngster of the kitchen who chances to meddle with her labors. You may hear her clattering eggs in a bowl, scolding servants, and screaming at Rip, who is perpetually in her way, amongst the sweetmeats : all of which matters, though enacted with a vinegar aspect, it is easy to see are very agreeable to her self-love.

There is no reverence like that of children for potentates of this description. Her very glance has in it something disconcerting to the young fry ; and they will twist their dumpling faces into every conceivable expression of grief, before they will dare to squall out in her presence. Even Rip is afraid of her. "When the old woman's mad, she is a horse to whip !" he told Ned and myself one morning, upon our questioning him as to the particulars of an uproar in which he had been the principal actor.

These exercises on the part of the old lady are neither rare nor unwholesome, and are winked at by the higher authorities.

Mrs. Winkle's complexion is the true parchment, and her voice is somewhat cracked. She takes Scotch snuff from a silver box, and wears a pair of horn spectacles, which give effect to the peculiar peakedness of her nose. On days of state she appears in all the rich coxcombry of the olden time; her gown being of an obsolete fashion, sprinkled with roses and sun-flowers, and her lizard arms encased in tight sleeves as far as the elbow, where they are met by silken gloves without fingers. A starched tucker is pinned, with a pedantic precision, across her breast; and a prim cap of muslin, puckered into a point with a grotesque conceit, adorns her head.—Take her altogether, she looks very stately and bitter. Then, when she walks, it is inconceivable how aristocratically she rustles,—especially on a Sunday.

CHAPTER IV.

MY picture of the family at Swallow Barn would be incomplete if I did not give a conspicuous place to my two young cousins, Lucy and Victorine. It is true they are cousins only in the second remove, but I have become sufficiently naturalized to the soil to perceive the full value of the relation; and as they acknowledge it very affectionately to me—for I was promoted to "Cousin Mark" almost in the first hour after my arrival—I should be unreasonably reluctant if I did not assert the full right of blood. Lucy tells me she is *only* fifteen, and that she is one year and one month older than Vic, "for all that Vic is taller than she." Now, Lucy is a little fairy with blue eyes and light hair, and partially freckled and sun-burnt—being a very pretty likeness of Rip, who, I have said, is an imp of homeliness; a fact which all experience shows to be quite consistent with the highest beauty. Victorine is almost a head taller, and possesses a stronger frame. She differs, too, from her sister by her jet-black eyes and dark hair; though they resemble each other in the wholesome tan which exposure to the atmosphere has spread alike over the cheeks of both.

These two girls are educated entirely at home, and are growing up together in the most confiding mutual affection. There is nothing more lovely than two sisters in this relation, tranquilly and unconsciously gliding onwards to womanhood amongst the familiar images and gentle influences of the household circle; their kindly impulses set in motion by the caresses of friends; their tastes directed by the simple and pure enjoyments of a refined home in the country, where nature supplies so many beautiful objects to attract the eye, and affection so much pleasant guidance to inform the heart; where lessons of love are received from parental teaching, or absorbed, rather, from looks that are more eloquent than words;. where useful instruction loses all its weariness in the encouragement of that fond applause which is assiduous to reward patient toil or to cheer the effort which has paused in the fear of failure. No over-stimulated ambition is likely there to taint the mind with those vices of rivalry which, in schools, often render youth selfish and unamiable, and suggest thoughts of concealment and stratagem as aids in the race of pre-eminence. Home, to a young girl, is a world peopled with kindly faces and filled only with virtues. She does not know, even by report, the impure things of life. She has heard and read of its miseries, for which her heart melts in charity, and she grows up in the faith that she was born to love the good and render kind offices to the wretched; but she conceives nothing of the wickedness of a world which she has never seen, and lives on to womanhood in a happy and guarded ignorance, which is not broken until her mind has acquired a strength sufficient to discern and repel whatever there may be dangerous in knowledge.

> "Affections are as thoughts to her,
> The measures of her hours"——

Poh!—bless me!—These children have actually brought me to lecturing and quoting verse. Let me get back to my appropriate function of narrative.

Lucy is rather meditative for her age—calm and almost
matronly. She is a little housekeeper, and affects to have cares.
Victorine is more intrepid, and attracts universal regard by the
jollity of her temperament, which is equally the index of her
innocence and her healthful organization. They pursue the same
studies, and I see them every morning at their tasks, often reading from the same book with their arms around each other's
waist. They have profound confidences in which they think
themselves very secure and exclusive ; but I can often tell them
their whole secret by watching their by-play ;—which shrewdness
of mine is so inexplicable to them, that they think I am something of a conjurer. I frequently walk with them in the evening
on the river bank. They are invariably attended upon these
rambles by two large white pointers, who gambol around them
with a most affectionate playfulness, and are constantly soliciting
the applause of their pretty mistresses by the gallant assiduities
which are characteristic of this race of faithful animals.

Meriwether is accustomed to have these girls read to him
some portion of every day. By this requisition, which he puts
upon the ground of an amusement for himself, he has beguiled
them into graver studies than are generally pursued at that time
of life. It is quite charming to notice the unwearying devotion
they bestow upon this labor, which they think gives pleasure to
their father. He, of course, looks upon them as the most gifted
creatures in existence. And truly, they have gained so much
upon me, that I don't think he is far wrong.

A window in the upper story of one of the wings of the building overlooks a flower-garden, and around this window grows a
profusion of creeping vine which is trained with architectural
precision along the wall to the roof. It is a prim, decorous
plant, with icy leaves of perdurable green, without a flower of its
own to give variety to its staid drapery. Here and there, how-

ever, an intruding rose has stolen a nest amongst its plexures, and looks pleasantly forth from this sober tapestry. In this window, about noon-tide, may be daily seen the profuse tresses of a head of flaxen hair scrupulously adjusted in glossy volume ; and ever and anon, as it moves to some thoughtful impulse, is disclosed a studious brow of fairest white. And sometimes, more fully revealed, may be seen the entire head of the lady as she sits intent upon the perusal of a book. The lady Prudence is in her bower, and pursues some theme of fancy in the delicious realm of poesy, or with pencil and brush shapes and gilds the wings of gaudy butterflies, or, peradventure, enricheth her album with dainty sonnets. And sometimes, in listless musing, she rests her chin upon her gem-bedizened hand, and fixes her soft blue eye upon the flower-beds where the humming-bird is poised before the honeysuckle. But howsoever engaged, it is a dedicated hour. I have said profanely, once before, that "a tall spinster" sat at the family board, and now here she sits in her morning guise, silent and alone, pondering over the creations of genius and the dreams of art.

Prudence Meriwether is an only sister of Frank's, and holds a station somewhat eminent amongst the household idols. She is rather comely to look upon—very neat in person, and is considered high authority in matter of dress. But Time, who notches mortal shapes with as little mercy as the baker, in his morning circuit, notches his tally-stick, has calendared his visits even upon this goodly form. A shrewd observer may note in sundry evidences of a fastidious choice of colors, and of what,—to coin a word,—I might call a scrupulous *toiletry*, that the lapse of human seasons has not passed unheeded by this lady. He may detect, sometimes, an overdone vivacity in her accost, and an exaggerated thoughtlessness ; sometimes, in her tone of conversation, a little too much girlishness, which betrays a suspicion of its opposite: and there are certain sober lines journeying from the mouth cheekward, which are ruminative, in spite of her light-heartedness. These are quite pleasant signs to an astute, experienced, perspicacious bachelor, like myself, who can read them with a learned skill; they speak of that mellow time when a woman captivates by complaisance, and overcomes her adver sary rather by marching out of her fort to challenge attack, than by standing a siege within it.

There is a dash of the picturesque in the character of this lady. Towards sunset she is apt to stray forth amongst the old oaks, and to gather small bouquets of wild flowers, in the pursuit of which she contrives to get into very pretty attitudes; or she falls into raptures at the shifting tints of the clouds on the western sky, and produces quite a striking pictorial effect by the skilful choice of a position which shows her figure in strong relief against the evening light. And then in her boudoir may be found exquisite sketches from her pencil, of forms of love and beauty, belted and buckled knights, old castles and pensive ladies, Madonnas and cloistered nuns,—the offspring of an artistic imagination heated with romance and devotion. Her attire is, sometimes, studiously simple and plain, and her bearing is demure and contemplative; but this is never long continued, for, in spite of her discipline, she does not wish to be accounted as one inclined to be serious in her turn of mind. I have seen her break out into quite a riotous vivacity. This is very likely to ensue when she is brought into fellowship with a flaunting mad cap belle who is carrying all before her: she then "overbears her continents," and becomes as flaunting a madcap as the other.

If Prudence has a fault—which proposition I prudently put with an *if*, as a doubtful question—it is in setting the domestic virtues at too high a value. One may, perhaps, be too inveterately

charitable. I think the establishment of three Sunday schools, a
colonization society membership, a management in a tract association, and an outward and visible patronage of the cause of
temperance, by the actual enrolment of her name amongst those
who have taken the pledge, smack a little of supererogation,
though I don't wish to set up my judgment too peremptorily on
this point. And I think, also, one may carry the praise of the
purity of country life, and of the benefits of solitude and self-
constraint, to an extent which might appear merciless towards
those whose misfortune it is to live in a sphere where these virtues
cannot be so fully cultivated. If a tendency in this direction be
a blemish in the composition of our lady, it is a very slight one,
and is amply compensated by the many pleasant aberrations she
makes from this phase of her character. She converses with
great ease upon all subjects—even with a dangerous facility, I
may say, which sometimes leads her into hyperbole : her diction
occasionally becomes high-flown, and expands into the incompre-
hensible—but that is only when she is excited. Her manner, at
times, might be called oratorical, particularly when, in imitation
of her brother, she bewails the departure of the golden age, or
declaims upon the prospect of its revival among the rejuvenescent
glories of the Old Dominion. She has an awful idea of the perfect respectability, I might almost say splendor, of her lineage,
and this is one of the few points upon which I know her to be
touchy.

Apart from these peculiarities, which are but fleecy clouds
upon a summer sky, even enhancing its beauty, or mites upon a
snow-drift, she is a captivating specimen of a ripened maiden,
just standing on that sunshiny verge from which the prospect
beyond presents a sedate autumnal landscape gently subsiding
into undistinguishable and misty confusion of hill and dale arrayed in golden-tinted gray. It is no wonder, therefore, that with

her varied perfections, and the advantages of her position, the James River world should insensibly have elevated Prudence Meriwether to the poetical altitude of the " cynosure of neighboring eyes."

CHAPTER V.

NED HAZARD.

Ned Hazard has become my inseparable companion. He has a fine, flowing stream of good spirits, which is sometimes interrupted by a slight under-current of sadness; it is even a ludicrous pensiveness, that derives its comic quality from Ned's constitutional merriment.

He is now about thirty-three, with a tolerably good person, a little under six feet, and may be seen generally after breakfast, whilst old Carey is getting our horses for a morning ride, in an olive frock, black stock, and yellow waistcoat, with a German forage-cap of light cloth, having a frontlet of polished leather, rather conceitedly drawn over his dark, laughing eye. This head-gear gives a picturesque effect to his person, and suits well with his weather-beaten cheek, as it communicates a certain reckless expression that agrees with his character. The same trait is heightened by the half swagger with which he strikes his boot with his riding-whip, or keeps at bay a beautiful spaniel, called Wilful, which haunts his person like a familiar. Indeed, I have grown to possess something of this canine attachment to him myself, and already constitute a very important member of his suite. It is a picture worth contemplating, to see us during one of those listless intervals. For, first, there is Ned lounging along the court-yard with both hands in his side pockets, and either telling me some story, or vexing a great turkey-cock, by imitating both his gobble and his strut;—before him walks Wilful, strictly regulating his pace by his master's, and turning his eye, every now and then, most affectionately towards him; then Meriwether's two pointers may be seen bounding in circles round him;—a little terrier, who assumes the consequence of a watch-dog, is sure to solicit Ned's notice by jumping at his hand; and, last in the train, is myself, who have learned to saunter in Ned's track with the fidelity of a shadow. It may be conjectured from this picture that Ned possesses fascinations for man and beast.

He is known universally by the name of Ned Hazard, which, of itself, I take to be a good sign. This nicknaming has a flavor of favoritism, and betokens an amiable notoriety. There is something jocular in Ned's face, which I believe is the source of his popularity with all classes; but this general good acceptation is preserved by the variety of his acquirements. He can accommodate himself to all kinds of society. He has slang for the stable-boys, proverbs for the old folks, and a most oratorical overflow of patriotism for the politicians. To the children of Swallow Barn he is especially captivating. He tells them stories with the embellishment of a deep tone of voice that makes them quake in their shoes; and with the assistance of a cane and cloak, surmounted by a hat, he will stalk amongst them, like a grizzly giant, so hideously erect, that the door is a mere pigeon-hole to him;—at which the young cowards laugh so fearfully, that I have often thought they were crying.

A few years ago he was seized with a romantic fever which manifested itself chiefly in a conceit to visit South America, and play knight-errant in the quarrel of the Patriots. It was the most sudden and unaccountable thing in the world; for no one could trace the infection to any probable cause;—still, it grew upon Ned's fancy, and appeared in so many brilliant phases, that there was no getting it out of his brain. As may be imagined, this matter produced a serious disquiet in the family, so that Frank Meriwether was obliged to take the subject in hand; and, finding all his premonitions and expostulations unavailing, was forced to give way to the current of Ned's humor, hoping that experience would purge the sight that had been dimmed by the light of a too vivid imagination. It was therefore arranged that Ned should visit this theatre of glory, and stand by the award of his own judgment upon the view. He accordingly sailed from New-York in the Paragon, bound for Lima, and, in due time, doubled Cape Horn. So, after glancing at the Patriots in all their positions, attitudes and relations,—with an eye military and civil,—and being well bitten with fleas, and apprehended as a spy, and nearly assassinated as a heretic, he carefully looked back upon the whole train of this fancy, even from its first engendering, with all the motives, false conclusions, misrepresentations, and so forth, which had a hand in the adopting and pursuing of it, and then came to a sober conclusion that he was the most egregious fool that had ever set out in quest of a wild goose. "What the devil could have put such a thing into my head, and kept me at it for a whole year, it puzzles me to tell!" was his own comment upon this freak, when I questioned him about it. However, he came home the most disquixotted cavalier that ever hung up his shield at the end of a scurvy crusade; and to make amends for the inconvenience and alarm he had occasioned,—for my cousin Lucretia expected to hear of his being strangled, like Laocoon, in the folds of a serpent,—he brought with him an amusing journal, which is now bound in calf, and holds a conspicuous place in the library at Swallow Barn. This trip into the other hemisphere has furnished him with an assortment of wonders, both of the sea and the land, the theme of divers long stories, which Ned tells

like a traveller. He is accused of repeating them to the same
auditors, and Frank Meriwether has a provoking way of raising
his hands, and turning his eyes towards the ceiling, and saying
in an under-tone, just as Ned is setting out:

> "A traveller there was who told a good tale;
> By my troth! it was true, but then it was stale."

This invariably flushes Ned's face; and with a modest expos-
tulation, in a voice of great kindness, he will say, "My dear sir, I
assure you I never told you this before—you are thinking of a
different thing." "Then, Uncle Ned"—as Rip said, on one of these
occasions, while he was lying on the floor and kicking up his
heels—"you are going to make as you go."—These things are
apt to disconcert him, and occasion a little out-break of a momentary peevish, but irresistibly comic thoughtfulness, which I have
said before formed a constituent of his temper. It is, however,
but for a moment, and he takes the joke like a hero. It is now
customary in the family, when any thing of a marvellous nature
is mentioned, to say that it happened round the Horn. Ned is
evidently shy of these assaults, and rather cautious how he names
the Horn if Meriwether be in company.

I have gleaned some particulars of Hazard's education, which,
as they serve to illustrate his character, I think worth relating.
When he was ten or eleven years old, he was put under the
government of a respectable teacher, who kept an academy on the
border of the mountain country, where he spent several years of his
life. In this rustic gymnasium, under the supervision of Mr. Crab,
who was the principal of the establishment, he soon became conspicuous for his hardiness and address in the wayward adventures
and miniature wars which diversified the history of this little
community. He was always an apt scholar, though not the most
assiduous; but his frank and upright qualities rendered him equally

a favorite with the master aud the pupils. He speaks of the attachments of this period of his life with the unction of unabated fondness. In one of our late rambles, he gave me the following sketch of the circumstances under which he quitted these scenes of his youth. His father was about removing him to college, and the separation was to be final. I have endeavored to preserve his own narrative, because I think it more graphic than mine would be; and at the same time it will show the gentle strain of affection that belongs to his nature.

"The condition of a schoolboy," said Ned, "forces upon the mind the import of a state of probation, more soberly than any other position in life. All that the scripture tells us about the transitoriness of human affairs,—of man being a traveller, and life a shadow,—is constitutionally part and parcel of the meditations of the schoolboy. He lives amidst discomforts; his room is small and ill-furnished; his clothes are hung upon a peg, or stowed away in a chest, where every thing that should be at the top, is sure to lodge at the bottom; his coat carries its rent from term to term, and his stockings are returned to him undarned from the washerwoman; his food is rough and unsavory; he shivers in a winter morning over a scant and smoky fire; he sleeps in summer in the hottest room of the house:—All this he submits to with patience, because he feels that he is but for a season, and that a reversion of better things awaits him.

"My preceptor Mr. Crab was, outwardly, an austere man; but his was the austerity which the best natures are apt to contract from long association with pupils. His intercourse with the boys was one of command, and he had but few opportunities of mingling in the society of his equals. This gave a rather severe reserve to his manners; but, at bottom, he had kindly feelings which awkwardly manifested themselves in frequent favors, conferred without any visible signs of courtesy. His wife was a fat,

shortwinded old lady, with a large round face, embellished above
with a large ruffled cap, and below, with a huge double chin.
This good lady was rather too fat to move about, so she maintained a sovereign station in an ample arm-chair, placed near the
door that led to the kitchen, where she was usually occupied in
paring apples to be baked up into tough jacks for our provender,
aud issuing commands for the regulation of her domestic police,
in shrill, stirring and authoritative tones. They had a reasonable
number of young scions growing around them, who, however, were
so mingled in the mass of the school as nearly to have lost all the
discriminating instincts which might indicate their origin.

"We were too troublesome a company to enlist much of the
domestic charities from our tutor; still, however, in the few gleams
of family endearment which fell to our lot, I had contracted a kind
of household attachment to the objects that surrounded me. Our
old master had the grave and solemn bearing of a philosopher;
but sometimes, of winter nights, when our tasks were done, he
joined in our sports,—even got down on the carpet to play marbles
with us, and took quite an eager interest in hearing our humming tops when we stealthily set them to bellowing in the room.
These condescensions had a wonderful effect upon us all, for, being
rare, they took us somewhat by surprise, and gave us something
of the same kind of pleasure which a child experiences in patting
a gentle and manageable lion.

"I had always looked forward, with a boyish love of change, to
the period when I was to be called to other scenes. And this
expectation, whilst it rendered me indifferent to personal comforts,
seemed also to warm my feelings towards my associates. I could
pardon many trespasses in those from whom I was soon to be separated. My time, therefore, passed along in a careless merriment,
in which all trivial ills were overborne and indemnified in the anticipations of the future.

" The summons to quit this little sylvan theatre was contained in a letter brought from my father by Daniel the coachman. It directed me to return without delay, and intimated, amidst a world of parental advice, that I was to be removed almost immediately to college. Notwithstanding the many secret yearnings I had felt for the approach of this period, I confess it overmastered me when it came. Daniel had brought me my pony,—a little, short-necked, piggish animal, which in the holidays I used to ride almost to bed—and he himself was ready to attend me on one of the coach-horses. I had no time to revolve the matter,—so with a spirit part gay and part melancholy, and with an alacrity of step assumed to conceal my emotions and to avoid the interchange with my school-fellows of words I was too much choked to utter, I went about my preparations. I collected my straggling wardrobe from the detached service of my comrades, to whom, scant as it was, I had lent it piece-meal; carefully paid off sundry small debts of honor, contracted at the forbidden game of all-fours; and distributed largesses, with a prodigal hand, amongst the negroes, with whom I had, for a long time, carried on an active commerce in partridge-traps, fishing tackle, and other commodities. I can remember now with what feelings I performed this last office, as I stood at the barn door, where the farm servants were threshing grain, and protracted, as long as I was able, that mournful shaking of hands with which the rogues gave me their parting benedictions;—for I always had a vagabond fondness for the blacks about the establishment. After this I went into the parlor, where our tender and plethoric mistress was employed in one of her customary morning duties of cleaning up the breakfast apparatus, and received a kiss from her, as she held a napkin in one hand and a tea-cup in the other. I bestowed the same token of grace upon all the little Crabs that were crawling about the room, and, in the same place, took my leave of the old monarch himself, who, relaxing into a grim manifestation of sorrow, took me with both hands, and conducting me to the window, placed himself in a seat, where he gave me a grave and friendly admonition,—saying many kind things to me, in a kinder tone than I had ever heard from him before. Amongst the rest, he bade me reflect, that the world was wide, and had many fountains of bitter waters, whereof—as I was an easy, good-natured fellow —it was likely to be my lot to drink more largely than others;— he begged me to remember the many wholesome lessons he had given me, and to forget whatever might seem to me harsh in his own conduct. Then, in the old-fashioned way, he put his hands upon my head, and bestowed upon me an earnest and devout blessing, whilst the tears started in both of our eyes. This last act he concluded by taking from his pocket a small copy of the Bible, which he put into my hands with a solemn exhortation that I should consult it in all my troubles, for every one of which, he told me, I should find appropriate consolation. I promised, as well as my smothered articulation permitted, to obey his instructions to the letter; and, from the feelings of that moment, deemed it impossible I ever could have forgotten or neglected them. I fear that I have not thought of them as much since, as they deserve. The little Bible I still keep as an affectionate remembrance of my very good old friend.

"My cronies, all this time, had been following me from place to place,—watching me as I packed up every article of my baggage, and asking me hundreds of unmeaning questions, out of the very fulness of their hearts. Their time came next. We had a general embrace; and after shaking hands with every urchin of the school-room and every imp of the kitchen, I mounted my plump nag, and on one of those rich mornings of the Indian summer, when the sun struggles through a soft mist, and sparkles on the hoar-frost, I broke ground on my homeward voyage.

Daniel, with my black leather trunk resting on his pommel—to be carried to the tavern where the mail stage was to receive it— led the way through the lane that conducted us beyond the precincts of this abode of learning and frolick, and I followed, looking back faint-heartedly upon the affectionate and envious rank and file of the school-room, who were collected in one silent and wistful group at the door, with their hard-visaged commander towering above their heads, and shading his brow from the sun with his hand, as he watched our slow progress. Every other face, white or black, upon the premises, was peering above the paling that inclosed the yard, or gleaming through the windows of the kitchen. Not a dry eye was there amongst us; and I could hear my old master say to the boys, "there goes an honest chap, full of gallantry and good will." In truth, this parting touched me to the heart, and I could not help giving way to my feelings, and sobbing aloud; until at last, reaching a turn in the road that concealed us from the house, the sound of a distant cheering from the crowd we had left, arose upon the air, and wafted to me the good wishes of some of the best friends I have ever parted from."

After the period referred to in this narrative, Ned was sent to Princeton. That college was then in the height of its popularity, and was the great resort of the southern students. Here he ran the usual wild and unprofitable career of college life. His father was lavish, and Ned was companionable,—two relative virtues which, in such circumstances, are apt to produce a luxuriant fruit. He was famous in the classical coteries at Mother Priestley's, where they ate buckwheat cakes, and discussed the state of parties, and where, having more blood than argument, they made furious bets on controverted questions, and drank juleps to keep up the opposition.

Amidst the distractions of that period there was one concern in which Ned became distinguished. They were never without a supply of goddesses in the village, to whom the students devoted themselves in the spirit of chivalry. They fell into despair by classes ; and as it was impracticable to allot the divinities singly, these were allowed each some six or seven worshippers from the college ranks, who revolved around them, like a system of roystering planets, bullying each other out of their orbits, and cutting all manner of capers in their pale light. But love, in those days, was not that tame, docile, obedient minion that it is now. It was a matter of bluster and bravado, to swear round oaths for, and to be pledged in cups at Gifford's. They danced with the beauties at all the merry-makings, and, in fact, metamorphosed Cupid into a bluff Hector, and dragged him by the heels around every tavern of the village.

As the mistresses were appurtenant to the class, they were changed at the terms, and given over to the successors ; whereby it generally fell out, that what advantage the damsels gained in the number of their admirers, was more than balanced by the disadvantage of age. But a collegian's arithmetic makes no difference between seventeen and thirty. Nay, indeed, some of the most desperate love affairs happened between the sophomores and one or two perdurable belles, who had been besonneted through the college for ten years before.

It was Ned's fortune to drop into one of these pit-falls, and he was only saved from an actual elopement by a rare accident which seemed to have been sent on purpose by his good genius ; for, on the very evening when this catastrophe was to have been brought about, he fell into a revel, and then into a row, and then into a deep sleep, from which he awoke the next morning, shockingly mortified to find that he had not only forgotten his appointment, but also his character as a man of sober deportment. The lady's pride took alarm at the occurrence, and Ned very solemnly took to mathematics.

Now and then, the affairs of this bustling little community were embellished with a single combat, which was always regarded as a highly interesting incident; and the abstruse questions of the duello were canvassed in councils held at midnight, in which, I learn, the chivalrous lore displayed by Ned Hazard was a matter of college renown.

Engrossed thus, like the states of the dark ages, in the cares of love, war, and politics, it is not to be wondered at, that the arts and sciences should have fallen into some disesteem. This period of Ned's life, indeed, resembled those feudal times, when barons fought for lady love,—swaggered, and swore by their saints,—and frightened learning into the nests of the monks. Still, however, there was a generous love of fame lurking in his constitution, which, notwithstanding all the enticements that waylaid his success, showed itself in occasional fits of close and useful study.

It pains me to say, that Hazard's days of academic glory were untimely cropped; but my veracity as a chronicler compels me to avow, even to the disparagement of my friend, that before his course had run to its destined end, he made shipwreck of his fortunes, and received from the faculty a passport that warranted an unquestioned egress from Nassau Hall;—the same being conferred in consideration of counsel afforded, as a friend true and trusty, to a worthy cavalier, who had answered the defiance of a gentleman of honor, to " a joust at utterance."

Thus shorn of his college laurels, Ned crept quietly back to Swallow Barn, where his inglorious return astounded the soothsayers of the neighborhood. For awhile he took to study like a Pundit,—though I have heard that it did not last long,—and in the lonely pursuits of this period he engendered that secret love of adventure and picturesque incident, that took him upon his celebrated expedition round the Horn. But it in no degree conquered his mirthful temper. His mind is still a fairy land, inhabited by pleasant and conceited images, winged charmers, laughing phantoms, and mellow spectres of frolick.

He is regarded in the family as the next heir to Swallow Barn; but the marriage of his sister, and soon afterwards, the demise of his father, disclosed the incumbered condition of the freehold, to which he had before been a stranger. He has still, however, a comfortable patrimony; and Frank Meriwether having by arrangement taken possession of the inheritance, together with the family, Ned has ample liberty to pursue his own whims in regard to his future occupation in life. Frank holds the estate, for the present, under an honorable pledge to relieve it of its burdens by a gradual course of thrifty husbandry, which he seems to be in a fair way of accomplishing; so that Ned may be said still to have a profitable reversion in the domain. But he has grown, in some degree, necessary to Meriwether, and has therefore, of late, fixed his residence almost entirely at Swallow Barn.

CHAPTER VI.

FROM the house at Swallow Barn, there is to be seen, at no great distance, a clump of trees, and in the midst of these an humble building is discernible, which seems to court the shade in which it is modestly embowered. It is an old structure built of logs. Its figure is a cube, with a roof rising from all sides to a point, and surmounted by a wooden weathercock which somewhat resembles a fish, and somewhat a fowl.

This little edifice is a rustic shrine devoted to Cadmus, and here the sacred rites of the alphabet are daily solemnized by some dozen knotty-pated and freckled votaries not above three feet high, both in trowsers and petticoats. This is one of the many temples that stud the surface of our republican empire, where liberty receives her purest worship, and where, though in humble and lowly guise, she secretly breathes her strength into the heart and sinews of the nation. Here the germ is planted that fructifies through generations, and produces its hundred-fold. At this altar the spark is kindled that propagates its fire from breast to breast, like the vast conflagrations that light up and purify the prairie of the west.

The school-house has been an appendage to Swallow Barn ever since the infancy of the last generation. Frank Meriwether has, in his time, extended its usefulness by opening it to the accommodation of his neighbors ; so that it is now a theatre whereon a bevy of pigmy players are wont to enact the serio-comic interludes which belong to the first process of indoctrination. A troop of these little sprites are seen, every morning, wending their way across the fields, armed with tin-kettles, in which are deposited their apple-pies or other store for the day, and which same kettles are generally used, at the decline of the day, as drums or cymbals, to signalize their homeward march, or as receptacles of the spoil pilfered from blackberry bushes, against which these barefooted Scythians are prone to carry on a predatory war.

Throughout the day a continual buzz is heard from this quarter, even to the porch of the mansion-house. Hazard and myself occasionally make them a visit, and it is amusing to observe how, as we approach, the murmur becomes more distinct, until, reaching the door, we find the whole swarm running over their long, tough syllables, in a high concert pitch, with their elbows upon the desks, their hands covering their ears, and their naked heels beating time against the benches—as if every urchin believed that a polysyllable was a piece of discord invented to torment all ears but his own. And, high above this din, the master's note is sounded in a lordly key, like the occasional touch of the horn in an orchestra.

This little empire is under the dominion of parson Chub. He is a plump, rosy old gentleman, rather short and thick set, with the blood-vessels meandering over his face like rivulets,—a pair of prominent blue eyes, and a head of silky hair, not unlike the covering of a white spaniel. He may be said to be a man of jolly dimensions, with an evident taste for good living ; somewhat sloven in his attire, for his coat,—which is not of the newest,— is decorated with sundry spots that are scattered over it in con- stellations. Besides this, he wears an immense cravat, which, as it is wreathed around his short neck, forms a bowl beneath his chin, and,—as Ned says,—gives the parson's head the appearance of that of John the Baptist upon a charger, as it is sometimes represented in the children's picture books. His beard is griz- zled with silver stubble, which the parson reaps about twice a week,—if the weather be fair.

Mr. Chub is a philosopher after the order of Socrates. He was an emigrant from the Emerald Isle, where he suffered much tribulation in the disturbances, as they are mildly called, of his much-enduring country. But the old gentleman has weathered the storm without losing a jot of that broad healthy benevolence with which nature has enveloped his heart, and whose ensign she has hoisted in his face. The early part of his life had been easy and prosperous, until the rebellion of 1798 stimulated his republicanism into a fever, and drove the full-blooded hero headlong into the quarrel, and put him, in spite of his peaceful profession, to standing by his pike in behalf of his principles. By this unhappy boiling over of the caldron of his valor he fell under the ban of the ministers, and tasted his share of government mercy. His house was burnt over his head, his horses and hounds (for, by all accounts, he was a perfect Ac- teon) were " confiscate to the state," and he was forced to fly. This brought him to America in no very compromising mood with royalty.

Here his fortunes appear to have been various, and he was tossed to and fro by the battledore of fate, until he found a snug harbor at Swallow Barn ; where, some years ago, he sat down in that quiet repose which a worried and badgered patriot is best fitted to enjoy.

He is a good scholar, and having confined his reading entirely to the learning of the ancients, his republicanism is somewhat after the Grecian mould.   He has never read any politics of later date than the time of the Emperor Constantine,—not even a newspaper;— so that he may be said to have been contemporary with Æschines rather than Lord Castlereagh, until that eventful epoch of his life when his blazing roof-tree awakened him from his anachronistical dream.   This notable interruption, however, gave him but a feeble insight into the moderns, and he soon relapsed to Thucydides and Livy, with some such glimmerings of the American Revolution upon his remembrance as most readers have of the exploits of the first Brutus.

The old gentleman has a learned passion for folios.   He had been a long time urging Meriwether to make some additions to his collections of literature, and descanted upon the value of some of the ancient authors as foundations, both moral and physical, to the library.   Frank gave way to the argument, partly to gratify the parson, and partly from the proposition itself having a smack that touched his fancy.   The matter was therefore committed entirely to Mr. Chub, who forthwith set out on a voyage of exploration to the north.   I believe he got as far as Boston. He certainly contrived to execute his commission with a curious felicity.   Some famous Elzivirs were picked up, and many other antiques that nobody but Mr. Chub would ever think of opening.

The cargo arrived at Swallow Barn in the dead of winter. During the interval between the parson's return from his expedition and the coming of the books, the reverend little schoolmaster is said to have been in a remarkably unquiet state of body, which almost prevented him from sleeping, and that the sight of the long expected treasures had the happiest effect upon him. There was ample accommodation for this new acquisition of ancient wisdom provided before its arrival, and Mr. Chub now spent a whole week in arranging the volumes on their proper shelves, having, as report affirms, altered the arrangement at least seven times during that period.

After this matter was settled, he regularly spent his evenings in the library. Frank Meriwether was hardly behind the parson in this fancy, and took, for a short time, to abstruse reading. They both, consequently, deserted the little family circle every evening after tea, and might have continued to do so all the winter but for a discovery made by Hazard.

Ned had seldom joined the two votaries of science in their philosophical retirement, and it was whispered in the family that the parson was giving Frank a quiet course of lectures in the ancient philosophy, for Meriwether was known to talk a good deal, about that time, of the old and new Academicians. But it happened upon one dreary winter night, during a tremendous snowstorm, which was banging the shutters and doors of the house, that Ned, having waited in the parlor for the philosophers until midnight, set out to invade their retreat,—not doubting that he should find them deep in study. When he entered the library, both candles were burning in their sockets, with long, untrimmed wicks; the fire was reduced to its last embers, and, in an arm-chair on one side of the table, the parson was discovered in a sound sleep over Jeremy Taylor's Ductor Dubitantium; whilst Frank, in another chair on the opposite side, was snoring over a folio edition of Montaigne. And upon the table stood a small stone pitcher containing a residuum of whisky-punch, now grown cold. Frank started up in great consternation upon hearing Ned's footstep beside him, and, from that time, almost entirely deserted the library. Mr. Chub, however, was not so easily drawn away from the career of his humor, and still shows his hankering after his leather-coated friends.

It is an amusing point in the old gentleman's character to observe his freedom in contracting engagements that depend upon his purse. He seems to think himself a rich man, and is continually becoming security for some of the neighbors. To hear him talk, it would be supposed that he meant to renovate the affairs of the whole county. As his intentions are so generous, Meriwether does not fail to back him when it comes to a pinch ;—by reason of which the good squire has more than once been obliged to pay the penalty.

Mr. Chub's character, as it will be seen from this description of him, possesses great simplicity. This has given rise to some practical jokes against him, which have caused him much annoyance. The tradition in the family goes, that, one evening, the worthy divine, by some strange accident, fell into an excess in his cups ; and that a saucy chamber-maid found him dozing in his chair, with his pipe in his mouth, having the bowl turned downward, and the ashes sprinkled over his breast. He was always distinguished by a broad and superfluous ruffle to his shirt, and, on this occasion, the mischievous maid had the effrontery to set it on fire. It produced, as may be supposed, a great alarm to the parson, and, besides, brought him into some scandal ; for he was roused up in a state of consternation, and began to strip himself of his clothes, not knowing what he was about. I don't know how far he exposed himself, but the negro women, who ran to his relief, made a fine story of it.

Hazard once reminded him of this adventure, in my presence, and it was diverting to see with what a comic and quiet sheepishness he bore the joke. He half closed his eyes and puckered up his mouth as Ned proceeded; and when the story came to the conclusion, he gave Ned a gentle blow on the breast with the back of his hand, crying out, as he did so, " Hoot toot,—Mister Ned !" —Then he walked to the front door, where he stood whistling.

CHAPTER VII.

VIRGINIA has the sentiments and opinions of an independent nation. She enjoyed in the colonial state a high degree of the favor of the mother country; and the blandishments of her climate, together with the report of her fertile soil and her hidden territorial resources, from the first attracted the regard of the British emigrants. Her early population, therefore, consisted of gentlemen of good name and condition, who brought within her confines a solid fund of respectability and wealth. This race of men grew vigorous in her genial atmosphere; her cloudless skies quickened and enlivened their tempers, and, in two centuries, gradually matured the sober and thinking Englishman into that spirited, imaginative being who now inhabits the lowlands of this state. When the Revolution broke out, she was among the first of its champions, ardent in the assertion of the principles upon which it turned, and brave in the support of them. Since that period, her annals have been singularly brilliant with the fame of orators and statesmen. Four Presidents have been given to the Union from her nursery. The first, the brightest figure of history; the others also master-spirits, worthy to be ranked amongst the greatest of their day. In the light of these men, and of their gallant contemporaries, she has found a glory to stimulate her ambition, and to minister to her pride. It is not wonderful that in these circumstances she should deem herself a predominant star in the Union. It is a feature in her education and policy to hold all other interests subordinate to her own.

Her wealth is territorial; her institutions all savor of the soil; her population consists of landholders, of many descents, unmixed with foreign alloy. She has no large towns where men may meet and devise improvements or changes in the arts of life. She may be called a nation without a capital. From this cause she has been less disturbed by popular commotions, less influenced by popular fervors, than other communities. Her laws and habits, in consequence, have a certain fixedness, which even reject many of the valuable improvements of the day. In policy and government she is, according to the simplest and purest form, a republic: in temper and opinion, in the usages of life, and in the qualities of her moral nature, she is aristocratic.

The gentlemen of Virginia live apart from each other. They are surrounded by their bondsmen and dependents; and the customary intercourse of society familiarizes their minds to the relation of high and low degree. They frequently meet in the interchange of a large and thriftless hospitality, in which the forms of society are foregone for its comforts, and the business of life thrown aside for the enjoyment of its pleasures. Their halls are large, and their boards ample; and surrounding the great family hearth, with its immense burthen of blazing wood casting a broad and merry glare over the congregated household and the numerous retainers, a social winter party in Virginia affords a tolerable picture of feudal munificence.

Frank Meriwether is a good specimen of the class I have described. He seeks companionship with men of ability, and is a zealous disseminator of the personal fame of individuals who have won any portion of renown in the state. Sometimes, I even

think he exaggerates a little, when descanting upon the prodigies
of genius that have been reared in the Old Dominion; and he
manifestly seems to consider that a young man who has astonished a whole village in Virginia by the splendor of his talents,
must, of course, be known throughout the United States;—for
he frequently opens his eyes at me with an air of astonishment
when I happen to ask him who is the marvel he is speaking of.

I observe, moreover, that he has a constitutional fondness for
paradoxes, and does not scruple to adopt and republish any apothegm that is calculated to startle one by its novelty. He has a
correspondence with several old friends, who were with him at
college, and who have now risen into an extensive political notoriety in the state:—these gentlemen furnish him with many new
currents of thought, along which he glides with a happy velocity.
He is essentially meditative in his character, and somewhat given
to declamation; and these traits have communicated a certain
measured and deliberate gesticulation to his discourse. I have
frequently seen him after dinner stride backward and forward
across the room, for some moments, wrapped in thought, and then
fling himself upon the sofa, and come out with some weighty
doubt, expressed with a solemn emphasis. In this form he lately
began a conversation, or rather a speech, that for a moment quite
disconcerted me. "After all," said he, as if he had been talking
to me before, although these were the first words he uttered—
then making a parenthesis, so as to qualify what he was going to
say—"I don't deny that the steamboat is destined to produce
valuable results—but after all, I much question—(and here he
bit his upper lip, and paused an instant)—if we are not better
without it. I declare, I think it strikes deeper at the supremacy
of the states than most persons are willing to allow. This anni-
hilation of space, sir, is not to be desired. Our protection against
the evils of consolidation consists in the very obstacles to our in-

tercourse. Splatterthwaite Dubbs of Dinwiddie—(or some such name,—Frank is famous for quoting the opinions of his contemporaries. This Splatterthwaite, I take it, was some old college chum who had got into the legislature, and I dare say made pungent speeches,) Dubbs of Dinwiddie made a good remark— That the home material of Virginia was never so good as when her roads were at their worst." And so Frank went on with quite a harangue, to which none of the company replied one word, for fear we might get into a dispute. Every body seems to understand the advantage of silence when Meriwether is inclined to be expatiatory.

This strain of philosophizing has a pretty marked influence in the neighborhood, for I perceive that Frank's opinions are very much quoted. There is a set of under-talkers about these large country establishments, who are very glad to pick up the crumbs of wisdom which fall from a rich man's table; second-hand philosophers, who trade upon other people's stock. Some of these have a natural bias to this venting of upper opinions, by reason of certain dependencies in the way of trade and favor: others have it from affinity of blood, which works like a charm over a whole county. Frank stands related, by some tie of marriage or mixture of kin, to an infinite train of connections, spread over the state; and it is curious to learn what a decided hue this gives to the opinions of the district. We had a notable example of this one morning, not long after my arrival at Swallow Barn. Meriwether had given several indications, immediately after breakfast, of a design to pour out upon us the gathered ruminations of the last twenty-four hours, but we had evaded the storm with some caution, when the arrival of two or three neighbors,— plain, homespun farmers,—who had ridden to Swallow Barn to execute some papers before Frank as a magistrate, furnished him with an occasion that was not to be lost. After dispatching their

business, he detained them, ostensibly to inquire about their
crops, and other matters of their vocation,—but, in reality, to
give them that very flood of politics which we had escaped. We,
of course, listened without concern, since we were assured of an
auditory that would not flinch. In the course of this disquisition,
he made use of a figure of speech which savored of some previous study, or, at least, was highly in the oratorical vein. "Mark
me, gentlemen," said he, contracting his brow over his fine
thoughtful eye, and pointing the forefinger of his left hand
directly at the face of the person he addressed, "Mark me,
gentlemen,—you and I may not live to see it, but our children
will see it, and wail over it—the sovereignty of this Union will
be as the rod of Aaron ;—it will turn into a serpent, and swallow
up all that struggle with it." Mr. Chub was present at this
solemn denunciation, and was very much affected by it.   He rubbed his hands with some briskness, and uttered his applause in a
short but vehement panegyric, in which were heard only the detached words—"Mr. Burke—Cicero."

The next day Ned and myself were walking by the school-
house, and were hailed by Rip, from one of the windows, who, in
a sly under tone, as he beckoned us to come close to him, told
us, "if we wanted to hear a regular preach, to stand fast."   We
could look into the schoolroom unobserved, and there was our
patriotic pedagogue haranguing the boys with a violence of action
that drove an additional supply of blood into his face.   It was
apparent that the old gentleman had got much beyond the depth
of his hearers, and was pouring out his rhetoric more from oratorical vanity than from any hope of enlightening his audience.   At
the most animated part of his strain, he brought himself, by a
kind of climax, to the identical sentiment uttered by Meriwether
the day before.   He warned his young hearers—the oldest of
them was not above fourteen—"to keep a lynx-eyed gaze upon

that serpent-like ambition which would convert the government
at Washington into Aaron's rod, to swallow up the independence
of their native state."

This conceit immediately ran through all the lower circles at
Swallow Barn. Mr. Tongue, the overseer, repeated it at the
blacksmith's shop, in the presence of the blacksmith and Mr.
Absalom Bulrush, a spare, ague-and-feverish husbandman who
occupies a muddy slip of marsh land, on one of the river bottoms,
which is now under mortgage to Meriwether ; and from these it
has spread far and wide, though a good deal diluted, until in its
circuit it has reached our veteran groom Carey, who considers
the sentiment as importing something of an awful nature. With
the smallest encouragement, Carey will put on a tragi-comic face,
shake his head very slowly, turn up his eyeballs, and open out
his broad, scaly hands, while he repeats with labored voice,
" Look out, Master Ned ! Aaron's rod a black snake in Old Virginny !" Upon which, as we fall into a roar of laughter, Carey
stares with astonishment at our irreverence. But having been
set to acting this scene for us once or twice, he now suspects us
of some joke, and asks " if there is'nt a copper for an old negro,"
which if he succeeds in getting, he runs off, telling us " he is too
'cute to make a fool of himself."

Meriwether does not dislike this trait in the society around
him. I happened to hear two carpenters, one day, who were
making some repairs at the stable, in high conversation. One
of them was expounding to the other some oracular opinion of
Frank's touching the political aspect of the country, and just at
the moment when the speaker was most animated, Meriwether
himself came up. He no sooner became aware of the topic in
discussion than he walked off in another direction,—affecting not
to hear it, although I knew he heard every word. He told me
afterwards that there was " a wholesome tone of feeling amongst
the people in that part of the country."

CHAPTER VIII.

ABOUT four miles below Swallow Barn, on the same bank of the river, is a tract of land known by the name of The Brakes. The principal feature in this region is an extensive range of low lands, reaching back from the river, and bounded by distant forest, from the heart of which tower, above the mass of foliage, a number of naked branches of decayed trees, that are distinctly visible in this remote perspective. These lowlands are checkered by numberless gullies or minute water-courses, whose direction is marked out to the eye by thickets of briers and brambles. From this characteristic the estate has derived its name.

A hill rises from this level ground, and on its top is placed a large plain building, with wings built in exact uniformity, and connected with the centre by low but lengthened covered ways. The whole structure is of dark brick, with little architectural embellishment. It was obviously erected when the ornamental arts were not much attended to, although there is an evident aim at something of this kind in the fancy of the chimneys which spring up from the sharp gable-ends of the building, and also in the conceited pyramids into which the roofs of the low square wings have been reared. The artist, however, has certainly failed in producing effect, if his ambition soared above the idea of a sober, capacious, and gentle-manlike mansion.

Seen from the river, the buildings stand partly in the shade of a range of immense lombardy poplars, which retreat down the hill in the opposite direction until the line diminishes from the view. Negro huts are scattered about over the landscape in that profusion which belongs to a Virginia plantation.

This establishment constitutes the family residence of Mr. Isaac Tracy, known generally with his territorial addition,—of The Brakes.

Mr. Tracy is now upwards of seventy years of age. He has been for many years past a widower, and seems to stand like a landmark in the stream of time, which is destined to have every thing gliding past it, itself unchanged. The old gentleman was a stark royalist in the days of the Revolution, and only contrived to escape the confiscation of his estate by preserving a strict and cautious neutrality during the war. He still adheres to the ancient costume, and is now observed taking his rides in the morning, in a long-waisted coat, of a snuff color, and having three large figured gilt buttons set upon the cuffs, which are slashed after an antiquated fashion. He wears, besides, ruffles over his hands, and has a certain trig and quaint appearance given by his tight, dark-colored small-clothes, and long boots with tops of brown leather, so disposed as to show a little of his white stockings near the knee. His person is tall and emaciated, with a withered and rather severe exterior. A formality, correspondent with his appearance, is conspicuous in his manners, which are remarkable for their scrupulous and sprightly politeness; and his household is conducted with a degree of precision that throws a certain air of stateliness over the whole family.

He has two daughters, of whom the youngest has already counted perhaps her twenty-third year, and an only son somewhat

younger. Catharine, the eldest of this family, has the reputation
of being particularly well educated; but her acquirement is
probably enhanced, in the common estimation, by a thoughtful
and rather formal cast of character,—a certain soberness in the
discharge of the ordinary duties of life,—and a grave turn of
conversation, such as belongs to women who, from temperament,
are not wont to enjoy with any great relish, nor perceive with
observant eyes, the pleasant things of existence.

Bel, the younger sister, is of a warmer complexion. Nature
has given her an exuberant flow of spirits, which, in spite of a stiff
and rigid education imposed upon her by her father, frequently
breaks through the trammels of discipline, and shows itself in the
various forms which a volatile temper assumes in the actions of
an airy and healthful girl. Still, however, her sentiments are
what nurture has made them, notwithstanding her physical
elements. She has been accustomed to the cautious and authoritative admonitions of her father, which have inculcated a severe
and exaggerated sense of personal respect, and a rather too
rigorous estimate of the proprieties and privileges of her sex.
These girls early lost their mother; and their father, at that
period advanced in years, had already parted with his fondness
for society. The consequence was that The Brakes, during the
minority of the children, was a secluded spot, cut off from much
of that sort of commerce with the world which is almost essential
to enliven and mature the sympathies of young persons.

Both Catharine and Bel are pretty, but after different models.
The eldest is a placid, circumspect, inaccessible kind of beauty.
Bel, on the other hand, is headlong and thoughtless, with quick
impulses, that give her the charm of agreeable expression, although
her features are irregular, and would not stand a critical examination. Her skin is not altogether clear; her mouth is large, and
her eyes of a dark gray hue.

Ralph, the brother, is a tall, ill made, awkward man, with black eyes, and black hair curled in extravagant profusion over his head. He contracted slovénly habits of dress at college, and has not since abandoned them; has a dislike to the company of women, fills up his conversation with oaths, and chews immense quantities of tobacco. He has an unmusical voice, and a swaggering walk, and generally wears his hat set upon one side of his head. He professes to be a sportsman, and lives a good deal out of doors, not being fond, as he says, of being stuck up in the parlor to hear the women talk. Ralph, however, is said to be a good fellow at bottom, which means that he does not show his best qualities in front. He is famous for his horsemanship, and avows a strong partiality for Bel on account of her skill in the same art, which, Ralph says, comes altogether from his teaching.

This family has always been on terms of intimacy at Swallow Barn, and of late years their intercourse has been much increased by the companionship which has been cultivated between the ladies of the two houses. Frank Meriwether holds the character of Mr. Tracy in great respect, and always speaks of him in a tone of affection, although the old gentleman, Ned says, is a bad listener and a painful talker, two qualities which sort but ill with the prevailing characteristics of Meriwether.

There are some points of family history, affecting the relations of these two gentlemen, which I shall find occasion hereafter to disclose.

CHAPTER IX.

AN ECLOGUE.

You have now, my dear Zack, the fruits of my first experiences, here at Swallow Barn, offered to you in a series of sketches, which will, at least, show you that I have not been idle in my traveller-vocation during my first fortnight. These labors of mine will reach you regularly chaptered and ticketed, after the most approved fashion of book-making, and will convince you that I am in earnest in my purpose. So far you have been *enter-tained*—you see, I take that for granted, assuming to myself the airs of an author—with a set of pictures from still life—(still enough, even to the point of drowsiness, you will say)—a little gallery of landscapes and portraits, which, in my judgment, were necessary as preliminaries to what I may write in future. You now understand exactly where I am, and what kind of good people I have around me, and will be all the better prepared for the little romance of domestic life which I am about to weave out of my every-day occurrences. What my romance will come to, it is impossible to foretell, as it is to grow up out of the events of the day. These sometimes naturally develop themselves through the regular stages of a story and a plot, but oftener run off into nothing. How it is to fare in my case, you will find out only by the reading. So, abandoning myself to my destiny in this particular, I resume my task at this ninth chapter, which, being of a bucolical character, I have entitled " an eclogue."

Hazard and I often take long rambles together—spending a whole morning, sometimes, on foot. In these idle wanderings we fall into strange caprices. The tide of animal spirits rises above the level which sober people call discretion, and we are apt to get, without being aware of it, into the empyrean of foolery. I believe many wise men, if they would make an honest confession, often find themselves in such a case ;—the best fellows in the world, if not the wisest,—and I am not sure that the best and wisest are so wide apart, as many think they are—but the best constructed men, I am quite convinced, are familiar with these vagaries. A genial, happy spirit has a great tendency to leap out of the circle of conventional proprieties, and now and then to make a somerset. I have read of seemingly very grave men doing this,—and liked them the better for it.

When Ned and I get into the woods, it is rather a favorite amusement to practise ludicrous caricatures of the drama, which Ned calls imitations of the most distinguished actors. Sometimes we deliver pompous harangues as if we were in a senate, and keep up a debate in a very impressive way, with abundance of parliamentary phrase and action.

A few mornings ago, about the first of July, we found ourselves abroad on one of these excursions. The weather was unusually pleasant and Ned was more buoyant than I had yet seen him, which gave an unwonted license to the range of his flights. Of course, I became almost as absurd as himself—for it is my nature to take such contagions violently. We strained the

strings of propriety until they were ready to crack.   Our madness ran this morning upon our feats of singing.

"Mark," said Ned to me, "I am truly astonished that you
can find amusement in this preposterous flourish of your voice.
Are you not aware that you make a dismal compromise of your
proper and inherent dignity—if it is inherent, which I don't
believe—by bawling in this fashion in the woods? What would
you think of yourself if any sober, solemn sort of person should
happen to be near and to overhear that execrable attempt at a
trill? Your voice, especially in its A sharp and its B flat, is perfectly horrid; your manner is bad, and your attitude altogether
too tame.   Now listen and look, and be instructed"—

Here Ned sent forth a vociferous stave, which he drew out
into manifold quavers.

"What do you think of that?" said he, with a brisk and peremptory look, as if he had done something to astound me.

"Tut—that's a mere squall—a servile imitation of Garcia,"
I replied.   "It wants force, expression, majesty.   Lend me your
ears"—

And here I returned him a flourish, greatly improving on his
style.

"Mark,—I see you are vain of that.   Perhaps you have a
right to be until you hear me again—but not afterwards.   So, sit
down and be attentive.   Let me have no interruptions of applause
by clapping of hands—no bravos.   Restrain your transports, and
bestow all your attention upon the pathos of this strain.   I challenge criticism"—

With this prelude, Ned assumed the attitude of a hero of the
opera, pressing his hands passionately upon his bosom, throwing
his elbows forward and eyes upward, as he poured forth a loud
and long bravura strain, which raised an echo in the depths of
the wood.   We had, throughout this farce, adapted our vocal ex-

travagancies to words not less ridiculous than the strain. Ned, in this effort, was expending the force of his burlesque humor in a series of repetitions, upon a couplet which was inspired by a lady whom I have mentioned in a former chapter. The words were,

> Bel Tracy against the field!
> Against the field, Bel Tracy!

The name was reverberated through the woods in a multitude of fantastical trills, set off with inordinately theatrical gestures.

"A merry morning, Mr. Edward Hazard!" said Bel Tracy, reining up her horse immediately at his back. "If I am to be put against the field, I should prefer to have it kept secret."

"My sister Bel," said Catherine, who was also on horseback close at hand, "feels greatly flattered by your considerate notice of her."

"The devil!" said Ned, hastily glancing his eye at me, "What a march they have stolen on us!"

"Decidedly, a most delicate compliment," said Harvey Riggs, a gentleman in the train, "such an unpremeditated expression of preference!"

"Humph!" uttered Ralph Tracy, the fourth and last of the party. "You call that singing, I suppose, Ned?"

Ned was utterly confounded by this quadruple assault, which was made not without a spirited accompaniment of laughter.

This cavalcade had been galloping with noiseless footfall along the sandy road, until they had got within a short distance of our position, where they had halted unobserved and had the full benefit of Ned's unlucky essay at the bravura; and as he drew to a close, they came stealthily upon our rear and affected the surprise I have related. Ned looked sheepishly at the invaders, in a state of comic perturbation,—for no man can stand such a flagrant exposure, even under the most favorable circumstances, much less when attended with such aggravation as the personal reference in this case presented—and after some little time necessary to collect his self-possession, bethinking himself of me to whom the whole company were strangers, he introduced me, saying, when he had done so—

"You have caught us, Bel, at our rehearsal. Odd enough that you should steal behind the scenes at such a moment. I have told Littleton all about you, and how fond you are of Italian music, so we determined to prepare a serenade for you."

"The music very soft and sentimental," interrupted Harvey—

"Quite satisfactory, Edward," said Bel.—"I think we are lucky in having heard it here, as that will save you the trouble of repeating it at The Brakes. My father's taste is not modern enough for such strains. Isn't it a pity, Mr. Littleton," she added, appealing to me,—"that Edward Hazard should be so merciless to his friends?"

"Hazard has already created so strong an interest in me to make your acquaintance, Miss Tracy," I replied, "that I scarcely regret the ludicrous accident which has brought it about so soon."

"Forgive me, Bel," said Hazard. "I own I am the most egregious buffoon, and the most unlucky one, besides, in the country. Littleton and I have been running riot all the morning—but whether in jest or earnest, I hope you will not think the worse of me that you are always uppermost in my thoughts."

As he said this he approached familiarly to her stirrup and offered his hand, which she took with great kindness. She remarked that they were then on their way to Swallow Barn, and would no longer interrupt our studies. Upon this she and Harvey Riggs rode forward at a gallop, Harvey looking back over his shoulder and calling out—

"Ned, of course, I shan't report you to Meriwether. I shall be tender of your reputation."

" The devil take his tenderness," said Ned, as they rode off;
" he'll make the most of this."

Catharine and Ralph followed more leisurely.

Ned stood looking at the retreating party for some moments.
Bel was mounted on a beautiful sleek bay mare, which sprang
forward with a gay, spirited motion. Her graceful and neat figure showed to great advantage as she flew out of our sight almost
at high speed. Her dress was a dark green riding habit, fanci-
fully braided over the breast and accurately fitting her shape.
She wore a light cap of the same color, with a frontlet sufficiently
prominent to guard her face, and over her right shoulder floated
a green veil which fluttered in the breeze like a gay pennon—but
not more gay than the heart it followed.

" Was there ever," said Ned, turning round to me, after this
troop had disappeared, " was there ever a more unlucky discovery
than that! Of all persons in the world, to be caught in the height
of our tomfoolery by that little elf Bel Tracy! Just to be taken
in the high flood of our nonsense! And with *her* name,
too, ringing through these grave and silent woods! I should
scarcely have regarded it if it had happened with any body else;
but she has such a superserviceable stock of conceit about elegance and refinement in her mind, that I don't doubt she will
find in this silly adventure a pretext to abuse me for the next
twelvemonth. And then, she will go home and tell that stiff old
curmudgeon, her father, that I am the very antipodes of a polished
man. Faith, she has said that before! And Harvey Riggs—"
added Ned, musing—" will not improve the matter, because he will
have his joke upon it. And then sister Kate!—she will pro-
nounce my conduct undignified;—that's *her* word : and so will
Bel, for that matter. Why, Mark, in the name of all the devils !
hadn't you your eyes about you ?"

" Egad," said I, " they surprised our camp without alarming

the sentinels. But after all, what is it? They can only say they met a pair of fools in the forest, and, certainly, they need not travel far to do that, any day!"

"By the by, Mark," said Ned, changing his mood, and brightening up into a pleasanter state of feeling, "did you note Bel's horsemanship,—how light and fearless she rides? And, like a fairy, comes at your bidding, too! She reads descriptions of ladies of chivalry, and takes the field in imitation of them. Her head is full of these fancies, and she almost persuades herself that this is the fourteenth century. Did you observe her dainty fist, 'miniardly begloved,'—as the old minstrels have it?—she longs to have a merlin perched upon it, and is therefore endeavoring to train a hawk, that, when she takes the air, she may go in the guise of an ancient gentlewoman. She should be followed by her falconer."

"And have a pair of greyhounds in her train," said I.

"Aye, and a page in a silk doublet," added Ned.

"And a gallant cavalier," I rejoined, "to break a lance for her, instead of breaking jokes upon her. I am almost tempted to champion her cause, against such a lurdan as you, myself. But let us hasten back to Swallow Barn, for our presence will be needed."

After this adventure we returned to the mansion-house, with some misgiving on the part of Hazard. He talked about it all the way, and dwelt somewhat fearfully upon the raillery of Harvey Riggs and Meriwether, who, he observed, were not likely to drop a joke before it was pretty well worn.

The servants were leading off the horses as we arrived at the gate, and the family, with their visitors, were collected in the porch, with all eyes turned to us as we approached. There was a general uproar of laughter at Ned, who took it in good part though with not many words.

When the mirth of the company had run through its course, Bel called Hazard up to her, and said:

"You are a shabby fellow, Edward. I have two causes of quarrel with you. You have not been at The Brakes for a week or more—and you know we don't bear neglect:—and secondly, I don't think you have a right to be frightening Mr. Littleton with my name, however lawful it may be to amuse the gentle geese of the James River with it."

"Bel," replied Hazard, "upon my honor, I never was more solemn in my life than at the very moment you rode upon us. And as to my remissness, I have had no sentiment on hand since Mark Littleton has been with me, and I did not know what I should say to you. Besides, I have a regard for Mark's health, and I was not disposed to interrupt it with one of your flirtations. He is a little taken already, for he has been praising you and your mare ever since you passed us. If he knew what a jockey you were in all things, he would give you very little encouragement."

"Pray heaven," said Bel, "if he be a virtuous man, he be not spoiled by such a madcap jester as yourself! Mr. Littleton, I hope you will not believe Edward, if he has been telling you any thing to my disadvantage;—I am never safe in his hands."

"I will tell you what I told him, Bel," said Hazard, getting round close to her ear, where he whispered what was too low to be heard.

"You are incorrigible!" cried Bel, laughing, and at the same time shaking her riding whip at him. And with these words she ran into the hall, and thence up stairs, followed by the rest of the ladies.

"'Isn't she a merry creature?" said Ned to me, in an affectionate tone, as we entered the door in the-rear of the party.

CHAPTER X.

THE party from The Brakes caused a great uproar within the whilom tranquil precincts of Swallow Barn. The ladies had congregated in one of the chambers, from whence might be heard that fitful outbreak of exclamation and laughter rising above a busy murmur of prattle, which, as far as my experience goes, is characteristic of every gathering of women. Below, the hall re-echoed with the bluff greetings of the gentlemen, the harsh tramp of boots upon the uncarpeted floor, and that noisy, mirthful play of frolic spirits which is equally characteristic of such assemblages of men.

I must say something of Harvey Riggs. Picture to your mind, a square-built, somewhat sturdy figure, of medium height, or rather below it; a weather-beaten visage and dry complexion, pock-marked not a little; the ripeness of forty brooding upon it and hatching a little nest of *thoughtlings* about the eyes, which are rather indefinitely of a greenish gray, short-sighted and sparkling; a small upturned nose, a large and well-shaped mouth, an uncommonly large head, rendered slightly gorgonic by a shock of disorderly iron-hued hair which curls upon the collar of his coat. Add to these a negligent style of dress, a coat rather too large, a black neckcloth much too loosely tied, with long ends pointing towards each shoulder, and a curious variety of color shown in the several garments; and you will have all the prominent features of his exterior. You may recognize in the blandness of his manners, and the mellowness of his general expression, a man who has had a full share of conversation with the world; who has seen it in its pleasant aspects, is familiar with revels, and has " sat up late o' nights," and often enough been caught by the dawn at a card-table. His countenance—I use this word in its ancient significance as including his whole apparition—though one of unquestionable and almost unmitigated homeliness, is far from displeasing; which may be ascribed to its perfectly natural keeping, and absence of all pretension.

It is not unusual to find men of this mould great favorites in female society. Women discriminate very shrewdly in personal qualifications, and have an instinctive appreciation of a warmhearted good fellow, as Harvey is. Every body here likes him. His strong and earnest good sense, his learned skill in the ways of society, and a certain happy waggishness of temper, give him great advantages. He is a kinsman of the Tracy family, and has recently come from Richmond upon a visit to The Brakes, which he does very often, I am told; being fond of his relations there, and equally fond of Ned Hazard.

Some refreshments were placed upon the sideboard in the parlor opening upon the hall. It is a common custom here in Virginia, about an hour before dinner, to prepare a bowl of toddy, which is generally made of the finest old Jamaica spirit, or rum of St. Croix, and being well brewed is iced almost to the freezing point. This is taken by way of whetting the appetite, which is generally sharp enough without such strapping. But appetite or not, this toddy, as I can avouch, is quite a pleasant thing to handle. Harvey Riggs has a distinguished reputation in the concoction of this beverage, and as it was now the time of day to be looking after it, he was already at the sideboard engaged in his vocation.

"Ned," said he, as with a small pitcher in each hand he was busy in pouring his brewage from one to the other, "how far do you call it from here to the spot where we *treed* you this morning?"

"What do you mean by *treed?*" asked Ned.

"Where you were caught, and couldn't help yourself, and looked so queer, when Bel heard you squalling her name so ferociously. How far is that from here?"

"A mile and upwards," said Ned. "Harvey, you might have given us notice. I know Bel thinks it was very unbecoming in me; and so it would have been if I had been aware she was within hearing."

"Bel, you know, has rather stately notions of decorum," replied Harvey, "but for your comfort, Ned, I can assure you we threw all stateliness to the winds this morning. Bel and I rode that mile in three minutes. There's a girl for you! Poor cousin Kate followed us at a demure gallop, with Ralph grumbling all the way, because she wouldn't race as we did. It was 'Bel Tracy against the field' sure enough. How does that music go, Ned? Let Meriwether hear it."

"You really did play that prank, Ned?" said Meriwether interrogatively—doubting the story as a mere jest. "Is it true that you were engaged in that way with our friend Littleton?"

"Perfectly and literally true, as you have heard it," said I.

"I am greatly astonished," returned Meriwether.

"Bel would have astonished you more," said Riggs, "if you had seen her flying this way afterwards. She thinks no more of a ditch or a moderate worm-fence, than she does of a demi-semi-quaver. She goes over them singing."

"The world, I fear, doesn't get wisdom with age," rejoined Frank. "I rather think this fantastical opera-singing—what do you call it Ned?—bravura?—which seems to have turned the heads

—now, even of such men as Ned Hazard here—I suppose you took a hand, Littleton, only from civility—these capers on the part of the men, and leaping ditches and fences by the women—I rather think we should have frowned upon such things twenty years ago in Virginia. But manners change, morals change also : the tendencies of government, as Burke remarks, in those masterly reflections on the French Revolution ''——

"I come as an ambassador from The Brakes," said Harvey Riggs, who had been too busy with his operations at the sideboard to note Meriwether's lapse into the philosophizing vein, and which he now broke in upon at this critical moment, when Frank was in the act of mounting a favorite hobby—"I come as an ambassador with a commission from Mr. Tracy to you. Here is an epistle, as the old gentlemen terms it, directed to you, Meriwether, and which I am to put into your hands, 'with care and speed,' as he was particular to say. Singleton Swansdown is expected ; and arrangements are to be made for the immediate settlement of that interminable boundary-line dispute, which has been vexed for forty years. My good kinsman, Mr. Tracy, is anxious that you should aid him to expedite Swansdown's departure, and I venture to add my own request, in the name of charity and all the cardinal virtues, that you will detain this gentle carpet-knight the shortest practicable time."

"I devoutly believe," replied Meriwether, "that if this old lawsuit between our families should be brought to a close by this device,—even if it should go in Mr. Tracy's favor,—it will cost him some unpleasant struggles to part with it."

"It is impossible to settle it," said Harvey: "all the oracles are against it. Mammy Diana, who is a true sibyl, has uttered a prophecy which runs thus—'That the landmarks shall never be stable until Swallow Barn shall wed The Brakes.' Ned, the hopes of the family rest upon you."

Meriwether opened the letter, and read as follows :

" Dear and Respected Friend,—Touching the question of the lawsuit which, notwithstanding the erroneous judgments of our courts, still hangs in unhappy suspense, I am moved by the consideration urged in your sensible epistle to me of the fifteenth ultimo, to submit the same, with all the matters of fact and law pertinent to a right decision thereof, to mutual friends, to arbitrate the same between us ; not doubting that the conclusion will be agreeable to both, and corroborative of the impressions which I have entertained, unaltered, from the first arising of this controversy with my venerated neighbor, the late Walter Hazard.

" What stake I have is insignificant in comparison of the value of vindicating the ground on which I have stood for forty years and upwards, and also of relieving our lineal and collateral kindred from vexatious disputes in time to come.

" I have written to my young friend, Singleton O. Swansdown, Esq. of Meherrin,—"

" Very young !" interrupted Harvey, " almost as juvenile as the lawsuit "—

" Son of my late worthy kinsman, Gilbert Swansdown, as a proper gentleman to act in my behalf ; and late letters from him signify his ready pleasure to do me this service. My advices inform me that he will be at The Brakes in this present week. Although I could have wished that this arbitrament should in nowise fall into the hands of lawyers—seeing that we have both had reason, to our cost, to pray for a deliverance from the tribe— yet. nevertheless, it is not becoming in me to object to your nomination of Philpot Wart, Esq. who is a shrewd and wary man, and will doubtless strive to do the right between us.

" I would desire, moreover, that it be understood as a preliminary, that no respect shall be had to the quibbles and law quirks wherewith the courts have entertained themselves, to my detriment, hitherto in these premises.

"Praying that unnecessary delay shall not hinder the speedy return of Mr. Swansdown, when his occasions shall call him hence, I beg leave to subscribe myself,

Respected and dear Sir,

Your very obedient and obliged servant,

ISAAC TRACY."

"Habit converts our troubles into pleasures," said Meriwether, as he stood with this letter in his hand, after he had finished reading it, and now began to descant, in one of his usual strains; "and my old friend Tracy has so long interested himself with this inconsiderable claim—for it is not of the value of a sharpshin—one hundred acres of marsh land, which no man would buy—that, to tell the truth, I would long since have given it up to him, if I did not think it would make the old gentleman unhappy to take the weight of it off his mind. Felicity, sir, is an accident; it is motion, either of body or mind; a mode of being, as the logicians call it. Let the best machine of man be constructed, with all the appurtenances of strength, faculty, thought, feeling, and with all the appliances of competence and ease, and it will rust from disuse; the springs and wheels will grow mouldy; the pipes become oppilated with crudities, and death will ensue from mere obstruction. But give it motion———"

"But what do you think," interrupted Harvey, "of the old gentleman's selecting Singleton Swansdown to reverse the decision of all the courts in Virginia, with Philly Wart, too, to back them?"

"The shrewdest person," replied Meriwether, smiling, and bringing down his left hand over his face, as he threw his head backward, "doubtless may be beguiled by his prepossessions.—Singleton's a right good fellow after all; and Mr. Tracy has a great respect for him, growing out of family connections, and his regulated tone of manners, which are very kind and conciliatory to the old gentleman."

" But he is such an ass," said Harvey, " and I had like to have blundered out as much, yesterday at dinner, when Mr. Tracy told us he was coming to The Brakes; but happily, I was afraid to swear before my cousin Kate."

" Why I dare say," rejoined Meriwether, " Swansdown will be entirely competent to this case, particularly with my friend Philly at his elbow, to show him his road.   I have been turning over in my mind," he continued, aside to Riggs, " to contrive to give the old gentleman the advantage in the lawsuit, if I can so arrange it as to let him win it upon a show of justice ; for if he suspected me of a voluntary concession to him, he would not be pleased; and, upon my conscience! I find a difficulty in managing it."

" Can't our friend Wart, " said Harvey, " patch up a case against you, that shall deceive even Mr. Tracy ?"

" I shall so instruct him," replied Meriwether, " and it will afford us some speculation to observe how reluctantly my good neighbor will part with this bantling of his, when it is decided."

" It has been his inducement," said Harvey, " to study the laws of Virginia from beginning to end ; and it has furnished him more conversation than any other incident of his life."

CHAPTER XI.

THE dinner hour found our company in that happy mood which belongs to the conviviality of country life. Eager appetite and that conscious health which grows upon out-door exercise, and which brings cheerfulness to the spirit as physical beauty brings pleasure to the eye,—these tell more visibly upon a party in the country, than they ever do in town. You will never know your friend so well, nor enjoy him so heartily in the city as you may in one of those large, bountiful mansions, whose horizon is filled with green fields and woodland slopes and broad blue heavens. Of all the conditions of life, give me ample country space, a generous, wide-sheltering roof, and my chosen cronies,—male and female,— gathered under it at my summons to spend weeks together! Then horses, sunshine, and pleasant breezes,—and a morning for the fields and the by-ways amongst the hills, with my little squadron of choice spirits to keep abreast with me and my fantasies! Then let us have dinner with its vigorous appetites:—I shall not be particular in the sauces.—And after that the placid evening, and the rich and honest old books,—or the pranks, I care not how boyish and girlish.—We have no age and no premeditated proprieties under my roof;—we go for good fellowship and a little harlequinade now and then. Merry Andrew is a king in his way.

These are my desires. I am glad to see something of this com·
plexion here at Swallow Barn. My narrative points to that.

We ordinarily dine about three o'clock. On the present oc
casion we were two hours before we left the table. Bel was on the
top-gallant of her spirits ; and Ned Hazard seemed to have devoted himself to the task of provoking her vivacity by continual
assault, which had a tone, sometimes, of satirical criticism upon
her imputed foibles, and sometimes of doubtful praise of her imputed perfections, well calculated to test her good nature and to
increase the animation of her defence. In both which particulars
she showed very pleasantly, and maintained her ground with a
skilful tact. Ned evidently found a gratification in her triumphs,
and studied occasions to make them agreeable to herself; though
his manner was perilously destitute of that reverence and gentle
submission which all women are pleased to exact, and which a
pretty woman, especially, considers as the least of her dues from
our sex.

Bel might even have found a pretext to be offended with
Hazard, but for the manifest good feeling which blazed up above
all his raillery.

Catharine was more prudish ; and Ned and Harvey were dis·
creet enough to attempt no jest with her, that was not as prudish
as herself. I cannot say so much for Hazard,—but of Harvey
Riggs it is quite observable that, under the externals of a volatile, swashing, trenchant manner, he maintains a careful guard to
give a complimentary flavor to his demeanor, which rather wins
upon the self-love of his company.

Prudence sustained her part variously, and was alternately
sentimental and mettlesome, thoughtless or grave, as the wind
blew towards those points.

When evening came, the tide of pleasant association was run·
ning so high that it was resolved to be inexpedient to interrupt

it by separation, and accordingly a messenger was dispatched to The Brakes, to say that the party would remain at Swallow Barn all night. Prudence, I observed, figured in the debate on that resolve, and rather startled us by repeating some lines, which, it strikes me, I have heard before. They ran something in this wise :—

> "Joy so seldom weaves a chain
> Like this to-night, that oh 'tis pain
> To break its links so soon."—

I am positive Prudence is not the author of these lines—she must have borrowed them.

After tea, the ladies made a concert at the piano. A few lively airs were so suggestive of a dance, that in a short time my cousin Lucretia was seated at the instrument, and our whole company, except Meriwether, was on the floor capering through alternate reels and cotillons.

The children were grouped about the room in an ecstasy of delight. Mistress Barbara, who had stolen quietly into the apartment, relaxed her features into a wormwood smile, and shook her head at Harvey Riggs's drolleries ; and the domestics, young and old, gathered about the doorway, or peeped in at the windows.

The thermometer of mirth rises with the heat of exercise. It was now getting above the point which society has established as the upper confine of elegant decorum. It was manifest that a romp was in the wind. The men were growing too energetic in their saltations ; and I am afraid I must say that the ladies did not decidedly discourage it. Now and then, indeed, Catharine bridled up and would not allow Harvey Riggs to give her such a gyratory fling in the reel, as he did the others ; but Bel gave way to it like a true child of nature, and permitted her swift-flowing

blood to guide her steps; and Prudence, at a little distance, followed her example.

In the midst of this confused and mingled scene, Lucy and
Victorine appeared the very personations of joy in the graceful
playfulness of their age; springing about with the easy motions
and delighted looks of young novices, to whom the world is a
sunny picture of pleasure and harmony.

Exhausted, at length, we took our seats, and gradually subsided into that lower and more equable temper which is apt to
follow violent excitements. Harvey Riggs and Ned Hazard
were observed to withdraw from the parlor, and it was some time
before they reappeared. In their absence they had been making
preparation for a melodrama, which was now announced by Rip.
The subject of this new prank was "the Babes in the Wood."
Rip and one of the little girls were to enact the babes; and accordingly, in due time, two candles were set upon the floor to
represent the stage lights; the company were arranged in front;—
the children were laid out, and ordered to keep their eyes shut;
a piece of baize covered them, instead of leaves, and Rip raised
his head, for an instant, to inform the audience that there was to
be a great storm. Suddenly a servant came in and put out the
candles,—all except the two on the floor. This was followed by
a tremendous racket in the hall, that was principally occasioned
by the violent slamming of doors, which was designed to imitate
thunder;—then came a flash of lightning that made our audience
start. It had an amazing sulphurous odor and a gunpowder
haze, that produced some terror amongst the children. And now,
to give a perfect verisimilitude to the storm, a most dismal hissing and pattering, as of rain, assailed every ear. This was a
very lively passage in the drama. It continued with unabated
violence for some moments, producing equal astonishment and
diversion amongst the spectators—but finally became rather op-

pressive by a volume of pungent vapor which was diffused through the apartment, and set us all to coughing. In the midst of this pother of the elements, Ned and Harvey entered, each with a huge sabre attached to his girdle, their faces smutted with burnt cork, and their figures disguised in old uniform coats oddly disproportioned to their persons. Here they strutted about, making tragic gestures and spouting fierce blank verse. The rain, at intervals, sank upon the ear as if dissolving into mist, and anon rose with redoubled fury into a kind of bubbling and boiling rage with increased pungency. The sabres were drawn, and the murderers were disputing the propriety of the uncle's famous order to put the babes to death, and had already crossed their weapons for a melodramatic fray, when an incident occurred which saved the innocents from the fatal execution of their truculent purpose. The rain by some unaccountable mismanagement came suddenly down to a mere drizzle, and when the tempest ought to have howled its loudest, dropped into entire silence.

"More rain!"—cried Ned, in a stage whisper, looking towards the hall where this department carried on its operations.

Instead of rain, however, came sundry distinct giggles from a group of servants on the outside of the door, in the midst of which Carey's voice was distinctly heard—

"It's no use, Master Ned;—the frying pan's got cold. It won't make no more noise."

The business-like sobriety of this disclosure at such a critical moment, raised a general laugh, which put an end to the tragedy. Ned had given orders to Carey to heat that implement of the kitchen, to which the old man referred, and to bring it near the parlor door, where it was his cue to supply it with lard, by which ingenious device the storm was to be kept hissing hot as long as it was wanted. This fortunate failure admonished the ladies of the lateness of the hour, and they soon afterwards bade us good night.

The two tragedians changed their dresses and washed the smut from their faces, and joined us in a short time on the porch at the front door, where we found ourselves in a very different mood.

The night was calm and clear, and our late boisterous occupations inclined us with more zest to contemplate the beautiful repose of nature. We sauntered a short distance from the house. The moon was up and flinging a wizard glare over the tree-tops, and upon the old roof and chimneys. A heavy dew had fallen upon the grass, and imparted an eager chilliness to the atmosphere. The grove resounded with those solemn invocations poured forth by the countless insects of the night, which keep their vigils through the livelong hours of darkness,—shrill, piercing, and melancholy. The house dogs howled at the moon, and rushed at intervals tumultuously forward upon some fancied disturber; for the dog is imaginative, and is often alarmed with the phantoms of his own thoughts. A distant cock, the lord of some cabin hen-roost, was heard, with a clear and trumpet-like cadence, breaking the deep stillness of this midnight time, like a faithful warder on the battlements telling the hour to the sleepers. Every thing around us was in striking contrast with the scenes in which we had just been engaged. We grew tranquil and communicative; and thoughtless of the late hour—or rather more alive to its voluptuous charm—we completed our short circuit, and had gathered again into the porch, where we lay scattered about upon the benches, or seated on the door-sill. Here, whilst we smoked segars, and rambled over the idle topics that played in our thoughts, Harvey Riggs engaged himself in preparing a sleeping draught of that seductive cordial which common fame has celebrated as the native glory of Virginia. It is a vulgar error, Harvey contends, to appropriate the mint sling to the morning. "It is," he remarked with solemn emphasis

" the homologous peculiar of the night,—the rectifier of the fancy,—the parent of pleasant dreams,—the handmaid of digestion,—and the lullaby of the brain; in its nature essentially anti-roral; friendly to peristaltics and vermiculars; and, in its influence upon the body, jocund and sedative." I have recorded Harvey's words, because in this matter I conceive him to be high authority.

Upon this subject Harvey is eloquent, and whilst we sat listening to his learned discriminations in the various processes of this manufacture, our attention was suddenly drawn to another quarter by the notes of a banjoe, played by Carey in the courtyard. He was called up to the door, and, to gratify my curiosity to hear his music, he consented to serenade the ladies under their windows. Carey is a minstrel of some repute, and, like the ancient jongeleurs, he sings the inspirations of his own muse, weaving into song the past or present annals of the family. He is considered as a seer amongst the negroes on the estate, and is always heard with reverence. The importance this gives him, renders the old man not a little proud of his minstrelsy. It required, therefore, but little encouragement to set him off; so, after taking a convenient stand, and running his fingers over his rude instrument by way of prelude, he signified his obedience to our orders.

The scene was quite picturesque. Carey was old, his head was hoary, and now borrowed an additional silver tint from the moonbeam that lighted up his figure. Our eager group, which stood watching him from the midst of the rose bushes in which we were partly embowered; the silent hour, interrupted only by the murmur of the occasional breeze; the bevy of idle dogs that lay scattered over the ground; the mistiness of the distant landscape; and the venerable mass of building, with its alternate faces of light and shade, formed a combination of images and circumstances that gave a rich impression to our feelings.

Carey, for a moment, tuned his instrument with the airs of a professor, smiled, and looking round to Hazard, asked, in a half whisper, "What shall I play, Master Ned?"

"What you like best, Carey."

"Well," said Carey, striking off a few notes, "I'll try this:"

> The rich man comes from down below,
>> Yo ho, yo ho.
> What he comes for I guess I know,
>> Long time ago.
> He comes to talk to the young lady,
>> Yo ho, yo ho.
> But she look'd proud, and mighty high,
>> Long time ago.

And in this strain, clothed in his own dialect, he proceeded to rehearse, in a doggerel ballad, sung with a chant by no means inharmonious, the expected arrival of Swansdown at The Brakes, and the probable events of his visit, which, he insinuated, would be troublesome to Ned Hazard, and would, as the song went,

> "Make him think so hard he couldn't sleep."

"Can't you give us something better than that?" interrupted Ned.

"Ah! that makes you very sore there, master Ned Hazard," said the old negro, putting his hand on Ned's breast.

"Tut!" replied Ned, "you croak like a frog to-night."

"Give us 'Sugar in a Gourd' or 'Jim Crow,'" cried Ralph— referring to two popular dances well known in this region, and for the execution of which Carey has some reputation.

"I've got a dream for you, Master Ned," said Carey, with the modest chuckle of a composer exhibiting his own music. "May be you'd like to hear that?" We encouraged him, and the minstrel struck up another kind of rattling air which went at a jangling gallop on his banjoe, accompanied by an improvisation in the same style as that which we had just heard.

It will not do to give his words, which, without the aid of all the accessories, the figure of the old man himself, and the rapid twang of his banjoe, and especially the little affectations of his professorial vanity, would convey but a bald impression of the serio-comic effect the whole exhibition had upon us. The purport of this recitative strain was, that as he, the bard, lay sleeping in his cabin, a beautiful lady appeared to him, in the dead of night, and told him that he must instruct his young master, when he went a wooing, that there were three things for him to learn: he must never believe his mistress to be light of heart because she laughed at him; nor, that she was really offended when she looked angry at him; and lastly, that he was not to be disheartened by a refusal, as that was no proof she would not have him: that women were naturally very contrary, and must be interpreted by opposites.

"Carey is a true seer," said Harvey Riggs, when the old man had finished, "and brings us great encouragement, Ned. Now, old gentleman, you have done your duty, and as you dream so well, come in and you shall have something to put you to sleep, that you may try it again—and there's something to cross your palm with."

The old negro was brought into the parlor, where Harvey regaled him with a glass of the julep he had been making.

"God bless you, master Harvey, and young masters all!" said Carey, with a polite and gentleman-like gesture, and with a smile of the utmost benignity. "Good night, gemmen," he added, as he retired with many formal bows.

We now betook ourselves to our chambers, whence, for some time after I had got to bed, I could hear the negroes dancing jigs to Carey's banjoe in the court-yard. In the midst of these

noises I fell asleep—thus terminating a day that had been
marked by a succession of those simple pastimes which give such
an agreeable relish to country life, and which the gravest man,
I think, would be over-wise to find fault with.

CHAPTER XII.

A CONFESSION.

THE ladies had announced their intention to return to The Brakes before breakfast. Accordingly, the next morning, soon after daybreak, the courtyard was alive with the stir of preparation, and by the time the sun was up, horses, dogs, and servants filled the inclosure with a lively bustle, and the inmates of the house thronged the door and porch. Bel, with the wholesome bloom of the morning on her cheek, exhibited that flow of buoyant good-humor which naturally belongs to a young and ardent girl, and more signally when she is conscious of being an object of admiration. She danced about the hall, and sang short passages from songs with a sweet and merry warbling.

"We owe you our thanks, gentlemen," she said, "for Mr. Carey's saucy ballad last night. Cousin Harvey, I set down all the impertinence of it to you. You have such a wicked conscience that you can't sleep yourself, and you seem to be resolved nobody else shall."

"Ah Bel," replied Harvey, "Ned has spoiled your taste for simple melodies, by those Italian graces of his."

"Not a word, you monster—but help me to my horse. I mean to get away from this house as quickly as I can; and when I have you on the road I will tell you a piece of my mind. With such a swift foot under me, you know I can run away from you, if you get angry."

Ned Hazard advanced, somewhat officiously, to lead the animal which Bel was to mount, to the steps—

" No, no," she said, " Edward, that's Harvey's business. I have trained him to it.—Now, Mr. Cavalier, your hand."

Harvey came round to the stirrup side of the mare, and stooping down, whilst he locked his two hands so as to form a step—

" Your left foot—so—bear on my shoulder. There you are," he said, as he tossed her lightly into the saddle.

" It isn't every one can do that as well as Harvey," said Bel, by way of apology to Ned for refusing his assistance, which she saw had a little discomfited him. " Bring Mr. Littleton, Edward, to see us, and you shall have the privilege of another rehearsal, if you like."

" I am afraid,"—replied Ned, " that I have practised too many antics already, to keep your favor. But you shall see us before long ; and I mean henceforth to be very grave."

" Good bye !"—said Bel—" the sun is beforehand with us.— " Now Grace,"—she added in a lively tone, to the petted animal on which she rode—" Forward !" The mare rose on her hind legs with an active motion, and sprang away at a brisk speed.

Catharine had all this time been quietly mounting by the aid of a chair, and talking in a subdued voice to Prudence. She now said some amiable things at parting, repeated the invitation of Hazard and myself to The Brakes, and rode forward with becoming propriety of gait, attended by Ralph. Harvey followed close upon the track of Bel, and whilst the sun's rays yet smote the fields in level lines, the equestrians were out of sight.

After breakfast I found Hazard sitting on the bench at the front door, examining a box of fishing tackle. Some rods were leaned against one of the pillars of the porch, and Rip, with a

little ape-faced negro, was officiously aiding in the inspection of
the lines, and teasing Ned with a hundred questions. These two
wanted to know how far it entered into his design to take them
with him, if he meant to go fishing. He told me that as the day
looked well for it, he thought we might find some pastime with
our rods in a ramble over the brook. Rip and his flat-nosed
compeer, the little black,—who seemed to think it was his business to take charge of Rip—were, of course, to accompany us.
To make them useful, Hazard dispatched them both to get us
some bait. Away they went—Rip, at a bound, across the railing
of the porch, and Beelzebub—this was Ned's nickname for the
other—down the steps, with a mouth distended from ear to ear,
cutting all manner of capers over the grass. In a few moments
the latter was on his way to the stable with a long-handled hoe
over his shoulder, and a small tin vessel to collect worms, whilst
Rip was making a foray upon the grasshoppers, and flapping down
his much-abused beaver upon them with a skill that showed this
to be a practised feat.

A brief delay brought in our active marauders with an abundant spoil, and we then set forth on our expedition, each provided with a long rod and its appropriate tackle—our young attendants shouldering their weapons and strutting before us with
amazing strides and important faces—jabbering unceasingly all
the way.

Ned seemed inclined to be serious ; and I soon perceived that
he wanted to make me his confidant,—I had already guessed upon
what point. He talked, as we loitered along the bank of the
stream, about Harvey Riggs, Catharine, Ralph, old Mr. Tracy—
about every body but Bel—except a slight allusion to her once
or twice, and in the most casual and apparently accidental manner. It was a touch-and-go manner which spoke volumes. I saw
that he wanted me to talk of her, and I was malicious enough not

to understand him.   It was very evident that I was soon to have
a revelation.

Ned, of course, is in love with Bel.   Any one might see that,
in the first five minutes he should find them together.   It is notorious to the whole family, and I believe to all the inhabitants
in these parts—as much as any piece of country gossip can be.   I
had no doubt of it, even before we were surprised in our burletta
on the road.   Rip, who is inconveniently shrewd in these matters, took occasion this morning, just after the ladies left us on
their return to the Brakes, to whisper to me, as we entered the
breakfast room,—" Uncle Ned wanted mightily to lift Bel to her
horse, because he likes the very ground she walks on." And Harvey Riggs doesn't mince matters when he speaks of it—and old
Carey had twisted it into rhyme that no one could misunderstand.
Yet, strange as it may be, Ned, with all these proofs against him,
was such an owl as to think I had no suspicion of such a thing,
or, in fact, that it was a secret to any body.

The transparency of Hazard's character, or what I might better call his unconscious frankness, gives a little coloring of comic
extravagance to his endeavor to conceal his feelings.   He is a
man who can no more hold a secret than a crystal decanter can
hold wine invisible.   His effort to disguise his admiration for Bel
has, in truth, been somewhat perilous in this affair, by inducing
him to counterfeit a rather disparaging indifference in his demeanor towards her.   This is the source of his inexpert and ill-
timed raillery, his falling pell-mell upon her foibles, and alarming
her pride, and making jests upon points which women are generally apt to take without complaisance—even in ill part, sometimes.   Instead of frequenting the society of his mistress, as more
skilful lovers would do, he is careful to regulate his approaches
in such a manner as to avoid all suspicion of particular intimacy.
His walks and rides, it is true, tend instinctively in the direction

of The Brakes, and he is seen often enough taking an observation of the house and grounds, and traversing up and down the roads that lead thither; but his heart fails him at the gate, and he does not go through it even once in a week, unless somebody can make a matter of business for him to go there; and then he is as bold as a lion. 'What's our duty,'—as he very cogently reasons, in such conjunctures, 'must be done at all hazards, regardless of consequences.' Ned, I observe also, loses his intrepidity in Bel's presence, which makes him awkward in his attentions. And then, again, he seems to have an unfortunate tendency—I might almost describe it as a destiny—to present himself to her under those drawbacks which most shock her conceptions of the decorum she is inclined to expect from a lover. Our woodland extravaganza —the burlesque melodrama of the last night, I perceived, notwithstanding her laughing at them, were neither of them exactly consonant with her ideas of dignified sportiveness. She has a vein of romance in her composition which engenders some fastidious notions touching propriety of manners, and gives her—if I can trust Hazard's opinion, which I find confirmed in what I have seen—a predilection for that solemn foppery which women sometimes imagine to be refinement,—and of which Ned has not the slightest infusion.

Bel's temper naturally is most uncongenial with these pretensions, as she constantly shows when off her guard;—but by a certain ply of her mind, got perhaps in some by-path of education, or nurtured by a fanciful conceit, or left upon her memory amongst the impressions of some character she has been taught to admire, or, peradventure, being the physical disclosure in her organization of some peculiarly aristocratic drop of blood inherited from some over-stately grandam, and reappearing at the surface after the lapse of a century;—from whatever cause produced—she has taught herself to consider an orderly, measured, graceful movement, a choice adaptation of language, reverence of deportment, and, above all, entire devotedness, essential to the composition of, what she terms, a refined gentleman—a character which runs a fair risk of being set down in the general opinion as sufficiently dull and insipid. Bel overlooks the total absence of these gifts in Harvey Riggs, and says his playfulness (she uses a soft expression) is quite delightful. I explain this anomaly by the fact that Harvey is entirely out of the question as a lover; and that Bel has unwarily permitted her nature to counsel her opinion in Harvey's case; by reason of which, her good-humored cousin has taken the citadel of her favor by surprise. Ned Hazard she regards in quite a different light. Her sentinels are all at their posts when he makes a demonstration.

I sometimes think there is a little spleen at the bottom of Ned's treatment of Bel, a momentary sub-acid fretfulness, occasioned by her professing to hold in estimation the grave and empty pedantry of Singleton Swansdown, the very model of a delicate and dainty gentleman. Bel says, "he is so like the hero of a novel;" which Ned has once or twice repeated to me, with the remark, that it was " cursed fudge."

I have said enough, in the way of composition of Ned's character and of the queer condition of his love affair, as well as of the quality of his mistress, to preface the account I am about to give of our conversation on the fishing excursion.

We had reached a wide-spreading old sycamore on the bank of the brook, and had thrown our lines into a deep pool which eddied under the roots of the tree, and where we had reason to expect some luck to our angling. Here we seated ourselves on the grass in the shade. I found that I was advancing in Ned's confidence. He was restless, and not very attentive to his rod, and somewhat thirsty, for he drank at the brook twice.—I was perfectly dull of apprehension, and asked the most simple questions. I was determined to give him no help, at least for the present. It is strange, but it is universally true, that no man of sober sense,—no sensible, well-ordered man, I mean—can with a calm and composed face disclose the fact of his being in love—even to his most intimate friend. Mankind always seem to treat this very natural incident of one's life as a foolish thing ; and a man, therefore, looks or feels like a fool,—attempt the disclosure when he will.

"Mark"—said Ned, in a rather abrupt transition from a literary topic we had been discussing, and which I had myself proposed in a mischievous humor to baulk a previous advance to the matter that was weighing upon his mind,—"Mark"—and here was a slight pause and some visible perturbation,—"don't you think Bel Tracy a very lively girl?"

"Don't you?" I asked.

"Very lively," replied Ned. "How would you like to make a visit to the Brakes?"

"Do you visit there much, Ned?"

"Occasionally; Bel rather reproaches me for not coming as often as I ought, perhaps."

"Rather a dull house, I should think, for a visit: the old gentleman, I understand, is very formal," said I.

"On the contrary," replied Ned, "a very pleasant family. I should like to take you there,—Bel's a great favorite with her father. I—I have seen a good deal of her:"—a pause in which Ned looked a little queer.—"That slippery little gudgeon!"—

"Who?" said I, "you don't mean to call Bel a gudgeon?"

Ned laughed. "No—what are you thinking of?—I mean this fish," said he, drawing up his line—"It has nibbled off three baits in succession, and I can't get him on my hook."

"Throw in again, Ned," said I, smiling, "perhaps you will have better luck next time. So Bel, you think, is a lively girl? and you go to make her a visit occasionally? That must be quite an effort. And she is of opinion that you don't come often enough.—What would you call often?"

"I was there the very morning of the day on which you arrived here," said Ned.

"Ten days ago!" I said, with an affected surprise—"and still she complains! What an unreasonable lady! I suppose she would have you galloping there twice a week, at least? These women exact a great deal of us poor men. Why, if you were a lover of hers,—as I know you are not—once a week I should say"—

"Well, I don't know"—said Ned, interrupting me.

"You don't know what?" I asked—"whether you are a lover of her's, or not?—Such a cool, unimpassioned fellow as you are never made a lover in the world. If I lived as near to the Brakes as you do, I should make it a point to be over head and ears in love with Bel Tracy—But there is a difference between you and me."

Ned laughed again, quite loud this time, but his mirth was manifestly artificial.

"You think so?"—he said, at last.

The confession was on his lips—but a hesitation of one moment drove it back. His heart failed him, and like a ship which misses her stays, he fell off again into the wind.

"They do say"—said I—"that this Mr. Swansdown, of whom I have heard so much lately, looks that way with an eager eye, and that something is likely to come of it. Her father is fond of him, I hear; and if that's true, I consider her as good as mortgaged already. Perhaps it is wise in you to keep out of a love-scrape against such odds?"

"Swansdown!" exclaimed Ned. "Who told you that?—Don't believe a word of it, Mark. Bel Tracy is a woman of sense, and discriminates amongst men with remarkable acuteness. She has some odd fancies—but Swansdown is not one of them. I don't believe she can abide him. D——n it, I know she can't. Women will do queer things sometimes—but Bel will never have Swansdown as long as her name is Bel Tracy."

"No, of course not," I replied. "She will consider it a point of propriety to change her name on the very day she weds him. As to her discrimination—she will settle that as Papa advises. Bel, I'll be bound, is a dutiful daughter, and will do as her father bids her. Moreover, when a woman of a lively imagination—as your country ladies generally are—once permits her fancy to light upon a lover, it is quite immaterial what manner of man he may be,—the fancy is apt to settle the business for itself. Fancy is a colt that will run away with as good a rider as Bel Tracy. I profess to know a little of these women myself, Ned."

"Swansdown,"—said Hazard, alarmed by the suggestion I had forced so confidently upon him, and flushed with a slight degree of fretful anger,—"is the most preposterous ass—the most enormous humbug—the most remarkable coxcomb in Virginia."

"No matter for that.—Bel, as you say, has a great admiration for an elegant, refined, sweet-spoken, grave, and dignified gentleman :—that's a hobby of hers, from your own account ; and it is hard to tell the counterfeit from the real in these things."

"Devil!" cried Ned. "She can't be mistaken in Swansdown. I acknowledge she is somewhat haunted by this crotchet of elegance, and all that,—and that such a thing does, once in a while, make a woman rather impracticable ; but Bel's good sense will get the better of that. However, you may argue about it as you will, I have reason to know what her feelings are—personal rea-son,"—he said with some warmth.

"How could you know ?—what reason have you?"

"If you will have it, Littleton, and will keep a secret, I will tell you. Bel and I have had a sort of understanding. I have been very much attached to her for some time, and she knows it. Indeed, between you and me, I told her so ; and although there was nothing specific came of it, yet I can assure you she does not care a brass button for Singleton Swansdown. Mark, you will not mention this, of course."

"Oh ho!—so the wind's in that quarter!"—said I. "Why did'nt you tell me this before? Here have I been taking your part against Bel Tracy all this time. And now it turns out I ought to have been on the other side."

"Well, I intended to tell you," said Ned, "but somehow it got out of my head. I did'nt think of it."

"You blind bat!" said I, "and hypocrite, to boot! Why, I knew you were in love the first day I saw you. You have had nothing in your head but Bel Tracy ever since I arrived here. You have been dying to tell me all day."

"I thought you would laugh at me—a love affair is always a foolish thing, and every body laughs at it."

"Indeed, I assure you, upon my honor, I think to be in love one of the most serious, nay solemn things in the world. It has made you a perfect stick. You have lost all your light-heartedness.—And so, she encourages you, you think?"

"I should say so," replied Ned. "That is, she don't discourage me. You know there are a thousand little movements in a woman's deportment that show how her humor lies. Not any thing to speak of singly, but take them—in the long run— you understand?"

"Are you very particular in your attentions?"

"Well—tolerably—when I have a chance."

"What do you call particular attentions, Ned?"

"Why—I don't know exactly how to answer that," he replied. "I am attentive to her,—that is to say, I keep an eye upon her. For instance, I have sent her partridges."

"Dead or alive?" I asked with great gravity.

"Some that I had shot," said Ned; "dead, of course."

"For her to eat?" said I. "Quite an appropriate present to a young lady. Is she gastronomic?"

"Nonsense!" exclaimed Ned. "The partridges were for her father, and I so explained it."

"Did you ever ask her at dinner to allow you to help her to some greens?"

"What the d——l do you mean, Littleton?"

"I mean that your attentions are rather odd for a lover. Can you think of any others?"

"Well, I can't recall what you would consider actuall₅ attentions. I am confident, however, that I have shown her many."

"Any verses, or love letters, or sketches for an album, any snug little inferences in a corner?"

"Oh no, nothing to that extent," said Ned.

"What then did you mean by telling me that you had personal reason to know her feelings, just now—that you have told her of your attachment? I think, too, you said nothing specific came of it?"

"I'll explain," replied Ned. "The fact is, I addressed her. It was'nt the luckiest thing in the world. About a year ago, we had a dinner party at the Brakes—rather a merry one, and I drank a little too much champagne; and being possessed with a devil—for I can't account for it in any other way—I got to walking with Bel after night-fall on the porch; and finding we were alone, with the moon shining bright above, and the roses and honey-suckles, and all that, perfuming the air with the incense of Araby, I naturally got to be sentimental and talked, I am inclined to believe, a good deal of nonsense—and, in the end, popped the question at her like the crack of a rifle."

"Well, what then?"

"Oh, she behaved with the most admirable spirit. She turned round promptly and went into the house, without saying a word; leaving me to construe that as I might choose to take it."

"Ah ha, I understand now what you mean by nothing *specific* coming of it. You think then she encourages you?"

"She did'nt refuse me," said Ned, "and I consider that encouragement. The truth is, Mark, Bel rather likes me, but she doesn't like to show it."

"You have never spoken to her since on the same subject?"

"Oh, never. I have ridden out with her frequently since that, and she is always in excellent spirits."

"Do you ride alone with her?"

"No. She always makes Ralph or Harvey Riggs, or some one else of the party. That shows she is sensitive on the subject, you perceive. She wishes to delay the matter—which is the most natural thing in the world. A woman gets tremulous, and likes to put off such things till the next day, and then the next,—and so on."

"Ah, my dear Ned, you are a coward. I thought you were a brave man. Why don't you tell her at once, you want to talk to her alone, and persevere till she agrees to give you an opportunity? You would soon find out whether she encourages you or not."

"My good fellow," replied Ned, with some emphasis, "that's harder to do than you think. There is a great difference in bravery man-ward and woman-ward. It is moral courage which is necessary in these affairs with women, and a good deal of it, too. I would as lief march up to an alligator to box him about the eyes, in kid gloves, as come up deliberately on a cool morning, in the drawing-room or any where else, to Bel Tracy with a straight, up-and-down, point-blank declaration of love. It is so hard to groove such a thing into conversation. A man gets his nerves flurried, and is so apt to become thick of speech. I don't know how to manage the topics that would carry me up naturally to the point, and save me from the awkwardness of an abrupt transition. There are men who can do it—men of genius in that line; but I am not one of them. Yet, when you come to reflect upon it, it ought not to be any such great matter. All the world is getting married every day ; every man has to go through it— an ordinance of nature : and it does come to pass. But how the thing is managed so universally and so successfully—by all sorts of persons, of course,—that's a great mystery. Like good Christians, we ought to help one another."

" To be sure we ought," said I, " and we will, Ned. We shall hold a council upon it, and conduct our seige of poor little Bel's heart, according to the rules of the most approved strategy. But there must be no flinching on your part."

" I sometimes feel in a mood," said Ned, " that would carry me through, off-hand, if I had a chance; but then again "—. Here he shook his head thoughtfully, as much as to say, that this mood was not the optative, to come at his wish. " I think," he added, with some animation, as if a new and ingenious thought had struck him, " the best time for it, Littleton, is after dinner— about twilight, between hawk and buzzard."

" We must try it with cool heads," I replied. " As much of the hawk as you please, Ned, but no buzzard will serve us."

Before we had come to this conclusion, we had several times changed our ground, and had now reached the centre of a grove of tall trees. Hazard, having in this conversation happily disburdened his mind of a weight that had oppressed it for some time, appeared quite a new man to me. He became rational, gay and confident, and was quite willing now to dismiss the topic we had agitated so long.

I was struck with the scenery around us. It was just such a landscape as a painter would delight to study in detail, and sketch from every point ; there was such variety of foliage, such beautiful contrasts of light and shade, such bits of foreground, and rich accessories to throw into a picture. The beech, the poplar, and the sycamore, all so different in form, and so majestical from age and size, rose in this forest from a carpet of matted grass of the liveliest verdure. There was no underwood to interrupt the view into the deep recesses of shade. An occasional straggling grape-vine swung across from tree to tree, embracing the branches of both in its huge serpent-like folds ; and, here and there, an erect, prim, and maidenish poplar was furbelowed, from the root all the way up to the limbs, with wild ivy, and in this sylvan millinery coquetted with the zephyr that seemed native to the grove.

Through this sequestered shade the stream crept with a devious course, brattling, now and then, at the resistance of decayed trunks which accident had thrown across the channel,—and then subsiding again into silence.

As we advanced, swarms of tad-poles darted from the shallow into deeper water; apple-bugs, as the country people call that black beetle-shaped insect which frequents summer pools, and which is distinguished for the perfume of the fruit that has given it its name—danced in busy mazes over the surface of the still water ; the large spider, resembling a wheel without its rim, shot forth over his little lake, in angular lines, as if making a trigonometrical survey of its expanse ; and schools of greedy little fish sprang up at every mote that fell upon the stream. Then the gray squirrel, with his graceful undulating tail, vaulted furtively across our path to some neighboring tree ; and our attention was frequently called to the water-snake with his head thrust under a stone and the folds of his body glistening in the sun as the stream washed over him.

Rip and his goblin page, both of whom had been long out of sight, were now in view. They had grown weary of their attendance upon us, and were seen at this time wading through the brook, with their trousers drawn above the knee—Rip leading the way and directing the motions of Beelzebub, who imitated all his gestures with a grin of saucy good nature. They were carrying on a destructive warfare against the frogs, and, by the capture of several distinguished individuals of the enemy, had spread consternation along the whole margin of the stream,—insomuch, as Rip declared, "that not a Frenchman amongst them dared to show his goggle-eyes above the water."

The sun was now some hour or more past his meridian, and we proposed a return. So, gathering up our spoils, some dozens of stone-heads, suckers, and other small fish, which we had taken at intervals during our colloquy, and calling in our skirmishers from the battle of the frogs, we took up our homeward line of march—the two dripping and muddy mignons of our suite bringing up the rear, each bearing a string of fish hung by the gills upon a willow withe. In this array we soon regained the courtyard of the mansion.

CHAPTER XIII.

A MAN OF PRETENSIONS.

It is to be remarked in regard to all love affairs, that whatever may be the embarrassment of the disclosure, there is by no means the same difficulty in conversing about them afterwards. When the ice is once broken, your genuine lover is never tired of talking about his mistress.

For twenty-four hours after our late ramble, Ned talked, almost incessantly, upon the same subject. He let it drop for a moment, but he was sure to come speedily back upon it with a new face, as if it were a matter that required a serious deliberation; and he insinuated, that, in the present stage of the business, my advice was important to determine whether he should go on with it; although it was easy enough to perceive that his mind was not only quite made up, but keenly set upon the prosecution of the affair. Then, he affected to be greatly undecided as to some minute particular of conduct. Again, he had his doubts whether, upon the whole, she really did encourage him. In this sentiment he was sincere, although he endeavored to persuade himself that the matter was reasonably certain. These doubts made him restless, droll and solemn; but again changing his mood, he presented the entire action to me, from beginning to end, as a laughable affair; and that made him swear at it, and say it was very queer—unaccountable—extraordinary;—that it put a man in such an awkward situation! But his conclusion to it all was, that there was no use in talking about it,—matters had gone so far that there was no alternative; he was committed on the point of honor, and bound as a gentleman to make his pretensions good. I vexed him a little by saying I did not think so; and that if it was distasteful to him, I thought he was at liberty to retire when he chose. This balked his humor. So I consented to admit his premises for the future, and allow that he was bound in honor. With this admission he proceeded in his argument. It all amounted to the same thing, and the only varieties I discovered after this, were in his positions. He argued it perpendicularly, walking, jumping, dancing; then horizontally, lolling over three chairs, stretched out on a bed, and perched in the windows; then manually, washing, dressing, whistling, singing and laughing. In short, he behaved himself throughout the whole debate, like a man in love.

We were at the height of this disquisition, on the morning following Ned's first confessions, about an hour before dinner, in my chamber, extended at full length upon the bed, with our feet up against the bed-posts, when Rip came running in, almost out of breath, saying, " that if we wanted to see something worth looking at, we should come down stairs quickly, for there was Mr. Swansdown spinning up to the house, and making the gravel fly like hail; and there was aunt Prue, in the drawing-room, fixing a book before her in such a hurry! and Mrs. Winkle scolding about the custards:—And wasn't there going to be fun!"

I went to the window, and could see the phenomenon that excited Rip's admiration approaching the mansion like a meteor. A new light blue curricle, with a pair of long-tailed bay horses in fine keeping, driven by a gentleman of a delicate, emaciated figure, and followed by a servant in livery, had just entered the court-yard. The plate of the harness and mouldings glittered with an astounding brilliancy in the sun, and the spokes of the wheels emitted that spirited glare which belongs to an equipage of the highest polish. The horses were reined up at the door, and the gentleman descended. It was very evident that Mr. Singleton Oglethorpe Swansdown was a man to produce a sensation in the country.

Hazard and myself repaired to the hall. Meriwether received his guest with the plain and cordial manner natural to him. Mr. Swansdown has a tall figure, and an effeminate and sallow complexion, somewhat impaired perhaps by ill health, a head of dark hair, partially bald, a soft black eye, a gentle movement, a musical, low-toned voice, and a highly finished style of dress. He was very particular in his inquiries after the family; and having gone through many preliminary civilities, he was shown to a chamber to make his toilet for dinner. Soon afterwards, he appeared in the drawing-room, where he was remarkable for his sober, winning affability. He flattered Mrs. Meriwether upon her good health, and the fine appearance of the children. Lucy and Victorine he thought were going to be very beautiful (Lucy and Victorine both blushed): they made him feel old, when he recollected their infant gambols; Master Philip (otherwise Rip) was growing up to be a fine manly fellow; (at this, Rip crept slyly behind him, and strutted in the opposite direction with many grimaces), it was time to give up his nickname; he didn't like nicknames. He was very complimentary to Prudence Meriwether, which had a visible effect upon her, and made her animated; and thought his friend Meriwether looked younger and more robust than when they last met. He told Hazard that he was very much wanting in Richmond, by a party of ladies who were going off to the North, and that he, Ned, had made a great impression upon them. In short, Mr. Swansdown seemed determined to please every body, by the concern which he manifested in their happiness; and this was done with such a refined address, and such practised composure, as to render it quite taking. There is nothing equal to the self-possession of a gentleman who has travelled about the world, and frequented the circles of fashion, when he comes into a quiet, orderly, respectable family in the country. It is pleasant to behold what delight he takes to hear himself talk.

Swansdown inherited from his father an estate on the Meherrin, in the most southern quarter of Virginia. He is now about the prime of life, and still a bachelor. Being therefore a gentleman without much to keep him at home, he has recently travelled over Europe, and is very conversant besides with the principal cities of the Union. He has twice been very nearly elected to Congress, and ascribes his failure to his not being sufficiently active in the canvass. Upon this foundation he considers himself a public man, and of some importance to the government. It is remarked of him, that he is a very decided Virginian when he is out of the state, and a great admirer of foreign parts when he is at home. His memory is stored with a multitude of pretty sayings, and many singular adventures that have befallen him in his sundry travels, which he embellishes with a due proportion of sentiment. He has the renown of a poet and of a philosopher, having some years ago published a volume of fugitive rhymes, and being supposed now to be engaged in a work of a grave, speculative character, which it is predicted will reflect credit upon the literature of the South.

That he is a bachelor is the fault only of his stars, for he has courted a whole army of belles between Maine and Georgia, in which divers wooing he has been observed to do remarkably well for the first two weeks; after which, somehow or other, he falls off unaccountably. And it is said that he can reckon more refusals on his head than a thorough-paced, political office-hunter. He is what the sailors call an unlucky ship. One misfortune in love matters makes many, and three are quite ill-omened in the calculation of a high-toned, fashionable dame. This calamity has been so often reduplicated upon Swansdown, that it is thought he begins to lower his pretensions, and talk in a more subdued tone upon the subject. He is believed now to encourage the opinion that your raging belles are not apt to make the best wives; that a discreet lady, of good family and unpretending manners, is most likely to make a sensible man happy; great beauty is not essential; the mad world of fashion is a bad school; and some such other doctrines which indicate reflection, if not disappointment.

In pursuance of this temperate philosophy, he is supposed to be casting his eye about the country, and investigating more minutely the products of those regions over which he has hitherto travelled with too much speed for accurate observation; like a military engineer whose first survey is directed to the most prominent points of the ground, and who retraces his steps to make his examination of the subordinate positions.

From an intimacy of long standing between Mr. Tracy and the father of Swansdown, the former has a strong prepossession in favor of the son, which is cherished by Singleton in a course of assiduous attentions, and, no doubt, enhanced in some degree by the studied and formal cast of his manners. Mr. Tracy does not fail to speak of him as a man of excellent capacity and solid judgment; and has therefore admitted him into a somewhat confidential relation. He says, moreover, that Singleton is remarkably vivacious, and a man of attic wit. This appears odd enough to those who have the honor of this worthy's society.

What I have said will explain how it came to pass that this gentleman had been selected as Mr. Tracy's arbitrator in the question of the boundary line. It was with a view to the final arrangement of this subject that Swansdown had lately arrived at The Brakes; and he had now visited Swallow Barn in respect to that identical negotiation.

The ladies had just retired from the dinner-table, and we were sitting over our wine, when Harvey Riggs and Ralph Tracy rode up to the door. This addition to our company gave a spur to the conversation of the table. Swansdown had become animated and eloquent. He descanted upon the occasion of his visit; that to gratify his old friend, Mr. Tracy, he had prevailed upon himself to proffer his service to terminate a difficult controversy, which, he had been given to understand, was of some duration. This was one of those imperfect obligations which appertain to the relation of friendship. He ventured to suggest an opinion, that the issue would be auspicious to their mutual interests, and took leave to indulge the hope, that neither of his amiable and excellent friends would find occasion to regret the arrangement.

Meriwether answered these diplomatic insinuations with a bend of the head implying entire acquiescence, and with an occasional remark which showed the little importance he attached to the matter. Ned and Harvey Riggs exchanged looks, drank their wine, and listened to the oracle. Swansdown, in the course of the evening, was continually reminded of something he had seen at Florence, or Vienna, or other places. The river, which was visible from our windows, put him in mind of the Lake of Geneva; it only wanted the mountains. Then, he had choice anecdotes to tell of distinguished personages in Boston or New-York; and a most pithy piece of scandal that had transpired last winter at Washington. Meriwether bowed his head again, but very much like a man who was at a loss how to reply, and con tinued to listen with the utmost suavity. Harvey Riggs, how-

ever, often drew the discourse into a parenthesis, as if to get at
such subsidiary particulars as were necessary to elucidate the
narrative, and generally, by this mischievous contrivance, took off
the finish which the speaker studied to give to his recital.

A neat little pamphlet of verses some time ago made its appearance at Richmond, in hot press, and on the finest paper. It
was a delicate effusion of superfine sentiment, woven into a plaintive tale ; and had dropped, apparently, from some bower of sun-
gilt clouds, as they floated, on one vernal evening, over the fashionable quarter of Richmond,—it was so dainty in its array, and
so mysterious in its origin. " From whence could it come, but
from the Empyrean, or from Hybla," said the ladies of Richmond ;
" or from the divine pen of the fastidious and super-sentimental
Swansdown ?" Ned Hazard had brought this beautiful foundling
to Swallow Barn, and had given it to Prudence Meriwether to
nurse. It was now upon the window-seat.

It is necessary to state, that amidst all the criticism of Richmond, and the concurring determination of every body to impute
the verses to Swansdown, and the consequent reiteration of that
imputation by all companies, he never gave a plain denial of his
paternity ; but, on the contrary, took pleasure in hearing the
charge, and was so coquettish about the matter, and insinuated
such gentle doubts, that it was considered a case of avowed detection.

This dapper and delicious little poetical sally was christened
" The Romaunt of Dryasdale," in the title-page, but was more
generally known by the name of " The Lapdog Romance," which
Harvey Riggs had bestowed upon it.

" I suppose you have seen this before ?" said Hazard to
Swansdown, as he threw the book upon the table before him.

Swansdown picked it up, hastily turned over the leaves, smiled,
and replied, " It has made some stir in its day. But things like

this are not long-lived, however well executed. This seems to have kept its ground much longer than most of its species."

"The common opinion," said Ned, "is not backward to designate its author."

"Of course," replied Swansdown, "if a man has ever been guilty in his life of stringing couplets, he becomes a scape-goat ever after. Is it not somewhat strange that I should be perpetually charged with this sort of thing? But it is long since I have abandoned the banks of the Helicon. I protest to you I have not time for this kind of idling. No, no, gentlemen, charge me with what indiscretion you please, but spare me from the verses."

"If we could believe the rumors," said Harvey, "we should not doubt the origin of this effusion; but I rely more on my own judgment. I can pretty surely detect the productions of persons I am acquainted with: there is a spice, a flavor, in a man's conversation, which is certain to peep out in the efforts of his pen. Now this work is diametrically opposite to every thing we know of Mr. Swansdown. In the first place, it is studied and solemn, and wants Swansdown's light and familiar vivacity. Secondly, there is an affectation of elegance utterly at war with his ordinary manners. Thirdly,"—

"Oh, my dear sir," cried Swansdown, "save me from this serious vindication of my innocence. You can't be in earnest in thinking any one believes the report?"

"They do say so," replied Harvey, "but I have always defended you. I have said that if you chose to devote your time in this way, something of a more permanent and solid character would be given to the world."

"I have been bantered with it by my friends in the North," added Swansdown, "but that is a gauntlet which every man, who dabbles in literature, must expect to run."

"I have forgotten the name of the poem," said Meriwether, with innocent gravity.

"It is called The Romaunt of Dryasdale," said Swansdown.

" Or The Lapdog Romance," added Ned.

Swansdown colored slightly, and then laughed; but without much heart.

"Fill up your glass, Mr. Swansdown," said Meriwether, " the truth of wine is a good companion to the fiction of poetry.   Is this thing much admired?"

" A good deal," replied Swansdown.

" Amongst the young ladies of the boarding-school. especially," said Harvey.

" If I were disposed to criticise it," said Ned, " I should say that the author has been more successful in his rhyme than in his story."

" Yes," added Harvey, " the jingle of the verse is its great merit, and seems to have so completely satisfied the writer, that he has forgotten to bring the story forward at all.   I have never been able to make out exactly what is the subject of it."

" Then the sentiment," continued Hazard, " in which it abounds is somewhat over-mystical ;—one flight runs so into the other that it is not very easy to comprehend them."

" That," said Harvey, " is an admirable invention in writing. The author only gives you half of what he means, leaving you to fill up the rest for yourself.   It saves time, and enables him to crowd a great deal into a small space."

At this, Swansdown gave another laugh, but somewhat dry and feeble.

" There is another thing about this poem," said Ned, " it has some strange comparisons.   There is one here that Prudence has marked ; I suppose she has found out its meaning, and as that is a fortunate enterprise, she has taken care to note it.   The poet has endeavored to trace a resemblance between the wing of Cupid and his mistress's breath ; and he sets about it by showing, that when Cupid takes a flight on a spring morning, with his wings bound with roses, he must necessarily, at every flutter, shake off some of these odoriferous flowers ; and then, as the lady's breath is redolent of aromatic flavors, the resemblance is complete. I'l. read the passage aloud, if you please."

" Meriwether," said Swansdown in evident embarrassment but still endeavoring to preserve a face of gayety, " suppose we take a turn across your lawn before dark ?—We want a little motion.'

" Won't you stay to hear this flight of Cupid ?" asked Ned, taking up the book.

" I have no doubt it is very fine," said Swansdown. " But your account of it is so much better, that I should not like to weaken the impression of it."

Saying this, he retreated from the dining-room, and waited at the front door for Meriwether, who almost immediately followed.

In the evening our party played at whist ; Prudence and the poet making partners against Meriwether and Harvey ; whilst the rest of us sat round as spectators of the game. Mr. Chub, as usual, smoked his pipe in the porch, and the children slept about the corners of the room. Swansdown had grown dull, and his particularly accomplished bearing appeared somewhat torpid, except now and then, when he had occasion to make an inquiry respecting the game, which he did in a manner that no vulgar whist-player may ever hope to emulate : as thus,—putting on an interrogative look, gently bending his body forward, extending his left arm a little outward from his breast, and showing a fine diamond ring on his little finger, and asking with a smile,—so soft that it could hardly be called a smile,—" spades are trumps ?"

CHAPTER XIV.

My grand uncle Edward Hazard, the father of Walter, was from all accounts, a man of an active, speculating turn. He was always busy in schemes to improve his estate, and, it is said, threw away a great deal of money by way of bettering his fortune. He was a gentleman who had spent a considerable portion of his life in England, and when he settled himself, at last, in possession of his patrimony at Swallow Barn, he was filled with magnificent projects, which, tradition says, to hear him explain, would have satisfied any man, to a mathematical demonstration, that with the expenditure of a few thousand pounds, Swallow Barn would have risen one hundred per cent. in value. He was a very authoritative man, also, in the province; belonged frequently to the House of Burgesses; and was, more than once, in the privy council. The family now look up to my grand uncle Edward, as one of the most distinguished individuals of the stock, and take a great deal of pride in his importance : they say he was a most astonishing rake in London, and a wonderful speaker in the provincial legislature.

Connected with these two developments of his character, there are two portraits of him at Swallow Barn. One represents him in an embroidered coat without a cape, a highly worked cravat, tied tight enough round his neck to choke him, which makes his eyes seem to start from their sockets; an inordinately bedizened waistcoat, satin small-clothes, silk stockings, and large buckles in his shoes. His complexion is of the most effeminate delicacy, and his wig seems to form a white downy cushion for a small fringed cocked-hat. By the portrait, he could not have been much above twenty years of age; and his air is prodigiously conceited. The second picture exhibits a gentleman with a fine, bluff, and somewhat waggish face, past the meridian of life, arrayed in brown and in an oratorical attitude, intended, doubtless, to represent him in the legislature.

Now it must be made known, that the tract of land, called The Brakes, belonging to the Tracy family, lies adjacent to Swallow Barn. In old times the two estates were divided by a small stream that emptied into the James River, and that is still known by the name of the Apple-pie Branch. This rivulet traverses a range of low grounds for some miles, occasionally spreading itself out into morasses, which were formerly, and in some places are now, overgrown with thickets of arrow-wood, nine-bark, and various other shrubs, the growth of this region. The main channel of the stream through these tangled masses, was generally distinct enough to be traced as a boundary line, although the marsh extended some distance from each bank. In the course of this stream there is one point where the higher ground of the country stretches in upon the bed of the marsh, from either side, so as to leave a gorge of about a hundred yards in width, from both of which eminences the spectator may look back upon the low lands of the swamp for nearly a mile.

Just at that period of the life of my grand uncle when his fever of improvement had risen to its crisis, and when he was daily creating immense fortunes,—in his dreams,—it struck him, upon looking at the gorge I have described, that with very little trouble and expense, he might throw a stout breastwork from one side to the other, and have as fine a mill-dam as any man could possibly desire.   It was so simple an operation that he was surprised it had never occurred to him before.   And then a flour mill might be erected a short distance below,—which would cost but a trifle,—and the inevitable result would be, that this unprofitable tract of waste land would thereupon become the most valuable part of the estate.

I am told that it belonged to the character of my grand uncle to fall absolutely in love with every new project.   He turned this one over in his mind for two or three nights ; and it became as clear to him as daylight, that he was to work wonders with his mill.

So, reflecting that he had but sixteen irons in the fire at this time, he went to work without a moment's delay.   The first thing he did was to send an order to Bristol, (for he never had any opinion of the mechanics at home,) for a complete set of mill machinery ; and the second, to put up a house of pine weather-boards, for the mill.   Contemporaneously with this last operation, he set about the dam ; and, in the course of one summer, he had a huge breastwork of logs thrown across the path of the modest, diminutive Apple-pie, which would have terrified the stream even if it had been a giant.

As soon as this structure was completed, the waters began to gather.   My grand uncle came down every day to look at them, and as he saw them gradually encroaching upon the different little mounds of the swamp, it is said he smiled, and remarked to his son Walter, whom he frequently took with him, "that it was strange to see what results were produced by human art."   And it is also told of him, that he made his way, during this rising of the waters, to a tree in the bed of the dam, to notch with his penknife a point to which the flood would ultimately tend ; that, while stooping to take a level with the breast of the dam, he lost his balance, and was upset into a pool, formed by the encroaching element; and that, when Walter expected to see him in a passion at this mishap, he rose laughing, and observed, "that the bed of the dam was a damned bad bed;" which is said to be the only pun that ever was made in the Hazard family, and therefore I have put it on record.

In a few days, with the help of one or two rains, the pool was completely full; and, to the infinite pleasure of my grand uncle, a thin thread of water streamed over one corner of the dam,—the most beautiful little cascade in the world; it looked like a glossy streamer of delicate white ribbon. My grand uncle was delighted. 'There, my boy," said he to Walter, "there is Tivoli for you ! We shall have our mill a-going in a week."

Sure enough, that day week, off went the mill. All the corn of the farm was brought down to this place; and, for an hour or two that morning, the mill clattered away as if it had been filled with a thousand iron-shod devils, all dancing a Scotch reel. My grand uncle thumped his cane upon the floor with a look of triumph, whilst his eyes started from his head, as he frequently exclaimed to the people about him, " I told you so; this comes of energy and foresight; this shows the use of a man's faculties, my boy !"

It was about an hour and a half, or perhaps two hours,—as my authority affirms,—after the commencement of this racket and clatter in the mill, that my grand uncle, and all the others who were intent upon the operation, were a little surprised to discover that the millstone began to slacken in its speed; the bolting cloth was manifestly moving lazily, and the wheels were getting tired. Presently, a dismal screech was heard, that sounded like all the trumpets of Pandemonium blown at once; it was a prolonged, agonizing, diabolical note that went to the very soul.

" In the name of all the imps of Tartarus,—(a famous interjection of my grand uncle,) what is that?" "It's only the big
wheel stopped as chock as a tombstone," said the miller, "and it
naturally screeches, because, you see, the gudgeon is new, and
wants grease." Hereupon a court of inquiry was instituted ; and,
leading the van, followed by the whole troop, out went my grand
uncle to look at the head-gate. Well, not a thing was to be seen
there but a large solitary bull-frog, squatted on his hams at the
bottom of the race, and looking up at his visitors with the most
piteous and imploring countenance, as much as to say, " I assure
you, gentlemen, I am exceedingly astonished at this extraordinary
convulsion myself, which has left me, as you perceive, naked and
dry." Then the court proceeded upon their investigation towards
the dam, to observe how that came on.

I can readily imagine how my grand uncle looked, when the
scene here first presented itself to his view. It must have been
a look of droll, waggish, solemn, silent wonder, which, for the
time, leaves it a matter of perfect doubt whether it is to terminate
in a laugh or a cry. In the first place, the beautiful ribbon cascade was clean gone. In the second, there were all the little tus-
socks of the swamp, showing their small green heads above the
surface of the water, which would hardly have covered one's shoe-
top ; and there were all the native shrubs of the marsh, bending
forwards, in scattered groups, like a set of rose bushes that had
been visited by a shower ; dripping wet, and having their slender
stalks tangled with weeds ; and there was, towards the middle, a
little line of rivulet meandering down to the edge of the dam,
and then holding its unambitious course parallel with the breastwork, deploying to the left, where it entered the race, and tripping
along gently, down to the very seat of the bull-frog. " Hoity,
toity," cried my grand uncle, after he had paused long enough to
find speech, " here is some mistake in this matter !"

Now, it is a principle of physics, that an exhausted receiver is the worst thing in the world to make a draught upon. The mill-dam was like a bank that had paid out all its specie, and, consequently, could not bare the run made upon it by the big wheel, which, in turn, having lost its credit, stopped payment with that hideous yell that wrought such a shock upon the nerves of my grand uncle.

In vain did the old gentleman ransack the stores of his philosophy, to come at this principle. He studied the case for half an hour, examined the dam in every part, and was exceedingly perplexed. " Those rascals of muskrats have been at work," said he. So, the examination was conducted to this point; but not a hole could be found. " The soil is a porous, open, filtrating kind of .soil," said the old gentleman.

" It seems to me, master," said an arch looking negro, who was gaping over the flood-gate upon the muddy waste, " that the mill's run out of water."

" Who asked you for your opinion, you scoundrel?" said my grand uncle in a great fury,—for he was now beginning to fret,— " get out of my sight, and hold your tongue !"

" The fellow is right," said the miller, " we have worked out the water, that's clear !"

" It's a two-hour-mill," added the negro, in a voice scarcely audible, taking the risk of my grand uncle's displeasure, and grinning saucily but good-humoredly, as he spoke.

It is said that my grand uncle looked at the black with the most awful face he ever put on in his life. It was blood-red with anger. But, bethinking himself for a moment, he remained silent, as if to subdue his temper.

There was something, however, in the simple observation of the negro, that responded exactly to my grand uncle's secret thoughts ; and some such conviction rising up in his mind, gradually lent its aid to smother his wrath. How could he beat the poor fellow for speaking the truth! It was,—and he now saw it written in characters that could not be mistaken,—it was, after all his trouble, and expense, and fond anticipations, " a two-hour-mill."

" Stop the mill," said my grand uncle, turning round, and speaking in the mildest voice to the miller, " stop the mill; we shall discontinue our work to day."

" 'Squire," replied the miller, " the mill has been as silent as a church for the last hour."

" True," said my grand uncle, recollecting himself; " come, Walter, we will mount our horses, and think over this matter when we get home. It is very extraordinary! Why didn't I foresee this? Never mind, we will have water enough there to-morrow, my boy!"

He slowly went to the fence corner, and untied his horse, and got up into his saddle as leisurely as if he had been at a funeral. Walter mounted his, and they both rode homeward at a walk; my grand uncle whistling Malbrouk all the way, in an under key and swinging his cane round and round by the tassel.

CHAPTER XV.

IT fortunately happened that a tolerably wet season followed this first experiment of the mill. But with all the advantages of frequent rains, the mortifying truth became every day more apparent, that my grand uncle's scheme of accommodating the neighborhood with a convenient recourse for grinding their corn, was destined to be balked, in the larger share of its usefulness, by that physical phenomenon which was disclosed to him on the first day of his operations; to wit, that his capacious reservoir was emptied in a much more rapid ratio than it was filled. It was like a profligate spendthrift whose prodigality exceeds his income. The consequence was that the mill was obliged to submit to the destiny of working from one to two hours in the morning, and then to stop for the rest of the day, except in the very wet weather of the spring, (and then there was no great supply of corn,) in order, by the most careful husbandry, to wring from the reluctant little water-course a sufficient fund for the next day's employment.

This was a serious loss to the country around ; for my grand uncle had talked so much about his project, and extolled his benefaction so largely, that the people had laid out their accounts to take all their grists to his mill. They came there, all through

the summer, in crowds; and nothing was more common than to
see a dozen ruminative old horses, with as many little bare-legged
negroes astride upon them, with the large canvas mill-bags
spread out for saddles, all collect of a morning round the mill
door, each waiting for his turn to get his sack filled.   Sometimes
these monkeys were fast asleep for hours on their steeds; and
sometimes they made great confusion about the premises with

their wild shouts, and screams, and rough-and-tumble fights in
which they were often engaged.   But it invariably fell out that
at least half were disappointed of their errands, and were obliged
to attend the next day.   In the dry spells the mill stopped
altogether.   These things gave great dissatisfaction to the neighborhood, and many good customers abandoned the mill entirely.
I am told, also, that the old gentleman was singularly unfortu-

nate in his choice of a miller. He had a great giant of a fellow
in that station, who was remarkable for a hard-favored, knotty,
red head, and a particularly quarrelsome temper. So that it often happened, when the neighbors expostulated in rather too
severe terms against the difficulty of getting their corn ground,
this functionary, who was a little of the mould of the ancient
miller as we read of him in the Robin Hood ballads, made but
few words of it, and gave the remonstrants a sound threshing,
by way of bringing them to reason. Then again, the dam formed
a large pestilent lake, and, by its frequent exposure of the
bottom to the sun, engendered foul vapors that made the country, in the autumn, very unhealthy.

These circumstances, in process of time, worked sadly to the
disparagement of my grand uncle's profits, and set the people to
talking in harsh terms against his whole undertaking. They
said the worst thing they could of it. " That it was a blasted
thundergust mill, and not worth a man's while to be fooling about
it with his corn, as long as he could get it ground any where else,
if it was ten miles off!"

In process of time the miller was turned away; and then the
machinery got out of order, and my grand uncle would not repair; and so the mill came to a dead halt. Following the course
of nature, too, the dam began to manifest symptoms of a prema-
ture old age. First, the upper beams decayed by the action of
the sun upon them; after these, the lower part of the structure
broke loose. But what with drift-wood, and leaves, and rubbish,
the mound, which constituted the breastwork, remained sufficently
firm to support the pond for some years. It was a famous place
for black snakes and sunfish in summer, and wild ducks in winter. All this time the stream found a vent through an opening
that had been worn in the breastwork; and, consequently, the
race had become entirely dry, and grown over with grass.

Year after year the surface of the pond grew gradually less. It retreated slowly from its former edge, and became narrower. At length, at the breaking up of one unusually boisterous, wet and surly winter, there came on, in the month of March, a week of heavy and incessant rain. This celebrated week closed with one of the most furious tempests ever remembered in that part of the country. The heavens poured down their wrath upon the incontinent mill-dam; the winds rushed, with a confounding energy, over this desolate tract, driving the waters before them in torrents; and away went the rickety old breastwork, with all the imprisoned pool behind it.

The next morning the tempest subsided. The sun smiled again over the chilly scene; and there was the fuming and affrighted little Apple-pie, in all its former insignificance. Not a trace of the breastwork was left; and there was to be seen the foul and slimy bed of the mill pond, exposed in shocking nakedness to the eye. Long green tresses of weed, covered with the velvet of many years' accumulation beneath the surface of the water, lay strewed about, wherever any stubborn shrub occurred to arrest their passage; huge trunks of trees, moss-grown and rotten, were imbedded upon the muddy surface; briers, leaves, and other vegetable wrecks were banked up on each other in various forms, mingled, here and there, with the battered and shapeless carcasses of the smaller vermin that frequented the pond. The wind swept with a brisk and whistling speed over this damp bottom, and visited, with a wintry rigor, the shivering spectators whom curiosity had attracted to witness the ravages of the night; but, in the midst of all, the feeble and narrow Apple-pie shot hastily along with a turbid stream, pursuing his course through, under, and around the collected impediments in his path, as near as possible in the very same channel which, ten or fifteen years before, he had been wont to inhabit; as if unconscious that this disturbance in the face of nature could be attributed, in the slightest degree, to such an inefficient and trifling imp as himself : by no means an unimpressive type of the confusion and riot which the most sordid and paltry passions may produce in the moral world, when suffered to gather up and gangrene in the system.

As I have introduced this narrative to make my reader acquainted with the merits of the controversy relative to the boundary line, it is necessary that I should inform him, that when my grand uncle first entered upon this project of the mill, he immediately opened a negotiation with Mr. Gilbert Tracy, his neighbor,—who was at that time the proprietor of The Brakes,—for the purchase of so much of the land, or rather of the marsh, which lay eastward of the Apple-pie Branch, as was sufficient for the projected mill-dam. I have already told my readers that the Branch itself was the dividing line between the two estates ; and, consequently, my grand uncle was already in possession of all westward of that line. In his communications with Mr. Gilbert Tracy on this subject, he unfolded his whole scheme, and, without the least difficulty, obtained the purchase he desired. There were several letters passed between them, which stated the purpose contemplated ; and the deed that was executed on the occasion also recites, that " Edward Hazard, Esquire, of Swallow Barn, conceiving it to be a matter of great importance to the good people residing on, frequenting and using the lands in the vicinage of the stream of water, commonly known and called by the name of the Apple-pie Branch, that a convenient and serviceable mill, adapted to the grinding of wheat, rye, and Indian corn, should be constructed on the said Apple-pie, &c. ;" and also, " that the said Edward Hazard, Esquire, having carefully considered the capacity, fall, force of water, head and permanency of the said Apple-pie Branch for the maintenance and supply of a mill as aforesaid ; and being convinced and certified of the full and perfect fitness of the same, for the purposes aforesaid;" the said Gilbert Tracy transferred, &c., a full title " to so much of the said land as it may be found useful and necessary to occupy in the accomplishment of the said design, &c.; the said Edward Hazard paying therefor at the rate of one pound, current money of Virginia, for each and every acre thereof."

By this conveyance, the western limit of The Brakes was removed from the channel of the Branch to the water edge of the mill-pond, as soon as the same should be created.

My grand uncle, after the failure of his scheme, could never bear to talk about it. It fretted him exceedingly; and he was sure to get into a passion whenever it was mentioned. He swore at it, and said a great many harsh things; for, I am told, he was naturally a passionate man, and was not very patient under contradiction. He would not even go near the place, but generally took some pains, in his rides, to avoid it. When they told him that the storm had carried away the dam, he broke out with one of his usual odd kind of oaths, and said, " he was glad of it; it was a hyperbolical, preposterous abortion ;—he must have been under the influence of the moon when he conceived it, and of Satan when he brought it forth; and he rejoiced that the winds of heaven had obliterated every monument of his folly." Besides this, he said many other things of it equally severe.

The date of this freak of the old gentleman was somewhere about the middle of the last century. The ruin of the mill is still to be seen. Its roof has entirely disappeared ; a part of the walls are yet standing, and the shaft of the great wheel, with one or two of the pinions attached, still lies across its appropriate bed. The spot is embowered with ancient beech trees, and forms a pleasant and serene picture of woodland quiet. The track of the race is to be traced by some obscure vestiges, and two mounds remain, showing the abutments of the dam. A range of light willows

grows upon what I presume was once the edge of the mill-pond;
but the intervening marsh presents now, as of old, its complicated
thickets of water plants, amongst which the magnolia, at its accustomed season, exhibits its beautiful flower, and throws abroad
its rich perfume.

Before the period of the Revolutionary war, Gilbert Tracy
paid the debt of nature. The present proprietor, his eldest son,
inherited his estate. Old Edward Hazard figured in that momentous struggle, and lived long enough after its close to share,
with many gallant spirits of the time, the glories of its triumph.
Isaac, the son of his old friend, preserved a neutral position in
the contest; and, being at heart a thorough-going loyalist, the intercourse between him and the family at Swallow Barn grew rare
and unsocial. The political principles of the two families were
widely at variance; and, in those times, such differences had their
influence upon the private associations of life. Still it is believed, and I suppose with some foundation for the opinion, that
the good offices of my grand uncle, secretly exerted, and without
even the knowledge of Mr. Tracy, had the effect to preserve The
Brakes from confiscation,—the common misfortune of the dis-
affected in the war: an affectionate remembrance of his old friend
Gilbert, and the youth of the successor to the estate at that time,
being imagined to have actuated Edward Hazard in this manifestation of kindness.

My grand uncle, very soon after the peace, was gathered to
his fathers, and has left behind him a name, of which, as I have
before remarked, the family are proud. Amongst the monuments which still exist to recall him to memory, I confess the old
mill, to me, is not the least endearing. Its history has a whimsical bearing upon his character, illustrating his ardent, uncalcu-
lating zeal; his sanguine temperament; his public spirit; his
odd perceptions; and that dash of comic, headstrong humorous-

ness that, I think, has reappeared, after the shifting of one gen·
eration, in Ned.

I, accordingly, frequently go with Ned to this spot; and, as
we stretch ourselves out upon the grass, in the silent shade of the
beech trees, or wander around the old ruin, the spot becomes
peopled to our imaginations with the ancient retainers of Swallow Barn; the fiery-headed miller; the elvish little negroes who
have probably all sunk, hoary-headed, to the grave, leaving their
effigies behind, as perfect as in the days when they themselves
rode to mill; and last of all, our venerable ancestors.

Out of these materials, we fabricate some amusing and touching stories.

CHAPTER XVI.

It was about the year 1790, that my uncle Walter began to turn his attention to the condition of the Apple-pie frontier.

Until this time, ever since the miscarriage of the unfortunate enterprise of the mill, this part of the domain had been grievously neglected. It was a perfect wilderness. No fences had ever been erected, on either side, to guard the contiguous territories from encroachment; and there were numerous cowpaths leading into the thickets, which afforded a passage, though somewhat complicated, from the one estate to the other. The soil was cold and barren, and no cultivation, therefore, was expended upon this quarter. In fact, it may be said to have belonged to the colts, pigs, heifers, racoons, opossums and rabbits of both proprietors. The negroes still consider it the finest place in the whole country to catch vermin, as they call the three latter species of animals; and I myself frequently, in my ranges through this region, en counter their various gins and snares set in the many by-paths that cross it.

The tract of marsh land, occupied by the dam in old times, did not exceed, on the Tracy side of the Branch, above thirty acres. It was a slip of about half a mile in length, and perhaps, at its widest part, not more than two hundred yards broad, that bordered on that side of the Branch. This slip, of course, constituted the subject matter of my grand uncle's purchase from Mr. Gilbert Tracy.

It occurred to Walter Hazard, about the period I have referred to above, that this bottom might be turned to some account, if it were well drained, cleaned of its rank growth of brushwood, and exposed to the sun and then set in grass. It would doubtless, he thought, make an excellent pasture for his cattle ; and, at all events, would contribute to render the surrounding country more healthy.

If my uncle Walter had been a man in the least degree given to superstitious influences, he would have seen, in the ill-fated schemes of his father in this direction, the most inauspicious omens against his success in his contemplated achievement. But he was a man who never thought of omens, and was now altogether intent upon adding a convenient meadow to his estate.

It seemed that the Apple-pie was to be the fountain of an Iliad of troubles to the Hazard family.

When Walter Hazard was ready to go to work, somewhere about midsummer, he turned in twenty hands upon the marsh, and forthwith constructed some rectangular ditches, traversing it upon both sides of the branch, sufficiently near to carry off the water. Whilst he was employed at this work, and not dreaming of any other obstacles than those that were before his eyes, he was exceedingly surprised to receive a letter from Mr. Isaac Tracy, which, in the most friendly and polite terms, intimated that the writer had just been made acquainted with Captain Hazard's (my uncle always bore this title after the war,) design of draining the marsh ; and regretted to learn that he had assumed a proprietary right over a portion of the domain that appertained to The Brakes. The letter proceeded to acquaint my uncle that this infringement involved a question affecting the

family dignity ; and, therefore, it was suggested, that it became
necessary to remonstrate against it, more from considerations of
a personal nature, than from any regard to the value of the soil
thus brought into dispute.

Now it so happened that Mr. Tracy had, for some time past,
been revolving in his mind this subject, to wit,—the right of
ownership over the bed of the mill-dam, after the accident that
brought it again into the condition in which it existed before the
erection of the mill. He had examined the deed from his father,
part of which I have recited in a former chapter, and that document favored the conclusion, that as the grant had been made for
a specific purpose, the failure of that purpose restored the original
owner to all his former prerogatives.

This brought him to studying the law of the matter, and he
soon became perfectly assured that he understood all about it.
In short, he took up a bold, peremptory and dogged opinion, that
he was in,—as he remarked,—of his former estate : that it was a
grant *durante* the existence of the mill-pond ; a feoffment defeasi-
ble upon condition subsequent, and a dozen such other dogmas
which tickled the worthy gentleman excessively, when they once
made a lodgment in his brain.   There is nothing in the world, I
believe, that produces a more sudden glory in the mind, than the
first conceits of a man who has made some few acquisitions in an
abstruse science ; he is never at rest until he makes some show
of his stock to the world ; and I have observed that this remark
is particularly applicable to those who have got a smattering of
law.   Mr. Tracy ran off with the thing at full speed.   He affected
to consult his lawyer upon the matter, but always silenced all attempts of that adviser to explain, by talking the whole time himself, and leaving him without an answer.

It was in the height of this fervor that he received the information of my uncle's proceedings ; and it was with a kind of ex-

ultation and inward chuckling over the certainty of his rights, that he sat down and addressed Captain Hazard the letter of which I have spoken. There was another sentiment equally active in Mr. Tracy's mind to spur him on to this action. The lord of a freehold coming by descent through two or three generations, and especially if he be the tenant in tail, is as tenacious as a German Prince of every inch of his dominions. There is a seigniorial pride attached to his position, and the invasion of the most insignificant outpost conveys an insult to the lawful supremacy; it manifests a contemptuous defiance of the feudal dignity. Mr. Tracy felt all this on the present occasion, and, perhaps, rather more acutely in consequence of the partial alienation between his own and his neighbor's family, produced by the late political events, and which was, at this period, but very little removed.

The letter came upon my uncle like a gauntlet thrown at his feet. He was somewhat choleric in temper, and his first impulse was to make a quarrel of it. It seemed to him to imply a dishonest intrusion.

However, when he came to consider it more maturely, he could find no fault either with its tone or its temper. It was a frank, polite, and seemly letter enough: "If it was Mr. Tracy's land," said my uncle, "he certainly had a right to say so:" and in truth, as he thought more about it, he came to the conclusion that it looked well to see a gentleman inclined to stand by his rights: it was what every man of property ought to do!

In this feeling, my uncle wrote his reply to Mr. Tracy's letter, and filled it with every observance of courtesy, but, at the same time, steadily gainsaying his neighbor's opinions of the right, and desiring that the matter should be investigated for their mutual satisfaction. This communication was followed by the instant withdrawal of his people from the debatable ground, and, for the time, with an abandonment of the meadow scheme.

Never were there, in ancient days of bull-headed chivalry, when contentious monk, bishop or knight appealed to fiery ordeal, cursed morsel, or wager of battle, two antagonists better fitted for contest than the worthies of my present story. My uncle had been a seasoned campaigner of the Revolution, with a sturdy soul set in an iron frame, and had grown, by force of habit, a resolute and impregnable defender of his point. Mr. Tracy, I have already described as the most enamored man in the world of an argument. And here they were, with as pretty a field before them as ever was spoiled by your peace-makers. The value of the controversy not one groat; its issue, connected with the deepest sentiment that lay at the bottom of the hearts of both,—the pride of conquest !

Mr. Tracy's first measure was to write a long dissertation upon the subject, in the shape of an epistle, to my uncle. It was filled with discussions upon reversionary interests, resulting uses, and all the jargon of the books, plentifully embellished with a prodigious array of learning, contained in pithy Latin maxims, in which the lawyers are wont to invest meager and common thoughts with the veil of science. It was filled, moreover, with illustrations and amplifications and exaggerations, the fruit of a severe and learned study of his case by the writer.

Then followed my uncle's reply, in which it was clear that he did not understand a word of the argument that was intended to prostrate him. After this came rejoinder and surrejoinder, and reduplications of both, poured in by broadsides. Never was there so brisk a tourney of dialectics known on the banks of the James River ! The disputants, now and then, became sharp, and my uncle, whenever this was the case, obtained a decided advantage by a certain caustic humor, which he handled with great dexterity.

Eventually, as it might have been foreseen, they resolved to go to law, and institute an amicable ejectment. Here a difficulty arose.

It was hard to determine which should be plaintiff, and which defendant; since it was not quite clear who was in possession. Mr. Tracy insisted, with all imaginable politeness, upon making my uncle the compliment of appearing as the plaintiff in the action, which the latter obstinately refused, inasmuch as he was unwilling it should be understood by the world that the suit had been one of his seeking. This was adjusted, at last, by Mr. Tracy's commencing the proceeding himself. It began in the county court; and then went to the superior court; and then to the court of appeals. This occupied some years. All the decisions, so far as they had gone had been in favor of my uncle; but there were mistakes made in important points, and proofs omitted, and papers neglected to be filed. Mr. Tracy was deeply vexed at the issue, and waxed warm. So, the whole proceedings were commenced anew, and carried a second time through the same stages. The principal points were still in my uncle's favor. His antagonist bit his lips, affirmed the utter impregnability of his first positions, and resolved not to give up the point. Never was there a case so fruitful of subdivisions! Jury after jury was brought to bear upon it; and twenty times every trace of the original controversy was entirely out of sight. At length they got into chancery, and then there was the deuce to pay!

Year after year rolled away, and sometimes the pretty little quarrel slept, like the enchanted princess, as if it was not to wake again for a century. And then again, all of a sudden, it was waked up, and shoved and tossed and thumped and rolled and racketed about, like Diogenes' tub.

It was observable, throughout all this din and bustle, that Mr. Tracy was completely driven out of every intrenchment of law and fact; which, so far from having the effect of moderating his opinion or his zeal, set him into a more thorough and vigorous asseveration of his first principles.

He affirmed that the juries were the most singularly obtuse and obstinate bodies he had ever encountered; and that the courts were, beyond all question, the most incurably opinionated tribunals that ever were formed.

In the height of this warfare, the death of the defendant, my uncle, occurred; which for some years again lulled all hostilities into a profound slumber. After a long interval, however, the contest was resumed; and it now fell to the lot of Frank Meriwether to enter the lists. No man could be more indisposed by nature to such an enterprise; and it was plainly discernible that our old friend of The Brakes was also beginning, in his old age, to relax into a pacific temper.

It must be remarked, that during the latter years of this struggle the two families had grown to be upon a very intimate footing, and that at no period had the legal disquiets the least influence whatever upon the private regards of the parties.

In order, therefore, to get rid of the troubles of carrying on the debate, Frank Meriwether had thrown out some hints of a disposition to settle the whole affair by a reference to mutual friends; and would gladly at any time have relinquished all claim to the disputed territory, if he could have contrived to do so without wounding the feelings of his neighbor, who was now singularly tenacious to have it appear that his only object in the pursuit was to vindicate his first decided impressions. The old gentleman, therefore, readily agreed to the arbitration, and still fed his vanity with the hope that he should find in the private judgment of impartial men, a sound, practical, common sense justification of his original grounds in the controversy.

This result is to be risked upon the opinions of Singleton Oglethorpe Swansdown and Philpot Wart, Esquires, who are immediately to convene for the consideration of this momentous subject.

CHAPTER XVII.

IT will be recollected, that before my digression to show the
merits of the question touching the boundary line, I left Mr.
Swansdown seated, after tea, at a game of whist. This game is
a special favorite in the low country of Virginia, and possesses an
absorbing interest for Meriwether. Prudence is not behind her
brother either in the skill or the devotion of a thorough-bred
player; and Harvey Riggs may very justly be set down as pre-
eminent in this accomplishment. The poet and philosopher was
the only one of the party at the table who may be said to have
ever been at fault during the evening.

I do not pretend myself to be well versed in the mysteries of
this silent and cogitative recreation; but I have often had occasion to observe that a genuine whist-player is apt, for the time,
to be one of the most querulous of mortals. He makes fewer
allowances for the frailty of his brethren than any other member
of society. The sin of not following suit, or losing a trick, or not
throwing out a good card in the right place, is, in his eyes, almost
inexpiable, and does not fail to bring down upon the delinquent
that sharp, unmitigated and direct rebuke that implies, "you
must be a blockhead, or you never would have thought of doing
so stupid a thing!" This is sometimes insinuated in a look,

sometimes conveyed in a question, and often inferred by a simple ejaculation.

Swansdown is not unfrequently taken to task by his antagonists. Harvey Riggs stops, puts down his cards upon the table, and, with a biting affectation of mildness, observes, "Really, Mr. Swansdown, if I could only count upon your observing the rules of the game, I should know what to play ; but as it is, I am exceedingly perplexed!" Even Frank Meriwether, with all his benignant impulses, sometimes throws himself back into his chair, and putting his hand across his forehead, draws it slowly down to his chin, as if studying a contingency which, from the play of the other party, has baffled his calculations ; and sometimes he breaks out into an interjectional whistle, and comes down suddenly with a card upon the table, as he says, "Now, Mr. Swansdown, I believe you have given me that trick!" To all these implied imputations against his dexterity, the gentleman replies in the most polite manner imaginable,—with a lambent smile upon his features,—by a compliment to the superior address of his partner, expressive of his reliance upon her ability to rescue him from the fatal tendency of his own errors.

It is quite perceivable that Prudence by no means joins in this vituperation of her coadjutor; but, on the contrary, frequently checks the license of the other two, and says many things in extenuation of his aberrations from the laws of the game. Indeed, I think she carries this vindication further than his case requires. But it never fails to produce a grateful recognition from him, and a frequent attempt to excuse himself upon the ground, that Miss Prudence has herself to blame, as her conversation is very much calculated to seduce such a tyro as he is from the proper study of his part in the play. At all such sallies, Prudence looks modestly ; readjusts herself in her seat, and smiles upon the poet.

Before the party broke up the lady was quite animated. Her demeanor was characterized by a certain restless attempt at composure, and a singularly vivacious kind of sobriety—partly sentimental, partly witty, and exceedingly lady-like. I will not say she has designs upon the peace of our new guest, but it looks prodigiously like it!

When she retired to her chamber, she was manifestly under some serious or strange influences. It is reported of her, that she sang one or two plaintive songs; showed a slight disposition to romp, above stairs, with Lucy and Vic; then she took a seat in her open window, looked out on the moon, and "fette a gentil sigh"—in the phrase of the lady of the ballads. It is, moreover, reported, that she remained in the window until long past midnight. Something ailed her; but it was not told! Perhaps some soft and blandishing vision floated before her pensive eye; some form from the fairy world of her imagination, at this hour wore its robes of light, and careered upon the moonbeam, or bounded with the silver ray along the tree-tops that fluttered in the dewy breeze! or, perchance, in the deep shades of the grove that slept in dark masses before her chamber lattice, the spectres of her thought beckoned her regards, and filled her mind with new and holy contemplations! I am all unlearned in the mystery of so serene a creature's secret communions; and it does not become me to indulge conjecture upon such a perilous question. I therefore content myself with reporting the simple fact, that in that window she sat, to all appearance doing nothing, until every other sentient being at Swallow Barn was hushed in sleep. What could it mean?

The next morning there was another phenomenon exhibited in the family, equally strange. An hour before breakfast, Prudence, arrayed with unusual neatness, was seated at the piano, apparently beguiling the early day with the rehearsal of a whole volume of sonnets. This was an unwonted effort, for her music had fallen, of late, into disrelish,—and it had been supposed, for a year past, that she had bidden a careless adieu to all its charms. But this morning she resumed it with a spirit and a perseverance that attracted the notice of all the domestics. It boded, in their simple reckonings, some impending disaster. Such a change in the lady's habits could import no good! They intimated, that when people were going to give up the ghost, such marvels were the not unusual precursors of the event. "It was as bad," one of the servant maids remarked, "as to hear a hen crow at night from the roost, and she shouldn't wonder if something was going to happen,—a burying, or a wedding, or some such dreadful thing!"

But Prudence was not melancholy. On the contrary, she smiled, and seemed more cheerful than ever.

After breakfast, Mr. Swansdown passed an hour or two in the parlor, and fascinated the ladies by the pleasantry of his discourse. He fell into a conversation with Prudence upon literary topics, and nothing could be more refreshing than to hear how much she had read, and how passionately she admired! It was hard to tell which was best pleased with this comparison of opinions—it was so congenial! Prudence proclaimed Cowper to be her favorite bard, and that was exactly Swansdown's preference. They both disliked the immorality of Byron, and admired Scott. And both recited delicious lines from "The Pleasures of Hope."—"'Tis distance lends enchantment to the view," declaimed Swansdown, following the line up with twenty more. "'Tis distance," echoed Prudence,—as if it had been a simultaneous thought,—and responded throughout, in a softer voice, and with an enraptured eye, to the whole recitation. Good souls! Delightful unison! Why has cruel fate—Pooh! Nonsense! I shall grow sentimental myself, if I say another word about them!

Before noon, Swansdown's equipage was at the door. Meriwether had arranged the examination of the boundary line to take place on Wednesday next. In the mean time, the belligerent parties, on either side, were to make their hostile preparations.

With the most gracious condescension, the philosopher, poet, patron, arbitrator, and aspiring statesman, ascended his radiant car, and whisked away with the brisk and astounding flourish that belongs to this race of gifted mortals.

CHAPTER XVIII.

THE NATIONAL ANNIVERSARY.

THE event with which I have closed the last chapter, took place on the morning of the Fourth of July, a day that is never without its interest even in the most secluded parts of our country. It was to be celebrated at "The Landing," a place about a mile and a half distant, on the bank of the river, where the small river boats aré usually moored to take in their cargoes. To this spot Ned proposed that we should ride after dinner.

It was a holiday; so Rip had permission to accompany us, and Carey was directed to have our horses at the door. We were amused to find that the old groom had not only brought out our own cavalry, but also a horse for himself; and there he stood holding our bridles, arrayed in his best coat, with a pair of old top-boots drawn over loose pantaloons of striped cotton which were scrupulously clean. He wore his spurs, and carried also a riding-whip. His mien was unusually brisk, and, after an ancient fashion, coxcombical. He ventured to tell us that Master Frank thought he ought to attend us to the Landing, " as there was goings on down there, upon account of the fourth of July." The truth was, that learning our destination he had slipped off to Meriwether to ask his permission to go with us.

Our aged squire rode at a mannerly distance behind us; and

Rip, on a hard-mouthed and obstinate colt, that belonged to him, trotted by our sides, with both hands pulling in the bridle, and his legs thrust forward to enable him to counteract the constant tendency of his steed to run away. Rip protests that Spitfire—for so he calls his colt—is the easiest-going animal on the place, although each particular step lifted him at least six inches above his saddle, and almost entirely stopped his talking, because the motion shook the words out of his mouth somewhat in the same manner that water comes out of a bottle. However, no man ever thinks ill of his horse.

Our road lay through thickets of pine, in the shade of which we advanced rapidly, and we soon reached the Landing. There are very few villages in the tide-water country of Virginia; it is intersected by so many rivers, that almost every plantation may be approached sufficiently near by trading vessels to gratify the demands of the population, without the assistance of those little towns which, in other parts of the United States, sprout up like mushrooms. There are yet, therefore, to be seen the vestiges of former trading stations on all the principal rivers; and the traveller is not unfrequently surprised, when, having consulted his map, and been informed of some village with a goodly name, he learns that he has unwarily passed over the spot without being conscious of any thing but a ruinous tenement standing on the bank of a river, embowered in deep and solitary shade.

The Landing, which we had now reached, had originally been used for a foreign trade, in which vessels of a large class, a long time ago, were accustomed to receive freights of tobacco, and deposit the commodities required by the country, in return. It is now, however, nothing more than the place of resort for a few river craft, used in carrying the country produce to market. There were two or three dilapidated buildings in view, and, among these, one of larger dimensions than the rest, a brick house, with a part of the roof entirely gone. A rank crop of Jamestown weed grew up within, so as to be seen through the windows of the first story. Indian corn was planted on the adjacent ground up to the walls, and extended partly under the shelter of a few straggling old apple-trees, that seemed to stand as living mementoes of an early family that had long since been swept from beneath their shade. An air of additional desolation was given to this ruin by an extensive swamp that reached almost up to the rear of the building, and over which the river spread its oozy tide, amongst a thick coat of bulrushes. This tenement, tradition says, was once the mansion of an emigrant merchant from Glasgow, who here ruminated in quiet over his small gains, and waited with a disciplined patience for the good ship which once a year hove in sight above the headland that bounded his seaward view. I can imagine now, how that harbinger of good tidings greeted his eye in the gloom of the great forest; and with what stir and magnified importance the fitting arrangements were made for her reception! How like a winged deity she came fluttering into this little road, with all her pomp of apparel—with foam upon her breast, and shouts upon her deck—gliding in upright stateliness to her anchorage, as she gathered up her sails in the presence of the wondering eagle and frightened heron!

What was once the warehouse, but now used for a ferry-house, stood with its gable end at the extremity of a mouldering wharf of logs. In this end there was a door studded with nails, and another above it opening into the loft. The ridge of the roof projected over these doors and terminated in a beam, where were yet to be seen the remains of a block and tackle. On the land side the building was enlarged by sheds, to which was appended a rude porch. A sun-dried post supported what was once a sign, whereon a few hieroglyphics denoted that this was a place of entertainment, notwithstanding its paper-patched windows and scanty means of accommodation.

Some thirty or forty persons were collected at the Landing. The porch of the shabby little hostelry was filled by a crowd of rough-looking rustics, who were laughing boisterously, drinking, and making ribald jokes. A violin and fife were heard, from within the building, to a quick measure, which was accompanied with the heavy tramp of feet from a party of dancers. A group of negroes, outside of the house, were enjoying themselves in the same way, shuffling through the odd contortions of a jig, with two sticks lying crosswise upon the ground, over which they danced, alternately slapping their thighs and throwing up their elbows to the time of the music, and making strange grimaces. A few tall, swaggering figures, tricked out in yellow hunting-shirts trimmed with green fringe, and their hats, some white and some black, garnished with a band of red cloth and ragged plumes of the same color, that seemed to have been faded by frequent rains, stood about in little knots, where they talked loudly and swore hard oaths. Amongst these were mingled a motley collection of lank and sallow watermen, boys, negroes, and females bedizened in all the wonders of country millinery. At the fences and about the trees, in the vicinity of the house, was to be seen the counterpart of these groups, in the various assemblage of horses of every color, shape and degree, stamping, neighing and sleeping until their services should be required by their maudlin masters. Occasionally, during our stay, some of these nags were brought forward for a race, which was conducted with increased uproar and tumult.

Contrasted with this rude and busy scene was the voluptuous landscape around us. It was a picture of that striking repose, which is peculiar to the tide-water views ; soft, indolent and clear, as if nature had retreated into this drowsy nook, and fallen asleep over her own image, as it was reflected from this beautiful mirror. The river was upwards of a mile in width, and upon its bosom were seen, for many a rood below, those alternate streaks of light and shade that are said to point out the channel, where its smooth surface was only ruffled by the frequent but lonely leap of some small fish above the water. A few shallops were hauled up on the beach, where some fishing-nets were stretched upon stakes, or spread upon the fences on the bank. At the distance of two or three hundred yards from the shore there was a slim pole planted in the river, probably to mark a fishing-ground, and upon the very top of this was perched, with a whimsical air of unsociableness, a solitary swallow, apparently ruminating on the beauteous waste of waters below him; whilst above this glittering expanse, some night-hawks skimmed, soared and darted in pursuit of the hordes of insects that bickered through the atmosphere.

The sun was within half an hour of his journey's end—and, nearer to theirs. were two negroes, who were rapidly approaching the shore with a boat load of crabs and cucumbers, the regular stroke of their oars falling on the ear as if measuring the stillness of the evening. Far below, and seemingly suspended in air amongst the brilliant reflections of the heavens, lay a small schooner at anchor, fixed as by a spell, and, nevertheless, communicating a sense of animation to this tranquil world by its association with the beings that trod its noiseless deck.

We had wandered, after dismounting from our horses, al. round the purlieus of the crowd. Rip had recognized some familiar features amongst the country volunteers, and had already found out the drummer, who had hung his martial instrument around his shoulders; and the delighted boy was beating away at it with all his might. Carey had collected about him a set of his old cronies, to whom he was delivering a kind of solemn harangue, of which we could only observe the energy of his gesticulations. The ferry-boat lay attached to the wharf, and on the stern-benches were seated three or four graver looking men in coarse attire, who were deeply discussing questions that occasionally brought them into a high tone of voice, and, now and then, into a burst of loud laughter. Ned had led me up to this group, and, in the careless indolence of the moment, we had thrown ourselves out at full length across the seats; Ned with his legs dangling over the gunwale, with Wilful lying close by, and reposing his head upon his lap.

The principal personage in this collection was Sandy Walker, a long, sun-burnt waterman, who was the proprietor of the hotel, and evidently a man of mark amongst his associates. One of the others was a greasy gentleman in a blue coat, out at elbows, with a nose lustrous with living fire. These two were the principal speakers, and they were debating an intricate point of constitutional law, with more vehemence than perspicacity. At length, an appeal was made to Ned, by Sandy, who was infinitely the most authoritative in his manner of the whole group.

" Can't Congress," said Sandy, " supposing they were to pass a law to that effect, come and take a road of theirn any where they have a mind to, through any man's land ? I put it to Mr. Ned Hazard."

" Not by the Constitution," said the gentleman in the greasy coat, with marked emphasis.

" Well," said Ned, " we'll hear you, Sandy."

Sandy rose up, and lifting his hand above his head, as he began,—

" I say it stands to reason —"

" It stands to no such thing !" rejoined the other, interrupting him, " if it's against the Constitution,—which I say it is undoubtedly,—to come and take a man's land without saying, by your leave ; if I may be allowed the expression, Mr. Ned Hazard, it's running against a snag."

" Silence," said Ned, " Mr. Walker has the plank; we can only hear one at a time !"

" Why, sir," continued Sandy, argumentatively, and looking steadfastly at his opponent, with one eye closed, and, at the same time, bringing his right hand into the palm of his left ; " they can just cut off a corner, if they want it, or go through the middle, leaving one half here, and t'other there, and make you fence it clean through into the bargain ; or," added Sandy, giving more breadth to his doctrine, " go through your house, sir."

" Devil a house have I, Sandy !" said the other.

" Or your barn, sir."

" Nor barn nother."

" Sweeping your bed right from under you, if Congress says so. Arn't there the canal to go across the Allegheny mountain ? What does Congress care about your state rights, so as they have got the money ?"

" Canals, I grant you," said his antagonist; " but there's a difference between land and water," evidently posed by Sandy's dogmatic manner, as well as somewhat awed by the relation of landlord, in which Sandy stood, and whom, therefore, he would not rashly contradict. " But," said he, in a more softened tone, and with an affected spice of courtesy in his accost, " Mr. Walker, I'd be glad to know if we couldn't nullify."

" Nullify !" exclaimed Sandy, " nullify what ?" said he, with particular emphasis on the last word. " Do you know what old Hickory said down there in the Creek nation, in the war, when the Indians pretended they were going to have a ball play ?"

" No."

" 'If you don't go and wash all that there paint from your faces, I'll give you the shockingest ball play you ever had in all your lives.' "

" You don't tell me so !" exclaimed the red-nosed gentleman with animation, and bursting out into a tremendous laugh.

" Didn't he say so, Ned Hazard ? I beg your pardon, Mr. Ned Hazard ?" ejaculated Sandy, and turning to Ned.

"I think I have heard so," said Ned, "though I don't believe he used that exact expression."

"It was something like it," said Sandy: "well, that's the sort of nullification you'd get."

"Things are getting worse and worse," replied the other. "I can see how it's going! Here, the first thing General Jackson did when he came in, he wanted to have the President elected for six years; and, by and by, they will want him for ten! and now they want to cut up our orchards and meadows, whether or no; that's just the way Bonaparte went on. What's the use of states if they are all to be cut up with canals and railroads and tariffs? No, no, gentlemen! you may depend, Old Virginny's not going to let Congress carry on in her day!"

"How can they help it?" asked Sandy.

"We hav'nt *fout* and bled," rejoined the other, taking out of his pocket a large piece of tobacco, and cutting off a quid, as he spoke in a somewhat subdued tone, "we hav'nt *fout* and bled for our liberties to have our posterity and their land circumcised after this rate, to suit the figaries of Congress. So let them try it when they will!"

"Mr. Ned Hazard, what do you call state rights?" demanded Sandy.

"It's a sort of a law," said the other speaker, taking the answer to himself, "against cotton and wool."

"That's a fact," cried Sandy, "and, in my thinking, it's a very foolish sort of a business."

"There's where you and me differs," responded the other.

"Well," said Ned, "it's a troublesome question. Suppose we wait until we hear what Old Virginia says about it herself? And as for us, Sandy, it is getting late, and we must go."

These words concluded the colloquy; and, soon after, having summoned our cavalcade, we set out on our return to Swallow Barn, where we arrived some time after night-fall.

Ned detailed the dialogue I have just described to Frank Meriwether, in the course of the evening, and, from what Frank let fall,—for he grew grave on the subject,—I have reason to think that he has some fearful misgivings of the ambitious designs of the general government. He is decidedly of the state rights party.

CHAPTER XIX.

THE COUNTY COURT.

On Monday morning Meriwether announced to us that the Coun
ty Court was to commence its session, and, consequently, that he
was obliged to repair to the seat of justice.

I have before intimated that my kinsman is one of the quorum, and has always been famous for his punctuality in the discharge of his judicial functions. It was, moreover, necessary for
him to be there to-day, because his business with Philly Wart, in
regard to the arbitration, enjoined it upon him to meet that legal luminary without delay.

He insinuated a wish that Ned and myself should accompany
him. I think Frank is a little vain of his appearance on the
bench. We readily assented to his proposal.

Meriwether never moves on these state occasions without old
Carey, who has a suit of livery that is preserved almost exclusively for this service. Accordingly, the old man this morning
was decorated with all his honors, of which the principal consisted in a thick drab coat, edged with green; and, as the day
was very hot, Carey suffered as much under his covering as an
ancient knight of the Crusades, in his linked mail, on the sandy
plains of Syria.

His master, too, had doffed the light and careless habiliments in which he accommodated himself, usually, to the fervors of the season, and was now pranked out in that reverential furniture of broadcloth which he conceived befitted the solemn import of the duties he was about to discharge.

He rides a beautiful full-blooded sorrel; and his pride in all matters that belong to his equitation is particularly conspicuous in the fresh and comfortable character of his housings and horse furniture. He has a large new saddle, luxuriously stuffed, and covered with a richly-worked coat of yellow buckskin. The stirrups hang inordinately low, so that it is as much as he can do to get the point of his boot into them. But he sits with a lordly erectness upon his seat, and manages his horse with a bold and dexterous hand. On horseback he is a perfect personation of an opulent, unquestioned squire,—the very guardian genius of the soil and its prerogatives—fearless, graceful, and masterly, his fine athletic figure appearing here to its greatest advantage.

Ned and myself formed a part of his retinue, like a pair of aids somewhat behind the commander-in-chief, insensibly accommodating our position to the respect inspired by his bearing and rank. Old Carey, in his proper place, brought up the rear. Our journey to the court-house was about twelve miles, and as we occasionally brought our horses to a gallop, we arrived there at an early hour.

The sitting of this court is an occasion of great stir. The roads leading to the little county capital were enlivened by frequent troops of the neighboring inhabitants, that rode in squadrons, from all directions. Jurors, magistrates, witnesses, attorneys of the circuit, and all the throng of a country side interested in this piepowder justice, were rapidly converging to the centre of business.

Upon our arrival, a considerable part of the population had already assembled, and were scattered about the principal places of resort, in decent and orderly groups, in which all seemed intent upon the quiet and respectful discharge of their several errands.

The court-house is a low, square, brick building, entirely unornamented, occupying the middle of a large area. It has an official appearance given to it by a huge door of a dingy exterior, and ample windows covered with dust and cobwebs. An humble and modest little building, of the same material, stands on one corner of the area, and by the well-worn path leading hence to the temple of Themis, it may be seen that this is the only depository of the county records. At a distance further off, a somewhat larger edifice claims a public character, which is denoted by one or two of the windows being grated. A few small forest trees have been set in the soil, over this space, which, by their feeble growth and shelterless condition, as well as by the formal and graceless precision with which they have been distributed, show that the public functionaries have at times had one or two abortive inspirations of a spirit of improvement, and a transient passion for beauty.

In front of the court-house there is a decayed and disjointed fixture, whose uses seem now to have gone by. It is a pillory, with the stocks below it, and was occupied at the moment of our visit as a place of meeting for a few idle negroes, who were seated on the frame at a game of pushpin. Immediately in this neighborhood the horses of the crowd whose occasions brought them to the scene, were fastened to racks erected for that purpose; and the adjacent fence-corners became gradually appropriated in the same way.

Half a dozen frame dwellings, partially obscured by trees and generally of a neat exterior, were scattered over the landscape, and made up the village—if so sparse an assemblage be entitled to that name. There are two places of entertainment. The first, a little shrunken, single-storied edifice, concealed behind a rough, whitewashed piazza. The second is an old wooden building of some magnitude, and, from the profusion with which its doors and windows have been supplied with architectural embellishments, must formerly have been a private residence of note. Our cavalcade stopped at the latter of these rival establishments ; and we dismounted under a broad flaunting sign, which screeched lazily upon its hinges in the breeze, and seemed to give a responsive note to a party of geese, that were greeting every fresh arrival with a vociferous, periodical cackle.

There were several respectable-looking gentlemen collected about the door ; and Meriwether was met with many kind and hearty expressions. We were shown into a room which, from its air of neatness, was evidently kept as an apartment of more worship than that in which the larger portion of the visitors of the hotel were assembled. This room was garnished with carvings and mouldings of an ancient date. The floor had suffered from the ravages of time, and had a slope towards an ample hearth, whose unsightly aperture was embowered by a tasteful screen of the tops of asparagus plants. Some pieces of mahogany furniture, black with age and glistening like ebony, stood against the wall ; and above them hung divers besmirched pictures representing game-cocks in pugnacious attitudes, trimly clipt of their feathers, the Godolphin Arabian, Flying Childers, and some other victors of the turf, all in black frames ; and which, from the hue that time had flung over the copperplate, seemed to be gleaming through an atmosphere obfuscated with smoke.

The hour soon came round for opening the court. This was announced by a proclamation, made in a shrill, attenuated voice, from the court-house door; and was followed by an immediate movement, from all directions, to that quarter. The little hall in which justice was administered was crowded almost to overflowing.

A semicircular gallery, raised five or six feet above the floor, at the further end of the hall, was already occupied with a bevy of justices—nearly a dozen, perhaps—some of whom had flung their feet upon the rail before them, and were lolling back upon their seats, ready to proceed to their judicial employments. Our friend Meriwether occupied his place with a countenance of becoming importance. Indeed, the whole bench presented a fine picture of solid faces and figures, that might be said to be a healthy and sturdy specimen of this pillar of the sovereignty of the state;— and was well calculated to inspire a wholesome respect for that inferior and useful magistracy which has always been so much a favorite of the people of Virginia.

Immediately under the gallery of the justices, sat the clerk of the court; and, on either side of his desk, within the area of the semicircle, were benches designed for the juries. Fronting this array of the court and jury, was a long, narrow platform, guarded all round with railing, and elevated a few feet above the floor, within whose constricted confines were disposed some five or six members of the bar, most incommodiously perched upon seats of a height out of all proportion to the human figure; and, before these, a narrow desk extended the whole distance, so as to give to the place of their accommodation somewhat of the dimensions of a pew.

These courts hold their sessions monthly, and their jurisdiction reaches almost all the ordinary legal requirements of the county; but, as the territorial limit over which they preside is generally small, it requires but a few days to dispatch the business of each term.

The first matter that occupied the attention of the court was the marshalling of the grand-jury, to whom the usual charge was delivered. This office was assigned by the court to one of the members of the bar, a young practitioner, who did not fail to embellish the summary of duties, which he unfolded to their view, with a plentiful garniture of rhetoric. Notwithstanding the portentous exaggeration of the solemnity of the occasion, and the multitudinous grave topics which were urged upon the grand inquest, it seems that this quintessence of the freehold dignity was sadly puzzled to find employment in any degree commensurate with the exaltedness of its function. It is said that the jurors revolved in their minds the whole list of national grievances. One party suggested the idea of presenting the established mode of electing the President of the United States as a grievance to the good people of the county; another thought of a formal denunciation of the Tariff; a few advocated an assault upon the Supreme Court; but all were happily brought into a harmonious concurrence in the design of presenting a mad-cap ragamuffin, by the name of Jemmy Smith, for disturbing the peace of a campmeeting by drinking whiskey and breeding a riot within the confines of the conventicle. Accordingly, after an hour's deliberation upon these various suggestions, they returned to the courtroom with a solitary bill, made out in due form against Jemmy; and, this matter constituting the sum total of their business for the term, they were thereupon discharged, with the thanks of the court for the able and vigilant administration of their inquisitorial duties.

Jemmy Smith had anticipated this act of authority; and was now in court, ready to stand his trial. He had already selected his counsel—a flowery and energetic advocate, whose strength lay, according to the popular opinion, in his skill in managing a jury. The name of this defender of Jemmy's fame was Taliaferro, (pronounced Tolliver,) or, as it was called for shortness, Toll Hedges, Esq., a gentleman whose pantaloons were too short for him, and whose bare legs were, consequently, visible above his stockings. Toll's figure, however, was adorned with a bran-new blue coat, of the most conceited fashion, which, nevertheless, gave some indications of having been recently slept in, as it was plentifully supplied with down from a feather bed. He was conspicuous, also, for an old straw hat, that had been fretted at the rim by a careless habit in handling it. This learned counsel had apparently been keeping his vigils too strictly the night before, for his eyes were red, and his face inflamed. His frame had all the morning languor of a sedulous night-watcher; and, altogether, Toll did not appear to be in the best condition to try his case. However, he had now taken his seat at the bar; and close beside him sat his client, Jemmy Smith, an indescribably swaggering, saucy blade, who had the irreverence to come into court without coat or waistcoat, and to show a wild, grinning, disorderly countenance to his peers.

Whilst the gentleman who conducted the case for the Commonwealth was giving a narrative of Jemmy's delinquencies to the jury, and was vituperating that worthy's character in good set terms, Toll was, to all appearance, asleep upon his folded arms, resting on the desk before him. When the charge was fairly explained, one witness was called to support it. This individual was pretty much such a looking person as Jemmy himself. He was rather down-faced and confused in his demeanor before the court, and particularly shabby in his exterior; but he told a plain, straight-forward story enough, in the main, and his evidence went the full length of all the traverser's imputed enormities. The truth was, Jemmy had certainly broke into the camp and played some strange antics, considering the sanctity of the place. But, during all this time, Taliaferro Hedges, Esq., maintained his recumbent position, except, now and then, when Jemmy, feeling himself pinched by the testimony, reclined his head to whisper in his counsel's ear, which act roused him enough to bring upon Jemmy a rebuke, that was generally conveyed by pushing him off, and injunction to be quiet. At length, the whole story was told, and bad enough it looked for Jemmy! The attorney for the Commonwealth now informed Mr. Hedges, that the witness was at his disposal. At this, Toll completely roused himself, and sitting bolt upright, directed a sharp and peremptory catechism to the witness, in which he required him to repeat the particulars he had before detailed. There was something bullying in the manner of the counsel that quite intimidated the witness, and the poor fellow made some sad equivocations. At last, said Toll, after admonishing the witness, in a very formal manner, that he was upon his oath, and explaining to him the solemnity of his obligation to speak the truth, " I will ask you one question ; answer it categorically, and without evasion."

" When you and Smith went down to camp-meeting, hadn't Smith a bottle of whiskey in the bosom of his shirt? Tell the truth."

The attorney for the Commonwealth objected to the question ; but the court overruled the objection.

" Why, yes, he had," replied the witness.

" Didn't Jemmy buy that bottle himself, and pay for it out of his own pocket? On the oath you have taken."

" Why, yes, he did."

" Well, now tell us. Didn't you drink some of that whiskey yourself, along the road ?"

" Why, yes, I did. I tell the truth, gentlemen."

" More than once?"

" Yes, several times."

" After you got down to camp?'

" Oh, yes! certainly. I don't deny it."

" Did you and Jemmy drink out of the mouth of the bottle, or out of a cup?"

" Certainly ; out of the mouth of the bottle. You will not catch me in any lies, lawyer Hedges."

"Really, Mr. Hedges," interrupted the attorney for the Commonwealth, " I don't see what this has to do with the question. I must apply to the court."

" Oh, very well," said Toll, " I see how it is! Gentlemen of the jury, I don't insist on the question, if the gentleman does not like to have it answered. But you can't help seeing the true state of the case. Here's this fellow, who has been all along drinking out of the very same bottle with Jemmy Smith,—and Jemmy's own whiskey too,—and now he comes out state's evidence. What credit can you attach to a cock-and-bull story told by a fellow that comes to swear against a man who has been dividing his liquor with him? For the honor of the Old Dominion, gentlemen !" cried Toll, concluding this side-bar appeal to the jury with an indignant gesticulation, and a look of triumph in his face, that might be said to be oratorically comic.

The look was a master-stroke. It took complete effect; and Jemmy was acquitted in spite of the facts.

As the crowd broke up, Toll, on leaving the court-room, walked up to the witness, and slapping him on the back, said, " Come, let us go take something to drink." And off the two went together to the tavern.

Hazard remarked to Hedges afterwards, that it was a little odd, as he had completely triumphed over the facts of his case by undermining the credit of the witness, he should be on such good terms with this person as to bring him down to drink with him.

" Ah !" replied Hedges, " if the jury knew that man as well as I do, they would have believed every word he said. For there is not an honester fellow in the county. But I know how to work these juries."

CHAPTER XX.

THE court resumed its session after dinner, having a prospect of concluding its business before noon the next day; and Meriwether was obliged to remain for the night. Neither Ned nor myself regretted the pretext this furnished us for the same delay.

During the afternoon many of the older inhabitants had taken to horse: and the crowd of the court-room was sensibly diminished. Still the out-door bustle assumed a more active and noisy character. The loiterers about the verge of the court had less business, but more to say. Indeed, it seemed to be difficult to keep those in attendance whose presence was necessary to the affairs of justice; for the crier of the court might be frequently heard summoning the absentees, as they were wanted, in his slender and shrill voice, by distinctly repeating thrice the name of each, from the court-house door, where he stood bareheaded, and with his hand shading his eyes.

The sun began, at last, to throw a merciless blaze upon the broken window-panes in the western fronts of some old buildings, whose raggedness was thus rendered painfully public. The ducks and geese of the village were already trooping homeward, from a small brook hard by, in their sober evening march, and with a sedate under-gabble, like that of old burghers in conversation.

The departing squadrons of horsemen became more frequent; and the alacrity with which these retreating bodies sprang forward from their starting points, showed that their temporary sojourn had been attended with an increase of animal spirits. At this hour the court put an end to its labors; and the throng that had been occupied there, all day, were now gathering about the doors of the two taverns.

Our host was an imperturbable, pleasant-faced old fellow, with a remarkably accommodating temper, which exhibited itself in lavish promises, though he was allowed to be very incommensurate in performance. He was unwieldy in bulk, and pertinacious in the enjoyment of his ease; and, to save the trouble of forming opinions, he gave an invariable answer to every speculation that was addressed to him. This was conveyed in the words "quite likely," no matter how inconsistent the averments to which they had reference. Ned and myself had put him, in the course of the afternoon, to some severe trials, but without being able either to ruffle his temper or enlarge his vocabulary.

The large room of the inn had a bar petitioned off at one corner; and this was the principal centre of reinforcement to the inhabitants of these precincts. As the shades of evening thickened, this resort became more crowded. The remnants, or more properly speaking, the sediment of the population, whose occasions had brought them to the court-house, had repaired thither to enjoy the compotations and arguments that are apt to abound in such assemblages. Some were in the middle of the floor, accompanying their diatribes with violent gestures; others were strewed around the room wherever seats were to be obtained. At a small table, lighted by a single candle in a most unsightly candlestick, sat a gentleman in a loose calico robe, with a dirty shirt, engaged at backgammon with a robust, well-knit man, who wore his hat drawn low over his eyes; the first was the Galen of

the country side, and the other a deputy sheriff. Our friend
Toll Hedges was a conspicuous personage in this checkered assembly. He had shaken off the dulness of the morning, and was
now playing a part that seemed more native to his disposition,
that of a familiar, confident, loud-talking interlocutor, who called
every man by his christian name, swore roundly after a pedantic
fashion, had some knowledge of every man's business, and bore
himself with the peremptoriness of one whose character partook
in equal degrees of the wag and the brawler. He was sarcastic,
shrewd, and popular ; and to all these, it may be added, that before bedtime he was in no small degree flustered. In this crowd
might also be observed one or two other members of the bar, of a
graver demeanor, and even some of the justices holding more
sedate conversations, apparently on matters connected with their
business. In one corner sat a quiet, neighborly shoemaker, in an
arm chair, contentedly taking a stiff beverage of whiskey and
water about once in fifteen minutes, and saying nothing to any
body.

Our host himself was a sober man, and a discreet ! He stood
at his post the whole evening, with a wooden pestle in his hand
—the symbol of his calling; one while laughing with a civil good
nature at the rough jokes that were aimed at himself, and at
another mixing toddy to meet the numberless demands of his
thirsty customers. Amidst this edifying display of toss-pot eloquence and genial uproar, my attention was particularly attracted
to the behavior of this exemplary publican. Though scant in
speech, he labored like a man who had the good of his family at
heart ; and bore himself through the tumultuary scene with the
address of a wily statesman who is anxious to win the applause
of all parties. The tide was in his favor, and his aim was to float
smoothly upon it. In times of great excitement, it may be observed that the party in power gain many advantages by a show

of moderation. With regard to them the maxim applies, " where
the least is said it is soonest mended." Now, our good landlord
stood pretty much in this predicament; for the whole assemblage
had fallen into an inflammatory discussion of some ticklish points
of politics, in which he might have lost friends by an inconsider-
ate participation. Whilst, therefore, the tempest raged he played
the part of moderator, and was perpetually crying out—" Now,
gentlemen !—if you please,—remember ;—we are all friends !"
and such like gentle admonitions ; and as often as he was taken
by the button by one of the speakers, and pinned up against the
wall, so that it seemed impossible for him to escape committing
himself, I could hear his old equivocation—" quite likely "—
uttered with an impregnable composure of nerve. In fact, a sober observer could have been at no loss to perceive that the cautious landlord had all the ambidexterity of a practised public
servant.

As the evening waned the disputants began to leave the
field ; and Hedges being thrown by chance into the bar-room,
alone with his good-natured host, addressed him very seriously
upon the subject of the countenance he had given to certain here-
sies that had been uttered in his presence, and, seemingly, with
his concurrence. " Lord ! Mr. Hedges," said he, in a quiet tone,
and looking round to see who was within hearing,—" you know
my ideas long ago about all that matter !—It isn't my business
to break with customers, or to be setting up against them. What
signifies opinion this way or that ! But," he continued, erecting
his figure to its full height and putting on a look of extraordinary
determination, " sentiments is another thing ! Let any man ask
me my sentiments !—that's all ;—Thar's no flinch in me, you may
depend upon it !"

Having learned this distinction between sentiments and
opinions, I retired to my chamber.

The next morning, after a short delay in court, Meriwether was released from his judicial cares, and we made preparations for our return to Swallow Barn. Philly Wart, who had been an active and conspicuous personage in the transactions of the term, and who is hereafter to make some figure in these annals, was to accompany us. About noon we were all mounted, Philly being perched upon a tall, raw-boned, gray steed, that seemed to have parted with his flesh in the severe duties of the circuit, but who was distinguished for his easy and regular pace. As to Philly himself, it is necessary that I should give him a chapter.

By the usual dinner hour, we were all comfortably seated at Swallow Barn.

CHAPTER XXI.

WITHOUT much reverence for the profession of the law itself, I have a great regard for its votaries, and especially for that part of the tribe which comprehends the old and thorough-paced stagers of the bar. The feelings, habits and associations of the bar in general, have a happy influence upon character. It abounds with good fellows: and, take it altogether, there may be collected from it a greater mass of shrewd, observant, droll, playful and generous spirits, than from any other equal numbers of society. They live in each other's presence, like a set of players; congregate in the courts, as the former in the green-room; and break their unpremeditated jests, in the intervals of business, with that sort of undress freedom which contrasts amusingly with the solemn and even tragic seriousness with which they appear, in turn, upon the boards. They have one face for the public rife with the gravity of the profession, and another for themselves, replete with mirth and enjoyment. The toil and fatigue of business give them a peculiar relish for their hours of relaxation, and, in the same degree, incapacitate them for that frugal attention to their private concerns which their limited means usually require. They have, in consequence, a prevailing air of unthriftiness in personal matters, which, however it may operate to the prejudice of the pocket of the individual, has a mellow and kindly effect upon his disposition.

In an old member of the profession,—one who has grown gray in the service,—there is a rich unction of originality, which brings him out from the ranks of his fellow-men in strong relief. His habitual conversancy with the world in its strangest varieties, and with the secret history of character, gives him a shrewd esti mate of the human heart. He is quiet, and unapt to be struck with wonder at any of the actions of men. There is a deep cur rent of observation running calmly through his thoughts, and sel dom gushing out in words : the confidence which has been placed in him, in the thousand relations of his profession, renders him constitutionally cautious. His acquaintance with the vicissitudes of fortune, as they have been exemplified in the lives of individu als, and with the severe afflictions that have " tried the reins " of many, known only to himself, makes him an indulgent and chari table apologist of the aberrations of others. He has an impreg nable good humor that never falls below the level of thoughtful ness into melancholy. He is a creature of habits ; rising early for exercise ; generally temperate from necessity, and studious against his will. His face is accustomed to take the ply of his pursuits with great facility, grave and even severe in business, and readily rising into smiles at a pleasant conceit. He works hard when at his task ; and goes at it with the reluctance of an old horse in a bark-mill. His common-places are quaint and pro fessional : they are made up of law maxims, and first occur to him in Latin. He measures all the sciences out of his proper line of study, (and with these he is but scantily acquainted,) by the rules of law. He thinks a steam engine should be worked with *due diligence,* and without *laches :* a thing little likely to happen, he considers as *potentia remotissima ;* and what is not yet in existence, or *in esse,* as he would say, is *in nubibus.* He

apprehends that wit best, which is connected with the affairs of
the term ; is particularly curious in his anecdotes of old lawyers,
and inclined to be talkative concerning the amusing passages of
his own professional life. He is, sometimes, not altogether free
of outward foppery ; is apt to be an especial good liver. and he
keeps the best company. His literature is not much diversified ;
and he prefers books that are bound in plain calf, to those that
are much lettered or gilded. He garners up his papers with a
wonderful appearance of care ; ties them in bundles with red
tape ; and usually has great difficulty to find them when he wants
them. Too much particularity has perplexed him ; and just so
it is with his cases : they are well assorted, packed and laid away
in his mind, but are not easily to be brought forth again without
labor. This makes him something of a procrastinator, and rather
to delight in new business than finish his old. He is, however,
much beloved, and affectionately considered by the people.

Philpot Wart belongs to the class whose characteristics I
have here sketched. He is a practitioner of some thirty or forty
years' standing, during the greater part of which time he has resided in this district. He is now verging upon sixty years of
age, and may be said to have spent the larger portion of his life
on horseback. His figure is short and thick-set, with a hard,
muscular outline ; his legs slightly bowed, his shoulders broad,
and his hands and feet uncommonly large. His head is of extraordinary size, inclining to be cubical in shape, and clothed with a
shock of wiry, dark gray hair. A brown and dry complexion ;
eyes small, keen, and undefined in color, furnished with thick
brows ; a large mouth, conspicuous for a range of teeth worn
nearly to their sockets ; and ample protruding ears, constitute
the most remarkable points in his appearance. The predominant
expression of his features is a sly, quick good nature, susceptible,
however. of great severity.

His dress is that of a man who does not trouble himself with the change of fashions; careless, and, to a certain degree, quaint. It consists of a plain, dark coat, not of the finest cloth, and rather the worse for wear; dingy and faded nankeen small clothes; and a pair of half boots, such as were worn at the beginning of this century. His hat is old, and worn until the rim has become too pliable to keep its original form; and his cravat is sometimes, by accident, tied in such a manner, as not to include one side of his shirt collar;—this departure from established usage, and others like it, happen from Mr. Wart's never using a looking-glass when he makes his toilet.

His circuit takes in four or five adjoining counties, and, as he is a regular attendant upon the courts, he is an indefatigable traveller. His habit of being so much upon the road, causes his clients to make their appointments with him at the several stages of his journeyings; and it generally happens that he is intercepted, when he stops, by some one waiting to see him. Being obliged to pass a great deal of his time in small taverns, he has grown to be contented with scant accommodation, and never complains of his fair. But he is extremely particular in exacting the utmost attention to his horse.

He has an insinuating address that takes wonderfully with the people; and especially with the older and graver sorts. This has brought him into a close acquaintance with a great many persons, and has rendered Philly Wart,—as he is universally called,—a kind of cabinet-counsellor and private adviser with most of those who are likely to be perplexed with their affairs. He has a singularly retentive memory as to facts, dates, and names; and by his intimate knowledge of land titles, courses and distances, patents, surveys and locations, he has become a formidable champion in all ejectment cases. In addition to this, Philly has such a brotherly and companionable relation to the greater number of

the freeholders who serve upon the juries, and has such a confiding, friendly way of talking to them when he tries a cause, that
it is generally supposed he can persuade them to believe any
thing he chooses.

His acquirements as a lawyer are held in high respect by the
bar, although it is reported that he reads but little law of later
date than Coke Littleton, to which book he manifests a remarkable affection, having perused it, as he boasts, some eight or ten
times; but the truth is, he has not much time for other reading,
being very much engrossed by written documents, in which he is
painfully studious.   He takes a great deal of authority upon himself, nevertheless, in regard to the Virginia decisions, inasmuch
as he has been contemporary with most of the cases, and heard
them, generally, from the courts themselves.   Besides this, he
practised in the times of old Chancellor Wythe, and President
Pendleton, and must necessarily have absorbed a great deal of
that spirit of law-learning which has evaporated in the hands of
the reporters.   As Philly himself says, he understands the currents of the law, and knows where they must run ; and, therefore,
has no need of looking into the cases.

Philly has an excellent knack in telling a story, which consists
in a caustic, dry manner, that is well adapted to give it point ;
and sometimes he indulges this talent with signal success before
the juries.   When he is at home,—which is not often above a
week or ten days at a time,—he devotes himself almost entirely
to his farm.   He is celebrated there for a fine breed of hounds ;
and fox-hunting is quite a passion with him.   This is the only
sport in which he indulges to any excess ; and so far does he carry it, that he often takes his dogs with him upon the circuit,
when his duty calls him, in the hunting season, to certain parts
of the country where one or two gentlemen reside who are fond
of this pastime.   On these occasions he billets the hounds upon

his landlord, and waits patiently until he dispatches his business; and then he turns into the field with all the spirit and zest of Nimrod. He has some lingering recollections of the classics, and is a little given to quoting them, without much regard to the appropriateness of the occasion. It is told of him, that one fine morning, in December, he happened to be with a party of brother sportsmen in full chase of a gray fox, under circumstances of unusual animation. The weather was cool, a white frost sparkled upon the fields, the sun had just risen and flung a beautiful light over the landscape, the fox was a-foot, the dogs in full cry, the huntsmen shouting with exuberant mirth, the woods re-echoing to the clamor, and every one at high speed in hot pursuit. Philly was in an ecstasy, spurring forward his horse with uncommon ardor, and standing in his stirrups, as if impatient of his speed, when he was joined in the chase by two or three others as much delighted as himself. In this situation he cried out to one of the party, "Isn't this fine; don't it put you in mind of Virgil? Tityre tu patulæ recubans sub tegmine fagi." Philly denies the fact; but some well authenticated flourishes of his at the bar, of a similar nature, give great semblance of truth to the story.

It sometimes happens that a pair of his hounds will steal after him, and follow him through the circuit, without his intending it; and when this occurs, he has not the heart to drive them back. This was the case at the present court: accordingly, he was followed by his dogs to Swallow Barn. They slink close behind his horse, and trot together as if they were coupled.

Philly's universal acquaintance through the country and his pre-eminent popularity have, long since, brought him into public life. He has been elected to the Assembly for twenty years past, without opposition; and, indeed, the voters will not permit him to decline. It is, therefore, a regular part of his business to attend to all political matters affecting the county. His influence in this department is wonderful. He is consulted in reference to all plans, and his advice seems to have the force of law. He is extremely secret in his operations, and appears to carry his point by his calm, quiet, and unresisting manner. He has the reputation of being a dexterous debater, and of making some sharp and heavy hits when roused into opposition; though many odd stories are told, at Richmond, of his strenuous efforts, at times, to be oratorical. He is, however, very much in the confidence of the political managers of all parties, and seldom fails to carry a point when he sets about it in earnest.

During the war, Philly commanded a troop of volunteer light-horse, and was frequently employed in active service, in guarding the hen-roosts along the river from the attacks of the enemy. These occasions have furnished him with some agreeable episodes in the history of his life. He gives a faithful narrative of his exploits at this period, and does not fail to throw a dash of comic humor into his account of his campaigns.

In our ride to Swallow Barn, he and Meriwether were principally engrossed with the subject of the expected arbitration. Meriwether particularly enjoined it upon him so to manage the matter as to make up a case in favor of Mr. Tracy, and to give such a decision as would leave the old gentleman in possession of the contested territory.

Philly revolved the subject carefully in his mind, and assured Frank that he would have no difficulty in putting Swansdown upon such a train as could not fail to accomplish their ends.

" But it seems strange to me," said the counsellor, " that the old man would not be content to take the land without all this circuity."

" We must accommodate ourselves to the peculiarities of our neighbors," replied Meriwether, " and, pray be careful that you give no offence to his pride, by the course you pursue."

"I have never before been engaged in a case with such instructions," said Philly. "This looks marvellously like an Irish donkey race, where each man cudgels his neighbor's ass. Well, I suppose Singleton Swansdown will take the beating without being more restive under it than others of the tribe!"

"I beseech you, use him gently," said Meriwether. "He will be as proud of his victory as ourselves."

Philly laughed the more heartily as he thought of this novel case. Now and then he relapsed into perfect silence, and then again and again broke forth into a chuckle at his own meditations upon the subject.

"You are like a king who surrenders by negotiation, all that he has won by fighting," said he, laughing again; "we shall capitulate, at least, with the honors of war,—drums beating and colors flying!"

"It is the interest of the commonwealth that there should be an end of strife; I believe so the maxim runs," said Meriwether, smiling.

"Concordia, parvæ res crescunt; discordiâ maximæ dilabuntur," added the counsellor. "But it seems to me to be something of a wild-goose chase notwithstanding."

Philly repeated these last words as he dismounted at the gate at Swallow Barn, and, throwing his saddle-bags across his arm. he walked into the house with the rest of the party.

CHAPTER XXII.

THE next morning opened upon us in all the beauty of the season. Every necessary preparation had been completed for the definite adjustment of the long abiding lawsuit. The household was in motion at an hour much earlier than usual, and a general anxiety seemed to prevail throughout the family to speed the issues of the day. Meriwether was animated by unwonted spirits; and Hazard and myself anticipated, with some eagerness, the entrance upon a business that promised to us nothing but amusement in its progress. The notoriety which all the preliminary movements in this matter had gained from the frequent conversations of Meriwether relating to it, had magnified its importance in a degree much disproportioned to its intrinsic merit. The day was therefore considered a kind of jubilee. Mr. Chub had expressed a strong wish to be present at the settlement; and had, accordingly, proclaimed a holiday in the school. The children were all in a state of riotous excitement. Rip was especially delighted with the prospect of the approaching bustle. Prudence partook of the common feeling with rather more restlessness than any one else. There was a studied sedateness upon her features, which was not altogether natural; and this was contrasted with her motions, which seemed to be unsettled, variable and perplexed.

Philly Wart had risen soon after the dawn, and had taken a walk of two or three miles before the family began to assemble. About an hour before breakfast, he had seated himself on the bench of the porch, alone with Mr. Chub, and was there chipping a stick with his penknife, as he kept up a desultory discourse with the parson, upon divers matters connected with the history, doctrine and discipline of the Presbyterian Church. What were the particulars of this conversation I could not learn, but it had a stimulating effect upon his companion, who took occasion to call me aside, as soon as it was finished, and said to me, " Faith, that Philly Wart, as you call him, is a sensible old fellow ! He's a man of a great deal of wit, Mr. Littleton ! He is a philosopher of the school of Democritus of Abdera, and knows as much about the kirk of Scotland as if he had been at the making of the covenant. And not very starched in his creed neither, ha, ha, ha ! a queer genius !"

Philly himself, after leaving the parson, was sauntering up and down in the hall, with his coat buttoned close about him, so as to cause a roll of papers which was lodged in one of his pockets to protrude somewhat oddly from above his hip. In this situation I joined him. " Your parson there, is a great scholar," said he, smiling; " we have had a bout together concerning church matters; and the old gentleman has been entertaining me with a speech, for an hour past. He is a very vehement orator, and has puzzled me with his Grecian heroes until I hadn't a word to say. I think he likes a good listener : but I am entirely too rusty for him. I must rub up the next time I talk with him.

Just before breakfast Harvey Riggs and Ralph, having in convoy Catharine and Bel Tracy, rode up to the door; and our attention was called to the party, by the loud salutations of Harvey. " Hark you, Ned ! spring to your post, and catch Bel before she touches ground."

Hazard succeeded in reaching the outer side of the gate just in time—not to catch Bel, who had already dismounted with the nimbleness of a bird—but to take the rein of her horse and fasten it to the fence, and then to conduct the lady to the door.

It was not long before we were ranged around the ample breakfast board. Mr. Wart was inclined to be jocular, and Meriwether indulged in some good-natured speculations upon the certainty of his success in the case. Harvey Riggs was placed next to Bel at the table, and took occasion to whisper in her ear, that he had no faith in these negotiations for a peace, and added, that he rested his hopes entirely upon the prophecy of old Diana; then, looking towards Ned, who sat opposite, he remarked, loud enough to be heard by the latter, " there is but one way of giving permanency to these family treaties."

Ned colored up to the eyes—affected not to understand, and asked for another cup of coffee. Bel was more self-possessed, and replied with perfect composure, " Cousin Harvey, look to yourself, or I shall dismiss you from my service."

After breakfast, it was determined that it would be necessary for the contending powers to have a personal inspection of the seat of war. The old mill was proposed as the trysting place, and the principal discussion, it was settled, should be held on the banks of the famous Apple-pie. Mr. Tracy's arrival with his privy counsellor, Swansdown, was looked for with impatience; and, in the mean time, our whole company had broken off into detachments.

Prudence and Catharine had gone out upon the grass-plot in front of the house ; and were slowly walking to and fro, without any covering upon their heads, and with their arms around each other's waists, in deep and secret communion, under the shade of the willow. Rip had run off with a whoop and halloo to the stable to order up the necessary cavalry for the expedition. The little

girls were jumping a rope on the gravel-walk. My cousin Lucretia was busy with household matters. Wart and Meriwether were
conning over some papers in the breakfast room; and Harvey
Riggs, Ralph Tracy, Hazard, and myself, were seated in the porch
patiently abiding the progress of events.

Bel, who had been roaming at large from group to group, and
making amusement for herself out of all, like one whose spirits
would not allow her to remain stationary, had picked up the dice
that belonged to a backgammon board in the parlor, and now
came to the porch where we were seated, rattling them in the box,
and making as much noise as she could.

"I mean to tell the fortune of the day," said she; "why are
not these dice just as good judges of boundary lines as all the
lawyers? Now, Mr. Littleton, observe if this be not a true oracle.
Here's for Mr. Meriwether," she continued, throwing the dice
upon the bench. "Four, one. That's a shabby throw for Swallow
Barn. Well, here's for Pa. Deuce, ace."

"Good-bye to The Brakes!" exclaimed Harvey.

"No, indeed!" interrupted Bel. "There's a great deal of
luck in deuce, ace. But we will give Swallow Barn another chance.
There's six, four; that's the parson's point, as Pa calls it."

"And now for The Brakes, Bel," said Ned; "this throw must
settle the question."

"Treys," cried Bel, flinging the dice, and clapping her hands.
"Havn't we gained it now?"

"No! certainly not!" said Hazard. "They make but six together, and Swallow Barn had ten."

"But," answered Bel, "you forget, Edward, that there is a
luckier number than any other; and we have got three, three
times out of the dice."

"The luck," replied Ned, "is in the highest number."

"Do you wait here, and I will go and ask Mr. Chub," said Bel,

" who will tell me all that he has ever read about fortunate numbers. Don't interrupt us, for the old gentleman is on such good
terms with me, that he says a great deal to me he would not let
any of you hear. You may listen to us through the windows."
The reverend gentleman was seated in the parlor window next
to the porch, with a book in his hand, when Bel entered and took
a seat beside him ; and, thus arranged, both of their backs were
towards the window.

Bel's accost was very grave.

" Mr. Chub," said she, with a gracious and respectful voice,
" do you think there is any thing in numbers?"

" Ha, ha !" cried the tutor, in a kind of bewildered laugh, as
if he did not exactly comprehend her purpose, " 'pon my honor,
madam, I don't know how to answer the question. There are
multipliers and multiplicands, and ——"

" I don't mean that," said Bel, " do you think there is any
luck in numbers?"

" If you mean in a number of lawyers to try the question of
the old mill-dam, I think the more there are, the worse the luck.
Upon my veracity, I would rather have Mr. Philpot Wart than
the whole bar ; judges, juries, and all, Miss Bell ! Ha, ha !"

" You don't understand me yet," answered Bell.

" I beg your pardon, my dear !" interrupted the tutor.

" I didn't speak with reference to the mill-dam question,
either, but I wanted to know, if there are not some numbers
deemed more fortunate than others. Were not the ancients a
little superstitious about the number of crows that flew across
the heavens of a morning, for instance ?"

" Assuredly, madam !" replied the old gentleman, now begin
ning to take Bel's meaning ; " all nations have had some leaning
to be superstitious about numbers. The number twelve has had
a great deal of distinction conferred upon it. The twelve apos-

tles, and the twelve hours of the day, and the twelve months of the year, in spite of the moon, Miss Bel! That looks as if there was some virtue in the number. And, you know, the Romans had their laws written on twelve tables ; and the Greeks celebrated the twelve labors of Hercules. And I believe, up to this day, it always takes twelve men to make a jury. There is something heathenish in that, Miss Isabella, ha, ha!"

This last burst was manifestly destined for a sally of wit, and the good old gentleman continued to laugh at it immoderately. Bel appeared to relish it herself. " And there are imagined to be some occult influences in the trines and nones," continued the tutor, after he had laughed his fill, " not to say any thing of seven, of which number, nevertheless, I will mention a few examples—for it was an especial favorite both of Jew and Christian. We well know that the week has seven days, Miss Isabella."

" Yes," said Bel, " that is very well known."

" And the Jews thought we should forgive our enemy seven times,—which the Scripture says, with reason, should be seventy times seven,—and the Revelation speaks of the seven phials of wrath, with divers other sevens : and we read of the seven ages of man, which I need not enumerate. You have heard, Mistress Isabella, of the seven sages of Greece, and of the seven wonders of the world ? Besides these, and many more that I could think of, the monkish legends tell us some strange adventures of the seven sleepers "—

" Mercy, what a list of sevens !" cried Bel.

—" Who slept in a cave for two hundred and thirty years, Saint Maximian, Saint Malchus, and their comrades. Wherefore I conclude seven to be a lucky number."

" It was undoubtedly a very lucky thing for the seven sleepers all to awake up again, after such a long sleep," said Bel.

" Ha, ha!" ejaculated the old gentleman, in another fit of laughter, " that's very well said, Miss Isabel! but the number three," continued the tutor, " is even more eminent in mystical properties. The most ancient Egyptians worshipped the holy Triangle Equilateral, as being the symbol of divine harmony; and Pythagoras and Plato have both taught the mysteries of this number. You are, moreover, aware, Miss Bel, that there were three Gorgons."

" I thought there were four!" said Bel, with an air of astonishment.

" Three, madam," replied the parson, " Stheno, Euryale, and Medusa. And there were three Furies too."

" What were their names, Mr. Chub?"

" Tisiphone, Mægara, and Alecto," said he, enumerating his triads slowly upon his fingers. And there were the three Graces, my dear! You know their names very well—Thalia, Euphrosyne, and Aglaia. The Fates,—there were three of them, you remember; and, faith, they have had work enough to do! Clotho, Lachesis, and Atropos:—if you had studied Greek, Miss Bel, you would understand how well their names became them.'

" Listen, if you would live and laugh!" exclaimed Harvey Riggs, who was sitting on the rail of the porch, and taking in every word of this odd discourse. " Here is the parson, pouring a whole dictionary of outlandish nonsense into Bel's ear, and she humoring all his pedantry with the most incomparable gravity!"

" There might be cited many more of these triple sisterhoods," continued Mr. Chub,—Bel still looking in his face with an encouraging earnestness, —" as for another example, there were the Horæ; namely, Dice, Irene, Eunomia: the Harpies,— Ce.œno, Ocypete, Aello (still counting with the same precision as before); we must not forget the Sirens,—bless me! no—the

ladies are often called Sirens themselves, ha, ha! Parthenope—
Parthenope—let me see—" He paused, with the forefinger of his
right hand upon the middle finger of his left: "Tut, it slips
my memory! I am very bad at remembering names."

"Particularly bad!" said Bel, interrupting him and smiling.

"Parthenope, Miss Tracy, child, I had it on my tongue! I
am getting old, Miss Isabel! I dare say, you can help me out."

"Indeed, I dare say I cannot," replied Bel; "you have
turned my brain so topsy-turvy with such a list of hard names,
that I have almost forgotten what I came to ask you."

"You have totally omitted, Mr. Chub, to mention the three
wise men of Gotham that went to sea in a bowl," said Hazard,
speaking to the parson from the porch.

"And the three blind mice, that lost their tails on a visit to
the farmer's wife," said Harvey Riggs.

"And the three fiddlers of old king Cole," said Hazard.

"Poh! Get along, Mr. Edward and Mr. Harvey! you are
both too much given to be waggish. I doubt you will never
mend your ways while you keep each other's company!" cried
the good old gentleman, completely overborne by this spirited attack upon him; and as he said this, he turned round upon them
a face full of queer perplexity at being caught in the high career
of this scholarly exercitation. He is especially sensitive to the
least jest that is aimed at this peculiarity.

"Well," said Bel, "I am really very much obliged to you,
Mr. Chub, for your instructive lecture; and I shall always remember hereafter, that the Graces were three young women, and
the Furies, three old ones: and that three is the luckiest number in arithmetic."

By this time two horsemen, followed by a servant, had come
in sight upon the road leading to the gate. They advanced at a
leisure pace, and were soon descried to be Mr. Tracy in company

with Swansdown. The old gentleman's face, even at a distance, exhibited careful thought, and his bearing was grave and mannerly. He was in deep conversation with his friend, up to the moment of their arrival at the gate. Meriwether went forth to meet him, and assisted him from his horse with an affectionate and highly respectful assiduity.

As soon as he was on his feet, he took off his hat and made Meriwether a formal bow; and then walked across the court-yard to the door, making many obeisances to the company. Swansdown followed with scarcely less ceremony; and they were ushered into the parlor.

"We have an agreeable day's work before us, Mr. Meriwether," said Mr. Tracy, with an air of sprightly politeness, but in a voice somewhat tremulous from years. "Permit me to assure you it is not a small gratification to me, that we come so amicably to the close of a controversy, which, in other hands, might have been embittered with many unkind feelings. This has been conducted with so much courtesy, from beginning to end, that I had almost flattered myself with the hope, I should have had the luxury of it for the rest of my life."

He concluded this complimentary speech with a dash of gayety in his tone, and a vivacious gesticulation of his body; and then turning round to the ladies, with smiles upon his face, he made many civil inquiries after family matters.

The parties now being all assembled, our next move was to the old mill.

CHAPTER XXIII.

WHEN mounted our muster consisted of ten persons, besides the servants, and included all the gentlemen assembled, with the addition of Rip, who, astride of Spitfire, caracoled and bounded from place to place, like a young adjutant of a squadron. The old walls of Swallow Barn had never echoed back the tramp, the hum, or the shouts of a more goodly company than that which now filed off from the gate. Our ranks were accommodated to the nature of the road we had to travel. At first, Mr. Wart, with his papers still peeping forth from his pocket, shot ahead of the troop by the common brisk and easy-racking gait to which his tall and ungainly steed was accustomed; and he did not seem to be aware of the inequality of his pace, until he had gained about a hundred yards upon the cavalcade, and was admonished by a call from two or three of the party, that he would soon leave us out of sight, if he went on at that speed. His two hounds were, as usual, jogging close at his horse's heels; and any one might very well have mistaken our whole equipment for a party setting out to beat a cover, with the principal huntsman in advance; for, in addition to Philly's hounds, we had every dog of Swallow Barn in our train. Never, since the deluge, was there a lawsuit to be determined by so grotesque an array of judges, counsellors, parties and witnesses, as this! And never before in the history of jurisprudence, perhaps, was there such a case!

Philly Wart was highly amused. He had brought himself to look upon the whole matter as a mere pastime, and he was now determined to make the best of it. He could not for a moment give his features a serious cast, but laughed in reply to every question, like a man tickled with his own thoughts. He had reined up his horse, in obedience to our call, and was looking back upon the approaching host, when I rode up to him.

"This is a mode of practice very much to my liking," said he. "The law would not be such a wearisome business, Mr. Littleton, if its affairs were to be transacted in the field o' horseback; and with a fine pack of dogs instead of a jury. Famous juries they'd make, for courses and distances, in an ejectment, ha, ha, ha! If it were only the right season, I think we should be likely to look over more boundary lines than one to-day."

The same tone of enjoyment seemed gradually to have visited even old Mr. Tracy, after we had left the gate. Before this, there was a deep-seated care upon his brow; but he now began to take the hue of the hour. We had entered, after riding some distance, upon a narrow and tangled path, beset with underwood, that indicated our proximity to the ground around the mill. Through this portion of our road we were constrained to pass in single files, thus elongating our line of march, until it resembled that of a detachment of cavalry exploring a suspected haunt of an enemy. The resemblance occasioned our venerable friend of The Brakes to turn round to Meriwether and remark, with a pleasant but precise form of address,—

"You perceive, Mr. Meriwether, that the most formidable invasion of the Apple-pie frontier continues now, as of old, to come from the direction of Swallow Barn."

"I could heartily wish, my dear friend," replied Frank, "that every invasion in the world were as certain to promote the ends of justice and peace as this. And I could wish, too, that every supposed encroachment upon right, should be as gallantly and honorably met."

" But not quite so obstinately defended," said Harvey Riggs, in a half whisper, as he turned round on his saddle to make the remark to Ned Hazard.

" Amen!" said Ned.

When we arrived at the mill there was a silent pause for some moments, in which every one seemed to be engaged in surveying the ragged, marshy and unprofitable features of the landscape, and wondering in his own mind (at least all but Mr. Tracy) how such a piece of land could possibly have furnished a subject for such a protracted litigation. Philly Wart appeared to be aware of the common surprise, and looking round, somewhat jestingly, in the faces of the group, remarked,—

" Yes, there it is! And all that we have to do is, to get down from our horses, organize the court, and fall to work to determine whether the heirs of Swallow Barn or of The Brakes are hereafter to be pestered with this fine garden of wankopins and snake-collards!"

We dismounted; and some moments elapsed before the parties were ready to proceed to the business in hand. In this interval, the counsellor had walked up to the tutor, who stood upon a hillock, with his glass up to his eye, surveying the scene.

" What do you think of the prospect, Mr. Chub?" asked Philly Wart. " By what name would you venture to describe this luxuriant, refreshing, and sightly piece of land? Is it *mariscus*, or *mora*, or *hulmus*, or simple *locus paludosus?*"

" Sure it is not to look at this ill-favored quagmire, that we have been risking our necks under boughs of trees, and dodging through brambles this morning!" exclaimed the tutor.

" Aye," answered Philly, " this is the very ground of conten-
tion that has enlivened the annals of two families and their descendants, for half a century. It has been a gay quarrel, Mr.
Chub, and has cost something more than breath to keep it up.
It has lost nothing of its dignity, I warrant you, for want of long
opinions and sober counsel! *Floreat Lex*, Mr. Chub, is our
motto! It is a merry day for our craft, when laymen take to
reading the statutes, and pride holds the purse-strings."

" This is a great Sirbonian bog," said the tutor. " It is as
worthless as the Pomptinæ Paludes,—Gad-a-mercy ! it should be
relinquished by unanimous consent to the skunks and the muskrats !"

" It is a hereditament, as we lawyers say, Mr. Chub, that
would pass under the name *runcaria*, which signifies, full of
brambles and briers, or rather, by the title in our law Latin, (I
doubt if you have studied that kind of Latin, Mr. Chub ?) of
jampna, which comes, as Lord Coke says, of *jonc*, the French for
bulrush, and *nower*, a waterish place."

" Truly, your dog Latin suits the description of the place
marvellously well, Mr. Philpot Wart," said the tutor, laughing.
" And what do you consider, Mr. Meriwether," he continued, addressing Frank, who had just come to the spot, " the value of
this ground to be, per acre ? "

" About sixpence," answered Frank, smiling.

" Too high ; you hold it all too dear," interrupted Philly,
" threepence at the outside, and dear at that.   But come, gentlemen,—Mr. Swansdown we lose time. Let us to business."

Upon this, the principal personages concerned in the business of the day withdrew to a convenient spot, and selecting a
piece of square timber, that constituted a part of the ruins of the
mill, they took their seats.

Old Mr. Tracy now very deliberately proceeded to empty his
pocket of a bundle of papers, neatly tied up together, and loosen-

ing the string that bound them, he spread them out upon his knees. Then, after some rummaging, he produced a pair of spectacles, which, with great caution, he adjusted upon his nose ; and taking up one of the papers, he presented it to the arbitrators, saying, "here is the first letter in the correspondence which arose between the lamented Mr. Walter Hazard, and myself, touching the present subject of difference. If you prefer it, gentlemen, I will give you the copy of the letters that passed in the year 1759, between my immediate ancestor and the first Mr. Edward Hazard, in regard to that latter gentleman's plan of erecting this mill, at that date."

"If you will be so kind," said Philly, with an air of affectionate courtesy towards the old gentleman, "as to leave these papers with us, Mr. Tracy, we will digest them at our leisure. In the mean time, we will look at the deed from Gilbert Tracy to Edward Hazard—I have it here—" Saying this, he produced the roll of papers which had been so conspicuous about his person all the morning, and took from it the deed in question.

Here Philly mounted his spectacles, and began to read, in a clear voice, such parts of the deed as related to the nature and character of the grant; and which parts, in order that my reader might thoroughly understand the precise question in dispute, I have substantially set forth in a former chapter.

"This deed, Mr. Swansdown," said Philly, as he finished reading, "lays the whole foundation of the controversy The pretensions of the parties, as based upon this instrument are well understood, and all that remains for us is to ascertain what was the specific meaning of the parties thereto."

"That must be seen," said Mr. Tracy, "by the letters which I have just given you."

"Upon that point," said Philly Wart, "the courts have uni formly decided —"

" We are not to be governed by the adjudications of the courts upon any of these questions," interrupted Mr. Tracy ; " it is understood that the case is to be adjudged according to the principles of equity."

" *Equitas sequitur legem,* my friend," said Philly, smiling. " If there be ambiguity patent, that is, apparent upon the face of the deed, the law allows testimony to be received as to the intent of the parties concerned in the covenants. But where the intention may be derived from the construction of the covenants themselves, according to their plain letter, the law doth not permit acts and matters *in pais* to be used to set up an intention *dehors* the written instrument."

" Pray, Mr. Wart," said Swansdown, " permit me to ask, whether this case, agreeably to your understanding of it, is governed by the Roman or civil law, or strictly according to the technical principles of the common law ?"

" Only, sir, according to the course of the laws of this commonwealth," replied Philly, with an air of surprise at the question, and as if nettled by the foppery of Swansdown's manner. " Your suggestion, Mr. Tracy, will be a subject for our consideration," he continued, assuming his former mild tone, to the gentleman he addressed.

Various other papers were now produced and read ; and when all this documentary evidence had been brought to view, Philly remarked, with a manner that seemed to indicate profound reflection upon the case in hand ;—

" An idea strikes me, which appears to have an important influence upon the subject under consideration. I confess I should like to be satisfied upon this point. Mr. Swansdown and myself, I presume, will not differ about the construction of the deed, nor upon the nature of the law by which it is to be determined," he added, smiling; " but, if my present suspicions be confirmed, it is more than probable that our labor will be very much abridged. I rather suspect that this case will be found, upon examination, to turn upon certain matters of fact which have never yet been brought into the view of the courts—"

" A very shrewd old gentleman that, Mr. Hazard," whispered the tutor, who stood by all this time, listening with profound attention; " a man of genius, I assure you, Mr. Edward !"

"—The facts to which I allude are these ; namely, in the first place, to what distance did the mill-dam anciently and originally extend, from the present margin of the Apple-pie, in upon the land belonging to the tract called The Brakes ? Secondly, how long did the mill-pond exist within the said original limits ; and when did it first begin to recede from the same ? And, thirdly, which is the most important point of all, did the same mill-pond contract in its dimensions by gradual and imperceptible stages, or did it sink into the present narrow channel of the Apple-pie, by any violent and sudden disruption of its banks ?"

" The bearing and value of these questions," continued the lawyer, " will be understood by referring to the conceded fact, namely, that the two contiguous estates were divided by the water-line or margin of the mill-dam on the side of The Brakes. Now, it is a principle of law, upon which Mr. Swansdown and myself cannot possibly disagree,—for it is asserted without contradiction by the ablest writers,—both in the common and civil law, Mr. Swansdown, that where a river, holding the relation which this mill-dam occupied between these two estates, changes its course by slow and invisible mutations, so as to leave new land where formerly was water, then he to whose territory the accretions may be made in such wise, shall hold them as the gain or increment of his original stock. But if the river change its course by some forcible impulse of nature, as by violent floods, or the like, then shall he who suffers loss by such vicissitude, be indemnified by the possession of the derelict channel. And it would seem to me, that in case the river, in the instance put, should merely dwindle and pine away, as this famous mill-pond seems to have done," said Philly, with a smile, " then, the possessors of the banks on either side should consider it to be the will of Heaven that they should be separated by narrower partitions, and should, straightway, follow the retreating waters ; and, when these become so small as to allow them to do so, they should shake hands from the opposite banks, and thank God they were such near neighbors."

" He's a man of a clear head, Mr. Riggs," said the tutor again, with incieased admiration, " and expounds law like a sage :—and with a great deal of wit too !—He reminds me of the celebrated Mr. Ponsonby whom I once heard at the Four Courts, in a cause—"

" I am entirely of Mr. Wart's opinion of the value of these considerations," said Swansdown.

" They seem to me sagacious and reasonable," said Mr. Tracy, " and concur to strengthen the first views which I took upon this subject."

" Let these facts then, gentlemen, be inquired into," said Meriwether.

Wart arose from his seat, and walking carelessly a short distance from the group, beckoned Meriwether to follow him, and, when they were together said,—

" I have thrown out enough to put Mr. Tracy upon a new scent, which, if it be well followed up, will answer our purpose ; and now, I think I will give our friend Swansdown a walk into the marsh."

" Since it is agreed Mr. Swansdown," said Philly, returning to the party, " that testimony should be heard upon the questions I have proposed, we shall be able to form a better judgment by a cautious survey of the ground ourselves. It is scarcely possible that the mill-pond should have vanished without leaving some traces to show whether it went off in a night, or wasted away, like a chestnut fence-rail under the united attacks of sun and wind. There is nothing like the Trial by View."

"In what manner do you suppose, Mr. Wart, to enjoy this view?" asked Swansdown, with some concern. "Can we see it from the hill-side? for it seems rather hazardous for a passage on horseback."

"By walking over it," replied Philly very cooly. "With a little circumspection we can get across tolerably dry. Leap from one tuft to another, and keep your balance. The thing is very easy."

"We shall find brambles in our way," said the reluctant Swansdown.

"*E squillâ non nascitur rosa*, Mr. Swansdown," replied the other. "It is not the first time I have explored a marsh. Why man, if you had your gun with you, the woodcock would take you twice through the thickest of it! This is a notorious place for woodcock—"

"There are snakes, and some of them of a dangerous species. I have an utter horror of snakes," persisted Swansdown.

"There are some copperheads and a few mocassins," replied Philly, "whose bite is not altogether harmless. As to the black snake, and viper, and common water snake, you may assure yourself with taking them in your hand. Or take St. Patrick's plan, Mr. Swansdown; cut a hazle rod, and if you use it properly you may conjure every snake of them out of striking distance."

"Ha, ha! A facetious man, that Mr. Philly Wart," said the parson again, to Harvey Riggs.

"Come, Mr. Swansdown, I will lead the way. Don't be alarmed: We shall be better acquainted with the boundary when we get back."

Saying these words, Philly walked forward along the margin of the marshy ground which was once the bed of the dam, and having selected a favorable point for entering upon this region, he turned into it with a prompt and persevering step, making advantage of such spots as were firm enough to sustain his weight, and, pushing the shrubbery to one side, was soon lost to view. Swansdown, ashamed of being outdone, but protesting his reluctance, and laughing with a forced and dry laugh, cautiously entered at the same point, and followed in Philly's footsteps. When they were both still within hearing, Philly's voice could be recognized, saying—

" Look where you step, Mr. Swansdown! That's the true rule of life, and particularly for a man who meddles with law. Have your eyes about you, man! *Latet anguis in herbâ*, ha, ha, ha !"

" Hark to him !" exclaimed the parson. " A prodigious smart man, that Philly Wart !"

" After a short interval, Philly's voice was heard calling out, " Mr. Swansdown, Mr. Swansdown, where are you ? Not lost, I hope! This way, man ; take the left side of the gum-tree, and you will reach the bank of the Apple-pie as dry as a bone. And a monstrous stream it is, as you will find when you get here !"

" I have encountered shocking obstacles, Mr. Wart," exclaimed the voice of Swansdown, at some distance ; " I have one leg submersed in water and mud, up to the knee ; and have had a score of black-snakes hissing at me, ever since I got into this abominable place. Pray allow me to return !"

" Come on man !" was the reply, " you will reach dry ground presently. What signifies a wet foot ! Here's a noble prospect for you."

Another interval of silence now ensued, and this being followed by a distant hum of conversation, showed us that the two wanderers had fallen again into company.

Whilst we sat amongst the willows that skirted the original margin of the dam, expecting to see the counsellor and his companion emerge from the thicket on the opposite side, our attention was all at once aroused by the deep tongue of Wart's hounds, who had been exploring the fastness cotemporaneously with their master. They had evidently turned out a fox; and the rapidly retreating and advancing notes informed us of the fact that the object of their pursuit was doubling, with great activity, from one part of the swamp to another. This sudden outbreak threw a surprising exhilaration into our party.

We sprang to our feet and ran from place to place, expecting every moment to see the fox appear upon the field: these movements were accompanied with a general hallooing and shouting, in which the voice of Philly Wart, amongst the recesses of the marsh, was distinctly audible. Rip, at the first note, had run to his horse, and now came galloping past us, half wild with delight. Mr. Chub was in a perfect ecstasy, jumping, flinging out his arms, and vociferating all the technical cries of encouragement usual amongst the votaries of the chase. Even old Mr. Tracy was roused by the vivacity of the scene. His eyes sparkled and his gestures became peculiarly animated. All the dogs of our train had taken into the swamp, and barked with a deafening clamor as they pursued the track of the hounds, whose strong musical notes were now fast dying away in distance, as these eager animals pursued their prey directly up the stream for more than a mile. For a time, they were even lost to the ear, until, having made another double, they were heard retracing their steps, and coming back to their original starting point, as their short and sonorous notes crowded upon the ear with increasing distinctness.

At length, the little animal, that had given rise to all this uproar, was descried on the opposite side of the swamp, some distance ahead of her pursuers, speeding with terrified haste, to a

hole in the bank, where she was observed safely to accomplish
her retreat.

The duration of this animating episode was not above half an
hour ; and for the greater portion of that period we had totally
lost all intelligence of Wart and Swansdown, but were now greatly
amused to perceive the old lawyer breaking out of the cover, immediately at the spot where the fox had taken to the earth.
And there he stood, guarding the place against the invasion of
the dogs, who seemed to be frantic with disappointment at not
being permitted to enter this entrenchment of their enemy.   By
whipping, hallooing and scolding, Philly succeeded in drawing
them away ; and now, for the first time during this interval,
turned his attention to the fate of his comrade.   Swansdown was
no where to be seen.   Wart called aloud several times without
receiving an answer ; and at length the party on our side, also,
began to vociferate the name of the lost gentleman.   This was no
sooner done than we were surprised to receive an answer from the
midst of the bushes, within ten paces of the spot where we stood.
In one instant afterwards, Mr. Swansdown reappeared, almost
exactly at the point where he had first entered the swamp.   His
plight was sadly changed.   A thick coat of black mud covered
the lower extremities of his pantaloons, and his dress, in places,
was torn by briars ; but as if glad to be extricated from his perils,
on any terms, he came forth with a face of good humor, and
readily joined us in the laugh that his strangely discomfited exterior excited.

" Well," he remarked, " to gratify Mr. Wart, I have seen the
Apple-pie ; and I can truly say that I have enjoyed more pleasure in my life, at less cost.   A fine figure I make of it !" he exclaimed, pointing to his clothes.   " We had no sooner reached
what Mr. Wart called the bank of the rivulet, than those whelps
of dogs set up such a hideous yelling as turned my excellent

friend, the counsellor, crazy upon the spot; and thereupon he set off at full speed, like an old hound himself, leaving me to flounder back or forward, as best I might. I scarcely know what course I took, and when I thought I had reached the other side, it seems I had arrived just where I started. I can't say I think as highly of Mr. Wart's trial by the view, as he does!

We gave the unfortunate gentleman all the consolation his case admitted of; and returning to the ruins of the mill, there took our seats to await the return of Mr. Wart.

It was not long before he appeared, followed by the two dogs. He had crossed from the side on which we left him, with as little concern as if he had been walking on the firmest ground, and joined our company, more in the guise of an experienced woodman than of a gentleman of the learned profession intent upon disentangling points of law.

It may well be supposed that the labors of the day terminated at this point. Our spirits had been too much roused by the events of the morning to allow us to sit down again to the business of the lawsuit; and the uncomfortable condition of Swansdown made it necessary that he should, as soon as possible, be allowed an opportunity to change his dress. It was therefore intimated by Mr. Wart, that the question of the boundary line should be adjourned until the next morning, when, he remarked, he thought he should be able to give testimony himself that would be material to the cause.

In accordance with this intimation, it was arranged that the parties should convene the next morning at the Brakes; and having determined upon this, old Mr. Tracy and Swansdown mounted their horses and pursued their road to the mansion house at the Brakes, which was not above two miles distant.

The rest of the party returned to Swallow Barn.

CHAPTER XXIV.

IT was at a late dinner hour when our party returned to the mansion, from the expedition of the boundary line. The absence of Mr. Tracy and his champion Swansdown, caused some solicitude in the family, which, together with the curiosity of the ladies to hear all the particulars of the day's adventure, gave rise to a multitude of inquiries that served to produce much animation at the dinner table. Ned and Harvey detailed what they called the facts, with exorbitant amplification, and with an assumed earnestness, that baffled all attempts to arrive at the truth. A great deal, they affirmed, was to be said on both sides. And then they gave a piteous account of Swansdown's misfortunes ; praising his calm and dignified composure, nothwithstanding he was so torn by brambles, and so disfigured with mud, and so frightened with snakes— "

" He was not attacked by these reptiles !" cried Prudence, with a marked concern.

" They did not absolutely strike their fangs into him," said Harvey ; " but they reared up their grizzly heads at his feet, and hissed hideously at him."

" And then he was so drenched to the very skin !" said Ned.

" Poor gentleman !" exclaimed Harvey, " an he 'scape a cold

or an ague, his friends should be thankful. Heaven knows what would become of the boundary line, if any thing were to happen to him at this critical juncture!"

"And he looked so forlorn!" continued Ned.

"And so interesting!" said Harvey, "with the black mud up to his knees, and his white pocket-handkerchief up to his face, wiping away the blood where the briars had made free with his chin."

"Don't you believe them, aunt Pru!" cried Rip. "Mr. Swansdown was laughing all the time,—for we had a most an elegant fox-hunt, only it was all in the swamp, and the bushes would not let us see any thing!"

"After all then, cousin Harvey," said Catharine, "tell us seriously how this famous arbitration has ended."

"Most appropriately," said Harvey. "About forty years ago, the law suit began with the quest of a wild-goose, and, having exercised the ingenuity of all the low-country lawyers in succession, during all this time, it has now turned into a fox-chase, and ended by earthing a poor little harmless quadruped, precisely at the place of beginning."

"That's true," said Philly Wart, laughing, "the hole was as nearly as possible at the commencement of the first line laid off in the survey of the mill-dam. But, Miss Tracy," he continued, "you must not suppose that there was any design on our part in putting up the fox this morning. This is not the time of the year for such sport, because these animals have all young families to take care of, and it is deemed cruel to disturb them : but my dogs happened to fall upon the trail of madam, as she was looking out for her breakfast. And so, off they went, Miss Catharine, making excellent music. It was a cunning thing for the little animal, too, to take right up the swamp; for, besides the wind being in that direction,—which you know would carry the

scent away from the dogs,—she had the water to wash away the
foot-prints; and, in addition to this, she was leading them off, as fast
as she could, from her den, which is a motherly trick these creatures
have. But, you see, Miss Tracy, the more she ran the warmer
she got; and so, she left her scent upon the bushes and brambles.
If you could have seen the dogs, you would have found them with
their noses up, as unconcerned as if they had had her in view all
the time. Presently, she got the foot of them so far, that she
found she could get back to her nest before they could come up;
and so, she doubled beautifully down the swamp again, and
straight to her hole, as fast as her legs could carry her. I knew
what her trick was from the first; and was, therefore, on the look-
out, which enabled me to reach her just as she entered it; and
there I defended her gallantly against the invasion of her enemies."

" For which you deserve the thanks of all mothers, Mr. Wart,"
said my cousin Lucretia.

" And of all sportsmen, too," said Harvey Riggs.

> " For a fox that is hunted and runs away,
> May live to be hunted another day."

Philly Wart had become exceedingly animated in the course
of the recital above detailed, and notwithstanding it was ludi-
crously out of place, considering the person to whom it was addressed, Philly was too full of his subject to let it drop. His
description was accompanied by a vivacious and expressive gesticulation, that prevented him from eating his dinner; and Catharine had become so much amused with his manner, that she
listened with a marked approbation, and encouraged him to proceed, by frequent nods of her head.

" It is quite lawful and customary, Miss Tracy," continued
the counsellor, " to hunt young foxes at this season, at moonlight; and it is a fine sport, I assure you! If you were to get

on your horse to-night, about twelve,— for we shall have a bright moon by that hour,—and ride over to the old mill-dam, and take my two dogs with you, you would be sure to get two or three of the cubs on foot almost immediately, and the mother besides; and then you might take a seat upon the rider of a fence, with your great coat well wrapped about you, and your hands in your pockets, and see a fine run. For, at this time of year, they (especially the young ones,) won't run far from the nest; but they are apt to play in circles round it, which gives you a chance, in a clear moonlight, to see them twenty times in an hour. And then, when they get tired, Miss Tracy, they have only to pop into the nest, and there they are as snug as you could wish them!"

" I have read," said Catharine, " of ladies indulging in the sports of the chase; but it would be a great novelty, Mr. Wart, to find one of our sex pursuing such a pastime alone, on the borders of a desolate marsh, at midnight, and seated, as you propose, on the top-rail of a fence, with her hands in her pockets!"

Here followed a general laugh from the company.

" To make the picture complete," said Harvey Riggs, " cousin Kate, you should have a scant mantle of scarlet, and a pipe in your mouth."

" And a broom-stick, I suppose you would say, cousin Harvey, instead of a pony," added Catharine.

" When I said you, Miss Tracy," said the counsellor, smiling, " I meant Ned Hazard here and his friends, who profess to be fond of manly exercises."

" I profess," said Ned, " a sovereign aversion to agues, and an especial proclivity to the comforts of a warm bed."——

Towards the hour of sunset the ladies from the Brakes were preparing to return home, and, as the arrangements for the following day contemplated a meeting at Mr. Tracy's, we promised to assemble there at an early hour. Prudence had yielded to the

entreaties of Catharine and Bel to accompany them that evening,
and a horse was accordingly brought to the door for her.   Our
guests, with this addition, soon afterwards left Swallow Barn.

When we had concluded our evening repast,—that substantial country meal which it would be altogether inadequate to call
by the feeble, but customary name of tea—the pleasant change
wrought upon the atmosphere by the dew, which in the low-
country, at this season, falls heavily after night, had, as usual,
brought the inmates of the house to the doors.   Mr. Wart and
Frank Meriwether had taken their seats in the porch; and here,
dismissing the tone of levity with which the events of the day
had been conducted, they fell into a grave conference upon sundry matters of public concern.   The rest of us sat quietly listening to the conversation, which became interesting from the sensible and shrewd character of the interlocutors.   Philly Wart,
nothwithstanding the mixture of jest and almost frivolity, that,
during the day, had shown itself in his demeanor, now exhibited
the thought and reflection of one versed in the secrets of his nature, and that keen insight into the merits of men and their actions, that can only be gained by extensive intercourse with the
world.   His remarks had a strong flavor of originality, and although now and then brought to the verge of the ludicrous by a
rash and unsuccessful attempt to be figurative, they were, nevertheless, pithy and forcibly illustrative of his subject.   Meriwether, with less pretensions to a knowledge of men, was calm,
philosophical and benevolent; his character principally manifesting itself in certain kindly prejudices, and in a tone of observation, which, in reference to political conclusions. might be said to
be even desponding.   Frank has never found the actions of those
who administer our government squaring with that lofty virtue
which the excellence of his own principles has taught him to exact from all men who aspire to control the interests of society

In fact, he speaks like an ancient stoic, removed from all ambition to figure on the theatre of life, and quietly observing the tumult of affairs from a position too distant to be reached by the sordid passions that sway the multitude; or, in other words, he discourses like an easy and cultivated country-gentleman.

It was in summing up a train of reflections, in this temper, upon the general aspect of the great political movements of the day, that he concluded—as we broke up our party—

" Well, Mr. Wart, you think better of these things than I do; but, to my mind, there is no satisfaction in this survey. Look which way I may, to the one side or to the other, to me it seems all equally vile and contemptible ; and so, good night !"

CHAPTER XXV.

THE OLD SCHOOL.

I AROSE on the following morning soon after day-light, and was quietly descending the staircase when I was saluted by the voices of Lucy and Vic, who at this early hour were equipped for the day. They were looking out with some eagerness at the clouds. A heavy rain had fallen during the night, but the eastern horizon was nevertheless tinted with the rosy flush of morning, and the indications were favorable to the dispersion of the few black vapors that still rolled across the heavens. My little cousins soon made me acquainted with the cause of their early appearance. They were to accompany us to the Brakes, and had planned it to ask me to take a seat with them in the carriage, telling me, that if I did not go with them they would be obliged to take Rip, which, as Vic said, " Rip never *did* like."

I assented heartily to their proposal; and upon this they fell to dancing round me, and amusing me with a great deal of prattle. They insisted upon my going with them to the stable yard, "just to make sure that uncle Carey was cleaning up the carriage, and getting ready." Here we found the old menial with a bucket of water and sponge, busily employed in the task the little girls had coaxed him to perform. He was affectionately obliging to his young mistresses, and spoke to them in a tone that showed how largely he partook of the family interest in them, although it was sufficiently apparent that he deferred but little to their authority.

As soon as breakfast was over, Carey brought the coach to the door. It was a capacious old vehicle, that had known better days, being somewhat faded in its furniture, and still clothed with its original cover of yellow oil-cloth, of which, I suppose, it had never been stripped, although now arrived at the latter stage of its existence. The plainness of this part of the equipage was compensated in a pair of high-mettled, full-blooded chestnut horses, in excellent keeping, but rather light in comparison with the size of the coach to which they were harnessed.

Meriwether having unexpectedly received intelligence that rendered his presence necessary at a remote part of the farm, was obliged to forego his visit to the Brakes; and Ned was accordingly commissioned by him to make his excuses and act as his representative. This matter being arranged, and all things being in readiness for our departure, Mr. Wart, attended by Ned Hazard and Rip, set out on horseback; whilst the two little girls and myself took our seats in the carriage, and old Carey, mounting the box, put off his horses at a brisk speed.

As we ascended the hill, and came in full view of the mansion house at the Brakes, we could observe Mr. Tracy walking backward and forward with his arms behind him, on a level plat at the door; and as soon as our party attracted his attention, he was seen to halt, with his hat raised off his head, and held in such a manner as to shield his eyes from the sun, until we got near enough for recognition. There was an unwonted alacrity in his salutations; and he helped Lucy and Vic from the carriage himself, with a gallantry that showed the cheerful state of his feelings, not forgetting to take a kiss from each as he handed them to the door.

When we entered the house, Harvey Riggs and Bel were observed walking leisurely up the lawn, from the direction of the river. At a parlor window sat Catharine and Prudence, in an absorbing conversation with Mr. Swansdown, who was apparently regaling his interested auditors with a narrative of deep attraction ; and perhaps it may have been an idle preconception of mine, but I thought Prudence, especially, listened with a more intelligent and changeful sympathy than was her wont. What was the topic, and in what language urged, I am altogether ignorant ; but to my prejudiced vision it seemed that either the story or the speaker had charmed " never so wisely."

In describing the mansion house at the Brakes, in a former chapter, I have informed my reader that it is without architectural embellishment. One front faces the river, from which it is separated by a long, sloping, and unshaded hill. At the foot of this slope the bank of the river is some eight or ten feet above the water, and is clothed with a screen of native shrubbery. The road winds round the hill from the river, so as to approach the house on the opposite side. This front of the dwelling differs widely from that I have described. Its plainness is relieved by a portico supported by stuccoed columns, massive and rough, and over which the second story of the building projects, so as to form a small apartment that has rather a grotesque appearance,—as it may be said to resemble a box perched upon a four-legged stool. This superstructure is built of wood painted blue, though a good deal weather-beaten ; and it is illustrated with a large bow-window in the front, surrounded with a heavy white cornice filled with modillions and other old-fashioned ornaments : it strikes the observer as an appendage to the edifice of questionable utility, and as somewhat incongruous with the prevailing simplicity that characterizes the exterior of the mansion. A range of offices, old, and interpolated with modern additions, sweeps rectangularly along the brow of the hill, and shows the ample provision made for the comforts of solid housekeeping. The whole of this quarter is thickly embowered with trees, amongst which the line of lombardy poplars, that I have before had occasion to notice, is marshalled along the avenue, from the mansion downwards, like a gigantic array of sylvan grenadiers. Over all the grounds in the vicinity of the buildings an air of neatness prevails, even to an extent that might be called pedantic.

The interior of the house is in full contrast with its outward appearance, and shows the relics of a costly grandeur. The rooms are large, and decorated with a profusion of wood-work, chiselled into the gorgeous forms of ancient pomp. The doors have huge pediments above them with figures carved upon the entablatures ; garlands of roses, as stiff as petrifactions, are moulded, with a formal grace, upon the jambs of the window-frames; and the mantel-pieces are thickly embossed with odd little mythological monsters, as various as the metamorphoses of Ovid. The walls are enriched with a fretted cornice, in the frieze of which cupids, satyrs and fauns are taking hands, and seem to be dancing country dances through thickets of nondescript vegetables. The fire-places are noble monuments of ancient hospitality, stately and vast, and on either side of them are deep recesses, surmounted by ornamented arches, and lighted by windows that look out from the gable-ends of the building.

The furniture of these apartments retains the vestiges of a corresponding splendor. The tables seem to have turned into iron from age, and are supported upon huge, crooked legs; the chairs, sofas, firescreens, and other articles of embellishment, though damaged by time, still afford glimpses of the lacker and varnish that gave effulgence to their days of glory. Amongst these remnants of the old time I recognized, with an affectionate interest, two elliptical mirrors,—no doubt the marvel of the country when they first reached this strand,—set in frames of tarnished gilt, and curiously carved into droll resemblances of twisted serpents, each swallowing his own tail.

I must return from this digression to continue my narrative of the important affair that had now brought us to the Brakes.

From an early hour, Mr. Tracy had been in a state of agitated spirits with the thoughts of the arbitration. Although his zeal had latterly subsided, it had been waked up by the recent movements, like a snake at the return of spring. The old gentleman rises from his bed, at all seasons, with the dawn of day; but this morning he was observed to make an unusual stir. It was remarked that his dress was even more scrupulously adjusted than ordinarily; the ruffles of his sleeves protruded over his hands with a more pregnant strut; his cravat was drawn, if possible, tighter round his neck; and his silvery hair was combed back into the small, taper cue that played upon his cape, with a sleekness that indicated more minute attention to personal decoration than the family were accustomed to expect. He is the very picture of a man for a law-suit. His tall figure and care-worn face have such an emaciated air! and when to this is added the impression made by his tight, brown kerseymere small-clothes, and his long, stocking-like boots, buttoned by straps to his knees, and the peculiar capacity of stride which this costume discloses, we have the personation of a man eminently calculated to face the biting blast of the law, or to worm through the intri-cacies of a tangled and long-winded suit, with the least possible personal obstruction.

Harvey Riggs told us that Mr. Tracy had scarcely eaten any breakfast, being in that fidgety state of mind that takes away the the appetite; and, what was a little out of his common behavior, he was even jocose upon the existing relations betwixt himself and Meriwether. It was also observable that, notwithstanding this elevation of spirits, he occasionally broke out into a slight expression of peevishness when any thing balked his humor. It fell upon Ned Hazard to encounter one of these passing rebukes, as will appear in the dialogue I am about to detail.

Mr. Tracy has reached that age at which old persons lose sight of the true relations of society. He considers all men, not yet rrived at middle age, as mere hair-brained boys; and does not scruple, especially in matters of business, to treat them accordingly. I believe he is of opinion that Frank Meriwether himself has scarcely attained to manhood. But as for Ned Hazard, or even Harvey Riggs, he thinks them not yet out of their teens. This temper is apparent when the old gentleman experiences any contradiction; for he is then apt to become dogmatic and peremptory, and sometimes a little harsh. But he likes Ned very well; and frequently, when he is in good humor, laughs at his pranks, until the tears come into his eyes, and roll over his dry cheeks, like vinegar trickling over a piece of leather.

Now it happens that Ned stands precisely in that category which renders him nervously solicitous to appear well in the eyes of Mr. Tracy. He is sadly aware that Bel's father has taken up an idea that he is a thoughtless, unballasted youth, and utterly deficient in those thrifty business-habits which are most pleasing to the contemplation of age; and he is therefore perpetually making awkward attempts to produce a different opinion. My reader has perhaps already had occasion to remark that Ned's character is utterly inauspicious to the management of such a matter. He is purblind to all the consequences of his own conduct, and as little calculated to play the politician as a child.

When the gentlemen of our party had gathered together, Mr. Tracy was anxious that no time should be lost to the prejudice of the principal concern of our meeting; and having announced this, he was approached by Ned, who, with a solemn face,—endeavoring

to assume as much of the look of a negotiator as he was able,—
made a formal communication of the cause of Meriwether's absence, and of the arrangement that he himself was to appear as
the representative of Swallow Barn. Mr. Tracy did not like it;
he could not imagine how any domestic engagement could claim
precedence over one so important as this. He was on the verge
of saying so; but, as if struck with a sudden thought, he paused,
stared at Ned, without uttering a word, grasped his nether lip
with his left hand, and fell into a study. Ned stood by, looking
as respectfully as he could. The conclusion was favorable; for
the old gentleman brightened up, and delivered himself, with some
hesitation, pretty much in this way:—

"Well, well! It is all right that you should give your attention to this matter. We old folks labor altogether for the young;
and they that come after us must live and learn. I wish I could
make my Ralph feel the interest he ought to take in this subject; but he is wayward, and plays his own game. As to you,
Mr. Hazard, although you are young and thoughtless, and not of
an age to take care of your property, this may be said to be your
own case, sir, seeing that you are the heir to Swallow Barn under
your father's will. And I am told Mr. Meriwether is clearing
the track for you; he is wiping off the incumbrances. So it is
your own case you have to look after."

"For my part, Mr. Tracy," replied Ned, with a timid deference, and with a singular want of shrewdness, considering the
person he addressed, "I have never seen the use of this controversy. Our family ought to have given up to you, rather than
trouble the courts with such an inconsiderable matter. I have
always expressed my willingness to end the affair by making you
a deed."

"Young gentleman," said Mr. Tracy, rather briskly, and
looking with an air of surprise at Ned, "you reckon without

your host if you consider this a matter of acres at all. Your father, sir, and I had an honest difference of opinion; he thought he was right; I thought I was; and we both knew that the other would expend twenty times the value of the land, before he would take an inch of it but as a matter of right. I am not accustomed to take up or put down opinions upon light grounds. In such matters I do not count the cost. A deed, sir!"—

"I beg pardon," replied Ned confusedly, and alarmed by this flash of temper, which set him, like a boy who has mistaken the mood of his master, to a speedy recantation. "You mistook my meaning,—I meant to say—"

"Yes, yes," interrupted the old gentleman, relapsing into the opposite tone of kindness, as if aware that his feelings had been unnecessarily roused, "so I suppose, my young friend! You are but a novice in the world; but you know Isaac Tracy well enough to be quite certain that he does not fling away five hundred pounds,—aye, twice five hundred,—to maintain his title to a bed of splatterdocks, unless there was something at the bottom of the dispute that belonged to his character."

This remark was concluded with an emotion that amounted almost to a laugh; and so completely reassured Ned, as to embolden him to venture upon a joke.

"Such character," said Ned, "is like the goose in the fable; it lays golden eggs."

"And there is nothing in it when you cut it up, Mr. Edward, that is what you were going to say," added the old gentleman, greatly amused with the remark. "You are a facetious young gentleman. You say pretty sharp things now and then, Edward, and don't spare such old codgers as I, ha, ha!" he continued, laughing, and tapping Ned familiarly on the back. "Why, what a plague! Here we are wasting our time with this merry Ned Hazard, when we ought to be at our business. Dogs

take you, for a jester as you are !" he exclaimed, jogging Ned
with his elbow. " You will trick us out of our proper vocation
with a laugh, would ye! Harvey, call Mr. Swansdown from the
parlor ; tell him he must leave the women ; we have our hands
full."

After this burst from the old gentleman, he opened a door
that admitted us to a small room which he calls his study. It is
an inner shrine that is deemed a prohibited spot to the members of the household, as the key of it is generally carried in Mr.
Tracy's own pocket. This apartment is so characteristic of its
inhabitant, that I must take advantage of my introduction to it,
to make my reader acquainted with its general appearance.

Some heavy volumes in quarto, such as constituted the guise
in which the best authors of Queen Anne's time were accustomed
to be exhibited to the public, were scattered over a range of
shelves that occupied one side of the room. There was one large
window only to the apartment, through which the sun flung a
broad light, that served to heighten the forlorn impression made
by the obsolete and almost shabby air of the furniture ; on the
sill of this window a collection of pods and garden seeds were
laid out to be dried. In another quarter of the room, a shelf
was appropriated to the accommodation of a motley assemblage
of old iron, of which the principal pieces were rusty hinges, bolts,
screws, bridle-bits, stirrups, and fragments of agricultural implements ; and upon the floor, below these, stood a chest of tools.
The fireplace had a ragged appearance, being strewed with scraps
of paper and other rubbish, and upon one side of it was placed an
old-fashioned secretary, with a lid like the roof of a house. One
or two paintings, too obscure to be guessed at, hung over the
mantel-piece ; and on the wall near the door, was suspended an
almost illegible map of Virginia. A small table was opened out
in the middle of the floor, and provided with a writing appara-

tus; around this table were three or four broad, high-backed mahogany chairs, with faded crimson seats stuck round with brass nails. The cobwebs on various parts of the walls, and the neglected aspect of the room, showed it to be an apartment not much resorted to or used by the old gentleman, except as a mere place of deposit for lumber.

When Mr. Swansdown, at Harvey's summons, made his appearance, our friend Philly Wart indulged in some little raillery upon the mischances of the day before, and accused the sentimental gentleman of deserting him; but finding old Mr. Tracy already provided with a mass of documents, and standing ready, with spectacles on nose, to plunge into the middle of affairs, the several parties sat down and addressed themselves to their tasks like men determined to make an end of matters. Ned put on a farcical gravity, and began to rummage over the papers, as if he was thoroughly acquainted with every document in the bundle, until Mr. Tracy, raising his glasses up to his forehead, asked him, with a fretful earnestness, what he was in search of. This simple interrogatory, and the look that accompanied it, so disconcerted the representative of Swallow Barn, that he was obliged to reply, for lack of something better to say, that " he was looking for nothing in particular !"

" I thought so, by your haste," said the old gentleman, as he brought his spectacles back to their original position. Ned, to conceal his confusion, picked up a large sheet of parchment, and set about reading its contents regularly through from the beginning.

As soon as we saw this little wittenagemote fairly at work with the lawsuit, Harvey and myself quietly stole away, not, however, without receiving a glance from Ned Hazard, who turned his head and gave us a look of sly perplexity as we disappeared at the door.

The ladies had retired to their rooms. Ralph had taken away our young cavalier Rip to the river ; and being thus left to ourselves, Harvey and I sat down at the front door, attracted by the commanding view of the scenery, and the appearance of a large ship that, with all her canvas spread, was winging her way round the headlands of the James River, towards the Atlantic.

In this situation, Harvey gave me the particulars of the scene I am about to describe in the next chapter.

CHAPTER XXVI.

THE RAKING HAWK.

I SAID that when we arrived at The Brakes, Bel and Harvey Riggs were seen approaching the house from a distance. The morning was still cool from the evaporation of the dew before the rays of the sun. A pleasant breeze swept across the lawn from the direction of the river. Bel was leaning upon Harvey's arm in earnest conversation; her face shaded by a kind of hood of green silk, and her dress such as ladies wear in the earlier part of the day, before they perform the more studied labors of the toilet; it was of a light fabric, neatly fitted to her person. Exercise had thrown a healthy hue over her cheek; and the fresh breeze fluttering amongst the folds of her dress imparted an idea of personal comfort that accorded with the coolness of the costume, and the blooming countenance of its wearer. It did not escape my notice, that her foot, which is exceedingly well shaped, appeared to great advantage in an accurately fitted shoe, bound to her ankle with black ribbons laced across stockings of spotless white. Her exterior was altogether remarkable for a becoming simplicity of attire, and seemed to speak that purity of taste which is the most beautiful and attractive quality in the character of a woman.

I must admonish my reader that, as my design in this work

has been simply to paint in true colors the scenes of domestic life as I have found them in Virginia, I do not scruple to record whatever has interested me ; and if, perchance, my story should not advance according to the regular rules of historico-dramatic composition to its proper conclusion, I do not hold myself accountable for any misadventure on that score.   I sketch with a careless hand; and must leave the interest I excite—if such a thing may be—to the due development of the facts as they come within my knowledge.   For the present, I have to tell what Harvey Riggs and Bel had been concerning themselves about, before we met them in the hall.   If any thing is to grow out of it hereafter, it is more than I know.

It had been hinted to me from two or three quarters, but principally by Ned Hazard, and I believe I have said as much to my reader in some former chapter, that Bel Tracy is a little given to certain romantic fancies, such as country ladies who want excitement and read novels are apt to engender.   Her vivacity and spirit show themselves in the zeal with which she ever cultivates the freaks that take possession of her mind.   For some time past, she had devoted her time to training a beautiful marsh-hawk, a bird resembling the short-winged hawk known by the name of the hen-harrier in the old books, and had nurtured it with her own hand from its callow state.   By an intimacy of one year she had rendered this bird so docile, that, at her summons, he would leave a large wicker cage in which he was ordinarily imprisoned, and which was suspended from an old mulberry-tree in the yard, to perch upon her wrist.   The picturesque association of falconry with the stories of an age that Walter Scott has rendered so bewitching to the fancy of meditative maidens, had inspired Bel with an especial ardor in the attempt to reclaim her bird.   In her pursuit of this object she had picked up some gleanings of the ancient lore that belonged to the art; and, fantastic as it may seem, began to think that her unskilful efforts would be attended with success. Her hawk, it is true, had not been taught to follow his quarry, but he was manned—as Bel said of him—in all such exercises as made him a fit companion for a lady. She had provided him with leather bewets, that buttoned round his legs, and to each of these was attached a small silver bell. A silver ring, or varvel, was fitted to one leg, and on it was engraved the name of her favorite, copied from some old tale, " Fairbourne," with the legend attached, " I live in my lady's grace." I know not what other foppery was expended upon her minion; but I will warrant he went forth in as conceited array as his " lady's grace " could devise for him. A lady's favorite is not apt to want gauds and jewels.

Immediately after breakfast, Bel stole forth alone to Fairbourne's perch. She held in her hand a pair of leather jesses, a leash, and a ball of fine cord, which she termed a creance. Now, the thought that had taken possession of her brain was, to slip off with Fairbourne into the field, and give him a flight; a privilege that he had never enjoyed during the whole period of his thraldom. Bel supposed that by fastening the jesses to his legs, —or I should say, speaking like one versed in the mystery, his arms,—and the leash to the jesses, and the creance to that, Fairbourne would be as secure in the empyrean as on his perch : she had only to manage him as a boy manages his kite. Her purpose, however, was to try the first experiment alone, and, upon its success, she designed to surprise her visitors, as well as the family, with the rare entertainment of a hawking scene.

As she stood under the mulberry-tree, looking at Fairbourne tiring at the limb of a pullet, or, in other words, whetting his voracious appetite with the raw leg of a chicken, and had just snatched the morsel from his beak to make him the more keen, Harvey Riggs accidentally came into the porch, and, stooping down, picked up from the floor a strange resemblance of a bird compacted of leather and feathers.

"What child's toy is this, Bel?" cried he, loud enough to startle the lady with the question. "What crotchet have you in your head now?"

"Pray, cousin Harvey, come this way," said she, turning round with the hawk upon her hand. "It is my lure; bring it to me, for I want your help. I am going to give Fairbourne a holiday. You shall see him presently dabbling his wing in yon-'der cloud."

Harvey approached with the lure in his hand; and Bel, patting the bird upon the back, as he alternately stretched out first one wing, and then the other, along his leg,—in the action known by the name of mantling,—explained her whole design to her cousin. Then binding on the jesses, with the leash and creance, each made fast to the other, she sallied out upon the lawn, attended by her squire, until she reached a spot at a distance from any tree, where she intimated to Harvey that she would now let Fairbourne fly.

"But if he should not come back, Bel?" inquired Harvey. "For it seems to me not altogether so safe to trust to his love of his perch, or even of his mistress; although in that he is not of my mind. In spite of your lure, which I know is a great temptation to some persons, my pretty cousin, there are creatures that prefer the open world to your hand, strange as it may seem!"

"Is not here my creance?" asked Bel, in reply. "And then, when the lure fails, have I not only to pull the string?"

"Your light flax is not so strong as a wild bird's love of freedom," said Harvey.

"Ah, cousin, you forget that Fairbourne is a gallant bird, and loves to hear me call him. I will whistle him down without compulsion. Now, mark how loth he is to leave my hand," continued Bel, rapidly endeavoring to cast the bird off, who, instead of flying, merely spread his wings with a motion necessary to preserve his balance. At length, she succeeded in disengaging him from her hand, when, instead of mounting into the air, he tamely lit upon the ground some few paces from her feet.

" Oh villain Fairbourne !" cried Harvey, "you grovel when you should soar."

" This comes of my not hooding him," said Bel. " But it seemed so cruel to pass a thread through his eyelids,—which is called seeling, and must be done before he would bear the hood,— that I could not think of it. I don't believe those ladies of the old time could have been so very tender-hearted. Cousin, if he will not fly, the direction is to strike at him with your wand."

" Which means my foot," said Harvey, " so, master Fairbourne, up, or my wand shall ruffle your feathers for you !" With these words, Harvey approached the bird, and, striking at him with his boot, had the satisfaction to see him spring briskly from the ground, and mount into the air with a rapid, bickering flight. He took his course against the wind, and, as he ascended, Bel played out her line, with rapturous exclamations of pleasure at the sight of her petted bird flinging himself aloft with such a spirited motion. When he had risen to the utmost reach of his creance, he was observed to dart and wheel through the air in every variety of perplexed motion, canceliering—as it was anciently termed— in graceful circles through the atmosphere, and turning, with quick flashes, the bright lining of his wings to the sun. It was beautiful to look upon the joyous bird gambolling at this lordly height, and the graceful girl watching his motions with a countenance of perfect transport.

" To my thinking," said Harvey, " Fairbourne is so well pleased with his pastime that he will not be very willing to re- turn."

" Oh, you shall see !" cried Bell ; " I can lure ' my tassel-gentle back again.' Look you now, cousin, here is Fairbourne shall come back to me like a spaniel !"

Saying this, she flourished her lure iñ the air, and called out the words of her customary salutation to the hawk as loud as she was able. " He sees and hears with extraordinary acuteness," she continued, as she still waved the lure above her head, " and will obey presently."

" Faith, if he hears or sees, he does not heed !" said Harvey.

" He has been so overfed with delicacies," replied Bel, a little disappointed at receiving no token of recognition, " that it is no wonder this lure has no charms for him. My whistle he never neglects."

Upon this, she put a small ivory pipe to her mouth, and blew a shrill note.

" You overrate your authority, Bel," said her cousin. " Fairbourne has no ear for music. He is fit for treason, stratagem and spoils."

" The wretch !" exclaimed Bel, playfully. " Does he dare defy my whistle ! then, master, I must need take a course with you ! there is some virtue in fetters, however, when milder means fail. So come down, scapegrace, and answer to your mistress for your truant behavior ! Aha ! you obey now !" she added exultingly, as she drew in the line, and compelled her hawk to dart towards the earth.

" After all," said Harvey, " there is no persuasion like a string. Trust me, a loop upon hawk or lover, coz, is safer than a lure any day."

" It did not require the flight of a silly bird to teach me that," said Bel, smiling, " or why did I bring this long line into the field with me ?"

At this moment, Fairbourne had almost reached the ground

by a swift flight that far outsped Bel's exertions, assisted by Harvey, to draw him down: then, skimming along the surface of the field with the slackened cord, he suddenly shot upwards with such vigor as to snap the string; and, frightened by the jerk that severed his fetters, he arose with an alarmed motion, to a soaring height, and then shaped his career directly up the river.

Bel and Harvey watched the retreating bird in equal amazement, as he winged his flight across the woody promontories in the distance, until he was reduced to a mere speck upon the sky.

Bel's emotion was one of mortification, not unmingled with admiration at the arrow-like swiftness with which her favorite sped from her hand. Harvey's was wonder, whether a bird nurtured in such household familiarity would soar so far from his accustomed haunts as to render his return hopeless.

" I can see him yet," said Harvey, straining his sight up the river, " and, if I am not mistaken, he has darted down to perch near Swallow Barn."

" He will come back," muttered Bel, in a distrusting tone of voice, and with a look of dejection, " I know he will come back! nothing that I have tended so kindly would desert me."

" Make yourself easy, my dear cousin," replied Harvey, " he belongs to an ungrateful tribe, and is not worth reclaiming."

" I could sit down and cry," said Bel.

" You should laugh rather, to think," replied her cousin, " what an arrant coxcomb you have sent abroad amongst the crows and kingfishers of the river. He, with his jangling bells, and his silver ring and dainty apparel! A marvellous fopling he will make in the sedate circles of owls and buzzards! I should not be surprised if, in three days' time, he should be whipped out of all good society in the woods, and be fain to come back to his perch, as torn-down and bedraggled as a certain other favorite of yours, who took refuge at The Brakes yesterday."

" Fie, cousin !" exclaimed Bel, laughing, " what harm has poor Mr. Swansdown done, that you should rail at him ?"

" True," said Harvey ; " if you had deigned to cast a loop round him, he would not have fled so willingly."

" What shall I do ?" asked Bel.

" I will tell Ned Hazard," said Harvey. " This is an incident in his line. Ned has not yet killed seven dragons in your service ; and therefore you frown upon him. So, pray let me put him in the way to signalize himself. He shall bring back Fairbourne, if the renegade is to be found in the Old Dominion."

" I would not give him the trouble," said Bel, carelessly.

" I will," replied Harvey ; " and by way of quickening his motion, will tell him that you would take it kindly."

" I am sure," said Bel, " Edward would do any thing I might ask of him."

" He would delight in it," replied Harvey. " He is most horribly in love. The search after this hawk would be occupation for him : it would divert his melancholy."

" Oh, cousin Harvey Riggs !" cried Bel with great animation, " to say that Ned Hazard is melancholy, or in love either, after what we heard on the bank of the river the other day, when we surprised him and Mr. Littleton !"

" Melancholy,—that is, your love-melancholy,—wears divers antics," said Harvey. " Ned was beguiling his sorrows in music, which is very common, as you will find, in all the old romances. It was one of the excesses of his passion, Bel."

" To be singing my name in doggerel couplets on the highway ! I assure you I don't forgive him for such passion !" interrupted the other.

" If the gods have not made him poetical," replied Harvey, " you should not blame him for that."

" Talk to me of my hawk, cousin, and pray spare your jests ; for you see I need comfort."

"Ned," said Harvey, "is all the comfort I can give you, and if he does not bring back Fairbourne, I would advise you to take the miserable swain himself."

"Why do you talk to me so?" asked Bel.

"To tell you the truth," replied Harvey, "I have a reason for it. Ned, you know, is a good fellow. And here,—what is very natural,—he has fallen in love. He could not help that, you know! Well, it makes him silly, as it makes every man, except those who are so by nature, and they grow wise upon it. He is afraid to talk to you, because his heart gets in his mouth, and chokes him. I can see plainly enough what he wishes to say, and therefore I am determined, as you are my cousin, to say it for him. He wishes to tell you, that as you are inexorable, he has made up his mind to leave this country with Mark Littleton; and then, heaven knows where the poor fellow will go!"

"If no man was ever more in love than Ned Hazard," answered Bel, "the world would be sadly in want of romances. Why, cousin, it is impossible for him to be in earnest long enough to sum up his own thoughts upon the subject."

"How little do you know," cried Harvey, "of my poor friend Ned!"

"Know him, cousin!" exclaimed Bel, laughing, "you won't be so rash as to say Ned Hazard is a man of mystery? Why he is mirth itself."

"You mistake his madness for mirth, Bel; he is distracted, and, therefore, unaccountable for his actions."

"You are as mad as he, cousin Harvey. That is a pretty kind of love that plays off such merry-andrew tricks as Ned's mummery, with you to back him! Your tragedy of the Babes in the Wood, and your serenades under our windows, look very much like the doings of a distracted lover! Give me a man of reverential manners and dignity for a lover. Now, you know, Ned has none of that, cousin."

"Bel, you are as mad as either Ned or myself," exclaimed Harvey with a laugh, and taking both of Bel's hands; "you will marry some grave rogue or dull pedant, after all!"

"Cousin Harvey, I will not be catechized any longer," interrupted Bel impatiently; "here I come to fly a hawk, and lo, you engage me in a parley about Ned Hazard!"

"Well," replied Harvey, "I have discharged my duty. I see Ned is in a bad way. Poor devil! he ought never to have fallen in love. But it was not his fault. I thought it but just to tell you what I feared. Ned will leave us: and who knows but he may take another trip around the Horn! He will then throw himself into the great struggle for freedom in that hemisphere; become a general, of course; push his conquests across the Andes; and perhaps, reaching the heights of Chimborazo, will fall in some splendid battle, having first engraved with his sword the name of the cold Bel Tracy upon the ice of the glacier. And there he will leave that mighty mountain to tell posterity how burning was his love, how frozen was his mistress! Now, there's dignity and superlative sentiment both for you! Let Swansdown himself beat that if he can!"

"Why what an irreclaimable jester are you!" cried Bel; "I do not wonder that Edward Hazard should be so little serious, with such a companion!"

"Then, Bel, you do not like him?"

"On the contrary," replied Bel, "I like him exceedingly; as well as a brother. But depend upon it, I cannot entertain him in any other relation, until perhaps—"

"He has learned to be more sentimental and scrupulous in his behavior," interrupted her cousin.

"At least," said Bel, in a more serious manner, and evidently as if she felt what she said, "until he ceases to jest upon me."

"That's in confidence," said Harvey; "I understand you.

Ned has some schooling to go through yet. At all events, he must not leave Swallow Barn."

" If you are in earnest, cousin,—for indeed I do not know how to take you,—and he thinks of such a thing, I should be very sorry for it," said Bel.

During this conversation, Bel had taken Harvey's arm, and they had wandered towards the bank of the river, and from thence homeward, so much engrossed with the topics that Harvey had brought into discussion, that Bel gradually forgot her hawk, and fell into a confidential communion upon a subject that was nearer to her feelings than she chose to confess. The particulars of this further discourse, which was continued until they had reached the house, after our arrival at The Brakes, was not all related to me by Harvey; but the impression made upon his mind was, that Ned Hazard had not taken the pains to conciliate Bel's favor, which the value of the prize deserved. He did not doubt that she had an affection for him; but still, she spoke as if there were prejudices to be overcome, and scruples to be conquered, which stood in the way of her decision. Harvey's object, under all his levity of manner, was to ascertain whether Ned's quest was hopeless or otherwise; and he had therefore availed himself of the adventure of the hawk, to draw her thoughts into the current indicated in the above conversation. His conclusion from it all was, that Ned must either reform his behavior towards Bel, or relinquish his pretensions. Harvey added, " Ned is falling rapidly into that privileged intimacy that is fatal to the pretensions of a lover. This jesting, careless friendship will lodge him, in a short time, high and dry upon a shoal in her regard, where he will become a permanent and picturesque landmark. He will acquire the enviable distinction of a brother, as she begins to call him already, and he will be certain to be invited to her wedding."

CHAPTER XXVII.

WHILST Harvey and myself were still discoursing over the matters I have imperfectly brought to my reader's attention in the last chapter, Ned Hazard opened the door of the study, and came towards us, with an animated step and a countenance full of merriment. He told us, with much boasting, of his own participation in the exploit, and of the inestimable value of his services, that the old family lawsuit, which had been so tempest-tost and weather-beaten, was at length happily towed into port: that the Apple-pie was once more elevated to the rank of a frontier stream, upon whose banks the whilom hostile clans of the Tracy and the Hazard might now assemble in peace: that after wading through a sea of manuscript to oblige Mr. Tracy, and hearing many wise legal apothegms from his lips, and turning Swansdown's brain topsy-turvy with points and discriminations, merely to prevent him from marring the decision, Mr. Wart had succeeded in bringing the matter to a close, and was now busy in drawing up a formal judgment upon the case. "Philly," continued Ned, "is like to suffer injury from retention. It is as much as he can do to prevent himself from bursting out into a horse-laugh at every line he writes. But he is, I believe, somewhat overawed by Mr. Tracy, who takes the whole matter as gravely as if it were a state business. The best of it is, Swansdown is in doubt as to the propriety of the decision, and, with very little encouragement, would bring in a verdict against The Brakes. Philly's whole endeavor, for the last hour, has therefore been to mystify the case in such a manner as to keep Swansdown from insisting upon the inquiry, whether the mill-pond oozed away in a series of years, or was carried of by some violent accident. Now, you know it is a fact of common notoriety, that it was swept off in a tremendous flood. Philly, finding Swansdown likely to dwell on this circumstance, has made a masterly diversion upon a point of law that has happily quieted the gentleman's scruples. He says, the act of God works no man injury, and that if the dam has been swept away suddenly, it makes no difference, because it would have wasted away at any rate, by this time; and that it is extremely probable it was very much diminished before the flood; that if, therefore, it was not an absolute, imperceptible decrease, it was *quasi* a decrease of that nature. I think Philly has written something of this sort in his report. This jargon has so confounded Swansdown, as to set him to gazing at the ceiling in a brown study, and has thrown Mr. Tracy into an ecstasy of admiration at Philly's learning and acuteness. All this time, however, Mr. Wart has had his mouth puckered up with repressed laughter, which so affected me, that I could not remain in the room. I have drunk half a dozen glasses of water, and have been thrumming my fingers against the window-panes ever since this debate has been in agitation, merely to escape notice. Mr. Tracy has, in consequence, given me some sharp rebukes for my inattention to the momentous principles that Philly has been expounding. In short, I was obliged to make my escape."

" Will they admit bystanders," asked Harvey, " to be present at the deliberation ?"

" Oh! cheerfully," replied Ned; " but you must be very careful how you behave. Mr. Tracy is in the most nervous state imaginable. He is greatly delighted with the result of the trial;
but I don't think he is quite satisfied with Philly's waiving an
opinion upon the points of law connected with the deed. It is a
little curious to observe how pertinaciously the old gentleman
adheres to his notion of the facts. He has twenty times asserted
that the site of the mill-dam was never surveyed: and there they
have the very document of the survey itself, which is shown to
him every time he makes the assertion; he looks at it, and, as
we all suppose, is convinced;—but, in the next minute, commen-
ces anew with the same objection. I remarked that at length he
began to get out of humor at this sort of contradiction."

" The old gentleman," said Harvey, " is turning a little sour
with age. His temperament is growing chilly; his constitution
resembles that waterish, gravelly soil that you see sometimes
around a spring, where nothing grows but sheep-sorrel."

In a few moments we all repaired to the study. Philly Wart
and Swansdown were standing together, at the moment of our
entrance, in one corner of the room. The former held in his hand
a sheet of paper upon which the award was written, and was
silently reading it over, whilst his features expressed that comic
perturbation which a man surprised by some droll incident in a
church might be supposed to wear. He looked at us, upon our
approach, from beneath his spectacles, as his chin rested upon
his waistcoat, and smiled, but read on. Swansdown's face wore
that air of gravity and doubt, which I can fancy was legible in
the countenances of the signers of the Declaration of Independence, after they had put their names to that important document. At the table, with his back to these two, sat Mr. Tracy,
with a silk handkerchief folded and laid upon his head, to guard
him against the breeze that blew in through the window. His

hands were spread flat upon the board, in such a manner as to throw his elbows directly outwards from his body ; and he was casting a keen glance over the field of papers that lay unfolded before him. As soon as he was aware of our approach, he raised his head, looked at us with an expression of good humor, and re-marked, with his usual slow and distinct utterance,—

" Our friends have had a serious job of it to-day," nodding to-wards the papers strewed over the table, " but I believe, by dint of perseverance, we have reached the bottom at last."

We offered him our congratulations upon the event; but he absolutely refused to allow us to express any pleasure at his suc-cess, lest it might be considered as triumphing over his friend Meriwether. He declared that moderation in victory was a sen-timent that he desired particularly to evince in this case ; and he therefore checked our advances with a gravity that made us laugh. The old gentleman, however, was too full of his victory to preserve his consistency in this humor; for when Harvey Riggs insinuated a compliment to his judgment, by reminding him that he had frequently predicted the result, whenever this case should come to be fairly considered, he laughed outright for some moments, with his hand across his eyes, and concluded by saying—

" I am not apt to take up fancies unadvisedly. I generally reflect upon my grounds. But, dogs take our friend Wart! he is for pruning the case so much, that he must needs slur over all my law touching the phraseology of the deed. Ha, ha, ha! I see his drift: he will spare our friend Meriwether. Well, well! it is quite immaterial what shot brings down the pigeon, so that we get him, ha, ha, ha !"

" A good judge," said Mr. Wart, speaking from the spot where we first found him, " will never decide more than the case requires. I am not apt to deal in *obiter dicta*."

" The commonwealth has done you injustice, Mr. Wart," said Mr. Tracy ; " you should have been on the bench long ago."

" I am afraid my chance has gone for ever now," replied Philly, " for here Mr. Swansdown and myself have overruled the opinions of the whole Court of Appeals."

" These courts are obstinate bodies," said the old gentleman ; " it is a difficult thing to bring them to reason, when they have once got a fantasy into their brains. And now, Mr. Wart, pray favor the gentlemen with the reading of your award."

" I will," said Philly, " if I can make out my own scrawl. It has been a rapid business. We have administered justice *velis levatis*, I may say, considering the nature of the case, and the time we have been at it."

Upon this, Philly began to read aloud. The document in his hand, although hastily prepared, was drawn out with all the technical verbiage that belonged to the nature of such an instrument. It gave a brief history of the controversy from the commencement, which part Philly ran over with a hurried voice ; but he assumed a more deliberate manner when he came to the grounds of the decision, stating, " that the said arbitrators, having duly considered all and singular the letters, declarations in writing, and other papers touching the exposition of the intent of the said parties, and their motives for making and receiving the said grant, and also duly considering the deeds appertaining thereunto, and all other matters connected therewith, have not found it necessary to declare their opinion upon the true intent and effect in law of the said deeds, by reason that certain facts and matters in evidence have come to the knowledge of the said arbitrators, whereby the original proprietary rights and relations of the said parties litigant—"

" I wish you would change that word ' litigant,' Mr. Wart," said Mr. Tracy, who during the reading of the award sat listening with fixed attention, and nodding his head, somewhat in the manner of one keeping time in a concert: "I don't like that word; it would imply that Mr. Meriwether and myself have been litigious, which is too strong a term."

Philly turned up his eyes with a queer expression, inclined his head sidewise, and raised one shoulder so as to touch his ear.

—"I wish you would say, 'of the parties laying claim to the land in dispute;' I think that would be better."

"As you please," replied Philly, approaching the table, and altering the phrase in conformity with this suggestion.

—"Of the said parties claiming the land in dispute," continued the counsellor, "have grown to be dependent upon the principles of law brought into view by the said facts and matters in evidence : which said facts and matters in evidence show that the said mill-dam, herein abovementioned, was originally bounded by courses and distances, as laid off and described in the survey thereof by a certain Jeremiah Perkins, made under the direction of the said Gilbert Tracy and Edward Hazard, as appears by the said survey filed in the proceedings in this case."

"I don't think the site of the dam was laid off by course and distance," said Mr. Tracy, interrupting the lawyer.

"The paper is here," replied Philly, stooping over the table, and producing it.

Mr. Tracy took it, and put it down again. "It must be a spurious document that," he remarked gravely.

The truth was, this paper, which had been always kept at Swallow Barn, presented a fact that completely overthrew one of Mr. Tracy's strongest positions, namely, that as the deed granted so much land only as might be used by the dam, the portion granted was necessarily mutable, and incapable of being confined to specific boundaries. This document of the survey, therefore, offended his sight whenever it was produced. And as it had but recently been brought to his consideration, he had pondered too long over the case, in its other aspects, to be able to accommodate his conceptions to this new state of things. It was impossible to break the crust of his prejudices, which now enveloped him like a suit of mail.

"I thought," said Philly, with a conciliatory inclination of his head, "we had settled this point before."

"Aye, aye," replied the old gentleman, recollecting himself, "go on, sir!"

—"And it hath also appeared that when the said grist-mill fell into disuse and decay, the mill-dam aforesaid was gradually drained of the water therein contained, by the action of wind and weather, in such wise that, during the space of twenty-one years, the bed or site of the said dam became derelict by slow and imperceptible degrees ; save and except that by a certain severe tempest, about the period of the vernal equinox, in the year seventeen hundred and ——, the actual date not being precisely known, a portion of the said dam was carried away ; which, being the act of God, that doth no man harm, it is considered ought not to prejudice the rights of the parties ; and the more especially as it hath appeared to these arbitrators, that the said mill-dam had before that time fallen into desuetude, and, notwithstanding the said tempest, would, in the nature of things, have dwindled down, contracted, and wasted away into the present natural and original channel of the said Apple-pie Branch.   And further, it hath appeared that neither of the said parties litigant —"

"I will alter the word here also," said Philly, taking the pen, and inserting the same periphrasis as before.

Mr. Tracy nodded, and the counsellor proceeded—

—"Has had occasion, during the time aforesaid, to exercise any acts of ownership over the said land, seeing that the same was barren and unproductive, and altogether unfit for any purpose of tillage,—"

" True," said Mr. Tracy.

—"Therefore the said arbitrators, carefully weighing the said several facts with full and ample consideration, and having heard all that the said Isaac Tracy on the one side, and Edward Hazard, for and on behalf of the said Francis Meriwether, on the other side, had to urge in respect of their said several pretensions —"

" Devilish little on behalf of Frank !" whispered Ned Hazard.

—"Do, in virtue of the powers vested in them by this reference, award, adjudge, and determine, for the complete and final ending of the said dispute, and for the quieting of actions in all time to come, that the land so left by the recession of the waters as aforesaid, shall henceforth be deemed and taken as followeth, that is to say; all that piece or parcel of land lying eastwardly between the bank of the said Apple-pie Branch, as the same now exists, and the former margin of the said mill-dam, bounding on the line of the tract called the Brakes, is hereby declared to have reverted to the original proprietors of the said tract called the Brakes, to them and their heirs for ever: and that the main channel of the said Apple-pie Branch shall be the only true and established conterminous boundary line of the said tracts of the Brakes and Swallow Barn respectively."

" Very conclusive and satisfactory !" cried Mr. Tracy, rising from his chair.

" There you are, gentlemen," said Philly, throwing the paper down upon the table, " exactly *in statu quo ante bellum.* It is a great thing, Mr. Swansdown, to pacify these border feuds."

" I have always permitted myself," replied the worthy thus addressed, " to indulge the hope that our intercession would prove advantageous to the permanent interests of the families. It has been a case, certainly, attended with its difficulties; and has given rise to some curious and recondite principles of jurisprudence."

"Very curious and recondite!" said Philly, looking archly around him. "It has been a perfect drag-net case. We have fished up a great deal of law, my dear sir!"

"I confess I have been sadly puzzled," replied Swansdown, "with the intricacies of this whole proceeding."

"So have I," said Philly. "But you have had much the worst of it. For there, in the first place, you were lost in the brambles; then, you were soused in the mud; and after that, you were torn with briers: you have some of the marks upon your face yet. Then, you lost entirely our chase of the fox; but I believe you are not fond of that, sir?"

"These were trifles," replied the other. "I alluded to the conflicting opinions."

"I understood you," interrupted the lawyer. "It takes a good nose and a fleet foot to follow one of these little old-fashioned ejectments through its doublings."

Saying this, Philly opened the door of the study, and walked into the hall, wiping his spectacles with his handkerchief, and casting strange and comic looks upon Hazard, Harvey, and myself, who followed him. He was highly excited with the proceedings of the morning, and being relieved from the restraint of Mr. Tracy's presence, gave vent to his feelings by amusing remarks, and a sly, half-quiet, and half jocular demeanor, which never broke out into any open fit of laughter, nor yet fell to the level of his ordinary calmness.

It was now the family dinner-hour, and the household assembled in one of the parlors, where the result of the arbitration was made known, and gave rise to a great deal of animated conversation.

The behavior of Mr. Tracy at the dinner-table was punctilious and precise. He was even more lavish than usual of the personal civilities that characterize his manners at all times; and it was observable, that during the whole time that he mingled in the family groups where the decision which had just been made was a subject of constant recurrence, he never permitted an expression relating to it to escape his lips. He sat but a few moments after the cloth was drawn, leaving the table in the occupation of his company, and retired to the study, where he employed himself amongst the papers belonging to the law-suit.

As the long afternoon wore away, the boundary line and all its concerns were forgotten ; and our party fell into the various amusements their situation afforded. At length, the hour came for our return to Swallow Barn. Prudence, at the persuasion cf the ladies, had consented to remain during the night. Ned Hazard informed Mr. Tracy that he was requested by Meriwether to invite the whole family, with Mr. Swansdown, to dinner at Swallow Barn the next day. The old gentleman expressed great pleasure in accepting the invitation, and the rest promised to keep the appointment without fail.

Having dispatched these matters, Mr. Wart and Rip mounted their horses, and rode slowly down the hill from the mansion. But just as Hazard, who had delayed a moment after his comrades, was leaving the door, his horse, grown restive by seeing his two companions moving off, after neighing, and tossing up his head, and champing his bit, made a sudden start, broke his bridle, and went off at full speed, leaping and flinging himself into wild and playful motions as he disappeared in the direction of the road.

All pursuit was vain. And as it was apparent that he would make the best of his way to his own stable, Ned got into the carriage with the little girls and myself ; and, followed by Wilful, we were wheeled off from the Brakes ·as rapidly as old Carey could urge his mettlesome cattle forward.

CHAPTER XXVIII.

THE GOBLIN SWAMP.

THE sun was not above half an hour high when we took our departure from the Brakes; and the heat of the atmosphere was beginning to yield to the partial distillation of the dew, and the slow invasion of the night breeze. The road lay principally along the river, upon a bank some ten or twelve feet above the tide, shaded with low black-jacks, dogwood, cedar, or tall pines. It occasionally digressed to head an inlet, or thread a brake; and sometimes extended, with a single meandering track, through the neighboring fields, which were guarded,—according to a common arrangement in the Old Dominion,—by a succession of peculiarly inconvenient, rickety, and weather-worn gates, that dragged heavily upon their wooden hinges, and swung to again, with a misdirected aim at their awkward bolts, to the imminent peril of the tails of all way-faring animals that travelled through them.

In a short time, we reached a point where the road turned abruptly from the river and took an inland direction, making a circuit of a mile or more, to pass the famous Apple-pie, which it does at some distance below the old mill, so conspicuous in my former sketches. At this turn Ned Hazard proposed that we should perform the rest of our journey on foot. He wished to show me the Goblin Swamp; a region of marsh, about half a mile distant, formed by the diffusion of the Apple-pie over the flat grounds, near its confluence with the James River. An old road had once traversed the swamp at this place; and the remains of the causeway were yet, Ned affirmed, sufficiently solid to afford a passage to pedestrians; besides, the Goblin Swamp showed to great advantage about twilight.

We accordingly committed our little companions to the guardianship of Carey; and, quitting the coach, entered a wood that bordered the road, where we soon found ourselves involved in a labyrinth of young pine-trees springing up so close together as almost to forbid a passage through them. The ground was strewed with a thick coat of pine-straw,—as the yellow sheddings of this tree are called,—so slippery as to render it difficult to walk over it; and the tangled branches caught in our clothes, and frequently struck our hats from our heads. But we succeeded at last in gaining an obscure path, so much embowered in shade as to be scarcely discernible. This conducted us through the mazes of the wood, and in a few moments we emerged upon the confines of an open country.

Before us lay a plain, surrounded by forest which in front towered above a copse that sprang from an extensive marsh at the further extremity of the plain. The earth was clothed with a thin vesture of parched grass; and the still distinct furrows of ancient cornfields furnished proof that the tract had been, at some remote period, under cultivation, but long since abandoned, perhaps on account of its sterility. A few clumps of meagre persimmon-trees were scattered over this forsaken region, and deep gullies, washed into the gravelly soil, exposed to view its signal poverty.

Somewhere near the middle of this open ground stood a solitary, low brick chimney, conspicuous for its ample fire-place, and surrounded by a heap of ruins, to which a more striking air of desolation was added by a luxuriant growth of weeds that had taken root in the rank compost formed by the wreck of household timber. Amongst these relics of former habitation were the vestiges of a draw-well, choked by the wash of the land; the weeds sprang from its mouth; and the tall post, with the crotch in its upper extremity, still supported the long piece of timber that balanced the bucket, according to a device yet in use in many parts of the country. Immediately around the ruin, in what was once the curtilage of the dwelling, a few crabbed fruit-trees, with chalky joints, and bowed down with years, flung their almost leafless and distorted limbs athwart the mouldering homestead. There were also to be seen, about fifty paces off, a black heap of dross, and some faint traces of the fire of a former smithy, of which the evidence was more unequivocal in the remains of a door, on which was burnt the figure of a horse-shoe.

When we arrived at this spot the sun was just peering, with his enlarged disk, through the upper branches of the trees, in the western horizon. The clouds were gorgeous with the golden and purple tints that give such magnificence to our summer evenings; and the waning light, falling on the volume of forest around us, communicated a richer gloom to its shades, and magnified the gigantic branches of some blasted oaks on the border of the plain, as they were seen relieved against the clear sky. Long and distorted shadows fell from every weed, bush, and tree, and contributed, with the forlorn aspect of the landscape, to impress us with an undefined and solemn sensation, that for a moment threw us into silence. Flights of crows traversed the air above our heads, and sang out their discordant vespers, as they plied their way to a distant roost; the fish-hawk had perched upon the highest naked branch of the tallest oak, and at intervals was seen to stretch forth his wing and ruffle his feathers, as if adjusting his position for the night. All animated objects that inhabited this region seemed to be busy with individual cares ; and the nocturnal preparations for rest or prey resounded from every quarter.

Hazard, taking advantage of the impression made by the sombre imagery around us, as we marched onward to the ruin, threw out some hints that we were now upon a haunted spot, and began to converse in a lower tone, and walk closer to my side, with an air of mystery and fear, put on to sort with the nature of the story he was telling. The ruin, he informed me, was formerly the habitation of Mike Brown, who had strange doings with the devil, and both Mike and his companion were frequently seen in the swamp after dark; the negroes, he said, and many of the white people about the country, held this place in great terror; which, he believed, was one reason why the road that formerly crossed the marsh at this place, had been disused. Certainly, the devil and Mike Brown could not have chosen a more secluded and barren waste for their pranks.

At length we reached the opposite side of the plain, where it became necessary to halt, and examine more minutely our road. Ned was under great embarrassment to discover the old causeway. The shrubbery had grown up so thick as to render this a task of uncertain accomplishment. There were several paths leading into the morass, made by the tramp of cattle. These so far perplexed my companion, that he was obliged to confess his ignorance of the right way. We determined, however, to go on ; the approaching night began already to darken our view, and the undertaking seemed to be sufficiently perilous, even in daylight. I kept pace with Hazard, and shared with him the difficulties of a path that at every step became more intricate; until, at last, we found ourselves encompassed by deep pools of stagnant water, with a footing no better than that afforded by a mossy islet, scarcely large enough for one person to stand upon, where we were obliged to cling to the bushes for support; whilst the soft texture of the earth yielded to our weight, and let in the water above our shoe-tops.

Here Ned began to swear that the place was strangely altered since he had last visited it, and to charge himself with a loss of memory, in not knowing better how to get through this wilderness. He protested that Mike Brown or his comrade had bewitched him, and brought him into this dilemma, as a punishment for his rashness. " I wish their devilships," he continued, " would condescend to favor us with the assistance of one of their imps, until we might arrive safely beyond the confines of their cursed dominion. What ho, good Mr. Belzebub!" he cried out jocularly, " have you no mercy on two foolish travellers ?"

Ned had no sooner made this invocation, which he did at the top of his voice, than we heard, at a distance from us, the indistinct rustling of leaves, as of one brushing through them, and the frequent plash of a footstep treading through the marsh. The sounds indicated the movement of the object towards us, and it became obvious that something was fast making its way to the spot where we stood.

"Truly," said Ned, " that Mr. Belzebub is a polite and civil demon. He scarce has notice of our distresses, before he comes himself to relieve them."

By this time a grotesque figure became faintly visible through the veil of twigs and branches that enveloped us. All that we could discern was the murky outline of something resembling a man. His stature was uncommonly low and broad ; apparently he wore no coat, and upon what seemed his head was an odd-shaped cap, that fitted closely to his skull.

" Who goes there?" cried Ned briskly, as the figure came to a halt, and looked wildly about; " ghost or devil?"

" Neither," replied the figure, with a husky voice,—such as that of a man with a bad cold,—and at the same instant stepping boldly before us, " but an old sinner, who is a little of both: a sort of castaway, that has more gray hairs than brains; yet not so much of a buzzard as to be ignorant that the round-about way is often the nearest home." Hereupon, the figure broke out into a loud, hollow, and unnatural laugh.

"What, Hafen? Is it possible? what, in the name of the foul fiend, brings you here?" cried out Ned, recognizing the speaker, who was Hafen Blok, a short, thick-set, bandy-legged personage, bearing all the marks of an old man, with a strangely weather-beaten face, intersected by as many drains as the rugged slope of a sand-hill. He had a large mouth, disfigured with tobacco, and unprovided with any show of teeth. He had moreover a small upturned nose, a low forehead, and diminutive eyes that glistened beneath projecting brows of grizzled and shaggy hair. For a man verging upon sixty-five, his frame was uncommonly vigorous; although it was apparent that he was lame of one leg. His headgear, which had attracted our attention even at a distance, was nothing more than the remnant of an antique cocked hat, now divested of its flaps, so as to form a close, round cap. His scraggy throat was covered with a prurient beard of half an inch in length, and laid open to view between the collar of a coarse brown shirt. Across his arm was flung a coat of some homely material, with huge metal buttons appearing to view; and his trowsers and shoes were covered with the mud of the swamp. A belt crossed his shoulder, to which was suspended a bag of hempen cloth; and in his hand he bore two or three implements for trapping. There was a saucy waggishness in his gestures, of which the effect was heightened by the fox-like expression of his countenance, and the superlatively vagabond freedom of his manners.

"You are well met, Hafen," continued Ned. " The devil of the swamp could never have sent us a better man. How are we to get through the bog?"

"It is easy enough, Mister Ned Hazard, for a traveller who knows a tussock from a bulrush," replied Hafen.

"And pray, how old should he be to arrive at that knowledge?"

"He should be old enough to catch a black snake in the water, Mister Ned; or, at least, he ought to have cut his eye-teeth," said Hafen, with another of his strange, hollow laughs.

"Save your jest for dry land, old fellow!" interrupted Hazard, "and tell us plainly how we shall find our way to Swallow Barn without going round."

"They who have the folly to get in, ought to carry wit enough with them to get out," replied Hafen dryly.

"Come, old gentleman," said Ned, with a tone of entreaty, "we shall take an ague if you keep us here. It grows late; and if we can save a mile by crossing the swamp, who knows but you may be all the better for it when we get safe to the other side?"

"You see, sir," said Hafen, with more respect in his manner than before, "a fool's counsel is sometimes worth the weighing; but an old dog, you know, Mister Ned, can't alter his way of barking; so you and that gentleman must excuse my saucy tongue; and if you will follow me, I will put you across the swamp as clean as a bridge of gold. Though I don't mean to insinuate, Mister Hazard, that you couldn't soon learn the way yourself."

Saying this, he conducted us back to the margin of the marsh, and passing some distance higher up, entered the thicket again by the path of the old causeway, along which we proceeded with no other caution than carefully to step in the places pointed out by Hafen, who led the way with the vigorous motion of a man in the prime of life; and in a brief space we found ourselves in safety on the opposite side.

Here we gave our guide a liberal reward for his services, which so elated the old man as to rouse all his talkativeness.

Hafen is a person of some notoriety in this district. He is a Hessian by birth, and came to America with Count Donop, during the war of the Revolution, as a drummer, not above fourteen years old; and he was present at the action at Red Bank on the Delaware, when that unfortunate officer met his fate. He was afterwards engaged in the southern campaigns, when he found means to desert to the American lines in time to witness the surrender of Lord Cornwallis. At the close of the war Hafen took up his quarters in the neighborhood of Williamsburg, where he set up the trade of a tinker, as being most congenial with his vagrant propensities. Being a tolerable performer on the violin, he contrived to amass a sufficient capital to purchase an instrument, with which he ever afterwards sweetened his cares and divided his business, wandering through the country, where he mended the kettles, and fiddled himself into the good graces, of every family within the circuit of his peregrinations. This career was interrupted by but one episode, which happened in the year seventeen hundred and ninety-one, when, being attacked by an unusual restlessness, he enlisted in the army, and marched with St. Clair against the Indians. The peppering he got in the disastrous event of that expedition, brought him home in the following year with a more pacific temper and a lame leg. It was like Cincinnatus returning to his plough. He took up his nippers and fiddle again, and devoted himself to the affairs of the kitchen and parlor. Being one of those mortals whose carelessness of accommodation is mathematically proportioned to their aversion to labor, Hafen was equally idle and ragged, and contrived generally, by a shrewd and droll humor, to keep himself in good quarters, though upon a footing that rendered him liable at all times to be dismissed without ceremony. He has always been distinguished for his stores of old ballads; and the women about the families where he gained a seat in the corner of the kitchen fire, were indebted to him for the most accepted versions of the Gosport

Tragedy, Billy Taylor, and some other lamentable ditties record-
ing the fates of "true lovyers" and "ladies fair and free," which
he taught them to sing in long metre, with a touching sadness,
and agreeably to their authentic nasal tunes. Besides this, he
was the depositary of much of the legendary lore of the neighborhood, picked up from the old people of the Revolutionary time :
and, according to his own account, he had a familiar acquaintance
with sundry witches, and was on good terms with every reputable
ghost that haunted any house along the James river.

These characteristics gave him many immunities, and often
gained him access to bower and hall ; and as he was gifted with
a sagacity which always knew how to flatter his patrons, he was
universally regarded as a well-meaning, worthless, idle stroller,
who, if he could not make himself useful, was at least in nobody's
way. On all festive occasions his violin was an ample recom-
mendation ; and as he could tell fortunes, and sing queer old
songs, he was connected in the imaginations of the younger folks
with agreeable associations. From these causes he was seldom
an unwelcome visitant ; and not being fastidious on the score of
personal entertainment, he was well content to get his supper in
the kitchen, a dram,—for which he had the craving of the daughter of the horseleech,—and the privilege of a corner in the hay-
loft.

Of late Hafen had lost some favor by his increasing propen-
sity for drink, and by the suspicion, that stood upon pretty strong
proofs, of not being over scrupulous in his regard for the rights
of property. Besides, for many years past, his tinkering had
fallen into disuse, by reason, as he said, of these Yankee pedlers
breaking up his honest calling. So that, at this time, Hafen may
be considered like an old hound whose nose has grown cold. His
employments are, in consequence, of a much more miscellaneous
character than formerly.

Such was the individual who had rescued us from the perils of the swamp, and who now, having brought us to firm ground, had no further pretext for keeping our company. But he was not so easily shaken off. His predominant love of gossip took advantage of the encouragement he had already met, and he therefore strode resolutely in our footsteps, a little in the rear, talking partly to himself and partly to us, without receiving any response. At length, finding that no further notice was likely to be taken of him, he ventured to say, in a doubtful tone—

" The next time the gentlemen have a fancy to cross this way, perhaps they'll think a few pennies in the tinker's pouch, better than a pair of swamp stockings."

" And many thanks beside, Hafen," said I. " But how came you to be so close at hand this evening ?"

" O sir," replied Hafen, availing himself of this overture, and coming up to our side, " bless you ! this is a quite natural sort of place to me. I am too good for nothing to be afraid of spirits, for I am not worth the devil's fetching, sir ;" here he laughed in his usual singular way. " The swamp is a very good mother to me, although I am a simple body, and can pick up a penny where rich folks would never think of looking for it."

" How is that ?" I asked.

" There is a power of muskrats about these parts, sir," he replied, " and with the help of these tools," holding up his snares, " I can sometimes gather a few ninepences with no more cost than a wet pair of breeches, which is fisherman's luck, sir, and of no account, excepting a little rheumatism, and not even that, if a man has plenty of this sort of physic."

So saying, he thrust his hand into his bag, and pulled out a green flask that contained a small supply of whiskey.

" Perhaps the gentlemen wouldn't be above taking a taste themselves ?" he continued, " for it's a mighty fine thing against the ague."

We excused ourselves; and Hafen put the flask to his mouth, and smacking his lips as he concluded his draught, observed—

"It's a kind of milk for old people. and not bad for young ones."

"What success have you had to-day, with your traps?" I inquired.

"I have come off poorly," he replied; "the vermin are getting shy, and not like what they used to be. Now, I have got no more than two rats. Some days even I don't get that much."

"Then, I take it, Hafen, you do not thrive much in the world," I remarked.

"Ah, sir," replied Hafen, still holding the flask in his hand, and beginning to moralize, "it is a great help to a man's conscience to know that he earns his bread lawfully: a poor man's honesty is as good as a rich man's gold. I am a hobbling sort of person, and no better than I ought to be, but I never saw any good come out of deceit. Virtue is its own reward, as the parson says; and away goes the devil when he finds the door shut against him. I am no scholar, but I have found that out without reading books—"

At this moment the half-smothered cluck of a fowl was heard from Hafen's bag.

"God never sends mouths," continued Hafen, "but he sends meat, and any man who has sense enough to be honest, will never want wit to know how to live; but he must plough with such oxen as he has: some people have bad names, but all are not thieves that dogs bark at."

"So, you have only taken two muskrats to-day?" said Ned. "Have you nothing else in the bag?"

"Nothing else, Mister Hazard."

"Are they dead or alive?" asked Ned.

"Oh dead! dead as old Adam! they were swinging by their necks long enough to strangle nine lives out of them."

"This swamp is haunted, Hafen," said Ned archly.

"Yes, sir," replied Hafen, "there are certainly some queer doings here sometimes. But, for my share, I never saw any thing in these hobgoblins to make an honest man afraid. All that you have to do is to say your prayers, and that will put any devilish thing out of heart."

"Did you ever know a dead muskrat," asked Ned, "to be changed into a live pullet? Now, master honest tinker! I can conjure up a devil to do that very thing."

Here Hafen put on a comic leer, and hesitated for a moment, as if collecting himself, whilst he was heard giving out a confused chuckling laugh. At length he observed,—

"Mister Ned Hazard has always got some trick. I often tell folks Mister Hazard is a pleasant man."

"See now," said Hazard, striking the bag with his hand, "does not that sound marvellously like a clucking hen?"

"Oh, I grant you," exclaimed Hafen, assuming a tone of surprise, "I had like to have forgotten; when I said there was nothing but the rats in my bag, I set no account upon a pullet that Sandy Walker gave me this evening, for putting a few rivets in his copper still."

"Come, Hafen," said Ned, "no lies amongst friends. Sandy Walker never owned a still in his life."

"Did I say a still, Mister Hazard? I spoke in a sort of uncertain way, which was as much as to signify,—" said Hafen, puzzling his brain for a better account of the matter, and twisting his face into some shrewd contortions, which at last ended by his coming close to Hazard, and putting his finger against his nose, as he said in a half whisper, "it was an old grudge against Sandy that I had, upon account of his abusing me before company for drinking, and insinuating that I made free with a shirt that his wife lost from the line in a high wind, last April, and some other old scores I had. So, I thought a pullet was small damages enough for such a scandal. Pick-up law is the cheapest law for a poor man, Mister Hazard; and possession is nine points out of ten. Isn't that true?" Here he laughed again.

" I think a gentleman who brags so much of his honesty and virtue, might practise a better code. But as between you and Sandy," said Ned, "your merits are so nearly equal, that take what you can, and keep what you get, is a pretty sound rule; although you are like to get the best of that bargain."

" Oh," replied Hafen, " I want nothing more than justice."

The night was now closing in fast. We were walking along a narrow tongue of land which stretched into the swamp, from the bosom of which, on either side, arose a forest of lofty trees, whose topmost branches were traced upon the sky with that bold configuration that may be remarked at the twilight, whilst the dusk rapidly thickened below, and flung its increasing gloom upon our path. Here and there a lordly cypress occurred to view, springing forth from the stagnant pool, and reposing in lurid shade. Half sunk in ooze, rotted the bole and bough of fallen trees, coated with pendent slime. The ground over which we trod took an easy impression from our footsteps; and the chilling vapor of the marsh, mingled with the heavy dew, was to be felt in the dampness of our clothes, and compelled us to button up our coats.

This dreary region was neither silent nor inanimate; but its inhabitants corresponded to the genius of the place. Clouds of small insects, crossed now and then by a whizzing beetle, played their fantastic gambols around our heads, displaying their minute and active forms against the western horizon, as they marshalled us upon our way. The night-hawk arose, at intervals, with a hoarse scream into this fading light, and swept across it with a graceful motion, sometimes whirling so near that we could hear the rush of his wing, and discern the white and spectral spot upon it, as he darted past our eyes. Thousands of fire-flies lit up the gloom, and sped about like sprites in masquerade; at one moment lifting their masks, as if to allure pursuit, and instantly again vanishing, as in a prankish jest. A populous congregation of frogs piped from the secret chambers of the fen with might and main. The whip-poor-will reiterated, with a fatiguing and melancholy recurrence, his sharp note of discord. The little catadid pierced the air with his shrill music. The foxfire,—as the country people call it,—glowed hideously from the cold and matted bosom of the marsh ; and, far from us, in the depths of darkness, the screech-owl sat upon his perch, brooding over the slimy pool, and whooping out a dismal curfew, that fell upon the air like the cries of a tortured ghost.

We trudged briskly upon our way, but almost without exchanging words; for the assemblage of striking objects in the scene had lulled us into silence. I do not wonder that a solitary traveller should grow superstitious, amidst such incentives to his imagination. Hafen followed our steps, and, as I fancied, completely subdued by faintheartedness. I thought he walked closer on our skirts than a man perfectly at ease would do, and his loquacity was entirely gone. He firmly believed in the stories of the Goblin Swamp, and I was anxious to get them from his own lips, as Hazard had given me to understand that I could not meet a better chronicler. With this purpose, I gave him timely encouragement to follow us to Swallow Barn. And now, having passed the confines of the wood, we found but little to attract our attention for the rest of the journey.

" You must tell me the story of Mike Brown to-night," said I to Hafen, as I invited him to bear us company.

In an instant, Hafen's imagination was full of the comforts of the kitchen at Swallow Barn, as well as of the self-consequence that belongs to a genuine story-teller. He consented with a saucy alacrity, and then remarked,—

"That the gentlemen always knew how to get something to please them out of Hafen; and that he always did like himself to keep company with quality."

It was after candlelight when we arrived at Swallow Barn.

CHAPTER XXIX.

STORY-TELLING.

In the time of the Revolution, and for a good many years after-wards, Old Nick enjoyed that solid popularity which, as Lord Mansfield expressed it, follows a man's actions rather than is sought after by them. But in our time he is manifestly falling into the sere and yellow leaf, especially in the Atlantic States. Like those dilapidated persons who have grown out at elbows by sticking too long to a poor soil, or who have been hustled out of their profitable prerogatives by the competition of upstart num-bers, his spritish family has moved off, with bag and baggage, to the back settlements. This is certain, that in Virginia he is not seen half so often now as formerly. A traveller in the Old Do-minion may now wander about of nights as dark as pitch, over commons, around old churches, and through graveyards, and all the while the rain may be pouring down with its solemn hissing sound, and the thunder may be rumbling over his head, and the wind moaning through the trees, and the lightning flinging its sulphurous glare across the skeletons of dead horses, and over the grizzly rawheads upon the tombstones ; and, even, to make the case stronger, a drunken cobbler may be snoring hideously in the church door, (being overtaken by the storm on his way home,) and every flash may show his livid, dropsical, carbuncled face,

like that of a vagabond corpse that had stolen out of his prison
to enjoy the night air ; and yet it is ten to one if the said traveller be a man to be favored with a glimpse of that old-fashioned,
distinguished personage who was wont to be showing his cloven
foot, upon much less provocation, to our ancestors. The old
crones can tell you of a hundred pranks that he used to play in their
day, and what a roaring sort of a blade he was. But, alas ! sin-
ners are not so chicken-hearted as in the old time. It is a terri-
bly degenerate age ; and the devil and all his works are fast
growing to be forgotten.

Except Mike Brown's humorsome pot-companion, I much
question if there is another legitimate goblin in the Old Dominion ; and in spite of Ned Hazard and Hafen Blok, who do all
they can to keep up his credit, I am much mistaken if he does
not speed away to the Missouri or the Rocky Mountains one of
these days, as fast and as silently as an absconding debtor. Lest,
therefore, his exploits should be lost to the world, I will veritably
record this " Chronicle of the Last of the Virginia Devils," as it
has been given to me by the credible Hafen, that most authentic
of gossips, as may be seen by the perusal of what I am going to
write.

The substance of this narrative—for I do not deny some
rhetorical embellishments—was delivered by Hafen after supper,
as we sat in the porch at Swallow Barn until midnight, Hafen
all the while puffing a short pipe, and only rising on his feet at
such times as his animation got beyond control, and inspired him
to act the scene he was describing. The witnesses were Mr.
Wart and Frank Meriwether, who sat just inside of the door, attended by Lucy and Vic, who for the greater part of the time
had their arms about Frank's neck ; and Mr. Chub, who, though
within hearing—for he was seated at the window, also smoking—
I do not believe paid much attention to the story ; although he

was heard once or twice to blow out a stream of smoke from his mouth, and say " balderbash !"—an epithet in common use with him. But there were Ned and myself close beside Hafen; and Rip, who sat on the steps in the open air, with his head occasionally turned over his shoulder, looking up at the story-teller with the most marked attention : and lastly, there were sundry wide-mouthed negroes, children and grown, who were clustered into a dusky group beneath the parlor window, just where a broad ray of candlelight fell upon them ; and who displayed their white teeth, like some of Old Nick's own brood, as they broke out now and then into hysterical, cowardly laughs, and uttered ejaculations of disbelief in Hafen's stories that showed the most implicit faith.

MIKE BROWN.

Mike Brown was a blacksmith, who belonged to Harry Lee's light-horse, and shod almost all the hoofs of the legion. He was a jolly, boisterous, red-faced fellow, with sandy hair, and light blue eyes so exceedingly blood-shot, that at a little distance off you could hardly tell that they were eyes at all. He had no leisure, during the Revolutionary war, to get them clarified ; for what with the smoke of his furnace, and keeping late hours on patroles, and hard drinking, his time was filled up to the entire disparagement of his complexion. He was a stark trooper, to whom no service came amiss, whether at the anvil or in the field, having a decisive muscle for the management of a piece of hot iron, and an especial knack for a marauding bout ; in which latter species of employment it was his luck to hold frequent velitations with the enemy, whereby he became notorious for picking up stragglers, cutting off baggage-wagons, and rifling rum-casks, and now and then, for easing a prisoner of his valuables. He could handle a broadsword as naturally as a sledge-hammer; and many a time has Mike brandished his blade above his beaver, and made it glitter in the sun, with a true dragoon flourish, whilst he gave the huzza to his companions as he headed an onset upon Tarleton's cavalry.

Towards the close of the war, he served with Colonel Washington, and was promoted to the rank of a sergeant for leading a party of the enemy into an ambuscade; and, in addition to this honor, the colonel made him a present of a full suit of regimentals, in which, they say, Mike was a proper-looking fellow. His black leather cap, with a strip of bearskin over it, and a white buck-tail set on one side, gave a martial fierceness to his red flannel face. A shad-bellied blue bobtail coat, turned up with broad buff, and meeting at the pit of his stomach with a hook and eye, was well adapted to show the breadth of his brawny chest, which was usually uncovered enough to reveal the shaggy mat of red hair that grew upon it. A buckskin belt, fastened round his waist by an immense brass buckle, sustained a sabre that rattled upon the ground when he walked. His yellow leather breeches were remarkable for the air of ostentatious foppery which they imparted to the vast hemisphere of his nether bulk; and, taken together with his ample horseman's boots, gave the richest effect to his short and thick legs, that, thus apparelled, might be said to be gorgeous specimens of the Egyptian column.

Such was the equipment of Sergeant Brown on all festival occasions; and he was said to be not a little proud of this reward of valor. On work days he exhibited an old pair of glazed, brown buckskin small-clothes, coarse woollen stockings, covered with spatterdashes made of untanned deer hide, and shoes garnished with immense pewter buckles; though, as to the stockings, he did not always wear them. Hose or no hose, it was all the same to

Mike! I am minute in mentioning the regimentals, because, for a
long time after the war, Sergeant Mike was accustomed to indue
himself in this identical suit on Sundays, and strut about with the
air of a commander-in-chief.

Mike's skill in horseshoes rendered him very serviceable in
the campaigns. On a damp morning, or over sandy roads, he
could trail Tarleton like a hound. It was only for Mike to examine the prints upon the ground, and he could tell, with astonishing precision, whether the horses that had passed were of his
own shoeing, how many were in company, how long they had gone
by, and whether at a gallop, a trot, or a walk ; whether they had
halted, or had been driving cattle, and, in fact, almost as many
particulars as might be read in a bulletin. Upon such occasions,
when appearances were favorable, he had only to get a few of his
dare-devils together, and Tarleton was sure to have some of Sergeant Brown's sauce in his pottage, before he had time to say
grace over it.

Mike used always to commence these adventures by drinking
the devil's health, as he called it ; which was done, very devoutly,
in a cup of rum seasoned with a cartridge of gunpowder, which,
he said, was a charm against sword cuts and pistol shot. When
his expedition was ended, he generally called his roll, marked
down the names of the killed, wounded and missing, by the scratch
of his black thumb-nail, and then returned the dingy scroll into
his pocket, with a knowing leer at the survivors, and the pithy
apothegm, which he repeated with a sincere faith, " that the devil
was good to his own." This familiarity with the "old gentleman,"
as Mike himself termed him, added to his trooper-like accomplishment of swearing till he made people's hair stand on end, begat a
common belief in the corps that he was on very significant terms
with his patron; and it was currently said, " that Mike Brown and
the devil would one day be wearing each other's shirts."

When the war was over, the sergeant found himself a disbanded hero, in possession of more liberty than he knew what to do with; a sledge and shoeing hammer; an old pair of bellows; a cabinet of worn-out horseshoes; a leather apron; his Sunday regimentals in tolerable repair; and a raw-boned steed, somewhat spavined by service :—to say nothing of a light heart, and an arm as full of sinew as an ox's leg. Considering all which things, he concluded himself to be a well-furnished and thriving person, and began to cast about in what way he should best enjoy his laurels, and the case the gods had made for him.

In his frequent ruminations over this momentous subject, he fell into some shrewd calculations upon the emolument and comfort which were likely to accrue from a judicious matrimonial partnership. There was at that time a thrifty, driving spinster, bearing the name of Mistress Ruth Saunders, who lived at the landing near Swallow Barn. This dame was now somewhat in the wane, and, together with her mother, occupied a little patch of ground on the river, upon which was erected a small one-storied frame house, the very tenement now in possession of Sandy Walker. Here her sire had, in his lifetime, kept a drinking tavern for the accommodation of the watermen who frequented the landing. The widow did not choose to relinquish a lucrative trade, and therefore kept up the house; whilst the principal cares of the hostelry fell upon the indefatigable and energetic Mistress Ruth, who, from all accounts, was signally endowed with the necessary qualifications which gave lustre to her calling.

Mike, being a free and easy, swaggering, sociable chap, and endowed with a remarkable instinct in finding out where the best liquors were to be had on the cheapest terms, had fallen insensibly into the habit of consorting with a certain set of idle, muddy-brained loiterers who made the widow Saunders' house their headquarters on Sunday afternoons, and as often on week days as they could find an excuse for getting together. And such had been Mike's habits of free entertainment in the army, that he acquired some celebrity for serving his comrades in the same manner that he had been used to treat the old Continental Congress; that is, he left them pretty generally to pay his scot.

By degrees, he began to be sensible to the slow invasion of the tender passion, which stole across his ferruginous bosom like a volume of dun smoke through a smithy. He hung about the bar-room with the languishing interest of a lover, and took upon himself sundry minute cares of the household, that excused some increase of familiarity. He laughed very loud whenever Mistress Ruth affected to be witty; and pounced, with his huge ponderous paws, upon the glasses, pitchers, or other implements which the dame fixed her eye upon, as needful in the occasions of her calling : not a little to the peril of the said articles of furniture :—for Mike's clutch was none of the gentlest, in his softest moods. In short, his assiduities soon made him master of the worshipful Mistress Ruth, her purse and person. She had seen the devil, according to the common computation, three times, and had been so much alarmed at his last visit that—the story goes—she swore an oath that she would marry his cousin-german, rather than be importuned by his further attentions. There is no knowing what a woman will do under such circumstances ! I believe myself, that Mistress Ruth chose sergeant Mike principally on account of his well known dare-devil qualities.

The dame whose worldly accomplishments and personal charms had dissolved the case-hardened heart of the redoubted black-smith of the legion, was altogether worthy of her lord. A succession of agues had spun her out into a thread some six feet long. A tide-water atmosphere had given her an ashen, dough face, sprinkled over with constellations of freckles, and exhibiting features somewhat tart from daily crosses. Her thin, bluish lips had something of the bitterness of the crab, with the astringency of the persimmon. Her hair, which was jet-black, was plastered across her brow with the aid of a little tallow, in such a manner as to give it a rigid smoothness, that pretty accurately typified her temper on holiday occasions, and also aided, by its sleekness, in heightening the impression of a figure attenuated to the greatest length consistent with the preservation of the bodily functions. A pair of glassy dark eyes, of which one looked rather obliquely out of its line, glared upon the world with an habitual dissatisfaction ; and in short, take her for all and all, Mistress Ruth Saunders was a woman of a commanding temper, severe devotion to business, acute circumspection, and paramount attraction for Mike Brown.

After the solemnization of the nuptials, Mike took a lease of Mr. Tracy of the small tract of land bordering on the Goblin Swamp, which, even at that day, was a very suspicious region, and the scene of many marvellous adventures. Of all places in the country, it seemed to have the greatest charm for Mike. He accordingly set up his habitation by the side of the old county road, that crossed the marsh by the causeway; and here he also opened his shop. Mistress Mike Brown resumed her former occupation, and sold spirits; whilst her husband devoted his time to the pursuits of agriculture, the working of iron, and the uproarious delights of the bottle : whereto the managing Ruth also attached herself, and was sometimes as uproarious as the sergeant.

In process of time they were surrounded by four or five imps, of either sex, whose red hair, squinting eyes, and gaunt and squat figures, showed their legitimate descent. As these grew apace, they were to be seen hanging about the smithy barefooted, half covered with rags, and with smutty faces looking wildly out of mops of hair which radiated like the beams of the sun in the image of that luminary on a country sign.

The eldest boy was bred up to his father's trade ; that is, he flirted a horse-tail tied to a stick, all day long in summer, to keep the flies from the animals that were brought to be shod ; at which sleepy employment Mike was wont to keep the youngster's attention alive by an occasional rap across the head, or an unpremeditated application of his foot amongst the rags that graced the person of the heir-apparent. Upon this system of training, it is reported, there were many family differences betwixt Mike and his spouse, and some grievously disputed fields. But Mike's muscle was enough to settle any question. So that it is not wonderful that the suffering Ruth should sometimes have taken to flight, and had recourse to her tongue.

In this way, the spoiler Discord stealthily crept into the litt'e Eden of the Browns ; and from one flower-bed advanced to another, until he made himself master of the whole garden. Quarrels then became a domestic diversion ; and travellers along the road could tell when the patriarch Mike was putting his household in order, by the sound of certain lusty thwacks which proceeded from the interior, and the frequent apparition of a young elf darting towards the shop, with one hand scratching his head, and the other holding up what seemed a pair of trowsers, but which, in reality, were Mike's old leather breeches. The customers at the shop, too, affirmed that it was a usual thing to hear Mistress Brown talking to herself, for two or three hours, in an amazingly shrill key, after Mike had gone to his anvil. And some persons went so far as to say, that in the dead hour of night, in the worst weather, voices could be heard upon the wind, in the direction of Mike Brown's dwelling, more than a mile off ; one very high, and the other very gruff ; and sometimes there was a third voice that shook the air like an earthquake, and made the blood run cold at the sound of it.

From this it may be seen that Mike's house was not very

comfortable to him ; for he was, at bottom, a good-natured fellow
who loved peace and quiet; or, at any rate, who did not like the
clack of a woman, which, he said, " wore a man out like water on
a drip-stone." To be sure, he did not care about noise, if it was
of a jolly sort ; but that he never found at home, and therefore,
" as he took no pride in Ruth," to use his own phrase, upon Hafen's report, " he naturally took to roaming."

He was an open-hearted fellow, too, who liked to spend his
money when he had it ; but the provident Mistress Mike began
to get the upper hand ; and in nothing are the first encroachments
of female despotism more decisively indicated than in the regulation of what is called the family economy. Ruth purl ined
Mike's breeches, robbed the pockets, and secured the treasure.
She forestalled his debtors, and settled his accounts, paralyzed
his credit, and, in short, did every thing but publish her determination to pay no debts of his contracting. The stout dragoon
quailed before these vexations tactics. He could never have been
taken by storm ; but to turn the siege into a blockade, and to
fret his soul with mouse-nibblings, it was enough to break the
spirit of any man ! Mike, however, covered himself with glory ;
for after being reduced to the last stage of vassalage, as happens
sometimes with an oppressed nation, he resolved to be his own
master again, (thanks to the lusty potations, or he would never
have made so successful a rebellion !) and gave Mrs. Brown, on
a memorable occasion, a tremendous beating, by which he regained the purse-strings, and spent where and when and as freely as
suited his own entertainment.

There was one thing in which Mike showed the regularity and
discipline of an old soldier. He was steady to it in the worst of
times. No matter where his vagrant humors might lead him, to
what distance, or at what hours, or how topsy-turvy he might have
grown, he was always sure to make his way home before morning.

From this cause he became a frequent traveller over the country in all weathers, and at all times of night. Time or tide did not weigh a feather. " He would snap his fingers," said Hafen, " at the foggiest midnight, and swear he could walk the whole county blindfold." The fact was, Mike was a brave man, and feared neither ghost nor devil,—and could hardly be said to be afraid even of his wife.

One winter night,—or rather one winter morning, for it was past midnight,—Mike was coming home from a carouse. The snow was lying about half-leg deep all over the fields; and there was a crust frozen upon it, that was barely strong enough to support his weight; at every step he took, it broke through with him, so that he floundered along sadly without a track; and there was a great rustling and creaking of his shoes as he walked. A sharp north-westerly wind whistled with that shrillness that showed the clearness of the atmosphere; and the moon was shining as bright as burnished silver, casting the black shadows of leafless trees, like bold etchings, upon the driven snow. The stars were all glittering with that fine frosty lustre which makes the vault of heaven seem of the deepest blue; and except the rising and sinking notes of the wind, all was still, for it was cutting cold, and every living thing was mute in its midnight lair. Yet a lonely man might well fancy there were sentient beings abroad besides himself, for on such a night there are sounds in the breeze of human tones, like persons talking at a distance. At all events, Mike was at such a time on his way home; and as he crossed the trackless field which showed him his own habitation at a distance, being in the best possible humor with himself, and whistling away as loud as he could—not from fear, but from inward satisfaction—he all at once heard somebody whistling an entirely different tune close behind him. He stopped and looked around, but there was nothing but the moon and trees and shadows; so, nothing daunted,

he stepped on again, whistling as before, when, to his great amazement, the other note was instantly resumed.　He now halted a
second time.　Immediately all was still.　Mike then whistled out
a sort of flourish, by way of experiment.　The other did the very
same thing.　Mike repeated this several times, and it was always
answered quite near him.

"Who the devil are you!" exclaimed Mike, holding his hand
up to his ear to catch the sound.

"Look behind you, and you will see," replied a harsh, screaming voice.

Mike turned suddenly around, and there he saw on the snow
the shadow of a thin, queer-looking man, in a very trig sort of a
dress, mounted upon a horse, that, by the shadow, must have been
a mere skeleton.　These were moving at full speed, although there
was no road for a horse to travel on either; but the shadow seemed
to go over shrubs and trees and bushes, as smoothly as any shadow
could travel; and Mike distinctly heard the striking of a horse's
hoofs upon the snow at every bound; though he could see nothing
of the real man or horse.　Presently, as the sound of the feet
died away, Mike heard a laugh from the voice in the direction of
the swamp.

"Hollo!" cried Mike, "what's your hurry?"　But there was
no answer.

"Humph!" said Mike, as he stood stock still, with his hands
in his breeches pockets, and began to laugh.　"That's a genius
for you!" said he, with a kind of perplexed, drunken, half-humor-
ous face.

As he found he was not likely to make much out of it, he
walked on, and began to talk to himself, and after a while to
whistle louder than ever.　Whilst he was struggling forward in
this way, he heard something like a cat-call down towards the
swamp; and immediately there rushed past him the shadows of a

pack of hounds, making every sort of yelping, and deep-mouthed cry. He could even hear the little chips of ice that were flung from their feet, whizzing along the crust of snow; but still he could see nothing but shadows; and the sounds grew fainter and fainter until they melted away in the bosom of the swamp.

Mike now stopped again, and folded his arms across his breast, —although he could not help tottering a little, from being rather top-heavy;—and, in this position, he fell gravely to considering. First, he looked all around; then he took off his hat and ran his fingers through his hair, and after that he rubbed his eyes. "Tut," said he, "it's all a botheration! There's no drag in the world will lie upon this snow. That's some drunken vagabond that had better be in his bed."

"What's that you say, Mike Brown?" said the same harsh voice he had heard before, "you had better look out how you take any freedom with a gentleman of quality."

"Quality!" cried Mike, turning his head round as he spoke. "You and your quality had better be abed, like a sober man, than to be playing off your cantrips at this time of night."

Mike looked on the snow, and there was the shadow of the horse again, standing still, and the figure upon it had one arm set a-kimbo against his side. Mike could now observe, as the shadow turned, that he wore something like a hussar-jacket, for the shadow showed the short skirt strutting out behind, and under this was the shadow of a tail turned upwards, and thrown across his shoulder. His cap appeared to be a fantastical thing perched on the very top of his head; and below the ribs of the skeleton horse he could perceive the legs dangling with hoofs, one of which was cloven.

"Aha!" exclaimed Mike, "I begin to understand you, sir. You are no better than you should be; and I will not keep company with such a blackguard."

" Then, good night, Mike Brown !" said the voice, " you are
an uncivil fellow, but I'll teach you manners the next time I meet
you ;" and thereupon the shadow moved off at a hard trot, rising
up and down in his saddle, like a first-rate jockey.

" Good night !" replied Mike; and he made a low bow, taking
off his hat, and scraping his foot, in a very polite fashion, through
the snow.

After this, Mike pushed home pretty fast, for he was growing
more sober, and his teeth began to chatter with cold. He had a
way of thrusting aside a back-door bolt, and getting into the
house without making a disturbance ; and then, before he went
to ʟed, he usually took a sleeping-draught from a stone jug which
he kept in the cupboard. Mike went through this manual on the
night in question, and was very soon afterwards stretched out
upon his couch, where he set to snoring like a trumpeter.

He never could tell how long it was after he had got to bed
that night, but it was before day, when he opened his eyes and
saw, by the broad moonlight that was shining upon the floor
through the window, a comical figure vaporing about the room. It
had a thin, long face, of a dirty white hue, and a mouth that was
drawn up at the corners with a smile. A pair of ram's horns
seemed to be twisted above his brows, like ladies' curls ; and his
head was covered with hair that looked more like a bunch of
thorns, with a stiff cue sticking straight out behind, and tied up
with a large knot of red ribbons. His coat was black, herring-
boned across the breast with crimson, and bound round all the
seams with the same color. It fitted as close to his body as the
tailor could make it ; and it had a rigid standing collar that
seemed to lift up a pair of immense ears, which were thus projected outwards from the head. The coat was very short, and
terminated in a diminutive skirt that partly rested upon a long,
pliant tail, which was whisked about in constant motion. He

wore tight crimson small clothes, bound with black; and silk
stockings of black and red stripes, one of which terminated in a
hoof instead of a human foot. As he walked about the room he
made a great clatter, but particularly with the hoof, that clinked
with the sound of loose iron. In his hand he carried a crimson
cap with a large black tassel at the top of it.

Mike said that as soon as he saw this fellow in the room, he
knew there was " something coming." He therefore drew his
blanket well up around his shoulders, leaving his head out, that
he might have an eye to what was going forward. In a little
time the figure began to make bows to Mike from across the room.
First, he bowed on one side, almost down to the floor, so as to
throw his body into an acute angle ; then, in the same fashion, on
the other side, keeping his eyes all the time on Mike. He had,
according to Mike's account, a strange swimming sort of motion,
never still a moment in one place, and passing from spot to spot
like something that floated. At one instant he brandished his
arms and whisked his tail, and took one step forward, like a dancing master beginning to dance a gavot. In the next, he made a
sweep, and retreated to his first position ; where he erected his
figure very stiffly, and strutted with pompous strides all round the
room. All this while he was twisting his features into every sort
of grimace. Then he shook himself like a merry-andrew, and
sprang from the floor upwards, flinging about his arms and legs
like a supple-jack, which being done, he laughed very loud, and
winked his eye at Mike. Then he skipped on the top of a chest,
and from that to a table, from the table to a chair, from the chair
to the bed, and thence off, putting his foot upon Mike's breast as
he passed, and pressing upon him so heavily, that for some moments Mike could hardly breathe. After this, he danced a mor-
rice dance close up to the bedside, and fetched a spring that
brought him astride upon Mike's stomach ; where he stooped down

so as to bring his long nose almost to touch Mike's, and there he twisted his eyebrows and made faces at him for several minutes. From that position he flung a somerset backwards, as far as the room permitted.

All this time the foot with the loose iron clanked very loud. Mike was not in the least afraid; but he tried several times to speak without being able to utter a word. He was completely tongue-tied, nor could he move a limb to help himself, being, as he affirmed, under a spell. But there he lay, looking at all these strange capers, which appeared so odd to him, that if he had had the power he would have laughed outright.

At last the figure danced up to him, and stood still.

" I have the honor to address myself to Sergeant Brown the blacksmith?" said he, interrogatively, making a superlatively punctilious bow at the same time.

" The same," replied Mike, having in an instant recovered the power of speech.

" My name," said the figure, " is———," here he pronounced a terrible name of twenty syllables, that sounded something like water pouring out of a bottle, and which Mike never could repeat; " I am a full brother of Old Harry, and belong to the family of the Scratches. I have taken the liberty to call and make my respects this morning, because I want to be shod."

Thereupon he made another bow, and lifted up his right foot to let Mike see that the shoe was loose.

" No shoeing to be done at this time of night," said Mike.

" It does not want but two new nails," said the figure, " and the clinching of one old one."

" Blast the nail will you get till daylight!" replied Mike.

" I will thank you, Mr. Brown," said the figure, " if you will only take my hoof in your hand, and pull out the loose nail that makes such a rattling."

"I can't do that," answered Mike.

" Why not ?"

" Because I am afraid of waking Ruthy."

" I'll answer for the consequences," said the other. " Mistress Brown knows me very well, and will never complain at your doing a good turn to one of my family."

" I'm sleepy," said Mike, " so, be about your business."

" Then, Mike Brown, I will waken you," cried the other, in a rage; " I told you I would teach you manners."

Saying these words he came close to Mike, and siezed his nose between the knuckles of the two first fingers of his right hand, and wrung it so hard that Mike roared aloud. Then, letting go his hold, he strutted away with a ludicrous short step, throwing his legs upwards as high as his head, and bringing them back nearly to the same spot on the floor, and, in this fashion, whistling all the time a slow march, he passed directly out of the window.

When Mike had sufficiently come to his senses, he found his gentle consort standing by his bedside, with a blanket wrapt round her spare figure, calling him all sorts of hard names for disturbing her rest.

Her account of this matter, when she heard from the neighbors Mike's version of this marvellous visit from the devil, was, that she did not know when he came into the house that night ; nor did she see any thing of his strange visitor ; although she was sure Old Nick must have been with him, and flung him into such an odd position as he was in ; for he made a terrible, smothered sort of noise with his voice, which wakened her up, and there she found him stretched across the bed with his clothes on, and his head inclined backwards over the side, with both arms down towards the floor. She said, moreover, that he was a drunken brute, and she had a great mind to tweak his nose for him.

"And I will be bound she helped the old devil to do that very thing!" said Rip.

"I don't know how that was," replied Hafen, "but Mike's nose got bluer and bluer after that, and always looked very much bruised, which he said was upon account of the devil's fingers being hot, and scorching him very much."

This adventure of Mike's gave him great celebrity in the neighborhood; and, by degrees, the people began to be almost as much afraid of Mike as they were of the goblin who was supposed to frequent the swamp. Mike added to this impression by certain mysteries which he used in his craft. He had the art of taming wild colts by whispering in their ears, which had such an effect that he could handle them at his shop as safely as the oldest horses. And he professed to cure the colt's distemper, sweeny, and other maladies, by writing some signs on a piece of paper, and causing the horse to swallow it in his oats.

These accomplishments, of course, were set down to the proper account; namely, to Mike's intimacy with his old companion, which was known now to be very great, as will appear by the following incidents.

Some years after the last adventure, in the summer, about the month of June, when the moon was in her third quarter, Mike was crossing the common late at night, just as the moon was rising. He was in his usual condition; for latterly Mike was scarcely ever sober. There had been rain that night, but the clouds had broken away, and he was talking to himself, and making the road twice as long as it was, by crossing and recrossing his path, like a ship tacking in the wind, and every now and then bringing himself up against a tree or sapling, and sometimes stepping, with a vast stride, across a streak of shadow, thinking it a gully; and at others, walking plump into a real gully without seeing it, until he came upon his back in the mud. On such accidents, he would swear out a good-natured oath, get up, and go on his way rejoicing, as usual.

It happened, as he was steering along in this plight, there suddenly stood before him his old friend in the herring-boned jacket.

"How do you do, Mike?" was his usual salutation.

"Pretty well, I thank you, sir." Mike was noted for being scrupulously polite when he was in his cups. So, he made a bow, and took off his hat, although he could hardly keep his ground.

"Sloppy walking to night, Mr. Mike."

"Sloppy enough, sir," replied Mike, rather short, as if he didn't wish to keep company with the devil.

"How is Mistress Brown this evening!" said the other, following Mike up.

"Pretty well, I thank you, sir," returned the blacksmith, walking as fast as he could.

"Trade brisk, Mr. Brown?"

"Quite the contrary," replied Mike; "there's nothing to do worth speaking of."

"How are you off for cash?" asked the other, coming up close along side.

"I have none to lend," answered the blacksmith.

"I did not suppose you had, sergeant; you and I have been acquainted a long while. I hope there is no grudge betwixt us."

"I never knew any good of you," said Mike.

"Let us drink to our better friendship," said the gentleman, taking a flat bottle from his pocket.

"With all my heart!" cried Mike, as he stretched out his hand and took the flask. "Here's to you, Mr. Devil!"

Hereupon they both took a drink.

"Now," said Mike, "let us take another to old Virginia."

" Agreed," answered the gentleman ; so they took another.

" You're a very clever fellow !" said Mike, beginning to brighten up.

" I know that," replied the gentleman.

" You are a man after my own heart," continued Mike, " here's your health again. Give us your paw, old fellow." Then they shook hands.

" Let us drink to Mistress Brown," said the gentleman, politely.

" Damn Mistress Brown ! I'll make you a present of her."

" I accept your offer," replied the other ; " here's her health."

" Well," said Mike, " here's the health of your wife."

" I am much obliged to you," replied the gentleman. " Mistress (here he pronounced his own unspellable name,) will thank you herself some of these days, when you may honor her with your company. But, Mike, as I have taken a liking to you, I'll make your fortune."

" Will you ?" cried the blacksmith ; " then I'm your man !"

" Come with me," said the other, " and I will show you where you may find as much gold as you can carry home in a bag. But you must not mind trouble."

" Trouble ! exclaimed Mike. " Any trouble for money !"

" Follow me," said the gentleman.

Upon this they both turned their steps towards the swamp, the broadest part of which they reached not very far from the scene of their colloquy. The morass here was covered with sheets of water, some of them ten or twelve yards in diameter. The gentleman in black and crimson easily traversed these, without soiling his habiliments more than if he had been in a drawing-room ; but Mike made his way with great difficulty, miring himself first in one hole, and then in another, and sometimes plunging up to his middle in water. But his companion exhorted him to persevere, and kept up his resolution by presenting him now and then with the flask, which, Mike said, was of great use to him.

At last they arrived at the inmost part of the swamp, upon the margin of one of the ponds, in the middle of which the water was about two feet deep, but shallow towards the edges.

"Now," said the gentleman, "Mike, my brave fellow! do you take a drink."

"Certainly," replied Mike.

"The bottom of this pond," continued the other, "is full of gold; and all that you have to do is to rake it out. I'll get you a light rake."

With this he withdrew for a few moments, and returned with a rake made of a white-oak sapling, with twelve iron teeth to it, each about a foot long, and put the implement in Mike's hand, who, having taken a good deal from his host's flask, had much ado to stand up. But still he was full of resolution, and very much determined to make money.

The image of the moon was reflected upon the water, whose surface being slightly agitated by the breeze and the frequent movement of small insects, broke the reflection into numberless fragments, that glittered upon Mike's vision like pieces of bright gold at the bottom.

"All that you have to do," said Mike's conductor, "is to rake out these scraps of metal, and put them in your pocket. Work hard, don't give up; and wet your feet as little as possible. So make yourself at home, for I must bid you good night."

"Good night," uttered Mike, "and joy go with you, my old boy!"

Finding himself alone in the bosom of the swamp at this hou', and on the high road to fortune, the blacksmith addressed h.m-self to his task as vigorously as the inordinate depth of his pota-tions would allow. He took up the rake, that was lying on the ground, and raised it perpendicularly, which was as much as he could do and keep his balance, considering the state of his head, and the slippery ground he had for a footing. Besides, the rake was very heavy, being made of green wood, and at least twenty feet long. When he had it well poised, and ready to make a stroke in the water, he took two steps forward to bring him immediately to the edge of the pond.

"Here goes!" he cried aloud, at the same time flinging the rake downwards, which motion disturbed his centre of gravity, and plunged him headlong into the pool. At the same moment with the plash were heard a dozen voices, laughing from the midst of the bushes, with a prolonged and loud ho, ho, ho! that echoed frightfully through the stillness of the night. Mike crawled out of the water, keeping hold of the rake, and once more stood upright on his former foothold.

"Well!" ejaculated Mike, with a thick utterance, and a kind of peevish gravity, "what do you see to laugh at in that? Never see a man in the water before?"

He now very seriously raised the rake a second time, and made a more successful pitch, driving it into the bottom, and breaking the water into a thousand ripples. Then, taking hold of the long shaft, which he straddled, as children when they ride a stick, he began to pull with might and main. He strained until the perspiration poured down his cheeks in large drops; but the teeth had sunk so deep in the mud, that the rake was immovable.

"Pretty tough work!" said Mike, stopping to run his finger along his brow.

But all his efforts proved unavailing; and he was therefore forced to wade into the pond again to release the iron teeth from their bed; and, resting them lightly on the bottom, he again began to pull, and succeeded in bringing the rake to the shore. Upon examination, the fruit of all this labor was nothing more than some decayed brushwood and grass.

"No great haul that!" muttered Mike to himself; and instantly the swamp was alive again with the same reverberations of the choir of laughers. Mike considering this as a taunt that he would bear from neither devil nor imp, returned it scornfully and in defiance, by an equally loud and affected ho, ho, ho! delivered in bass tones. "I can laugh as well as the best of you," he said, nodding his head towards the quarter from which the noises came.

Mike's temper now began to give way; and as he grew angry, he toiled with proportionate energy, but with the same disappointment, which was always mocked by the same coarse laugh. The violence of his exertions, the weight of the implement with which he worked, and his frequent drenchings, gradually overcoming his strength, he grew disheartened, and began to wake up to the real nature of his employment. The chill of the night slowly dispelled the fever of his brain, and at last the full conviction of the truth broke upon him.

"If I was not a born fool," said he, "I should think I was drunk. I see how it is : that fellow who left the marks of his hot fingers upon my nose, has been playing his tricks upon me again. It is unaccountable ; but if I don't have my revenge, he may bridle and saddle me both, and ride me over the swamp as much as he pleases."

So saying, Mike threw down his rake, and resolutely retraced his steps through the marsh. As soon as he set his foot upon the firm land, he heard the voice of his late companion calling out, "Good night, Sergeant Brown!" which was instantly followed with the accustomed laugh.

"Good night, you blackguard!" cried Mike, as loud as he could bawl. "Your liquor is as bad as your lodgings!" and posted off homeward as fast as his legs could carry him.

All the next day Mike ruminated sullenly over this adventure,

and the more he thought upon it the more wroth he became.
There is nothing more to be dreaded than a pleasant-tempered,
sociable, frolicksome fellow, of good bone and muscle, when he is
once roused. Quarrel not being one of his habits, he manages it
roughly and with great energy,—or as Mike would say,—" like a
new hand at the bellows." The affront put upon him the night
before went very hard with Mike, and he therefore resolved to
call his false friend to an account. It was singular that after this
thought took possession of his mind, there seemed to be a relish
in it that almost brought him into a good humor. The idea of
standing upon his prowess with the devil, and giving him a
fair beating, was one of those luxurious imaginings that no man
ever dreamt of but Mike Brown. There was a whimsicalness in
it that vibrated upon the strongest chord in his character. Mike
had never met his match in daylight, and he had a droll conviction
that he could master any thing in darkness, if he could only come
to it, arm to arm. His first and most natural suggestion was, to
put himself in order for the projected interview, by making a
merry evening of it, and then to depend upon his genius for his
success in the subsequent stages of the adventure.

Mike followed one half of the old Scythian custom in all
affairs of perplexity : he first considered the subject when he was
drunk, but he did not revolve it again in a sober mood. On the
present occasion his reflections had the advantage of being matured
under circumstances of peculiar animation, induced by the disturbed state of his feelings ; for he has often said that when any
thing fretted him it made him awfully thirsty. There was one
determination that was uppermost in all the variety of lights in
which he contemplated his present purpose ;—and that was, as it
was a delicate affair, to treat it like a gentleman, and to give his
adversary fair play. Accordingly, as soon as Mike had cast off
work for the day, he put on his regimentals, took his broadsword,

and set out for his usual haunt to prepare himself for the business in hand. Never did he enter upon a campaign with a more wary, circumspect, or soldier-like providence.

He remained at the tavern in the neighborhood until he had fairly put all his compotators asleep; and then, in the dead hour of the night, when the moon was but a little way above the horizon, and divided her quiet empire with Mike's own nose, he crept forth silently upon his destined exploit. It was a goodly sight to see such a valiant blacksmith, so martially bedight, with his trusty sword tucked under his arm, stealing out at such an hour, and wending his silent way to the Goblin Swamp, there to have a pass at arms with the fiend ! the night breeze blowing upon his swarthy cheek, and his heavy, sullen tramp falling without an echo upon his own ear, and not a thought of dread flickering about his heart.

With his head spinning like a top, and his courage considerably above striking heat, Mike, after many circumgyrations, arrived in about half an hour on the frontier of the field of action. Here he halted, according to a military fashion ; and, like a cautious officer entering upon an enemy's territory, he began to explore the ground. Then, drawing his sword and straightening his person, he commenced an exhortation to himself in the manner of a general addressing his troops.

" Now, my brave boy, keep a stiff upper lip ! mind your eye ! look out for squalls ! don't fire until you see the whites of their eyes ; carry swords ; advance !"

All this he uttered with a solemn, drunken wisdom, and with the flourish of an old soldier. At the words he stepped forward, and continued to approach the swamp, muttering half articulated sounds, and occasionally falling one step backward, from carrying himself rather too erect. As soon as he reached the edge of the morass, he gave the word " halt" in a loud and defying tone of voice, as if to inform his adversary of his presense. He did not wait long before he heard a crackling noise as of one breaking through the thick shrubbery ; and full before him stood, on an old log within the swamp, his adversary, in his customary dress, with the addition of a Spanish cloak of scarlet that was muffled about his neck.

Mike, immediately upon seeing this apparition, brought his sword with an alert motion up to his breast, with the blade reaching perpendicularly upward in the line of his face ; then, with a graceful sweep of his arm, he swung it down diagonally, with the point to the ground, in the usual manner of a salute.

" Your honor !" said Mike, as he performed this ceremony.

" Walk in, Sergeant Brown !" said the devil, with a husky voice, that was scarcely above a whisper. " I did not expect to see you to night ; I have caught a bad cold, and am not able to stir abroad."

" I am come to night," said Mike very stiffly, and with an affectation of cold politeness, " to see you on a piece of business. I require satisfaction for the affront you put upon me last night."

" You shall have it. What's your weapon?"

" It is in my hand," answered the sergeant.

" Then follow me," said the devil with great composure.

They both stepped forward into the swamp ; and, after traversing some defiles, and passing around ponds, and making many tiresome circuits through the most intricate parts of the marsh, Mike at length stopped to inquire which way the devil meant to lead him.

" As I am the challenged party, I have the right to choose my own ground," said the other.

" Certainly !" rejoined Mike. " It is all one to me."

At length they reached a spot that was covered with tall trees, at the foot of which the earth seemed to be of a more firm texture than in the rest of the fen. There was a fire smoking through a heap of rubbish near the middle of the ground, and a little, peaked old woman, almost black with the smoke, sat upon her haunches so near the fire that by the flash of the small flame Mike could perceive that she was smoking a pipe. Her elbows were placed upon her knees, and her chin rested in the palms of her hands in such a manner that her long fingers were extended, like the bars of a gridiron, over her cheeks. Her eyes looked like burning coals, and could be seen through the dark at a great distance.

"Wife," said the devil, "Mike Brown. Mike Brown, my wife."

"Your servant," said Mike, with one of his best flourishes, and a bow.

"Pish!" cried the old woman with a sort of scream, "sit down!"

"Much obliged to you, ma'am," replied Mike, "I'd rather stand."

"What brings you with Mike Brown into my bedroom at this time of night?" said the old woman to her husband.

"Mind your own business," was the reply, "and give me my sword. I have an affair of honor to settle with this gentleman."

"Get it yourself," said the wife.

So the devil stepped inside of a hollow tree, and brought out a huge old fashioned, two-handed straight sword, that was covered with rust, and immediately began to feel the edge with his thumb.

"It is very dull; but it will do. Now, sergeant, we will go a little way further, and settle this matter in a twinkling."

"Agreed! and remember, as you set up for a gentleman, I expect fair play."

"Honor bright!" said the devil, putting his hand to his breast.

"No striking till each says he is ready."

"By no means," said the devil.

"Nor no hit below the knee."

" Of course not," said the devil.

" Time to breathe, if it is asked."

" Assuredly !"

" Points down at the first blood."

" Just as you say," replied the devil.

" Then," said Mike, " move on."

" We ought to drink together, sergeant, before we get to blows. I am for doing the thing civilly," said the devil.

" So am I," replied Mike. " I am entirely of your opinion."

So the devil put into Mike's hands a large gourd, that had a stopper in the top of it, which the sergeant pulled out, and applying the orifice to his mouth, took a hearty drink, first turning to the old woman, who sat all this time in silence by the fire, and saying, " My service to you, ma'am !" The devil having likewise performed his part in this ceremony, they once more resumed their walk.

In their progress towards the ground which the devil had chosen for the theatre of this mortal rencounter, they came to two small islands, the soil of which was a yielding black mud covered with moss. These little parcels of ground arose out of the marsh, with well-defined banks, perhaps twelve inches high, and were separated from each other by a channel of deep water, not more than five feet in width, so that to pass from one to the other required a leap that was somewhat perilous, because the foothold on the opposite bank was not only very soft, but the ground itself scarcely one pace in breadth. The chances were, therefore, that in leaping to it, the momentum employed would precipitate the leaper into another pond of water beyond it. The devil skipped over this strait with great ease, and called on Mike to follow. The sergeant, however, hesitated, and looked for some moments upon the spot with anxious concern. He traversed the ground in the neighborhood, to observe if there was any other passage

round this hazardous channel; meditated upon the consequences
of a failure in the attempt to cross it; looked at his legs, as if to
compare their capabilities with the obstacle before him; and, at
last, wisely determined that the risk was more than he ought, in
prudence, to run. So, taking the next expedient,—which was to
make a long step, in such wise as to plant one foot on the opposite bank, and rely upon the assistance of his adversary to drag
him over,—he forthwith essayed the effort. By one prodigious
stride, he succeeded in fixing his left foot on the desired spot, his
legs being extended in the endeavor to their greatest possible
compass; and there he remained in his ludicrous position, like
the colossus of Rhodes, his feet sliding imperceptibly outward in
the slimy material of the banks, thus more effectually splitting
him asunder, whilst the great weight of his body denied him all
power to extricate himself, even if he had stood upon a firmer
base, and with a less relaxed frame. He was, of course, wholly
at the mercy of his antagonist, upon whose generosity he relied
with the confidence of a true soldier ; if this failed him, he had
nothing better left than to fall sidewise, in the manner of a pair
of distended compasses, into the water, and abide the consequences
of going headlong to the bottom of a stagnant pool, where, for
aught he knew, he should not only be compelled to swallow a portion of the noxious liquid, but come into familiar contact with
toads, snakes, snapping-turtles, and other abominable inhabitants
of such a place. For the present, therefore, he began to entreat
the aid of his old companion in the most supplicating terms. To
his utter dismay, the gentleman in the scarlet mantle not only
refused him a hand, but answered his request with a malignant
laugh, so loud as to make the swamp ring with its reverberations.

" Blood and fury ! why don't you give me your hand ?" cried
Mike at last, in an extremity of torture; " where are your manners ?"

"What ails you?" said the devil, "that you roar so loud?"

"I'm in a quandary!" bellowed the sergeant. "Is this the way you treat a gentleman in distress? Don't you see I'm splitting up to my chin?"

"When I fight," replied the other calmly, "I choose my own ground, and if you can't reach it, it is no fault of mine."

"Don't you mean to give me satisfaction?" asked Mike.

"All the satisfaction in the world, Sergeant Brown. Rare satisfaction," said the devil, laughing and holding his sides.

"You are a coward," cried Mike, drawing his sword, and flourishing it over his head.

"Step out, sergeant, and make your words good."

"You are no gentleman."

"Granted," said the devil; "I never set up for one. But I don't think you are much better, or you would never stand vaporing there with your sword, and straddling as if you thought yourself a man of consequence."

"What's the use," said Mike, in a gentle persuasive tone, "of keeping a man here all night, tearing the life out of him by inches? Just give us a hand, like a genteel Christian; and as to the quarrel, I'll not be particular about it."

"Good night, Sergeant Brown," said the devil; "I see you have no mind to fight; and as I did not come here to trifle, I will wait no longer for you."

So the devil turned round and disappeared from Mike's view, with a bitter, scoffing laugh.

The sergeant being thus left alone without relief, found his torment becoming every moment more insupportable; and therefore, without further effort to reach the ground on either side, he plunged head-foremost into the pond, from which he rose in a moment covered with black mud, and with a multitude of ropes of green slime clinging to his shoulders, and platted about his throat.

This shock had the effect to bring the blacksmith partially to his senses. He awoke from his intoxication, like one from a dream, wondering at the chances that brought him into such a predicament, and with a confused recollection of the strange adventure he had just been engaged in. His conclusion was, "that the old chap had taken him in again," and he therefore set off homeward, very much ashamed of the failure of his expedition, and not less vexed to hear, as he once more arrived on dry land, the usual valedictory, "Good night!" with its hoarse, wild and fiendish accompaniment.

I will not pretend to give any further avouch for these facts than the authority of Hafen, who affirmed that he had them from Mike himself; and as Mike was a little prone to exaggerate when his personal prowess was in question, the judicious reader will make some grains of allowance on that score.

There were various incidents in Mike's life similar to those above narrated; but it is only material to know, that not long after this last adventure, Mike began to grow jealous of his old crony's attentions to Mistress Brown. There was a spirited intercourse kept up between this worthy and the family, which resulted at last in the sudden disappearance of the matron from the neighborhood. The folks in these parts have their own notions of the matter; but they don't like to speak freely on the subject. Mike, however, bore his misfortune like a philosopher. He very sedately increased his allowance of comfort by doubling the strength of his cups, and, in consequence, was more frequently than ever beside himself,—a very refreshing expedient for a man who has been left alone in the world. The heir-apparent and the rest of the progeny abdicated their birthright, and wandered off, it is supposed, in search of food. The shop was deserted, the anvil was sold, and the bellows fell a victim to a pulmonary attack. The roof of the dwelling had decayed so as to give the wind and rain free admission. The relics of the smithy were, one windy night, blown down. The frame of the house first became twisted out of its perpendicular line, and gradually sunk to earth, at the base of the brick chimney that stands, at this day, a monument to show that another of the host of Revolutionary heroes has departed. The well grew to be choked up with weeds; the balance-pole waxed stiff, and creaked in its swivel; and, finally, Mike ceased to be seen in the country side.

It is now many years gone by, since these mysterious events employed the gossip of the neighborhood; and many credible witnesses,—amongst the rest Hafen Blok,—affirm that Mike and his wife are yet seen to hold occasional conventicles with their old associate, in that part of the swamp known as the devil's bed-chamber.

"Well, Hafen," said I, when this story of Mike Brown was concluded, "do you believe it all?"

"Why, I don't know," replied Hafen, "it does seem to me as if it might be partly true. But Mike was a monstrous liar, and an uncommon hard drinker."

"It is reasonable," said Hazard, "to suppose that the devil should be fond of such a fellow as Mike Brown."

Said Rip, "For my share, I don't believe it. Hafen's making fun: how could the devil walk over the swamp in silk stockings, and not get them muddy?"

CHAPTER XXX.

AN INTERLUDE.

About the same hour of the night when Hafen Blok was regaling his circle of auditors in the porch at Swallow Barn, it fell out that two sympathetic souls, who have frequently been brought to view in this narrative, were weaving closer the network of sentimental affinities in a quiet conference in one of the chambers at The Brakes. As this contemporary incident may serve to give my readers some insight into the family history, I will relate it as it was told to me by Harvey Riggs; only premising that Harvey is somewhat dramatic in his nature, and therefore apt to put words into the mouths of his actors, which, if the matter were investigated, it might be discovered they never spoke. Be that as it may, if the story be not a positive fact, (Harvey makes a distinction between a positive and a simple fact,) it is at least founded on a real event.

The bustle attending the negotiation of the treaty that had just been concluded by our plenipotentiaries at The Brakes, had subsided, upon the departure of the Swallow Barn cavalcade, into an unusual calm. The family retired from the tea-table with a sedateness that might be ascribed to exhausted spirits; and, what was most worthy of observation, Swansdown, neglectful of his customary assiduities, relinquished the company of the ladies,

and sauntered with Mr. Tracy towards the back door, where, in a
chair inclined against a column of the portico, he fixed himself,
with one foot resting upon the front bar, and with his right leg
thrown across his left knee in such fashion as to point upwards at
an angle of forty-five ; and in this posture he incontinently
launched into a long, prosing discourse with Mr. Tracy, who sat
opposite to him, which lasted all the evening. He was tuned to
too high a key for light company. The achievement of the award
had wrought him into that state of self-complacency which generally attends upon ambition when saturated with a great exploit.
He had done a deed of mould, and was pleased to float upon the
billow of his vanity, high borne above all frivolous things.

This humor did not pass unobserved, nor, perhaps, unre-
sented : for as soon as affairs had fallen into the posture I have
described, Prudence Meriwether and Catharine Tracy, in an apparently careless spirit, set to walking up and down the hall, and
afterwards sallied forth, amidst the lingerings of the twilight,
upon the open hill-side, and, with no better protection against
the damps of the evening than their handkerchiefs thrown across
their shoulders, strolled at a snail's pace towards the river ; and
talked—heaven knows what!—or, at least, they only know, who
know what ruminative virgins, on river banks at dewy eve, are
wont to say

It was nine by the clock,—or even later,—when they returned
to the front door and sat down upon the steps, still intent upon
the exchange of secret thoughts. After a brief space, they rose
again, and with locked arms stepped stately through the hall, to
and fro. Still the interminable Swansdown pursued his incessant
discourse. Another interval, and the two ladies slowly wended
their way up stairs, and in the eastern chamber, looking towards
the river, lighted by a solitary taper which threw a murky ray
across the room, they planted their chairs at the window ; beneath

which, until late at night, was heard a low, murmuring, busy note of ceaseless voices, like the flutter of the humming-bird in a wilderness of honeysuckles.

Harvey pretends that the subject of this long communing between our thoughtful dames had a special regard to that worthy personage whom but now my reader has seen seated at the porch, with his foot as high as his head. I have said somewhere that Prudence was oratorical; and, indeed, I have heard it remarked that the ladies of the Old Dominion, in general, are not sparing of their tropes. Upon that subject I have no opinion to give, but leave the world to draw its own conclusions from the following authentic conversation; authentic as far as Harvey Riggs is a credible witness.

It is characteristic of Prudence Meriwether,—as it is of sundry other ladies of my acquaintance,—to lavish much fervor of imagination in the advocacy of any favorite opinion. The glow of her feelings is, of course, reflected upon her subject, and the glow of her subject is again reflected back upon her feelings; and thence, backward and forward successively, until the greatest possible degree of heat is obtained by the process; exactly as we see the same result produced between two concave mirrors. It seems to me that an attentive observation of this phenomenon may go a great way to explain the mystery of a love affair.

The present theme was one of those upon which Prudence was wont to expatiate with a forcible emphasis. Her rhetoric might be said to be even hyperbolical, and her figures of speech were certainly of the most original stamp. First, she gave an inventory of Swansdown's gentle qualities. "He was amiable, mild, soft, and polished." Then again, "his voice was silvery, his motion graceful, his manners delicate." In this enumeration of dainty properties she sometimes paused to ask Catharine if she did not think so.

Catharine thought so, of course.

" There was a gravity in his demeanor," said Prudence, " which gave authority to his presence, and seemed to rebuke familiarity ; and yet it was so mixed up with the sallies of a playful imagination, that it won the good opinion of the world almost by stealth."

" He is very generally respected," said Catharine.

Prudence continued the catalogue with increasing warmth ; and although Catharine was not so figurative, she was not less energetic in her panegyric. She not only echoed Pru's sentiments, but even magnified their proportions. Where two persons agree, the debate must be short. Such congeniality of thinking occludes discussion, and the two ladies therefore travelled rapidly through the inventory.

Prudence rose to the height of the stature of his mind, and descanted upon his abilities.

" He had the art," she said, " to impart a charm to the dullest subjects. His discrimination was intuitive, and facilitated his journey through the mazes of research, like one that wandered over a shorn meadow. Who but a man of genius could unravel the occult darkness of the boundary line, and shed certainty, in one day, upon an important question, in opposition to all the courts and all the lawyers of a state that boasted of both, with that forensic jurist Mr. Wart (manifestly prejudiced against his opinion) on the other side ! There was a moral romanticity in it. It was like casting a spell of " gramarie" over his opponents. The world would talk of this thing hereafter !"

" It is very surprising," muttered Catharine.

" Think of it, my dear !" cried Prudence. " The country, before long will discover his dormant talents, and he will be compelled to forego his reluctance to guide the destinies of his native state."

" It can be nothing but his modesty," rejoined Kate, " that

keeps him in the background now. He never would have been beaten three times for Congress, if he had not been so diffident."

"He is what I denominate emphatically," said Prudence, "a man of lofty sentiments : nothing sordid, nothing paltry, nothing tawdry, nothing—"

"Nothing," replied Kate, "nothing of the sort."

"Such sound opinions !"

"And spoken in such chaste language !"

"Such a strain of charity ! such a beautiful commingling of the virtues that mollify, with the principles that fortify, the heart !"

"Such a rare union !" echoed Kate.

Never has the world seen more perfect harmony than that which ruled in the counsels of our two damsels.

At length they fell into a speculation upon the question, why he did not marry. Women consider, very naturally, life to be a sort of comedy, and constantly look to see the hero pairing off by way of preparation for the catastrophe. They agreed that there were not many of the sex who would not think themselves fortunate in an overture from Mr. Swansdown. But it was allowed that he was fastidious. It resulted from the peculiar nature of his organization.

"I confess," said Prudence, "it puzzles me. It is one of the inexplicable arcana of human action that I cannot explain."

"Nor I, neither," replied Kate.

"There are men," said Miss Meriwether, "of such attenuated fibre, that they shrink at the rude touch of reality. They have the sensitiveness of the mimosa, and find their affections withering up where the blast of scrutiny blows too roughly upon them. Such a man is Singleton."

"I believe that is very true," rejoined Miss Tracy; "and

besides, I think Mr. Swansdown is a little dashed by being refused so often."

To this succeeded a shrewd inquiry as to what was his present purpose.

"For," said Prudence, "it is quite clear to me that he meditates an important revolution in his fate."

"Prudence, I have lately taken up the same idea."

"There is something," continued Prudence, "in his thoughts that disturbs him. He is variable, vacillating, and visionary : sometimes, you would suppose, all mirthful exuberance,—if your opinion were governed by the beaming expression of his face,—but, when he speaks, it is only to say some common-place thing, with an air of earnestness, that shows his thoughts to be looking upon some invisible idea. He is, at other times, so pensive, that one would think 'melancholy had marked him for her own.' What can it signify ?"

"Can he have taken a religious turn?" asked Kate, with an air of wonder.

"No," replied the other, thoughtfully.—"It has the fitfulness of genius distracted by its own emotions. It is not religion : we should wish it were so. But it is not that. It is the agitation of sensibility.—An imaginative temperament recreating amidst the attractive creations of its own handiwork."

"Oh, Prudence ! how much that is like Swansdown himself?"

"I think," returned Miss Meriwether, "I have studied his character well. And, to tell you the truth, my dear Catharine, I fancy he recognizes some affinity between us. I perceive that when he is anxious to share his thoughts with a friend, he flies to me ; and it strangely happens, that some secret instinct brings us into that holy confidence, where friendship puts on its garb of naked simplicity, and ideas flow together on the same high road, without reserve."

" Indeed! I did not know you were so intimate with Mr.
Swansdown. It is strange it should have escaped me."

".Why, it was sudden. It is wonderful to think how long
two spirits may associate in the same sphere without striking
upon that chord which vibrates in unison in the hearts of both.
But for an accidental walk we took three or four mornings ago,
before breakfast, I doubt if I should ever have been brought to
that conviction which I entertain of his high qualities. And,
take him altogether, Kate, I think him a timid man. He is even
timid in his intercourse with me ; although he passes so many
moments in my company."

" I did not think him timid," said Kate.

" Oh, I am sure that he is so, my dear! To tell you the truth,
with that frankness which should preside over the breathings of
inviolable friendship, I have no question, from his manner, that
he has something of a very delicate nature."—

" No! Prudence! You don't think so! My dear, you deceive yourself. You are entirely mistaken in his views. Indeed,
I know you are," cried Catharine with energy.

" Indeed, I am sure I am not, Kate. I have it in every thing
but words."

" Then," said Kate with emphasis, " there's no faith in man!"

" Why not, my dear Catharine ?"

" It is of no consequence," replied the other, in a tremulous,
murmuring voice. " The thing is not worth investigating. From
any other lips than yours, Pru, I never would have believed that
Swansdown harbored such a thought. Well, I wish you joy of
your conquest. I renounce—"

" Heavens, Catharine! Do I understand you right? What
a dreadful truth do you divulge to my mind! I comprehend
your silence, my dearest Catharine, and do not ask an explanation,
because I see it all. This is one of the cruelest bolts that Fate
has treasured up in her quiver."

"What shall we do, my dear Prudence? I am all amazement!"

"Do! What ought we to do, but banish him from our favor as a false-hearted minion; banish him to the antarctic circle of our regard, and fix upon him the indelible stain of our displeasure? From this moment I discard him from my heart."

"And I from mine," said Catharine.

"Now we are free," cried Prudence. "Is it not lucky that we have had this interview?"

"Most fortunate. But are you sure, my dear Prudence, that you have not made some mistake? Do you think he seriously aimed at entrapping your affections?"

"Sure, my love! He did every thing that man could do, and said every thing that man could say, short of falling on his knee and offering me his hand."

"What unparalleled perfidy! When I contrast what you tell me with what I know, and for seven long months have so frequently experienced—"

"For seven months?"

"For seven months, believe me, my dear Prudence, for seven months."

"Why he told me, Catharine, only this morning, that he never could grow intimate with you. That you had a reserve in your manners which repelled all advances; that—"

"Good heavens! does Swansdown say so? There is an hypocrisy in that, my dear Prudence, which shocks me. He has had some sinister design."

"Oh! forbear, Catharine. Do not mention it. I always thought him somewhat worldly-minded; a little hollow-hearted, He shows it in the expression of his countenance."

"Particularly," replied Catharine, "about the eyes, when he smiles. Do you know, I always suspected him. I have a horror of a man of extravagant professions, and have often doubted the sincerity of Swansdown."

" Sincerity! Let not the word be profaned by wedding it with his name. It is plain, that all those apparently deep emotions by which he vainly endeavored to wrench from me—yes, to wrench from me, my affections, were but the false glitter that plays about the sunny summit of worldly profession."

" But when you tell me," said Catharine, interrupting her friend, "that he has made an assault upon your affections, I am lost in amazement. He has twenty times insinuated to me, that although he thought you a woman of some pretensions, yet you were the last woman in the world that could interest his regard. He said he thought your manners unnatural, and your tone of feeling superficial. I recollect his very words."

" What reason have I to be thankful," exclaimed Prudence, clasping her hands, " that I have escaped the snare he has infused into my cup! He has been lavish of expedients to entrap me. Would you believe it, Catharine, he has actually written a long, and, I must do him the justice to say, talented letter, depicting the misery of the Greek matrons, and their devotion to the cause of their country, with a view to gratify me, and inspire me with a loftier sentiment of admiration for him. He was aware of my zeal in that cause."

" The Greeks !" said Catharine. " Does he pretend to be an advocate for the cause of the Greeks ? His precise words to me were, that he thought the Greeks the most barbarous, the most uninteresting, and the vilest wretches in the world."

" The infidel! the preposterous man ! What a fatal mildew must have struck its fangs into the understanding and the heart of the being that uttered such a sentiment ! And then, what hypocrisy must have varnished his face, whilst his pen traced his appeal to the sensibilities of Virginia in behalf of the suffering patriots !

" It could not have been his own," replied Catharine.

" Indeed, I should doubt it myself," said Prudence, " if it were not remarkable for those affected ornaments of style which disfigure even the best of his effusions. You may easily see that it abounds in those vicious decorations which betray a false taste, those superfluous redundancies that sparkle out in his compositions, like the smothered embers of an extinguished furnace."

" I think," added Catharine, " that it will invariably be found that a bad heart—"

" Yes, my dear, that is perfectly true : a bad heart never puts pen to paper, but its guardian imp stands at its elbow, and infuses into the composition a spice of hypocrisy. And had he the assurance to say that he thought my manners unnatural ?"

" Yes ; he said you were stiff and formal, and almost inaccessible."

" That shows his poverty of thought, Catharine ; for he made use of the same terms in reference to you."

" He said he thought it strange," continued Catharine, " that you should fancy you were doing good by circulating tracts. He observed this was another of your follies ; that these tracts—"

" And so he had the effrontery to attack the Tract Society !"

" He had, and went further ; he remarked that the society was a mere invention to give employment to busy-bodies and country-gossips."

" Heavens and earth ! had he the rashness to question my motives ?"

" To be sure he had ; and called you one of the immaculates."

" Then, I am done with man. Depend upon it, Catharine, the sex is not to be trusted. There is a natural propinquity—proclivity I mean—in this baser part of creation, to undervalue all that is virtuous. I never saw one man whose impulses were not essentially wicked."

" Nor I, neither, except my father," replied Catharine.

" Of course, I except my brother Frank," said Prudence.

" Henceforward I abjure the sex."

" I think I will too," said Catharine in a lower tone.

" Well now, Catharine," continued Miss Meriwether, " it becomes us to take a decided part in reference to this Mister Swansdown."

" What do you propose, Pru ?"

" To treat him with that cutting coldness which we both so well know how to assume."

" I don't think we ought to make him of so much importance."

" My dear," said Prudence, after a moment's hesitation, " perhaps you are right. There is nothing puffs up these lords of creation so much as to find our sex guilty of the weakness of even the homage of contempt. Suppose we indicate to him by our manner that we have unveiled his treachery, and show him, that although it has been so assiduous to insinuate himself into our good opinion, we regard him as an object of perfect indifference."

" As one," added Catharine, " whose ways were known to us."

" Whose fate," said Prudence, in continuation, " is a subject that has never occupied our thoughts."

" Whose duplicity has failed of its aim," said Catharine.

" Whose tergiversation and ambidexterity have alike excited our ridicule," replied Prudence.

" Agreed ! let us do so," continued Catharine ;—" how shall we manage it ?"

" By our looks, my dear Catharine ! I will look into the deepest recesses of his heart with a glance, and wither him into a spectacle of scorn."

" Looks may do a great deal," replied Catharine, " and I will regulate my demeanor by yours. " I am glad we have found him out !"

" Let us retire to rest, my dear," said the other.   " Let us to
our prayers, and be thankful that we have escaped these impending dangers."

For a while, all was silent.   But at midnight again, and long
afterwards, a buzzing sound of suppressed voices was heard from
the chamber.

CHAPTER XXXI.

In the country every thing wears a Sunday look. The skies have a deeper blue, the clouds rest upon them like painting. The soft flutter of the groves hushes one into silence. The chirp of the grasshopper, as he leaps in his short semi-circles along your path, has the feebleness of a whisper; and the great vagabond butter-fly, which gads amongst the thistles, moves noiseless as a strag-gling leaf borne upon a zephyr. Then, there is a lowing of cows upon a distant meadow, and a scream of jay-birds, heard at inter-vals; the sullen hammer of a lonely woodpecker resounds from some withered trunk; and, high above, a soaring troop of crows, hoarse with cawing, send forth a far-off note. Sometimes a huge and miry mother of the sty, with her litter of querulous pigs, steps leisurely across the foreground; and a choir of locusts in the neighboring woods spin out a long stave of music, like the pupils of a singing-school practising the elements of psalmody. Still, this varied concert falls faintly upon the ear, and only seems to measure silence.

Our morning pursuits at Swallow Barn partake somewhat of the quiet character of the scenery. Frank Meriwether is an early riser at this season, and generally breakfasts before the rest of the family. This gives him time to make a circuit on horseback, to inspect the progress of his farm concerns. He returns before the heat of the day, and, about noon, may be found stretched upon a broad settee in the hall, with a pile of books on the floor beneath him, and a dozen newspapers thrown around in great confusion : not unfrequently, too, he is overtaken with a deep sleep, with a volume straddling his nose ; and he will continue in this position, gradually snoring from a lower to a higher key, until he awakens himself by a sudden and alarming burst that resembles the bark of a mastiff. He says the old clock puts him asleep, and, in truth, it has a very narcotic vibration ; but Frank is manifestly growing corpulent. And, what is a little amusing, he protests in the face of the whole family that he does not snore.

The girls get at the piano immediately after breakfast ; and Ned and myself usually commence the morning with a stroll. If there happen to be visitors at Swallow Barn, this after-breakfast hour is famous for debates. We then all assemble in the porch, and fall into grave discussions upon agriculture, hunting, or horsemanship, in neither of which do I profess any great proficiency, though I take care not to let that appear. Some of the party amuse themselves with throwing pebbles picked from the gravel walk, or draw figures upon the earth with a cane, as if to assist their cogitations ; and when our topics grow scarce, we saunter towards the bridge, and string ourselves out upon the rail, to watch the bubbles that float down the stream ; and are sometimes a good deal perplexed to know what we shall do until dinner time.

There is a numerous herd of little negroes about the estate ; and these sometimes afford us a new diversion. A few mornings since, we encountered a horde of them, who were darting about the bushes like untamed monkeys. They are afraid of me, because I am a stranger, and take to their heels as soon as they see me. If I ever chance to get near enough to speak to one of

them, he stares at me with a suspicious gaze; and, after a moment, makes off at full speed, very much frightened, towards the cabins at some distance from the house. They are almost all clad in a long coarse shirt which reaches below the knee, without any other garment: but one of the group we met on the morning I speak of, was oddly decked in a pair of ragged trowsers, conspicuous for their ample dimensions in the seat. These had evidently belonged to some grown-up person, but were cut short in the legs to make them fit the wearer. A piece of twine across the shoulder of this grotesque imp, served for suspenders, and kept his habiliments from falling about his feet. Ned ordered this crew to prepare for a foot-race, and proposed a reward of a piece of money to the winner. They were to run from a given point, about a hundred paces distant, to the margin of the brook. Our whole suite of dogs were in attendance, and seemed to understand our pastime. At the word, away went the bevy, accompanied by every dog of the pack, the negroes shouting and the dogs yelling in unison. The *shirts* ran with prodigious vehemence, their speed exposing their bare, black, and meager shanks, to the scandal of all beholders; and the strange baboon in trowsers struggled close in their rear, with ludicrous earnestness, holding up his redundant and troublesome apparel with his hand. In a moment they reached the brook with unchecked speed; and, as the banks were muddy, and the dogs had become tangled with the racers in their path, two or three were precipitated into the water. This only increased the merriment, and they continued the contest in this new element, by floundering, kicking, and splashing about, like a brood of ducks in their first descent upon a pool. These young negroes have wonderfully flat noses, and the most oddly disproportioned mouths, which were now opened to their full dimensions, so as to display their white teeth in striking contrast with their complexions. They are a strange

pack of antic and careless animals, and furnish the liveliest picture that is to be found in nature, of that race of swart fairies
which, in the old time, were supposed to play their pranks in the
forest at moonlight. Ned stood by, enjoying this scene like an
amateur; encouraging the negroes in their gambols, and hallooing to the dogs, that by a kindred instinct entered tumultuously
into the sport and kept up the confusion. It was difficult to decide the contest. So the money was thrown into the air, and as
it fell to the ground, there was another rush, in which the hero
of the trowsers succeeded in getting the small coin from the
ground in his teeth, somewhat to the prejudice of his finery.

Rip asserts a special pre-eminence over these young serfs, and
has drilled them into a kind of local militia. He sometimes has
them all marshalled in the yard, and entertains us with a review.
They have an old watering-pot for a drum, and a dingy pocket-
handkerchief for a standard, under which they are arrayed in
military order. As they have no hats amongst them, Rip makes
each stick a cock's feather in his wool; and in this guise they
parade over the grounds with a riotous clamor, in which Rip's
shrill voice, and the clink of the old watering-pot, may be heard
at a great distance.

Besides these occupations, Hazard and myself frequently ride
out during the morning; and we are apt to let our horses take
their own way. This brings us into all the by-places of the
neighborhood, and makes me many acquaintances. Lucy and
Victorine often accompany us, and I have occasion to admire
their expert horsemanship. They have each a brisk little, pony
and these are wonderful favorites with them ; and, to hear them
talk, you would suppose them versed in all the affairs of the
stable.

With such amusements, we contrive to pass our mornings,
not listlessly, but idly. This course of life has a winning quality

that already begins to exercise its influence upon my habits. There is a fascination in the quiet, irresponsible, and reckless nature of these country pursuits, that is apt to seize upon the imagination of a man who has felt the perplexities of business. Ever since I have been at Swallow Barn, I have entertained a very philosophical longing for the calm and dignified retirement of the woods. I begin to grow moderate in my desires; that is, I only want a thousand acres of good land, an old manor-house, on a pleasant site, a hundred negroes, a large library, a host of friends, and a reserve of a few thousands a year in the stocks,—in case of bad crops,—and, finally, a house full of pretty, intelligent, and docile children, with some few et ceteras not worth mentioning.

I doubt not, after this, I shall be considered a man of few wants, and great resources within myself.

CHAPTER XXXII.

A COUNTRY GATHERING.

The day that followed our adventure in the Goblin Swamp was a busy one. We were to have our dinner party at Swallow Barn. At an early hour, before breakfast a servant waited at the front door for Hazard's orders. This was a negro boy equipped for service on horseback. He was rather more trig in his appearance than I was accustomed to see the servants. From his jockey air, and the conceited slant he had given to an old dark-colored cap with a yellow band, which stuck upon one side of his head, I was not wrong in my conjecture that he had something to do with the race-horses. He was mounted upon one of this stock, a tall, full-blooded bay, just ready to start, when Hazard came to instruct him in the purpose of his errand.

"Ganymede," said Ned, "you will go to the Court House, and give my compliments—"

"Yes, sir," said the messenger, with a joyful countenance.

—"To Mister Toll Hedges and the doctor, and tell them that we expect some friends here at dinner to day."

"Yes, sir," shouted the negro, and striking his heels into his horse's sides at the same instant, plunged forward some paces.

"Come back," cried Ned; "what are you going after?"

"To ax Mas Toll Hedges and the doctor to come here to dinner to-day," returned the impatient boy.

"Wait until you hear what I have to tell you," continued Ned. "Say to them that your Master Frank will be glad to see them; and that I wish them to bring any body along with them they choose."

"That's all!" exclaimed the negro again, and once more bounded off towards the high road.

"You black rascal!" cried Ned at the top of his voice, and laughing, "come back again. You are in a monstrous hurry. I wish you would show something of this activity when it is more wanting. Now, hear me out. Tell them, if they see the 'squire, to bring him along."

"Yes, sir."

"And as you pass by Mr. Braxton Beverly's, stop there, and ask him if he will favor us with his company. And if he cannot come himself, tell him to send us some of the family. Tell him to send them, at any rate. Let me see; is there any body else? If you meet any of the gentlemen about, give them my compliments, and tell them to come over."

"Yes, sir."

"Now can you remember it all?"

"Never fear me, Mas Ned," said the negro, with his low-country, broad pronunciation, that entirely discards the letter R.·

"Then be off," cried Hazard, "and let me hear of no loitering on the road."

"That's me!" shouted Ganymede, in the same tone of excessive spirits he evinced on his first appearance. "I'll be bound I make tracks!" and, saying this, the negro flourished his hand above his head, struck his heels again on the horse's ribs, hallooed with a wild scream, and shot forward like an arrow from a bow.

Soon after breakfast the visitors from The Brakes began to appear. First came Prudence Meriwether with Catharine, in Mr. Tracy's carriage. About an hour afterwards, Swansdown's glittering curricle arrived, bringing Bel Tracy under the convoy of the gentleman himself. After another interval, Harvey Riggs and Ralph followed on horseback. Mr. Tracy had not accompanied either of these parties ; but Harvey brought an assurance from him that he would be punctual to the engagement.

A dinner party in the country is not the premeditated, anxious affair it is in town. It has nothing of that long, awful interval between the arrival of the guests and the serving up of the dishes, when men look in each other's faces with empty stomachs, and utter inane common-places with an obvious air of insincerity, if not of actual suffering. On the contrary, it is understood to be a regular spending of the day, in which the guests assume all the privileges of inmates, sleep on the sofas, lounge through the halls, read the newspapers, stroll over the grounds, and, if pinched by appetite, stay their stomachs with bread and butter, and toddy made of choice old spirits.

There were several hours yet to be passed before dinner-time. Our company, therefore, began to betake themselves to such occupations as best sorted with their idle humors. Harvey Riggs had already communicated to me the incidents I have recorded of the interview between Prudence and Catharine, and our curiosity had been accordingly aroused to see in what way the two damsels intended to pursue the measures which both had voted. necessary in their emergency. An occasion now occurred to put them in practice. Prudence was seated at the piano strumming a tune ; Swansdown was in the courtyard, looking through the open window, with a flower in his hand regaling his nose, and listening to the strains, the syren strains, that fell from his fair enemy. Presently the piano ceased, the maiden turned carelessly towards the window. Swansdown put on a winning smile, said some unheard, gallant thing, and presented the nosegay to the lady. She smelt it, and sat down at that very window. This position brought her ear right opposite the gentleman's lips. It is pretty obvious what must follow, when a cavalier has such an advantage over even an angry dame. Soon Prudence was obser- ved to smile ; and, straightway, the conference became soft and low, accompanied with earnest, sentimental looks, and ever and anon relieved by a fluttering, short, ambiguous, and somewhat breathless laugh. It was plain, Prudence was enforcing her tactics. She was heaping coals of fire upon the head of the luck- less swain. In truth, if she yet nursed her wrath, it seemed to have grown monstrous charitable. Perhaps she relented in her stern purpose, and gave way to the gentler emotions of pity, in the hope of converting the sinner. Perhaps she had tempered her censure of man's obliquities, by the spontaneous and irresist- ible overflow of her own tenderness ; or, perhaps she had been altogether in a mistake. Whatever was the truth, her present purpose, motive, and action, certainly seemed to me marvellously inexplicable.

Whilst this private interview was going on, the members of the household passed freely along the hall. A drawing would show my reader how one might have looked thence into the par- lor, and seen the position of the speakers ; and how from the lit- tle porch where Harvey and I were seated, we could discern Swansdown through a screen of rose-bushes, as he stood with his head rather inside of the casement. But, for want of a good map or sketch of the premises, these things must be conceived. At length Catharine, who till now had been engaged with other cares, and who had, I presume, supposed that the war against the per- fidious poet, philosopher, and future pillar of the state, was to be one of extermination, came flaunting along the hall, carolling a gay tune, and wearing an outside of unaccustomed levity. When she arrived opposite the parlor door, the same phenomenon that had put us at fault seemed all at once to strike her. An emotion of surprise was visible upon her countenance. She passed, went back, looked into the parlor, hesitated, returned towards the front door, stood still a moment in a fit of abstraction, wheeled round, and finally entered the room with a face all smoothness and pleasure. Her plans were concerted during these motions. Her accost was playful, loud, and even unusually gracious ; and from that moment the trio fell into an easy, voluble, and pleasant discourse, in which the two ladies talked without intermission, and without listening to each other, for a good half-hour.

"That's strange !" said Harvey, looking at me with a face full of wonder.

"You have misrepresented them, Harvey," said I.

"Not a jot ; for Bel has had the whole detailed to her, not exactly in the words I have given you, but in substance, from each of them separately this morning. They have both, in turn, confided to her the conversation of last night ; and, like a good secret-keeper, she has told it all to me,—knowing my anxiety in the matter,—but with a strict injunction that it was to go no further. And so I, in order that I may have a witness to my fidelity, have told it all to you, who of course will understand it as confidential, and not permit a word of it to escape your lips. There you have the whole pedigree of the secret, and you see that I am as close as a woman. In the detail, I have not in any degree impaired the excellence of the story, I assure you."

"Then the wind blows from another quarter to-day," said I.

"The thing is perfectly plain," said Harvey ; "that solemn ass, Swansdown, has a greater hold on these women than they are willing to allow to each other. Prudence is not quite agreed to trust Kate ; and Kate is half inclined to disbelieve every word that Prudence has told her. And both of them think it at least very probable that there is some mistake in the matter. So, for fear there might be a mistake, Pru has set about making a demonstration for herself; and Kate has taken the alarm from what she has discovered, and is afraid that Pru, if let alone, will get the whip-hand of her. In this state of things, they have dissolved the alliance, and each one is coquetting on her own account. It is something like a panic against a bank, when the creditors are all dashing in to get the preference in the payment of their notes."

Swansdown was at last relieved from the spirited run that had been made upon his courtesy. The two ladies drew off to other engagements, and the disencumbered gentleman came round to the door where we were sitting. It happened that Rip, a few moments before, had been released from school, and had walked into the parlor where Prudence and Catharine were entertaining the poet; but, finding them earnestly occupied, had made a circuit round the room and out again without stopping, and then came and seated himself on the sill of the front door, where he remained when Swansdown joined our party. What had previously been occupying Rip's brain I know not, for he sat silent and abstracted; but at last, drawing up his naked heels on the floor, so as to bring his knees almost in contact with his chin, and embracing his legs with his arms, in such manner as to form a hoop round them with his fingers interlaced, he looked up at us with a face of some perplexity, as he broke out with the exclamation,—

"Dog them women! If they ar'nt too much!"

"Whom do you mean, Rip?" inquired Harvey.

"Aunt Pru and Catharine."

"What have they been doing? you seem to be in a bad humor."

"Oh, dog 'em, I say! they won't let Mr. Swansdown do any thing he wants: always tagging after him. (Swansdown was a great favorite of Rip's, principally on account of his horses.) I don't wonder he don't like to stay with them."

"What fault have you to find with the ladies, Rip?" asked

Swansdown, amused with the boy's manner.   "You are not angry with them on my account, I hope?"

"Yes, I am.   They're always a talking about you.   For my share, I think they must be in love with you."

Here Harvey laughed aloud.   "What do they say of Mr. Swansdown, Rip?"

"You needn't laugh, Mr. Riggs," said Rip.   "Havn't I heard them both talking about Mr. Swansdown?   Oh, oh! I wouldn't like any body to talk about me so!"

"I hope they said nothing ill of me, Rip?" said Swansdown, a little confused.

"I guess they didn't," replied Rip.   "But you had better look out, else every body will say that you are going to get married to both of them.   That would be queer, wouldn't it?"

"But you havn't told us what they said," interrupted Harvey.

"No matter, Rip, about that," said Swansdown.   "We must not tell tales out of school, you know."

"Catch me!" replied Rip, "I'm not going to tell."

Saying these words, he jumped up and ran off to his sports, with his natural careless and irresponsible manner, not dreaming that the slightest consequence could be attached to any thing he had uttered.

This simple incident had a sensible influence upon the conduct of Swansdown during the rest of the day.   He had of late been haunted by an apprehension that he was almost ashamed to acknowledge, namely, that it was possible his civilities both to Prudence and Catharine might be overrated and misconstrued. They had both flattered his vanity, and allured him by that means into a somewhat intimate intercourse, although it was very far from kindling up a serious interest in his feelings.   Still, this attention was agreeable to him ; and once or twice the suspicion might have crossed his mind, that he was permitting matters to go too far; an indiscretion which he foresaw might produce some unpleasant consequences. It was in this state of doubt that he had left the ladies but a few moments since; and it was, therefore, with something of trepidation and alarm that he heard Rip's abrupt disclosure, made with the boyish recklessness I have described. Harvey Riggs saw this, and was inclined to make advantage of it; but Rip took the caution inculcated by Swansdown, and frustrated the object. The most amusing feature in the whole transaction was, that it brought about the very state of things, by the voluntary choice of Swansdown, that Prudence and Catharine, on their part, had resolved the night before to compel; but which their uncertain and distrustful policy to-day had countervailed. Swansdown came to the sudden determination to allay the false hopes he had raised, by assuming, for the future, a more circumspect and reserved behavior, and, as soon as the opportunity favored, to decamp from the field of action, and make his way back to his native oaks, where, he hoped, his absence would in a short time—at least in as short a time as so sore a disease allowed—heal up the wounds his innocent and unwary perfections had inflicted upon the peace of two unquiet and unhappy spinsters. Full of this sentiment, he suddenly became pensive, formal, punctilious, prosy, and cold. Never did the thermometer fall more rapidly to zero.

Whilst these things were going on, our company continued to assemble. Two odd-looking figures arrived on horseback at the gate, followed by our trusty boy Ganymede, who had staid behind to accompany the guests he had been sent to invite. The older of the two was the doctor, a fat, short-winded gentleman, dressed, notwithstanding the heat of the season, all in woollen cloth. Behind his saddle he carried a small valise, such as gentlemen of his profession use in the country for the conveyance of drugs and medicines. The other was our old friend Taliaferro Hedges, considerably improved in attire, but with his pantaloons—some white cotton fabric—rubbed up, by the action of his horse, almost to his knees. He wore his broad, shapeless, and tattered straw hat, that flapped over his eyes with a supreme air of waggishness; and as he dismounted at the gate, he deliberately disburdened his mouth of a quid of tobacco, and walked up to the door. It was now past one o'clock; and as it is usual in this part of Virginia to follow up the introduction of a guest at this hour of the day with an invitation to take some of the toddy, our new comers were ushered into a back room, where an immense bowl had been prepared by Ned Hazard, who was there present with Meriwether and Mr. Wart to administer it.

In the midst of the jest, clamor, and laughter of the convocation that was now assembled, admiring and doing homage to the icy and well-flavored bowl, other visitors were introduced, amongst the rest Mr. Braxton Beverly, an extensive breeder of sheep and blooded horses. He was a tall, thin, talkative gentleman, who had an authoritative way of besieging the person he addressed, and laying down the heads of his discourse by striking the fingers of his right hand upon the palm of his left, and shaking his head somewhat as I have seen a bullying school-boy, when he was going to fight. Mr. Chub formed a part of this group, but stood rather in the background, with his hands tucked under the skirts of his coat, so as to throw them out like the tail of a bantam cock, whilst he erected his figure even beyond the perpendicular line. For a time, this was a busy and a gay scene, characterized by the exhibition of that good-humored and natural freedom from the constraint of forms, which constitutes one of the most unequivocal features of a genuine hospitality. The tumult gradually subsided, as the several personages in the room retreated towards the hall; and it was not long before the whole party seemed to be entirely domesticated, and had separated into as many fragments as whim or chance produced. Some sauntered towards the bridge, and thence to the stable; some sat in the shade of the porch, and discussed the topics that interested the country; and others wandered as far as the schoolhouse, whence might be heard an occasional obstreperous laugh, the sudden consequence of some well-told story.

As the dinner hour drew nigh, our scattered forces were fast concentrating upon one point. The ladies had assembled in the drawing-room; and there were many signs that could not be mistaken, that the hour dedicated to the imperious calls of appetite was near at hand. Still, Mr. Tracy had not yet appeared. Divers speculations were set on foot as to the cause of his absence. Perhaps he had forgotten his engagement; but that was not probable, considering how careful he was known to be in all such matters; and especially after the interest he had expressed to relieve Meriwether from the sense of mortification which he supposed his friend felt in his defeat. He could not have lost his way; nor could he have mistaken the hour. A general anxiety, at length, began to prevail on the subject. Meriwether was particularly desirous to meet his neighbor at this moment of pacification; and the rest of the party were curious to note the old gentleman's behavior at so critical a juncture.

The dinner hour had now come, and every one was still on the lookout for our ancient guest. Most of the gentlemen were congregated about the door, watching every object that came in sight upon the road leading to the gateway. At last, slowly emerging from behind a clump of trees, at some distance off, where the road first occurred to view, was seen the venerable veteran himself. He had dismounted from his horse, and, unattended by any servant, was walking leisurely with his arms behind his back, the bridle dangling from one hand, and his horse dodging along after

him, as slow as foot could fall. Both the steed and the rider
looked patiently and pensively upon the ground. A long interval
elapsed before they reached the gate. The worthy gentleman,
all unconscious of the lateness of the hour, or of his proximity
to his point of destination, and the impatient crowd that were
gazing at him, advanced in deep thought. The exterminated
lawsuit disturbed him. He thought sorrowfully over the extinguished controversy. A favorite fancy had been annihilated,
untimely cropped, as a flower of the field. He could not realize
the idea. The privation had left him no substitute. All this
was plainly read in his movements. He travelled forward a few
paces, then stopped, raised his head, by a careful, circuitous motion of his hand, took his handkerchief out of his pocket, paused
and adjusted it in his grasp, then, stooping forward, applied it to
his nose, and returned it, with the same deliberation, to its place
of deposit. This operation was several times repeated, and accompanied with looks of bewildered abstraction. Poor gentleman! He had parted with a friend when he gave up his suit.
He arrived, at length, at the gate, where he was met by Meriwether, and almost by the whole company. It was a surprise to him
to find himself so near; and, immediately dismissing the meditative air which had rendered his march so tardy and perplexed, he
put on his accustomed demeanor of studied and sprightly civility, and replied to the numerous greetings with an alacrity that
astonished every one.

"I fear I have kept you waiting, my friend," said he to Meriwether; "that, you know, is not my way; but, body-o'-me! I had
like to have made a slip; my timepiece is to blame. We old fellows," he continued, looking at his watch, "havn't so much of this
commodity to lose either, Mr. Meriwether, ha, ha! Time does
not spare such an old curmudgeon as I: he has handled me pretty
well already."

"Papa, what made you stay so long?" asked Bel. "We have been waiting for you until I began to be alarmed lest something had happened to you."

"My dear," replied the father, "I thought I would just ride round by the Apple-pie to take a look at the grounds; and I believe I staid there rather too long."

"And what had you to look at there, all by yourself, I should like to know?"

"Nothing, my dear, but we must not talk of the Apple-pie,— not a word! That subject is to be buried for ever. It is done, I assure you, my dear, it is done."

With these words, the old gentleman entered the hall and mingled with the crowd.

CHAPTER XXXIII.

THE DINNER TABLE.

ABOUT half after three, Carey, with a solemn official air wnich was well set off by a singularly stiff costume,—assuming for the nonce the rank and station of head-waiter,—announced that dinner was on the table. The greater part of the company was collected in the drawing-room; some two or three loitered through the hall. At the summons, Mr. Tracy, with that alacrious motion which sometimes belongs to old men, sprang upon his feet and hastened to the opposite side of the room, where my cousin Lucretia was seated, took her hand, and, with a repetition of formal bows after a fashion in vogue in the last century, led her to the dining-room. Meriwether stood at the door beckoning to one after another of his guests, with that kind smile and unstudied grace which are natural to a benevolent temper; his tall figure somewhat constrained in its motion by an infusion of modesty, which is always discernible in him when placed in any conspicuous position. As soon as Mr. Tracy led the way, Swansdown, with some particularity, offered his arm to Bel. The other ladies found an escort among the more gallant of the gentlemen; and after them the rest of the party pressed forward pell-mell towards the dining-room, leaving Meriwether to bring up the rear, who, upon arriving at the table, with that considerateness which never

forsakes him in the smallest matters, placed Mr. Wart, Mr.
Chub, and one or two of his elder guests near his own seat.

I must not forget to mention, that before we had taken our
chairs, Mistress Winkle, decked out in all the pomp of silk and
muslin, sailed, as it were, with muffled oars into the room from a
side door ; and, with a prim and stealthy motion, deposited her
time-worn person near to my cousin Lucretia. It is a custom of
affectionate courtesy in the family, to accord to this venerable
relic of the past generation the civility of a place at table. Mr.
Tracy was aware of Meriwether's feelings towards the aged dame;
and, prompted by his overflowing zeal on the present occasion to
manifest his deference to his host, he no sooner observed her than
he broke out into a jocose and gallant recognition :—

"Mistress Winkle! what, my old friend! It rejoices me to
see you looking so well—and so youthful! The world goes merrily with you. Gad's-my life! if Colonel Tarleton were only
alive again to make another visit to the James River, it would
be hard to persuade him that time had gained so small a victory
over the romping girl whom he had the impertinence to chuckle
under the chin so boldly. A saucy and stark trooper he was in
those days, Mistress Winkle! But the gout, the gout, I warrant,
did his business for him long ago! Ha, ha! You hav'nt forgot
old times, Mistress Winkle, although they have well nigh forgotten you."

The housekeeper, during this outbreak, courtesied, hemmed
and smiled; and, with much confusion, rustled her silken folds
in her chair, with somewhat of the motion of a motherly hen in
the process of incubation. Mr. Tracy had touched upon an incident which, for nearly half a century, had been a theme that
warmed up all her self-complacency, and which owed its origin to
one of the English partisan's forays upon the river side, during
the Revolution, in which he was said to have made himself very

much at home at Swallow Barn, and to have bestowed some com-
plimental notice upon the then buxom and blooming dependant
of the family.

The table was furnished with a profusion of the delicacies
afforded by the country ; and, notwithstanding it was much more
ample than the accommodation of the guests required, it seemed
to be stored rather with a reference to its own dimensions than
to the number or wants of those who were collected around it.
At the head, immediately under the eye of our hostess, in the
customary pride of place, was deposited a goodly ham of bacon,
rich in its own perfections, as well as in the endemic honors that
belong to it in the Old Dominion. According to a usage worthy
of imitation, it was clothed in its own dark skin, which the imaginative mistress of the kitchen had embellished by carving into some fanciful figures. The opposite end of the table smoked
with a huge roasted saddle of mutton, which seemed, from its
trim and spruce air, ready to gallop off the dish. Between these
two extremes was scattered an enticing diversity of poultry, prepared with many savory adjuncts, and especially that topical luxury, which yet so slowly finds its way northward,—fried chickens,—sworn brother to the ham, and old Virginia's standard dish.
The intervening spaces displayed a profusion of the products of
the garden ; nor were oysters and crabs wanting where room
allowed ; and, where nothing else could be deposited, as if scrupulous of showing a bare spot of the table-cloth, the bountiful
forethought of Mistress Winkle had provided a choice selection
of pickles of every color and kind. From the whole array of the
board it was obvious, that abundance and variety were deemed no
less essential to the entertainment, than the excellence of the
viands.

A bevy of domestics, in every stage of training, attended upon the table, presenting a lively type of the progress of civiliza-

tion, or the march of intellect; the veteran waitingman being well-contrasted with the rude half-monkey, half-boy, who seemed to have been for the first time admitted to the parlor; whilst, between these two, were exhibited the successive degrees that mark the advance from the young savage to the sedate and sophisticated image of the old-fashioned negro nobility. It was equal to a gallery of caricatures, a sort of scenic satire upon man in his various stages, with his odd imitativeness illustrated in the broadest lines. Each had added some article of coxcombry to his dress; a pewter buckle fastened to the shirt for a breast-pin; a dingy parti-colored ribbon, ostentatiously displayed across the breast, with one end lodged in the waistcoat pocket; or a preposterous cravat girding up an exorbitantly starched shirt collar, that rivalled the driven snow, as it traversed cheeks as black as midnight, and fretted the lower cartilage of a pair of refractory, raven-hued ears. One, more conceited than the rest, had platted his wool (after a fashion common amongst the negroes) into five or six short cues both before and behind; whilst the visages of the whole group wore that grave, momentous elongation which is peculiar to the African face, and which is eminently adapted to express the official care and personal importance of the wearer.

As the more immediate, and what is universally conceded to be the more important, business of the dinner was discussed, to wit, the process of dulling the edge of appetite, the merriment of the company rose in proportion to the leisure afforded to its exercise; and the elder portion of the guests gently slid into the vivacity of the younger. Mr. Tracy did not lose for an instant that antiquated cavalier air which he had assumed on entering the room. As Harvey Riggs expressed it, " he was painfully polite and very precisely gay." The ladies, for a time, gave their tone to the table; and, under this influence, we found ourselves falling into detached circles, where each pursued its separate

theme, sometimes in loud and rapid converse, mingled with frequent bursts of laughter that spread an undistinguishable din
through the room; and sometimes in low and confidential mur-
murings, of which it was impossible to say whether they were
grave or gay. Swansdown's voice was poured into Bel's ear in
gentle and unremitting whispers, of which Ned Hazard alone, of
all the guests—to judge by his intense and abstracted gaze—was
able to unriddle the import. Prudence, equally abstracted, was
unnaturally merry, and laughed much more than was necessary
at Harvey's jokes. Catharine talked with singular sagacity, and
listened, with still more singular earnestness, to Mr. Beverley,
who was instructing her, with equal interest and eloquence, upon
the wholesome effects he had found in the abundant use of flannel
—which he described with unnecessary amplitude of details—in
repelling the assaults of an ancient enemy, the rheumatism. Now
and then a loud and rather obstreperous laugh, not altogether
suited to the region he inhabited, and which some such consciousness seemed abruptly to arrest, was set up by Taliaferro Hedges.
This worthy had already begun to occupy that questionable ground
which a gentleman of loose habits and decaying reputation is
pretty sure to arrive at in his descending career. Dissipation
had lowered him somewhat in the world, and had already introduced him to a class of associates who had made a visible impression on his manners, a circumstance which very few men have so
little shrewdness as not to perceive, nor so much hardihood as not
to be ashamed of. In truth, Toll had imbibed some of the slang,
and much of the boisterousness of the bar-room; but he had not
yet given such unequivocal indications of the incurableness of his
infirmity, as to induce his acquaintances (who for the most part
upheld him on some family consideration) to exclude him from
their houses. On the contrary, a certain strain of disorderly but
generous companionship, breaking out and shining above the vices

to which it was akin, still recommended him to the favor of those who were unwilling to desert him as long as his case was not absolutely hopeless. The course of intemperance, however, gravitates by a fatal law downwards: it is unfortunately of the most rare occurrence, that the mind which has once been debauched by a habit of intoxication, ever regains that poise of self-respect which preserves the purity of the individual. It was easy to perceive that Hedges labored under a perpetual struggle to constrain his deportment within even the broader boundaries that limit the indulgence of the class of gentlemen.

Amidst these diversified exhibitions, Mr. Wart ate like a man with a good appetite, and gave himself no trouble to talk, except in the intervals of serving his plate ; for he remarked, " that he was not accustomed to these late hours, and thought them apt to make one surcharge his stomach ;" whilst the parson, who sat opposite to him, wore a perpetual smile during the repast; sometimes looking as if he intended to say something, but more generally watching every word that fell from Mr. Wart's lips.

The courses disappeared ; a rich dessert came and went: the spirits of the company rose still higher. The wine, iced almost to the freezing point, moved in a busy sphere ; for the intense heat of the weather gave it an additional zest. We had made the usual libations to the ladies, and exchanged the frequent healths, according to the hackneyed and unmeaning custom which prevails unquestioned, I suppose, over Christendom, when the epoch arrived at which, by the arbitrary law of the feast, the womankind are expected to withdraw ; that time which, if I were a sovereign in this dinner-party realm, should be blotted from the festive calendar. I should shame me to acknowledge that there was any moment in the social day when it was unseemly for the temperate sex to look upon or listen to the lord of creation in his pastimes ; but I was neither monarch nor magician, and so we were left alone to pursue unreproved the frolic current upon which we had been lifted. Before us glittered the dark sea of the table, studded over with " carracks," " argosies," and " barks" freighted with the wealth of the Azores, Spain, Portugal and France ; and with the lighters by which these precious bulks were unladen, and deposited in their proper receptacles. In sooth, the wine was very good.

Almost the first words that were spoken, after we had readjusted ourselves from the stir occasioned by the retreat of the ladies, came from Mr. Tracy. He had been waiting for a suitable opportunity to acquit himself of a grave and formal duty. The occasion of the dinner, he conceived, demanded of him a peculiar compliment to the host. His strict and refined sensitiveness to the requirements of gentle breeding would have forbidden him to sleep quietly in his bed with this task unperformed ; and therefore, with a tremulous and fluttered motion, like that of a young orator awe-struck at the thought of making a speech, he rose to command the attention of the table. A faint-hearted smile sat rigidly upon his visage, " like moonlight on a marble statue,"— his eye glassy, his cheek pale, and his gesture contrived to a faint and feeble counterfeit of mirth. It was evident the old gentleman was not accustomed to public speaking : and so he remarked, as he turned towards Meriwether, and continued an address somewhat in the following terms :—

" Since we have, my dear sir, so fortunately succeeded in putting an end to a vexatious question,—which, although it has resulted in throwing upon my hands a few barren and unprofitable acres, has given all the glory of the settlement to you ;—(here his voice quavered considerably,) for it was indubitably, my very worthy and excellent friend, at your instance and suggestion, that we struck out the happy thought of leaving it to the arbitrement of our kind friends :—and to tell the truth, (at this point the old gentleman brightened up a little and looked jocular, although he still had the quaver,) I don't know but I would as lief have the lawsuit as the land,—seeing that it has been the occasion of many merry meetings :—I will take upon myself to propose to this good company of neighbors and friends, that we shall drink,—ha ha! (continued the veteran, waving his hand above his head, and inclining towards the table with a gay gesticulation,) that we shall drink, gentlemen, a bumper; (here he took the decanter in his hand, and filled his glass.) " Fill your glasses all around,—no flinching !"

" Fill up ! fill up !" cried every one, anxious to help the old gentleman out of his difficulties, " Mr. Tracy's toast in a bumper !"

" Here," continued Mr. Tracy, holding his glass on high with a trembling hand, " here is to our admirable host, Mister Francis Meriwether of Swallow Barn !—a sensible and enlightened gentleman,—a considerate landlord,—a kind neighbor, an independent, upright, sensible,—enlightened—(here he became sadly puzzled for a word, and paused for a full half minute,) reasonable defender of right and justice ; a man that is not headstrong (his perplexity still increasing) on the score of landmarks, or indeed on any score ! —I say, gentlemen, here's wishing him success in all his aims, and long life to enjoy a great many such joyous meetings as the present; besides—"

" Health of our host, and many such meetings !" exclaimed Mr. Wart, interrupting the speaker, and thus cutting short a toast of which it was evident Mr. Tracy could not find the end.

" Health to our host,—joyous meetings !" cried out half a dozen voices.

And thus relieved from his floundering progress, the old gentleman took his seat in great glee, remarking to the person next to him, " that he was not much practised in making dinner speeches, but that he could get through very well when he was once pushed to it."

Meriwether sat out this adulatory and unexpected assault with painful emotions, sinking under the weight of his natural diffidence. The rest of the company awaited in silence the slow, drawling and distinct elocution of the speaker, with an amused and ludicrous suspense, until Mr. Wart's interruption, which was the signal for a shout of approbation; and in the uproar that ensued, the wine was quaffed; while Mr. Tracy chuckled at the eminent success of his essay, and Meriwether stood bowing and blushing with the bashfulness of a girl.

When the clamor subsided, Philly Wart remarked in a quiet tone,—

" I think our friend Meriwether will scarcely escape a speech in reply to this compliment.   The fashion is to return the broadside whenever it is given."

" I pray you," said Meriwether, with an emotion amounting almost to alarm, " do not ask me to say any thing.   I have an insuperable aversion to such efforts : my nerves will not stand it. Mr. Tracy knows how kindly I take the expression of his regard."

Harvey Riggs, who observed Meriwether's real embarrassment, rose to divert the attention of the company to another quarter; and putting on an air of great solemnity, observed that he was unwilling to lose so favorable an opportunity of paying a tribute to two very worthy, and on the present occasion he might say, conspicuous persons ; " I mean, gentlemen," said he, " Mr. Philpot Wart and Mr. Singleton Oglethorpe Swansdown.   Replenish, gentlemen !   Here's to the health of the pacificators ! the men whose judgments could not be led astray by the decisions of courts, and whose energies could not be subdued by the formidable difficulties of the Apple-pie !"

" Bravo !" rang from every mouth.

" A speech from Mr. Swansdown !" exclaimed Ned Hazard.

" A speech from Mr. Swansdown !" echoed from all quarters.

The gentleman called on rose from his chair. Harvey Riggs rapped upon the table to command silence ; there followed a pause.

" I do not rise to make a speech," said Swansdown with great formality of manner.

" Hear him !" shouted Harvey.

" I do not rise, gentlemen," said the other, " to make a speech ; but custom, in these innovating times, almost imperatively exacts that the festive, spontaneous and unmerited encomiums of the table,—that, I remark, the festive, spontaneous and unmerited encomiums of the table, generated in the heat of convivial zeal, should meet their response in the same hilarious spirit in which they find their origin. Gentlemen will understand me ; it is not my purpose to rebuke a custom which may, and doubtless does, contribute to the embellishment of the social relations. It is merely my purpose, on the present occasion, as an humble, and, if I know myself, an unpretending individual, to respond to the free and unbidden expressions of the good-will of this company to myself, and my distinguished colleague, with whom my name has been associated. In his name therefore, and in my own, I desire to acknowledge the deep sense we entertain of the compliment conveyed in the toast of our worthy fellow-guest. (Philly Wart bowed and smiled.) It will be amongst the proudest topics of re- membrance left to me, gentlemen, amidst the vicissitudes of a changeful life, that the personal sacrifices I have made and the toil I have bestowed, in the successful endeavor to define and establish the complex relations and rights of two estimable friends, have found a favorable and flattering approval in the good sense of this enlightened company. If it should further result, that the great principles developed, and, to a certain extent, promulgated in this endeavor, should hereafter redound to the advantage of the generation amongst which I have the honor to live, I need not say how sincerely I shall rejoice that neither my friend nor myself have lived in vain. I propose, gentlemen, in return,—"The freeholders of the Old Dominion; the prosperity of the Commonwealth reposes securely upon their intelligence!"

"Amen!" said Hazard in an under tone, intended only for my ear, "and may they never fail to do honor to *unpretending* merit!"

"I suppose," said Mr. Wart, speaking in an unusually placid tone, as he rose with a face reefed into half its ordinary length with smiles, and, at the same time, expressing arch waggery, "I suppose it is necessary that I also should speak to this point. There are, if your honor pleases—Mr. President—ordinarily two different motives for proposing the health of an individual at table. The one is a *bonâ fide* purpose to exalt and honor the person proposed, by a public manifestation of the common feeling toward him, by reason of some certain act or deed by him performed, entitling him, in the estimation of the persons proposing, to applause. In this point of view, my worthy friend who has just spoken, seems to have considered the case in hand. The second motive for the act, may it please you,—Mr. Meriwether,—may be, and such I take it, a certain intent, *inter alia*, to promote and encourage cheerful companionship. With whatever gravity the *res gesta* may be conducted, I hold that it is to be looked upon *diverso intuitu*, according to the temper and condition of the company for the time being.

"Now, sir, I will not venture to say that my learned friend has not wisely considered the toast in the present instance, as intended and made in all gravity of purpose; but, seeing that this company did certainly manifest some levity on the occasion,

I choose, sir, to stand on the sunny side of the question, as the safest, in the present emergency. *Vere sapit*, sir, *qui alieno periculo sapit* : I, therefore, sir, go for the joke. I have sometimes seen an old hound tongue upon a false scent ; but then there is music made, and, I believe, that is pretty much all that is wanting on the present occasion.

"When a man is praised to his face, gentlemen of the jury," he continued, rising into an energetic key, and mistaking the tribunal he was addressing,—"I beg pardon, gentlemen, you see the ermine and the woolsack will stick to my tongue : *Omnibus hoc vitium cantoribus*, as an ancient author (I forget his name) very appropriately remarks. What is bred in the bone,—you know the proverb. But when a man is praised to his face,"— here the speaker stretched out his arm, and stood silent for a moment, as if endeavoring to recollect what he intended to say,— for he had lost the thread of his speech,—and during this pause his countenance grew so irresistibly comic that the whole company, who had from the first been collecting a storm of laughter, now broke out with concentrated violence.

"Poh, Ned Hazard ! you put every thing I had to say out of my head with that horse laugh," continued the orator, looking at Ned, who had thrown himself back in his chair, giving full vent to his merriment.

Philly patiently awaited the blowing over of this whirlwind, with an increased drollery of look ; and then, as it subsided, he made a bow with his glass in his hand, saying, in an emphatic way, "your healths, gentlemen !" swallowed his wine, and took his seat, amidst renewed peals of mirth. At the same moment, from the depths of this tumult, was distinctly heard the voice of Mr. Chub, who cried out, with his eyes brimful of tears, and a half suffocated voice,—" A prodigious queer man, that Mister Philly Wart !"

Segars were now introduced, the decanters were filled for the
second time, and the flush of social enjoyment reddened into a
deeper hue.   Some one or two additional guests had just arrived,
and taken their seats at the table, a full octave lower in tone than
their excited comrades of the board : it was like the mingling of
a few flats too many in a lively overture ; but the custom of the
soil sanctions and invites these irregularities, and it was not long
before this rear-guard hastened on to the van.   The scene presented a fine picture of careless, unmethodized and unenthralled
hospitality, where the guests enjoyed themselves according to
their varying impulses, whether in grave argumentation or top-
pling merriment.   Now and then, a song,—none of the best in
execution,—was sung, and after that a boisterous catch was trolled,
with some decisive thumpings on the table, by way of marking
time, in which it might be perceived that even old Mr. Tracy was
infected with the prevailing glee, for his eyes sparkled, and his
head shook to the music, and his fist was brandished with a downward swing, almost in the style of a professed royster.   In the
intervals of the singing a story was told.   Sometimes the conversation almost sank into a murmur; sometimes it mounted to a
gale, its billow rolling in with a deep-toned, heavy, swelling roar,
until it was spent in a general explosion.   Not unfrequently, a
collapse of the din surprised some single speaker in the high road
of his narrative, and thus detected him recounting, in an upper
key, some incident which he had perhaps addressed to one auditor,
and which, not a little to his disconcertment, he found himself
compelled to communicate to the whole circle.   It was in such
an interval as this, that Hedges was left struggling through the
following colloquy with Ralph Tracy :—

"I made a narrow escape."

"How was that ?" asked Ralph.

"Oh, a very serious accident, I assure you ! I came within

an ace of getting yoked that trip ; married, sir, by all that's
lovely !"

" No•!" exclaimed Ralph, " you didn't, sure enough, Toll ?"

" If I didn't," replied Toll, " I wish I may be——(here he
slipped out a round, full and expressive malediction.) I'll tell you
how it was. At the Sweet Springs I got acquainted with a pre-
posterously rich old sugar planter from Louisiana. He had his
wife and daughter with him, and a whole squad of servants.
Forty thousand dollars a year! and the daughter as frenchified
as a sunflower : not so particularly young neither, but looking as
innocent as if she wa'nt worth one copper. I went in for grace,
and began to show out a few of my ineffable pulchritudes,—and
what do you think?—she was most horribly struck. I put her
into an ecstasy with one of my pigeon-wings. She wanted to find
out my name."

" Well, and what came of it ?"

" *Thar* were only three things," said Toll, " in the way. If
it had not been for them, I should have been planting sugar this
day. First, the old one didn't take to it very kindly ; and then,
the mother began to rear a little at me too ; but I shouldn't have
considered that of much account, only the daughter herself seemed
as much as to insinuate that the thing wouldn't do."

" Did you carry it so far as to put the question to her ?"

" Not exactly so far as that. No, no, I was not such a fool
as to come to the *ore tenus ;* I went on the non-committal principle. She as much as signified to a friend of mine, that she didn't
wish to make my acquaintance : and so, I took the hint and was
off :—wa'nt that close grazing, Ralph ?"

This concluding interrogatory was followed up by one of
Toll's loud cachinations, that might have been heard a hundred
paces from the house, and which was, as usual, chopped short
by his perceiving that it did not take effect so decidedly as he

expected upon the company.   Upon this, Hedges became rather silent for the next half hour.

The dining-room had for some time past been gradually assuming that soft, mellow, foggy tint which is said by the painters to spread such a charm over an Indian-summer landscape.   The volumes of smoke rolled majestically across the table, and then rose into the upper air, where they spread themselves out into a rich, dun mass, and flung a certain hazy witchery over the scene. The busy riot of revelry seemed to echo through another Cimmerium, and the figures of the guests were clad in even a spectral obscurity.   Motionless, exact and sombre as an Egyptian obelisk, old Carey's form was dimly seen relieved against the light of a window, near one end of the table; all the other domestics had fled, and the veteran body-guard alone remained on duty.   The wine went round with the regularity of a city milk-cart, stopping at every door.   A mine of wit was continually pouring out its recondite treasures : the guests were every moment growing less fastidious ; and the banquet had already reached that stage when second-rate wit is as good as the best, if not better.   The good humor of our friend Wart had attracted the waggery of Riggs and Hazard, and they were artfully soliciting and provoking him to a more conspicuous part in the farce of the evening.   Like Munchausen's frozen horn, the counsellor was rapidly melting into a noisy temperature.   He had volunteered some two or three stories, of which he seemed, somehow or other, to have lost the pith.   In short, it was supposed, from some droll expression of the eye, and a slight faltering of the tongue, that Mr. Wart was growing gay.

Harvey Riggs, when matters were precisely in this condition, contrived, by signs and secret messages, to concentrate the attention of the company upon the old lawyer, just as he was setting out with the history of a famous campaign.

"You all remember the late war," said Philly, looking around, and finding the eyes of every one upon him.

This announcement was followed by a laugh of applause, indicating the interest that all took in the commencement of the narrative.

"There is certainly nothing particularly calculated to excite your risible faculties in that!" said he, as much amused as his auditory.—"I was honored by his Excellency the Governor of Virginia with a commission as captain of a troop of horse, having been previously elected to that station by a unanimous vote at a meeting of the corps."

"Explain the name of the troop," said Ned Hazard.

"The Invincible Blues," replied the other; "the uniform being a blue bobtail, and the corps having resolved that they would never be vanquished."

"I am told," interrupted Harvey Riggs, "that you furnished yourself with a new pair of yellow buckskin small-clothes on the occasion; and that with them and your blue bobtail you produced a sensation through the whole country."

"Faith!" said Mr. Chub, speaking across the table, "Mr. Riggs, I can assure you I don't think a horseman well mounted without leather small-clothes."

"I took prodigious pains," continued Philly, not heeding the interruption, "to infuse into my men the highest military discipline. There wasn't a man in the corps that couldn't carry his nag over any worm fence in the country,—throwing off the rider—"

"The rider of the fence, you mean," said Hazard, dryly.

"To be sure I do!" replied Philly, with briskness, "you don't suppose I meant to say that my men were *ex equis dejecti*—exephippiated, if I may be allowed to coin a word? No, sir, while the horse kept his legs, every man was like a horse-fly."

"What system of discipline did you introduce?" inquired Harvey.

"The system of foxhunting," answered Mr. Wart; "the very best that ever was used for cavalry."

"Go on," said Harvey.

"We received intelligence, somewhere in the summer of eighteen hundred and thirteen, that old Admiral Warren was beginning to squint somewhat awfully at Norfolk, and rather taking liberties in Hampton Roads. *Ratione cujus,* as we lawyers say, it was thought prudent to call into immediate service some of the most efficient of the military force of the country; and, accordingly, up came an order addressed to me, commanding me to repair with my men, as speedily as possible, to the neighborhood of Craney Island. This summons operated like an electric shock. It was the first real flavor of gunpowder that the troop had ever snuffed. I never saw men behave better. It became my duty to take instant measures to meet the emergency. In the first place, I ordered a meeting of the troop at the Court House;— for I was resolved to do things coolly."

"You are mistaken, Mr. Wart," said Harvey, "in the order of your movements; the first thing that you did was to put on your new buckskin breeches."

"Nonsense!" said the counsellor; "I called the meeting at the Court House, directing every man to be there in full equipment."

"And you sent forthwith to Richmond," interrupted Hazard, "for a white plume three feet long."

"Now, gentlemen!" said Philly, imploringly, "one at a time! if you wish to hear me out, let me go on. Well, sir, the men met in complete order. Harry Davenport, (you remember him, Mr. Meriwether, a devil-may-care sort of a fellow, a perfect walking nuisance in time of peace, an indictable offence going at large!)

he was my orderly, and the very best, I suppose, in Virginia. I
furnished Harry (it was entirely a thought of my own) with a
halbert, the shaft twelve feet long, and pointed with a foot of
polished iron. As soon as I put this into his hands, the fellow
set up one of his horse-laughs, and galloped about the square like
a wild Cossack."

" I should think," said Meriwether, " that one of our countrymen would scarcely know what to do with a pole twelve feet long,
after he had got into his saddle : however, I take it for granted
you had good reason for what you did."

" The Polish lancers," replied Philly, " produced a terrible
impression with a weapon somewhat similar."

" No matter," said Ned, " about the Polish lancers ; let us get
upon our campaign."

" Well," continued Mr. Wart, " I thought it would not be
amiss, before we started, to animate and encourage my fellows
with a speech. So, I drew them up in a hollow square, and gave
them a flourish that set them half crazy."

" That was just the way with Tyrtæus before Ithome !" exclaimed Mr. Chub, with great exultation, from the opposite side
of the table. " I should like to have heard Mr. Wart exhorting
his men !"

" I will tell you exactly what he said, for I was there at the
time," said Ned Hazard ; " Follow me, my brave boys ! the eyes
of the world are upon you ; keep yours upon my white plume,
and let that be your rallying point !"

" Pish !" cried Philly, turning round and showing his black
teeth with a good-natured, half-tipsy grin, " I said no such thing.
I told them, what it was my duty to tell them, that we had joined
issue with the British Government, and had come to the *ultima
ratio ;* and that we must now make up our minds to die on the
field of our country's honor, rather than see her soil polluted with

the footsteps of an invader; that an enemy was at our door, threatening our firesides."

" You told them," interrupted Hazard again, " that the next morning's sun might find them stark and stiff and gory, on the dew-besprinkled sod. I can remember those expressions as well as if it were yesterday."

" I might have said something like that," replied Philly, " by way of encouragement to the men. However, this you recollect well enough, Ned, that there was not a man in the corps whose mind was not as perfectly made up to die as to eat his dinner."

" All, except old Shakebag, the tavernkeeper," said Ned, " and he was short-winded and pursy, and might be excused for preferring his dinner."

" I except him," replied Mr. Wart, and then proceeded with his narrative. " As soon as I had finished my address, I dissolved the square, and instantly took up the line of march."

" You should say rather that you took up the charge," said Ned, " for you went out of the village in line, at full speed, with swords brandishing above your heads. You led the way, with Harry Davenport close at your heels, thursting his long lance right at the seat of your yellow buckskins, and shouting like a savage."

" What was that for?" I asked with some astonishment.

" Ned puts a coloring on it," replied the counsellor ; " I did go out from the court house at a charge, but there was no brandishing of swords ; we carry our swords, Mr. Littleton, in the charge, at arm's length, the blade being extended horizontally exactly parallel with the line of the eyes. I did this to give the men courage."

" How near was the enemy at this time ?" I inquired.

" They had not landed," answered Ned gravely, " but were expected to land at Craney Island, about one hundred miles off."

Here was a shout of applause from the table.

" I can tell you what," said Mr. Wart, for he was too much flustered to take any thing in joke that passed, " there is no time so important in a campaign as when an army first breaks ground. If you can keep your men in heart at the starting point, you may make them do what you please afterwards."

" That's true !" said Mr. Chub, who had evinced great interest in Philly's narrative from the beginning, and was even more impervious than the lawyer himself to the waggery of the table. " Cyrus would never have persuaded the Greeks to march with him to Babylon, if he had not made them believe that they were going only against the Pisidians. Such stratagems are considered lawful in war. It was a masterly thing in my opinion, this device of Mr. Wart's."

" Had you severe service ?" asked Meriwether.

" Tolerably severe," replied Philly, " while it lasted. It. rained upon us nearly the whole way from here to Norfolk, and there was a good deal of ague and fever in the country at that time, which we ran great risk of taking, because we were obliged to keep up a guard night and day."

" You had an engagement I think I have heard ?" said I.

" Pretty nearly the same thing," answered Mr. Wart. " The enemy never landed whilst I remained, except, I believe, to get some pigs and fowls on Craney Island : but we had frequent alarms, and several times were drawn up in a line of battle, which is more trying to men, Mr. Littleton, than actual fighting. It gave me a good opportunity to see what my fellows were made of. Harry Davenport was a perfect powder-magazine. The rascal wanted us one night to swim our horses over to the Island. Gad, I believe he would have gone by himself if I hadn't forbidden him !"

" Your campaign lasted some time ?" said I.

" About a week," replied Philly. " No, I am mistaken, it was rather more, for it took us three days to return home. And such

a set of madcaps as we had all the way back to the court house !
Nothing but scrub races the whole distance !"

"Now," said Harvey Riggs, looking at Mr. Wart with a face
of sly raillery, " now that you have got through this celebrated
campaign, tell us how many men you had."

" Seven rank and file," said Ned, answering for him.

" Fiddle-de-dee !" exclaimed Mr Wart.   " I had twenty !"

" On your honor, as a trooper ?" cried Ned.

" On my *voir dire*," said Philly, hesitating.—" I had nine in
uniform, and I forget how many were not in uniform,—because
I didn't allow these fellows to go with us ; but they had very good
hearts for it.   Nine men, bless your soul, sir, on horseback, strung
out in Indian file, make a very formidable display !"

" Well, it was a very gallant thing, take it altogether," said
Harvey.   " So, gentlemen, fill your glasses.   Here's to Captain
Wart of the Invincible Blues, the genuine representative of the
chivalry of the Old Dominion !"

As the feast drew to a close, the graver members of the party
stole off to the drawing-room, leaving behind them that happy
remnant which may be called the sifted wheat of the stack.
There sat Harvey Riggs, with his broad, laughing face mellowed
by wine and good cheer, and with an eye rendered kindly by long
shining on merry meetings, lolling over two chairs, whilst he urged
the potations like a seasoned man, and a thirsty.   And there sat
Meriwether, abstemious but mirthful, with a face and heart brimful of benevolence; beside him, the inimitable original Philly
Wart.   And there, too, was seen the jolly parson, priestlike even
over his cups, filled with wonder and joy to see the tide of mirth
run so in the flood ; ever and anon turning, with bewildered
eagerness, from one to another of his compotators, in doubt as to
which pleased him most.   And there, too, above all, was Ned
Hazard, an imp of laughter, with his left arm dangling over the

back of his chair, and his right lifting up his replenished glass on high, to catch its sparkling beams in the light; his head tossed negligently back upon his shoulder; and from his mouth forth issuing, with an elongated puff, that richer essence than incense of Araby : his dog Wilful, too, privileged as himself, with his faithful face recumbent between his master's knees.

Such are the images that gladden the old-fashioned wassail of Virginia.

CHAPTER XXXIV.

A BREAKING UP.

THEY who remained at the dinner table were at last summoned to tea and coffee in the adjoining apartment, where the ladies of the family were assembled. It was about sunset, and Mr. Tracy's carriage, with two or three saddle-horses, was at the door. As soon as this short meal was dispatched, Catharine and Bel made their preparations for departure. Ned, like a flustering lover, was officiously polite in his attentions to the lady of his affections : he had brought Bel her bonnet, and assisted in adjusting it to her head, with supererogatory care ; and, as he led her to the carriage, he took occasion, with many figures of speech, to tell her how much he participated in the affliction she had experienced by the loss of Fairbourne ; and, as he was sure the recreant did not meditate a total separation from his mistress, he vowed to bring him back to her if he was to be found alive in the county. Bel endeavored to evade the service tendered ; and, getting into the coach, she and Catharine were soon in full progress homeward.

Mr. Tracy's horse was led up to the steps, and the old gentleman, after some civil speeches to the company, a little bragging of his ability as a horseman, and a respectful valedictory to Meriwether, clambered up with a slow but unassisted effort into his saddle.

" I should make a brave fox-hunter yet, Mr. Wart," said he
with some exultation, when he found himself in his seat, "and
would puzzle you to throw me out on a fair field. You see I can
drink, too, with the best of you. I am good pith yet, Mr. Meriwether!"

" Upon my word, sir," said Meriwether, smiling, " you do
wonders! There is not to-day in Virginia, a better mounted
horseman of the same age."

" Good eating and drinking, Mr. Meriwether, and good wine,
warm the blood of an old grasshopper like me, and set him to
chirping, if he can do nothing else. Come, Ralph, you and Harvey must get to your horses : I will have my aide-de-camps.
Mount, you young dogs, and never lag! I allow no grass to grow
to my horse's heels, I warrant ye! Mount and begone!"

The two attendants obeyed the order, and reined their steeds
near to his.

" Now don't run away from us," said Harvey.

" Why, as I think upon it again, Harvey, more maturely,"
replied the old gentleman, " I think we will jog along slowly ; we
might alarm the horses of the carriage if we got to any of our
harum-scarum pranks. So, good evening! good evening!"

With these words the cavalcade set forward at a brisk walk,
Mr. Tracy gesticulating in a manner that showed him to be engaged in an animated conversation with his companions.

Soon after this, Mr. Swansdown's curricle was brought to the
door. This gentleman, with a languid and delicate grace, ap-
prized Meriwether that he was about " to wing his flight " to
Meherrin, there to immerse himself in pursuits which his present
visit had suspended ; and, consequently, he could not promise
himself the pleasure of soon again meeting his worthy friend at
Swallow Barn. He reminded his host, however, that he would
carry into his retirement the agreeable consciousness that his

visit had not been a fruitless one, since it had contributed so hap-pily to the termination of an ancient dispute. He particularly insisted on the honor of a return visit from Meriwether and his friends.

His parting with the ladies might be said to have been even touching. It presented an elegant compound of sensibility and deference. Prudence could not possibly mistake the impression he designed to convey to her. He gently shook her gloved fin-ger, as he said, with a gentle and embarrassed smile, " I particu-larly regret that the nature of the occupation to which I am about to return is such as to engross me for some months, and most probably may compel me again to cross the Atlantic. It is likely, therefore, that I shall have added some years to my ac-count before we meet again. Your fate will be doubtless changed before that happens : as for mine, I need scarcely allude to it ; I am already written down a predestined cumberer of the soil. I still may hope, I trust, to be sometimes remembered as a passing shadow."

" He means to write a book, and die a bachelor, poor devil ! That is the English of this flourish," said Ned to Prudence, as soon as Swandsdown walked towards the front door.

Pru was silent, and inwardly vexed. At length she said to Ned, " He attaches more consequence to his movements than any body else."

Shortly after this, the glittering vehicle, with its dainty bur-den, was seen darting into the distant forest.

One after another our guests followed, until none were left but Mr. Wart and Hedges, who having determined to ride to-gether as far as the Court-House, were waiting, as they said, un-til the night should fairly set in, in order that they might have the coolness of the "little hours" for their journey.

" Well, Mr. Chub," said Philly, " what do you think of our friend Swansdown?"

"I am glad he is gone," replied the parson ; "in my opinion he is very fatiguing."

In a few minutes after this, the counsellor dropped asleep in his chair, leaving Meriwether in an unusually argumentative mood, but unfortunately without a listener. Frank had drawn up to the window, and thrown his feet carelessly against the sill, so as to give himself that half recumbent posture which is supposed to be most favorable to all calm and philosophic discussions. He had launched upon one of those speculative voyages in which it was his wont to circumnavigate the world of thought ; and as there were no lights in the room, he continued to pour into the unconscious ears of his friend Wart his startling random-shots of wisdom, for half an hour before he became aware of his unedifying labor. Finding, however, that no answer came from the quarter to which he addressed himself, he suddenly stopped short with the exclamation, "God bless me! Mr. Wart, have you been asleep all this time? truly, I have been sowing my seed upon a rock. But sleep on, don't let me disturb you."

"Asleep!" replied Philly, waking up at hearing himself addressed by name, as a man who dozes in company is apt to do ; "not I, I assure you: I have heard every word you have said. It was altogether just ; indeed I couldn't gainsay a word, but I think, Mr. Hedges, it is time for us to be moving."

Meriwether laughed, and remarked that Mr. Hedges had left the room some time since with Mr. Chub.

"At all events," said Philly, "we will have our horses. It is time we were upon our journey."

Every effort was made to detain him and his companion until the next morning ; but the counsellor was obstinate in his resolve to be off that night, observing that he had already taken a longer holiday at Swallow Barn than he had allowed himself in the last fifteen years ; "and as to the hour," said he, "I am an old stager on the road, and have long since lost all discrimination between night and day."

"But it is very dark," said Hazard, "and threatens rain. You will assuredly be caught in a thunder-storm before you get three miles."

"Wet or dry," replied the other, "it makes but a small matter in the account.   I don't think a shower would take much of the gloss from my old coat," he added, looking round at his skirts, "and as for Hedges here, I know he is neither sugar nor salt."

"With a julep before we go," said Hedges, "and another when we stop, you may put as much wet and darkness between the two as you please, for me.   So let us pad our saddles according to the old recipe, ' A spur in the head is worth two on the heel.' "

Saying this, he went to the sideboard and helped himself rather beyond the approved allowance.   " I have a laudable contempt for thin potations, Mr. Wart," he added as he took off his glass.

The horses were at the door ; it was now about ten o'clock ; when the two travellers were mounted, Philly whistled up his hounds, and they set forward on their dark journey.

CHAPTER XXXV.

KNIGHT ERRANTRY.

THE next morning Hazard appeared a little perplexed. Notwithstanding the apparent recklessness of his character, it belongs to him, as it does to the greater number of those persons who put on an irresponsible face in the world, to feel acutely any supposed diminution of the esteem of his friends induced by his own indiscretion. In the present instance he was particularly obnoxious to this sentiment. Bel's good opinion of him was the very breath of his nostrils, and her rigid estimate of the proprieties of life the greatest of his terrors. His perplexity arose from this, that he had given way the day before at the dinner-table to the natural impulses of his character, and in spite of the admonitory presence of the lady of his soul, nay, perhaps elevated into a more dangerous gayety by that very circumstance, he had possibly (for such a temper as his is least of all others able to know the true state of things), in her very sight and hearing, committed a thousand trespasses upon her notions of decorum. Whether he had or not, he was in doubt, and afraid to inquire. All that he knew of the matter was, that, like a man in a dream, he had passed through a succession of agreeable changes; had begun the day with a certain calm pleasure, rose from that into a copious flow of spirits, thence to an exuberant merriment, and thence into—what he could not precisely tell: heavens knows if it were

riot or moderate revelry, outrageous foolery or lawful mirth!—
the prospect from that point was a misty, dreamy, undefined
mass of pleasant images. Of this he was conscious, that after
drinking much wine, and while reeking with the fumes of tobacco, (a thing utterly abhorrent to Bel,) he had certainly ventured
into her presence, and had said a great many things to her in
very hyperbolical language, and, if he was not mistaken, in somewhat of a loud voice. Perhaps, too, he might have been rather
thick of speech! The recurrence of the scene to his thoughts
this morning rather disturbed him.

There was one consolation in the matter. Bel's father, the
very personation, in her view, of all that was decorous and proper
—the Nestor of the day—the paragon of precision—had, it was
admitted on all hands, left Swallow Barn very decidedly exhila-
rated with wine. If Bel believed this, (and how could she fail
to see it?) the fact would go a great way towards Ned's extenuation. And then the occasion too!—a special compliment to Mr.
Tracy. Tut! It was as pardonable a case as could be made
out!

Amidst the retrospects of the morning Hazard had not forgotten the promise he had made Bel the night before, to attempt
the recovery of her hawk. Harvey Riggs before dinner had informed him of Bel's loss, and of his, Harvey's, engagement that
Ned should bring back her bird. Hazard was not aware that I
had heard him pledge himself to this task as he assisted Bel to
the carriage; nor did he mention it to me to-day, when he announced after breakfast that he had ordered our horses to the
door for a ride. Without questioning his purpose, I readily
agreed to accompany him; and, therefore, at an early hour we
were both mounted, and, followed by Wilful, we took the road
leading from Swallow Barn immediately up the river.

"Now," said I, after we had ridden some distance, "pray

tell me what is the object of this early and secret enterprise, and what makes, you so abstracted this morning?"

" I wish to heaven, Mark," replied Ned, half peevishly, " that this business were settled one way or another!"—Ned always spoke to me of his courtship as " this business;" he had a boyish repugnance to call it by its right name. " Here am I," he continued, " a man grown, in a girl's leading-strings, ' turned forehorse to a smock,' as Shakspeare calls it. Saint David speed us, and put me out of misery! Now, what do you think, Mark, of all the adventures in the world, I am bound upon at this moment?"

" Why, sir," I answered, " upon the most reasonable wild-goose chase that ever a man in love pursued. I never knew you before to do so wise a thing; for I take it that you and I are already in search of Bel's hawk. There are not more than a million birds about; and I'll be bound Fairbourne is one of them! He is certainly within a hundred miles, and I have no doubt anxiously expecting us."

" Conjurer that thou art!" said Ned, " how did thy foolish brain find that out?"

" Didn't I hear you last night, when you were so tipsy that you could hardly stand, bleat into Bel's ear that you would neither take rest nor food until you restored her renegade favorite to her fist?"

" Did I say that?" exclaimed Ned. " Was I not supremely ridiculous?"

" I can't pretend to do justice to your language on the occasion. It would require higher poetical powers than I boast of to imitate, even in a small degree, the euphuism of your speech. The common superlatives of the dictionary would make but poor positives for my use, if I attempted it."

" Look you, now!" said Hazard, " Is not this deplorable, that a man should have a mistress who hates a fool above all worldly plagues, and yet be so bestridden by his evil genius that he may never appear any thing else to her! I am not such a miserable merry-andrew by nature, and yet, by circumstances, wherever Bel is concerned, I am ever the v--y crown-piece of folly!"

"And do you think," said I, "that this little girl, so instinct, as she is, with the liveliest animal impulses,—a laughing nymph, —is such a Cato in petticoats as to be noting down your nonsense in her tablets for rebuke? Why, sir, that is the very point upon which you must hope to win her!"

"I am afraid I wasn't respectful," said Ned.

"I assure you," I replied, "that, so far from not being respectful, you were the most ridiculously observant, reverential, and obsequious ass,—considering that you were in your cups,—I ever saw."

"Was I so?" exclaimed Ned. "Then I am content; for, on that score, Bel is as great a fool as I am or any other. Now, if I can only bring her back her bird," he said exultingly,—"and I have some presentiment that I shall get tidings of him,—I shall rise to the very top of her favor."

Saying this, Ned spurred forward to a gallop, and flourished his whip in the air as he called to me to follow at the same speed

"Mark, watch every thing that flies," he cried out; "you may see the harness about his legs; and listen for the bells, for the truant can't move without jangling,—'I live in my lady's grace,' —remember the motto!"

"Now, by our lady!—I mean our lady Bel," said I, "for henceforth I will swear by none but her,—I am as keen upon this quest as yourself. I vow not to sleep until I hear something of this ungrateful bird."

My reader would perhaps deem it a hopeless venture to attempt the recovery of a bird under the circumstances of this case ; but it will occur to him, if he be read in romance, that it was not so unusual an exploit to regain a stray hawk as he might at first imagine. A domesticated bird will seldom wander far from his accustomed haunt ; and, being alien to the wild habits of his species, will, almost invariably, resort to the dwellings of man. Fairbourne having been known to direct his flight up the river, we had good reason to hope that the inhabitants of this quarter might put our search upon a successful track.

For a good half mile, therefore, we rode at speed along the highway leading to the ferry. The velocity of our motion, combining with the extravagant nature of the enterprise, and the agreeable temperature of the morning, cloudless and cool, had raised our spirits to a high pitch. In this mood we soon arrived at Sandy Walker's little inn upon the river. All that we could learn here was, that the hawk had been seen in the neighborhood the day before, and had probably continued his flight further up the river.

With this intimation we proceeded rapidly upon our pursuit. It was near noon when, through many devious paths, visiting every habitation that fell in our way, we had gained a point about five miles distant from Swallow Barn. Some doubtful tidings of Fairbourne were obtained at one or two houses on the road : bu. for the last hour our journey had been without encouragement, and we began to feel oppressed with the mid-day fervors of the season. It was, therefore, somewhat despairingly that we halted to hold a consultation whether or not we should push our expedition farther.

Not far distant from the road we could perceive the ridge-pole of a log cabin showing itself above a patch of luxuriant Indian corn. This little dwelling stood upon the bank of the river ; and, as a last essay, we resolved to visit it, and interest its inmates in the object of our enterprise.   It was with some difficulty that we made our way through a breach in the high worm-fence that bounded the road ; and, after struggling along a path beset with blackberries and briars, we at length found ourselves encompassed by the corn immediately around the hut.   At this moment Wilful sprang from the path, and ran eagerly towards the yard in the rear of the dwelling.   He did not halt until he arrived at an apple-tree, where hung a rude cage ; under this he continued to bark with quick and redoubled earnestness, until Ned called him back with a peremptory threat, that brought him crouching beneath the feet of our horses, where he remained, restless and whining, every now and then making a short bound in the direction of the tree, and looking up wistfully in Hazard's face.

In the mean time an old negro woman had come to the door ; and, as Ned engaged her in conversation, Wilful stole off unobserved a second time to the tree, where he fell to jumping up against the trunk, uttering, at the same time, a short, half-subdued howl.

" There is something in the branches above the cage," I exclaimed, as I followed the movements of the dog with my eye. " It is Fairbourne himself ! I see the silver rings upon his legs glittering through the leaves !"

" For heaven's sake, Mark, keep quiet !" cried Ned, springing from his horse. " If it be Fairbourne in truth, we may get him by persuasion, but never by alarming him.   Dismount quickly. Wilful—back, sir."

I got down from my saddle, and the horses were delivered into the charge of the old woman.   Wilful crept back to the door of the hut.   Ned and myself cautiously advanced to reconnoitre.

As soon as all was still, to our infinite joy, Fairbourne in proper identity descended from his leafy bower and perched upon the top of the cage. Some association of this abode of the mock-ing-bird with his own prison in the mulberry-tree at the Brakes, had, possibly, attracted and bound him to this spot ; and there he sat, seemingly quiet and melancholy, and struck with contrition for the folly that had tempted him to desert his mistress and his mew. I thought he recognized an acquaintance in Wilful ; for as the dog moved about, Fairbourne's quick eye followed him from place to place ; and, so far from showing perturbation at Wilful's presence, he composedly mantled his wing and stretched his neck, as if pleased with the discovery.

Assured by these manifestations, Ned addressed the bird in the words of endearment to which he had been accustomed, and slowly stepped forward towards the tree. Fairbourne, however, was distrustful, and retreated to the boughs. After much solici-tation on the part of Hazard, and a great deal of prudery on that of the hawk, we had recourse to some morsels of meat obtained from the hut. These Ned threw upon the earth, and Fairbourne, pinched by hunger and unable to resist, pounced upon them with an unguarded voracity. Still, as Ned advanced upon him he retreated along the ground, without flying. A piece of the cord which Bel had used as her creance, some three or four feet in length, was attached to his jesses, and served in some degree to embarrass his progress, as it was dragged through the grass. Hazard endeavored to place his foot upon the end of this line, but as yet had been baffled in every effort. Wilful seemed to comprehend the purpose, and with admirable sagacity stole a cir-cuit round the bird, drawing nearer to him at every step, and then, with a sudden and skilful leap, sprang upon him, in such a manner as effectually to secure his captive, scarcely ruffling a feather. Hazard rushed forward at the same instant, and made good his prize, by seizing his wing and bearing him off to the hut.

The good fortune of this discovery and the singular success that attended it, threw us into transports. Ned shouted and huzzaed, and tossed up his hat in the air, until the old negro woman began to look in his face to see if he were in his senses. The hawk, the unconscious cause of all this extravagance, looked like a discomfited prisoner of war, bedraggled, travel-worn and soiled,—a tawdry image of a coxcomb. His straps and bells hanging about his legs had the appearance of shabby finery; and his whole aspect was that of a forlorn, silly, and wayward minion, wearing the badge of slavery instead of that of the wild and gallant freebooter of the air so conspicuously expressed in the character of his tribe.

Congratulating ourselves on our good luck, we began to prepare for our homeward journey. The negro received an ample bounty for the assistance afforded in the capture; the jesses were repaired and secured to Fairbourne's legs, and the bird himself made fast to Hazard's hand. In a few moments we were remounted and cantering in the direction of Swallow Barn, with a lightness of spirits in Hazard that contrasted amusingly with his absolute despondence half an hour before.

CHAPTER XXXVI.

A JOUST AT UTTERANCE.

WE had not travelled far on our return to Swallow Barn, before we arrived at a hamlet that stands at the intersection of a cross-road. This consists of a little store, a wheelwright's shop, and one or two cottages, with their outhouses. The store was of that miscellaneous character which is adapted to the multifarious wants of a country neighborhood, and displayed a tempting assortment of queensware, rat-traps, tin kettles, hats, fiddles, shoes, calicoes, cheese, sugar, allspice, jackknives and jewsharps,—the greater part of which was announced in staring capitals on the window-shutter, with the persuasive addition, that they were all of the best quality and to be had on the most accommodating terms. The rival establishment of the wheelwright was an old shed sadly bedaubed with the remainder colors of the paint-brush, and with some preposterous exaggerations in charcoal of distinguished military men mounted on preternaturally prancing steeds; and, near the door, a bran-new blue wagon and a crimson plough showed the activity of the trade.

As may readily be conjectured, this mart of custom was not without its due proportion of that industrious, thriving and reputable class of comers who laudably devote their energies to disputation, loud swearing, bets and whisky,—a class which, to the glory of our land, is surprisingly rife in every country side. Some six or seven of these worthies were congregated on the rail of the piazza, which extended across the front of the store, like so many strange fowls roosting along a pole. The length of our previous ride and the heat of the day made it necessary that we should stop here for a short time to get water for our horses. We accordingly dismounted.

Fairbourne excited the curiosity of the inhabitants of the porch; and Ned, who seemed to be well acquainted with the persons about him, answered their many questions with his customary good-humor. During this brief intercourse, one of the party approached with a swaggering step, and began to pry, with rather an obtrusive familiarity, into the odd equipment of the hawk. His air was that of a shabby gentleman : He had an immense pair of whiskers, a dirty shirt, and a coat that might be said to be on its last legs; but this, however, was buttoned at the waist with a certain spruce and conceited effect. As Ned held the bird upon his hand, this complacent gentleman brought himself into a rather troublesome contact, and finally threw his arm across Hazard's shoulder. Ned, at first, gently repelled him, but as the other still intruded upon him, and placed himself again in the same situation—

"Softly, Mr. Rutherford!" he said, slipping away from beneath the extended arm; "you will excuse me, but I am averse to bearing such a burden."

"You are more nice than neighborly, Ned Hazard," replied the other, stiffly erecting his person. "I think I can remember a time when even you, sir, would not have found me burdensome: that time may come again."

"I am not in the habit," rejoined Ned, "of arguing the right to shake off whatever annoys me."

"Aye, aye!" said the other, walking to the opposite end of

the porch. "There are dogs enough to bark at the wounded lion, that dare not look him in the face when he is in health. It is easy enough to learn, as the world goes, what is likely to annoy a fair-weather friend. Honesty is of the tailor's making—"

These and many other expressions of the like import were muttered sullenly by the speaker, with such glances towards Hazard as indicated the deep offence he had taken at the rebuke just given.

This man had been originally educated in liberal studies, and had commenced his career not without some character in the country, but had fallen into disgrace through vicious habits. An unfortunate reputation for brilliant talents, in early life, had misled him into the belief that the care by which a good name is won and preserved is a useless virtue, and that self-control is a tax which only men of inferior parts pay for success. This delusion brought about the usual penalties; first, disappointment, then debauch, and after that, in a natural sequence, the total wreck of worldly hopes :—a brief history which is often told of men, and varied only in the subordinate incidents which color the common outline.

Rutherford still retained, (as it generally happens to a vain man,) unimpaired by the severe judgment of the world, his original exaggerated opinion of the extent of his abilities; but, having lost the occasions for their display, he became noted only by a domineering temper, a boastful spirit, a supreme hatred of those in better circumstances than himself, and, sometimes, by excessive and ferocious intemperance.

His conduct on the present occasion passed unheeded. Hazard had no disposition to embroil himself with a man of this description, and therefore made no reply to these muttered overflowings of his spleen.

"I have seen your bird before, Mr. Ned Hazard," said a plain

countryman, who sat without a coat on the bench of the piazza.
"If I am not mistaken, that hawk belonged to one of Mr. Tracy's
daughters, over here at the Brakes."

"It did," replied Ned; "she has nursed it with her own
hand."

"Well, I have been studying," said another, "ever since you
came here, to find out what all these things are stuck about its
legs for. It is the most unaccountablest thing to me! I don't
consider one of these here hawks no more than vermin. What
is it good for, Mr. Hazard, any how?"

"Indeed, I declare I can't exactly tell," answered Ned. "In
the old time they kept hawks pretty much as we keep hounds,—
to hunt game with."

"Oh, they are amazing swift, and desperate wicked,—that's
a fact!" said the first speaker. "Did you never see how spiteful
these little king-birds take after and worry a crow? They are a
sort of hawks too—"

"Many's the time," said another of the company, "that I have
known how to follow a fox from looking at the crows tracking
him across a field; and I have seen hawks take after vermin just
in the same way."

"But what is the use," asked the second speaker again, "of
these here silver rings? and here are words on one of them, too.
Let me see,—'I live—in my lady's—grace,'" he continued,
straining his sight to make out the legend.

Rutherford had now approached to the skirts of the group,
and stood leaning against the balustrade of the porch, with an
unsocial and vexed air, as if disposed to take advantage of whatever might occur to vent his feelings.

"My lady's grace!" said he, tartly, "My lady's grace! I
suppose we shall hear of my lord's grace, too, before long! There
are some among us who, if they durst do it, would carry their

heads high enough for such a title. If that stark old English tory, Isaac Tracy, of the Brakes,—as he calls himself—"

"Miles Rutherford," interrupted Hazard, angrily, "look to yourself, sir! I am not disposed to put up with your moody humor. Do not give me cause to repent my forbearance in not punishing your insolence at its first outbreak."

"A better man than you, Ned Hazard," said the other, "proudly as you choose to bear yourself, might have cause to repent his rashness in making such a threat. Insolence, do you call it, sir! Take care that I do not teach you better to know who I am!"

"I know you already," replied Ned, "for a brawling bully—a disturber of the common peace—a noisy churl—a nuisance, sir, to the whole country round."

"I know you," said Rutherford.——

"Silence!" cried Ned; "Not another word from your lips, or, by my life! unworthy as you are of the notice of a gentleman, I will take the pains to chastise you here upon this spot."

"Good gentlemen! Good gentlemen! Mercy on us! Stop them!" exclaimed our old acquaintance, Hafen Blok, who, until this moment, had been seated in the store, and now came limping to the porch, on having recognized Hazard's voice. "For God's sake, Mr. Ned Hazard, don't put yourself in the way of Miles Rutherford! Take a fool's advice, Mister Edward," he continued, coming up to Ned, and holding him by the coat: "It isn't fit for such as you to concern yourself with Miles Rutherford; the man's half in liquor, and of no account if he wasn't."

Several others of the company crowded round Hazard to beg him not to be disturbed by his antagonist. In the mean time Rutherford had worked himself up to a pitch of fury, and, springing over the balustrade upon the ground, he took a station in front of the house, where, vociferating in his wrath a hundred opprobrious epithets, he challenged Hazard to come out of the crowd if he dared to face him.

I interposed to remind Hazard that he should restrain his anger, nor think of matching himself with such an enemy. He listened calmly to my remonstrance, and then laughing, as if nothing had occurred to ruffle his temper, though it was manifest that he was much flurried, he remarked in a tone of assumed good humor,—

"You mistake if you imagine this ruffian moves me; but still I think it would be doing a public service if I were to give him a sound threshing here on his own terms."

"Don't think of such a thing, Mister Edward!" said Hafen; "you are not used to such as Miles. He is close built, and above fourteen stone. You are hardly a feather to him."

"You underrate me, Hafen," replied Ned, smiling, "and I have a mind to show you that weight is not so great a matter as a good hand."

"You are bold to speak amongst your cronies," said Rutherford. "You can make a party if you can't fight. But I shall take the first opportunity, when I meet you alone, to let you know that when I choose to speak my mind of such hoary-headed traitors as old Isaac Tracy, I will not be schooled into silence by you."

At these words Hazard turned quickly round to me, and whispered in my ear, with more agitation of manner than was usual to him, "I will indulge this braggart; so, pray don't interrupt me. You need not be anxious as to the result;" then, speaking to the assemblage of persons who surrounded him, he said, "Now my good friends, I want you to see fair play, and on no account to interfere with me as long as I have it."

With this he left the porch, and stepping out upon the ground where Rutherford stood, he told him that he would save him the trouble of any future meeting, by giving him now what he stood especially in need of,—a hearty flogging.

Rutherford in a moment threw off his coat. Ned coolly buttoned his frock up to the chin.

"Good Lord, preserve us!" exclaimed Hafen Blok again— "Mr. Hazard's gone crazy! Why, Miles Rutherford ought to manage two of him."

"I can tell you what," said one of the lookers-on, after surveying Ned for a moment, "Ned Hazard's a pretty hard horse to ride, too; only look at his eye,—how natural it is!"

By this time the two combatants had taken their respective positions. Ned stood upon a practised guard, closely eyeing his antagonist, and waiting the first favorable moment to deal a blow with effect. It was easy to perceive that, amongst his various accomplishments, he had not neglected to acquire the principles of pugilism. Rutherford's figure was muscular and active; and, to all appearance, the odds were certainly very much in his favor. Not a word was spoken, and an intense interest was manifested by the whole assembly as to the issue of this singular encounter.

During the first onset Ned acted entirely on the defensive, and parried his opponent's blows with complete success. In the next moment he changed the character of the war, and pressed upon Rutherford with such science and effect, as very soon to demonstrate that he had the entire command of the game. From this period the contest assumed, on the part of Hazard, a cheerful aspect. He struck his blows with a countenance of so much gayety, that a spectator would have imagined he buffeted his adversary in mere sport, were it not for the blood that streamed down Rutherford's face, and the dogged earnestness that sat upon the brow of the belabored man. Wilful seemed to take a great interest in the affray, and curveted around the parties, barking, sometimes violently, and springing towards his master's opponent. On such occasions Ned called out to him, with the utmost composure, and ordered him away, but without the least interruption to his employment; and Wilful, as if assured by his master's cool tone of voice, yielded instant obedience to the mandate, and took his place amongst the by-standers.

For the space of two or three minutes nothing was heard but the sullen sound of lusty blows, planted with admirable adroitness on the breast and face of Miles Rutherford, whose blows in return were blindly and awkwardly spent upon the air. At last, the furious bully, worn down by abortive displays of strength, and perplexed by the vigorous assaults of his enemy, began to give ground and show signs of discomfiture. Ned, as fresh almost as at first, now pressed more severely upon him, and, with one decisive stroke, prostrated him upon the earth.

At this incident a shout arose from the crowd, and every one eagerly interceded to exhort Ned to spare his adversary farther pain. Ned stepped a pace back, as he looked upon his recumbent foe, and composedly said—

" I will not strike him whilst he is down. But if he wishes to renew the battle, I will allow him to get upon his legs,—and he shall even have time to breathe."

Rutherford slowly got up ; and, without again placing himself in an attitude of offence, began to vent his displeasure in wild and profane execrations. Several of the persons nearest took hold of him, as if with a purpose to expostulate against his further prosecution of the fight ; but this restraint only made him the more frantic. In the midst of this uproar, Ned again approached him, saying, " Miles Rutherford, it little becomes you as a man to be unburthening your malice in words. We have come to blows, and if you are not yet satisfied with the issue of this meeting, I pledge you a fair field, and as much of this game as you have a relish for. Let the crowd stand back !"

After looking a moment at Hazard in profound silence, Rutherford's discretion seemed suddenly to sway his courage; and, dropping his arms by his side in token of defeat, he muttered, in a smothered and confused voice, "It's no use, Ned Hazard, for me to strike at you. You have had the advantage of training."

"You should have counted the cost of your insolence," replied Ned, "before you indulged it. The tongue of a braggart is always more apt than his hand," he continued, taking a white handkerchief from his pocket, and wiping his brow, and, at the same time unbuttoning his coat and adjusting his dress. "You have disturbed the country with your quarrelsome humors long enough; so take the lesson you have got to-day, and profit by it. Hafen, get me some water; my hands are bloody."

At this instant the group of amused and gratified spectators mingled promiscuously together, and made the welkin ring with cheers of triumph and exultation.

"That I should have lived to see such a thing as this!" vociferated Hafen, as he went to get the water. "Didn't I always say Mister Ned Hazard was the very best bottom in the country!"

"I fight fair," murmured Miles Rutherford, as if struggling under the rebuke of the company, and endeavoring to make the best of his situation, "but I am not conquered. Another time— by hell!—another time! and Ned Hazard shall rue this day. That proud coxcomb has practised the art and strikes backhanded. The devil could not parry such blows."

"What does he say?" asked Ned.

"Miles, you are beaten!" exclaimed half a dozen voices, "and you can't make any thing else out of it. So be off!" saying this, several individuals gathered round him to persuade him to leave the ground.

"It is immaterial," said Miles; and taking up his coat from

the ground, he walked towards the neighboring dwellings in a sad and confused plight.

"I am a fool," said Hazard in my ear, "to permit myself to be ruffled by this scoundrel; but I am not sorry that I have taken advantage of my anger to give him what he has long deserved."

Ned now began gradually to recover his gayety, and, after a short space, having washed his hands and recruited himself from the severe toil in which he had been engaged, he took Fairbourne from one of the crowd, to whom the charge of the bird had been committed, and we mounted our horses amidst the congratulations of the whole hamlet for the salutary discipline which Ned had inflicted upon his splenetic antagonist.

In less than an hour we regained Swallow Barn: returning like knights to a bannered castle from a successful inroad,—flushed with heat and victory,—covered with dust and glory; our enemies subdued and our lady's pledge redeemed.

CHAPTER XXXVII.

MOONSHINE.

WE were too much elated with having achieved the recapture of the hawk, to postpone the communication of our good fortune to the family at The Brakes longer than our necessary refreshment required ; and accordingly, about five o'clock in the evening, having then finished a hearty dinner, and regained our wasted strength, we were on our way to the habitation of our neighbors.

Whether it was that the rapid succession of scenes, through which we had past during the forepart of the day, and the vivid excitements we had experienced, had now given place to a calmer and more satisfied state of feeling; or whether it arose only from some remaining sense of fatigue from previous toil, our present impulse was to be silent. For more than a quarter of an hour, we trotted along the road with nothing to interrupt our musings but the breeze as it rustled through the wood, the screams of the jay-bird, or the tramp of our horses. At length Ned, waking up as from a reverie, turned to me and said—

"Mark! not a word about that fight to-day."

"Truly, you speak with a discreet gravity," said I. "What would you have?"

"Not the slightest hint that shall lead Bel Tracy to suspect I have had a quarrel with Miles Rutherford."

"I pity you, Ned," said I, laughing. "Out, hyperbolical fiend! why vexest thou this man?"

"Ah!" replied Ned," that is the curse of the star I was born under. The most innocent actions of my life will bear a reading that may turn them, in Bel Tracy's judgment, into abiding topics of reproof. I dread the very thought that Bel should hear of this quarrel. She will say—as she always says—that I have de· scended from my proper elevation of character. I wish I had a hornbook of gentility to go by! It never once occurred to me when I was chastising that blackguard, that I was throwing aside the gentleman. My convictions always come too late."

"Why, what a crotchet is this!" said I. "To my thinking, you strangely misapprehend your mistress, Ned, when you fancy she could take offence at hearing that you had punished an inso-lent fellow for reviling her father."

"It is the manner of the thing, Mark," replied Ned. "The idea that I had gone into a vulgar ring of clowns, and soiled my hands in a rough-and-tumble struggle with a strolling bully. Now if I had encountered an unknown ruffian in the woods, with sword and lance, on horseback, and had had my weapon shivered in my hand, and then been trussed upon a pole ten feet long,— Gad, I believe she would be thrown into transports!—that would be romance for her; it would be a glorious feat of arms; and, I doubt not, she would attend me in my illness, like the king's daughter in the ballad,—the most bewitching of leeches! But to be pommeled black and blue, with that plebeian instrument a fist—pugh!—she will turn up her nose at it with a magnificent disdain. Do you see any traces of the fight about me? have I any scar or scratch? do you think I may pass unquestioned?"

"You may thank your skill in this vulgar accomplishment," I answered, "that you do not carry a black eye to The Brakes. As it is, you have nothing to fear on that score; and, I promise you, although I doubt your apprehension of Bel, that I will say nothing that shall lead to your detection."

"This is only of a piece with my other miseries," said he. "It is another proof of the tyranny to which a man is exposed who is obliged to square his conduct to the caprices of a mistress. I declare to you I feel, at this moment, like a schoolboy who is compelled to rack his wits for some plausible lie to escape a whipping."

"Truly, Ned, you are a most ridiculous lover," said I. "Of all men I ever knew, I certainly never saw one who took so little trouble to square his conduct to any rule. This is the merest farce that ever was acted. Little does Bel suspect that she has in her train such a trembling slave. Why, sir, it is the perpetual burthen of her complaint that your recklessness of her rises to the most flagrant contumacy: and, to tell you the truth, I think she has reason on her side."

"Well, well!" said Ned, laughing, "be that as it may; say nothing about the feat to-day, because, in sober earnest, I am not quite satisfied with the exploit myself. I certainly was under no obligation to drub that rascal Rutherford."

In the discussion of this topic we arrived at The Brakes, where both joy and surprise were manifested at finding Fairbourne brought back in fetters to his prison. Harvey Riggs clapped his hands and called out "Bravo! Well done Hazard! Did'nt I say, Bel, that Ned would perform as many wonders as the seven champions altogether? Is there such another true knight in the land?"

As for Bel, she was raised into the loftiest transports. She laughed,—asked a thousand questions,—darted from place to place, and taking Fairbourne in her hand, smoothed his feathers, and kissed him over and over again. The rest of the family joined in similar expressions of pleasure, and Ned gave a circum-

372   MOONSHINE.

stantial detail of all the facts attending the recovery, carefully
omitting the least allusion to the affair that followed it.   When
this was done, Harvey again heaped a torrent of applause upon
the Knight of the Hawk, as he called Hazard, and with a lively
sally sang out, in a cracked and discordant voice,—

> "Oh, 'tis love, 'tis love, 'tis love, that rules us all completely,
> Oh, 'tis love, 'tis love, 'tis love commands, and we obey—"

—which he concluded with sundry antics, and danced out of the
room.   Bel, upon hearing the part that Wilful acted in the recapture, declared that she would take him into high favor, and
that thenceforth he should have the freedom of the parlor; saying this, she patted him upon the back, and made him lie down
at her feet.

"Hey day! this is a fine rout and pother about a vagabond
bird!" said Mr. Tracy.   "Will you lose your senses, good folks!
Mr. Edward, you see what it is to gather toys for these women.
You have made Bel your slave for life."

Bel blushed scarlet red at this intimation; and Ned observing it, followed suit: their eyes met.   A precious pair of fools,
to make so much of so small a thing!

Fairbourne was carried to his perch, and regaled with a meal;
and the composure of the family being restored, after the conclusion of this important affair, we sat down to talk upon other matters.   Swansdown, we were told, had taken his departure after
breakfast.   Mr. Tracy, Harvey assured us, had been in his study
nearly all day, conning over the papers of the arbitration.   "The
old gentleman," he said, "was not altogether satisfied with the
award, inasmuch as there were certain particulars of fact which
he conceived to be misstated, especially in regard to a survey
affirmed to be made of the mill-dam, which did not appear in his
notes.   I have no doubt," Harvey added, "that before a month

my venerable kinsman will be in absolute grief for this untimely cutting short of the law-suit in the vigor of its days."

Ned sat beside Bel, occupied in a low, tremulous, and earnest conversation, until the stars were all shining bright, and even then, he unwillingly broke his colloquy at my summons. Our horses had been waiting at the door for the last hour.

We galloped nearly the whole way back to Swallow Barn; Ned rapidly leading the way, and striking his whip at the bushes on the road side, whistling, singing, and cutting many antics upon his saddle.

" What the deuce ails you?" I called out.

" I feel astonishingly active to-night," said he. " I could do such deeds !" and thereupon he put his horse up to full speed.

" The man is possessed," said I, following, however, at the same gait.

That night we did not go to bed until the moon rose, which I think the almanac will show to have been near one o'clock.

CHAPTER XXXVIII.

THE LAST MINSTREL.

As I do not at all doubt that you, my dear Zack, have by this time become deeply interested in the progress of Ned Hazard's love affairs; and as I find, (what greatly surprises myself,) that Ned has grown to be a hero in my story; and that I, who originally began to write only a few desultory sketches of the Old Dominion, have unawares, and without any premeditated purpose, absolutely fallen into a regular jog-trot, novel-like narrative,—at least, for several consecutive chapters,—it is no more than what I owe to posterity to go on and supply such matters of fact as may tend to the elucidation and final clearing up of the present involved and uncertain posture into which I have brought my principal actors. Feeling the weight of this obligation, as soon as I had closed the last chapter I began to bethink me of the best means of compassing my end; for, like a true historiographer, I conceived it to be, in some sort, my bounden duty to resort to the best sources of information which my opportunities afforded. Now, it must have been perceived by my clear-sighted readers, that I am already largely indebted to Harvey Riggs for the faithful report of such matters as fell out at the Brakes when I was not there myself to note them down; and I therefore thought, that in the present emergency I might, with great profit to my labor, have recourse to the same fountain of intelligence. In this I do but imitate and follow in the footsteps of all the illustrious chroniclers of the world, who have made it their business to speak primarily of what they themselves have seen and known, and secondarily, to take at second-hand, (judiciously perpending the force of testimony,) such things as have come to them by hearsay: for, nothing is more common than for these grave wights to introduce into their books some of their weightiest and most important morsels of history by some such oblique insinuation as this;—" I have heard people say," or "the renowned Gregory of Tours, or William of Malmsbury, or John of Nokes affirms," or, " it was currently reported and believed at the time,"—or some such preface, by which they let in the necessary matter. Henceforth, then, let it be understood, that as I profess to speak in my own person of what happened at Swallow Barn, so I rely mainly on my contemporary Harvey, as authority for all such synchronous events as transpired at The Brakes. With this explanatory advertisement, I proceed with my story.

I have described, in the last chapter, the unnatural speed with which Hazard and myself had ridden to Swallow Barn. Bel too, it seems, was possessed in some such strange mood after we were gone ; for she moved about the house singing, dancing, talking unconnectedly, and manifesting many unaccountable humors. I devoutly believe that both she and Hazard were bewitched. It might have been the hawk,—or some other little animal with wings on his shoulders.—But I leave this to the consideration of the Pundits, and pass on to events of more importance.

We had not left the Brakes above half an hour when the scraping of a violin was heard in the yard, near the kitchen door The tune was that of a popular country-dance, and was executed in a very brisk and inspiring cadence.

"That sounds like Hafen Blok's fiddle," said Ralph. "He has come here for his supper, and we shall be pestered with his nonsense all night."

"If it be Hafen," said Bel, "he shall be well treated, for the poor old man has a hard time in this world. He is almost the only minstrel, cousin Harvey, that is left.

> "'The bigots of this iron time,
>   Have called his harmless art a crime.'

"And truly, I wish we had more like him! for, Hafen has a great many ballads that, I assure you, will compare very well with the songs of the troubadours and minnesingers."

"There you go," cried Harvey, "with your age of chivalry. I don't know much about your troubadours and minnesingers: but, if there was amongst them as great a scoundrel as Hafen, your age of chivalry was an arrant cheat. Why, this old fellow lives by petty larceny; he hasn't the dignity of a large thief: he is a filcher of caps and napkins from a washerwoman's basket; a robber of hen-roosts; a pocketer of tea-spoons! Now, if there was any romance in him, he would, at least, steal cows and take purses on the highway."

"Pray, cousin," exclaimed Bel, laughing, "do not utter such slanders against my old friend Hafen! Here, I have taken the greatest trouble in the world to get me a minstrel. I have encouraged Hafen to learn ditties, and he has even composed some himself at my bidding. Once I gave him a dress which you would have laughed to see. It was made after the most approved fashion of minstrelsy. First, there was a long gown of Kendal green, gathered at the neck with a narrow gorget; it had sleeves that hung as low as the knee, slit from the shoulder to the hand and lined with white cotton; a doublet with sleeves of black worsted; upon these a pair of points of tawny camlet, laced along the wrist with blue thread points, with a welt towards the hand, made of fustian; a pair of red stockings; a red girdle, with a knife stuck in it; and, around his neck, a red riband, suitable to the girdle. Now what do you think, cousin, of such a dress as that?"

"Where did you get the idea of this trumpery?" cried H•rvey.

"It is faithfully taken," said Bel, "from the exact description of the minstrel's dress, as detailed by Laneham, in his account of the entertainment of Queen Elizabeth at ' Killingworth Castle.'"

"And did Hafen put it on?"

"To be sure he did!" replied Bel, "and paraded about with it here a whole evening."

"Bel," said Harvey, after a loud laugh,—"I like your nonsense: it is so sublimated and refined, and double-distilled, that, upon my soul, I think it throws a shabby air over all other folly I ever saw! Minstrel Blok, Hawk Fairbourne, and Childe Ned, Dragon-killing Ned, are altogether without a parallel or a copy in the whole world. A precious train for a lady! And so Hafen has been learning ballads, too?"

"Certainly," returned Bel, "I have taken the trouble to get him some very authentic collections. Now, what do you think of ' the Golden Garland of Princely Delights?' that is an old book I gave him to learn some songs from, and the wretch lost it, without learning one single sonnet."

"Good reason why," said Ralph;—"he never could read."

"I didn't know that, Ralph, when I gave it to him," said Bel. "But Hafen has an excellent memory. Hark! he is beginning to sing now. Listen, cousin, and you will hear something to surprise you."

At this moment, Hafen's voice was heard commencing a stave,

with a nasal tone, in a monotonous, but quick tune, which accompanied words that were uttered with a very distinct articulation.

"Let us have this in the porch," said Harvey; and he immediately led the way to the back-door; where Hafen being called, took his seat and recommenced his song as follows:—

> "November the fourth, in the year ninety-one,
> We had a sore engagement near to Fort Jefferson.
> St. Clair was our commander, which may remembered be.
> For there we left nine hundred men, in the Western Territory
> Our militia was *attackted*, just as the day did break;
> And soon were overpowered and forced to retreat.
> They killed Major Ouldham, Levin and Briggs likewise,
> With horrid yells of savages resounded thorough the skies;
> Major Butler was wounded, the very second fire—"

"Well, that will do, Hafen," interrupted Harvey; "we don't like such a bloody song as this; it is the very essence of tragedy."

"It's as true as preaching, Mister Riggs," said Hafen. "I was there myself, in Colonel Gibson's regiment."

"No doubt!" replied Harvey. "But Miss Tracy wants something more sentimental, Hafen; this butchering of militia men does not suit the ladies so well as a touching, sorrowful song."

"Ay, ay!" said Hafen, "I understand you, Mister Harvey. I have just the sort of song to please Miss Isabel. It goes to the tune of 'William Reilly.'

> "'While I rehearse my story, Americans give ear,
> Of Britain's fading glory, you presently shall hear;
> I'll give a true relation, attend to what I say,
> Concerning the taxation of North America.

"There is a wealthy people who sojourn in that land,
Their churches all with steeples most delicately stand,
Their houses, like the lily, are painted red and gay;
They flourish like the gilly in North America.'"

"Poh! this is worse than the other!" exclaimed Harvey.
"Do you call this sentimental? Why don't you give us something pitiful? Bel, your minstrel is as badly trained as your hawk."

"Hafen," said Bel, "I fear you have not thought of me lately, or you would have brought me something more to my liking than these songs."

"Bless your young heart, mistress!" replied Hafen, "I can sing fifty things that you'd like to hear, in the love line: There's 'the Manhattan Tragedy,' and 'the Royal Factor's Garland,' and 'the Golden Bull,' and 'the Prodigal Daughter,' and 'Jemmy and Nancy,' commonly called the Yarmouth Tragedy, showing how, by the avariciousness and cruelty of parents, two faithful lovyers were destroyed: and there's 'the Gosport Tragedy,' that shows how a young damsel was led astray by a ship's carpenter, and carried into a lonesome wood; and how her ghost haunted him at sea;—

"'When he *immediantly* fell on his knees,
And the blood in his veins with horror did freeze.'"

"Oh, very well," said Harvey, "stop there; we don't wish to hear the music. Go get your supper, Hafen; the servants are waiting for you. These are entirely too sentimental; you run into extremes." Hafen obeyed the order; and, as he limped towards the kitchen, Harvey remarked to Bel, "This is a fine smack of war and love that Hafen has favored us with;—

"'The last of all the bards was he
Who sang of Border Chivalry.'"

Truly, Cousin Bel, these shreds and patches of romance are wonderfully picturesque. Hafen does honor to your zeal in behalf
of the days of knighthood and minstrelsy."

"You may laugh, Harvey, as much as you please, but there
is something pleasant in the idea of moated castles, and gay
knights, and border feuds, and roundelays under one's window,
and lighted halls where ladies dance *corantos* and ' trod measures'
as they called it !"

"And when hawks," added Harvey, "were not flown like kites,
with a string, but came at a whistle, and did as they were told;
and troubadours were not Dutch tinkers; and when bachelors
could win mistresses by hard blows, and were not sent off because
they were merry and like other people."

"Pshaw! cousin," interrupted Bel. "You havn't one spark
of genuine romance in your whole composition. It is profane to
listen to such a recreant as you are."

"Well, Bel, I will tell you," said Harvey. "It is not to be
denied that Hafen shines as a fiddler, however questionable may
be his merits as a ballad monger. So if cousin Kate here and
Ralph will dance, we will bring him into the parlor and have a
four-handed reel. We will call it a *coranto*, if you prefer the
name; and, to give you a lighted hall, I will have two more candles put on the mantle-piece."

"Agreed," said Bel; "so tell Hafen to bring in his instrument."

Hafen appeared at the summons, and an hour was merrily
spent in dancing.

When the dance was over, Bel gave Hafen a glass of wine,
and slipped into his hand a piece of money.

"Many thanks to my young lady!" said the old man. "You
deserve a good husband, and soon."

"You have travelled, Hafen, to very little purpose," said

Harvey, "if you are not able, at your time of life, to tell this lady's fortune."

" Oh, bless you !" replied Hafen, "I can do that very truly. You are not afraid, young mistress, to show me the palm of your hand ?"

" Not she !" said Harvey. " Bel, open your hand ; let the venerable Hafen disclose to you the decrees of fate."

" Take care, Hafen," said Bel, holding out her hand ; "if you say one unlucky word I will for ever dismiss you from my service."

Hafen took from his pocket an old pair of spectacles, and proceeded, very minutely, to examine the open hand.

" Here is a line that has not more than six months to run : that is the line of marriage, young mistress. It is not so smooth a line, neither, as ought to be in such a palm, for it breaks off in two or three places, with some crossings."

" Defend me !" cried Bel. " What does that mean ?"

" It means," replied Hafen, " that the lady is hard to please, and can scarcely find heart to make up her mind."

" True !" exclaimed Harvey. " Worshipful soothsayer Hafen go on !"

" The lady does not sleep well o' nights," continued Hafen ; " and here are cloudy dreams ; the hand is mottled, and yet her blood ought to flow smoothly too, for it has a healthy color ; the palm is moist and shows a warm heart : I fear the lady has fancies. Well, well, it is all nothing, as there is a good ending to it. Here is a person who has done her great service lately. He will do her more : and,—let me see,—he is a gentleman of good blood, and more in love than I think it right to tell. He travels on a line that runs to marriage. Fie, my young mistress, you would not be obstinate with such a gentleman ! But here is a stop and a cross line. 'There is many a slip 'twixt the cup and the lip.' No, no, it is better than it looks."

" Excellent well !" cried Harvey again.

" It is not excellent well, cousin," said Bel, playfully with·
drawing her hand.   " Hafen, you have to learn the beginnings of
your art.   You know nothing about palmistry !   Couldn't you
see, with half an eye, that the marriage line on my hand was a
mile from the end ?   I wonder at you !"

" Not so fast, not so fast, Miss Isabel !" cried Hafen, with a
sly laugh.   " You can't deceive me.   I saw the very man to-day.
And a proper gentleman he is—a brave one, as I said before.
Why, gentle bred as he is, he can handle any man, in the way of
boxing, 'twixt this and Richmond.   It is a real pleasure to see
him strike a blow."

" His name," said Harvey.

" It would not be a strange name to these walls, if I was to
tell it," answered Hafen.   " But I never thought such a pair of
arms belonged to a gentleman, as he showed this morning."

" Ned Hazard !" said Harvey.   " Pray, what did you see of
him this morning ?"

" I will tell you and our pretty young lady here what I saw,"
replied Hafen.   " Up here at the cross-roads, you must know,—
about noon or a little later,—comes along Mister Edward Hazard
and that strange gentleman his friend, on horseback, with that
same hawk that's out here in the cage.   Well, there was a parcel
of neighbors drinking, and such like, about the store.   Mister
Edward never stands much upon ceremony ; so, he got down,
and then the other got down, and ' good morning,' and ' good
morning,' went round.   Mister Edward's not one of your proud
men, for he got to showing them the bird, and told them, bless
your heart ! whose it was—Miss Isabel's here.   I suspected something then," said Hafen, putting his finger against the side of his
nose and looking at Harvey.   " Well, one word brought on
another, and somehow or 'nother, Miles Rutherford gives Mister

Edward the lie. So, out jumps Mister Edward, and calls to the others to stand by him, and swears out pretty strong, (you know, Miss Isabel, Mister Ned's like any other man at swearing when he's angry,) and tells Miles to step out if he dares, and says, he will lick him to his heart's content,—or something to that effect. Well, Miles had whipped almost every fighting man in the county, and he wa'nt going to be baulked by Ned Hazard; and, accordingly, out he comes. Mercy on me! says I, now Mister Edward will give Miles such a mouthful to stay his stomach, as he never tasted in his life before. I knew Mr. Hazard of old, and told Miles what he'd get. And sure enough, it would have done your heart good, Miss Isabel, if you had seen how Mister Edward did drub Miles! And the best of it was, he did it so genteel, as if he didn't want to bloody his clothes. And when he was done he wiped his face, as natural as if he had been at his dinner, and I brought him some water to wash his hands; and then off he and the tother gentleman rode after bidding the company good day.— Upon which we gave them three cheers."

"Are you telling us the truth, Hafen?" asked Harvey, earnestly.

"I would not tell you a lie, Mister Harvey," replied Hafen, "if it was to save my right hand from being chopped off this minute."

"This morning, do you say this happened?"

"As I am a Christian man," said the tinker.

"Ned fought with that bully, Miles Rutherford?—and with fists?"

"As fair a fight, Mister Riggs," replied Hafen, "and as pretty a one as you ever saw."

"What brought it about? You have told us nothing about the cause of the quarrel."

"I'm not particular about that," said the other; "but it was words. The truth is, I suspect Miles was impertinent, and Mister Edward wanted to beat him; for he said he did it on account of the good of the public. Both on 'em might have been a little in the wrong, but Mister Hazard's hand was in; and, you know, a man don't stand much persuasion when that's the case. But, you may depend, Mister Edward gained a great deal of glory."

" Edward didn't say a word about this to us," said Bel.

" I can't unriddle it," replied Harvey, shaking his head.

Hafen was now dismissed from the parlor; and Bel and Harvey fell into a long conversation, in relation to the disclosure that was just made. Bel uttered a deep and sincere complaint in Harvey's ear, that the waywardness of Hazard's temper should be so continually driving him off his guard. It was so unbecoming his station in society to permit himself to appear in these lights to the world! When would he learn discretion? How could he hope to win the affections even of his intimate friends, when he was perpetually offending against the plainest duties he owed them? She admitted his goodness of heart, and the value she set upon the many excellent points in his character; but it seemed as if fate had unalterably decreed that every day he was to be farther removed from all hopes of making himself agreeable to her.

To these suggestions Harvey could frame no defence, except that Hafen had, perhaps, misrepresented the facts.

" I do not wish to inquire into the details," said Bel, " because no provocation, in my opinion, could excuse a gentleman in making such a figure before a set of low-bred rustics. I cannot express to you, cousin Harvey, how much this thing shocks me."

" There are provocations, Bel," replied Harvey, " that would render such an exploit meritorious—even in a gentleman."

" I cannot think it,—cousin:—I cannot think so," replied Bel, musing over the matter; " I wish I could."

"I'll tell you, Bel, what we will do," said Harvey, with a gay air; "we will get our old minnesinger Hafen to hitch it into verse and sing it to the tune of 'The Lay of the Last Minstrel.'"

"Incorrigible sinner!" exclaimed Bel, "how can you jest upon such an incident! as for your friend Edward, I pity him; you know why. But do not make me think as hardly of you. Good night!"

"Pleasant dreams to you!" cried Harvey. "Fancy that you have heard of a tilting match between a bull and a cavalier, and that the bull was beaten. Romance and chivalry are sovereign varnishes for cracked crowns and bloody noses. Good night!"

CHAPTER XXXIX.

SIGNS OF A HERO.

While Hazard was indulging the luxurious fancy that he had sailed, at last, into the harbor of Bel's good graces; and was casting about to see how he should best make good his moorings, Hafen, like a lame Vulcan, was forging a thunderbolt that was destined to descend upon Ned's slender pinnace, and either tear up one of the principal planks, or at least, give him such a lurch as should make him think he was going straight to the bottom.

Happy would it have been for Hazard if he had not forbidden me to say any thing to his mistress about his unfortunate quarrel with Miles Rutherford ; for then I could have given the matter such a gloss as must have entirely satisfied any reasonable woman whatever. But to have this incident mangled by Hafen Blok, disgraced by his slang, and discolored by his officious zeal to contribute to Ned's glorification, was one of those unlucky strokes of fortune to which the principal actors in romance have been subject from time immemorial. This, therefore, gives me strong hopes that he is really destined to be a hero of some note before I am done with him. It has thrown him, for the present, into a deep shade. And yet,—shortsighted mortal !—so little suspicious was he that affairs had taken this turn, that all the next day (being Sunday) he was more like a man bordering upon insanity than a rational Christian. His first impulse was to go over to The Brakes immediately after breakfast: then, he checked himself by the consideration that it was pushing matters too fiercely. After this, he thought of sending for Harvey Riggs to join us at dinner: then, he reflected that it wasn't Harvey he wished to see. He then sat down with a book in his hand, but soon discovered that he could not understand one sentence that he was reading. He got up, and walked as far as the gate; looked critically at the plum-tree, that had not the smallest appearance of fruit upon it and very few leaves, and then returned to the house whistling, where Lucy and Vic told him, " it was Sunday and he must not whistle." At length, as a last resort, he went up to his chamber, and dressed himself out with extraordinary particularity in white drilling pantaloons, as stiff with starch as if they were made of foolscap paper, a white waistcoat, his dark-green frock, a black stock, boots and his hair-cloth foragecap. In this attire he appeared in the hall, with a riding-whip in his hand, walking up and down in profound abstraction.

" Where are you going, Ned?' asked Meriwether.

" Going?" he replied, " I am going to stay at home."

" I beg your pardon! I thought you were about to ride." Meriwether passed on. Ned continued his walk.

" Where are you going, Edward?" asked my cousin Lucretia.

" Nowhere," said Ned.

" Edward, where are you going?" inquired Prudence.

" I am not going out," said Ned.

" Uncle Ned, may I go with you? shall I get Spitfire?" cried Rip, running into the hall.

" Where?" asked Ned, with some surprise.

" Wherever you are going to ride," answered Rip.

" Good people!" exclaimed Hazard. " What has got into the family! where would you have me go? what do you see? what do you want?"

"Arn't you going to ride?" asked Rip.

"By no means, my dear."—Away went Rip.

All this I saw from the porch. So, getting up from my seat, I also accosted him with the same question. "Where are you going?"

"The Lord knows, Mark! I have just dressed myself, and have been walking here, for want of something better to do. I wish it were to-morrow! for I don't like to go over yonder to-day. I think a man ought not to visit more than three times a week. —I feel very queerly this morning: I have been every where, gaping about like an apprentice-boy in his Sunday clothes. I have seen the horses in the stable, the fowls in the poultry-yard, the pigs, the negroes, and, in fact, I don't know what in the devil to do with myself. Mark, we will go over to The Brakes to-morrow morning?"

"Oh, certainly. I think our affairs require some attention in that quarter. Why not go this evening?"

"I should like it very much," said Ned. "But it would alarm the family. I feel qualmish at being seen there too often. People are so fond of gossipping! No, no, we will wait until to-morrow."

These particulars will show the state of Hazard's mind, the day following the recovery of the hawk,—a day that passed heavily enough. Ned pretended to impute all this tediousness to Sunday, which, he remarked, was always the most difficult day in the week to get through.

On Monday morning we were at The Brakes by ten o'clock. Bel was busy with Fairbourne, and looked uncommonly fresh and gay. Her manner was affable, and too easy, I thought, considering the peculiar relation of her affairs, at this moment, towards Hazard. She addressed her conversation principally to me; and, once or twice, refused Ned's services in some little matters wherein it was natural he should offer them. I observed, moreover, that she did not second his attempts at wit as freely as she was used to do : they made me smile; but upon her they fell harmless and flat, like schoolboys' arrows headed with tar. All this seemed strange and boded ill. Hazard observed it; for it made him awkward; his cheek grew pale, and his words stuck in his throat.

In a short time some household matters called Bel away.

"The wind has changed," said Ned, in a half-whisper to me, as we walked to the parlor ; "the thermometer is falling towards the freezing point. I wish this business was at the——"

"Whist, Ned!" I exclaimed, "don't swear! There is some mistake in this matter: we'll talk to Harvey."

Harvey Riggs took a seat with us at the front door; and there, in a long, confidential and grave conference, he explained to us all that he knew of this perplexing affair. He said that he had been trying to bring Bel to reason, because he thought, to use his own phrase, "it was all flummery in her to be so hyperbolical with Ned ;" but that she was struck, just between wind and water, with Hafen's rigmarole about Ned's boxing match ; and that it would require some time to get this warp out of her fancy; that there was no question she was deeply wounded by all she had heard ; but still he had hopes, that he would be able to set matters right again. "Ned," said he, "my dear fellow, let me warn you, at least until you are married, (if you are ever to have that luck,) to care how you make a fool of yourself ; because it is sure immediately to turn Bel into a greater one. Mark, they are a miraculous pair of geese !" cried Harvey, breaking out into a loud laugh; and then singing out with a great flourish, to the tune of a popular song, the following doggerel—

> And grant, oh Queen of fools! he said—
> Thus ran the mooncalf's prayer—

That I may prove the drollest knight
And wed the queerest fair.

Ned absolutely raved. He thought he had the fairest occasion in the world to get into a passion; and he, accordingly, fell
to swearing against all womankind, in the most emphatic terms.
As soon as he had "unpacked his heart" in this way, he dropped
into another mood, and began to deplore his fate, pretty much as
he had done on some of those former occasions that I have described; and last of all,—which he ought to have done at first,—
he became very reasonable; and, in a calm, manly defence of
himself, narrated circumstantially the whole affair; showing, in
the most conclusive manner, that he had been induced to accept
Miles Rutherford's challenge, only because he did not choose to
hear that graceless brawler pour out his vile abuse upon one so
venerable in his eyes as Mr. Tracy.

"What could I do," said he, "but chastise such a scoundrel,
for the irreverent mention, in such a circle, of the excellent old
gentleman? and, I humbly think, that, of all persons in the
world, Bel Tracy is the last that has a right to complain of it."

"This sets the matter in a new light," said Harvey; "I told
Bel, I was certain Hafen had lied. Her worshipful minstrel, her
rascally minnesinger makes a great figure in this business!"

Here Hazard's mood changed again. Nothing is so brave as
a lover who has found good ground to rail against his mistress.
He may be as gentle as a pet squirrel, or a lamb that is fed by
hand, as long as he has no confederate to encourage him in rebellion; but no sooner does he receive a compassionate word from a
by-stander, or enlist a party, than he becomes the most peremptory and fearful of animals. Harvey's words stirred up Ned's
soul into a sublime mutiny; and, for some minutes, he was more
extravagant than ever. He would let Bel see that she had made
a sad mistake, when she imagined that he was going to surrender

his free agency, his judgment, his inclinations, his sense of duty to her! It became a man to take a stand in affairs of this nature! He scorned to put on a character to win a woman, that he did not mean to support afterwards, if he should be successful: it would be rank hypocrisy! What, in the devil's name, did she expect of him!—to stand by; and acknowledge himself a man, when she—yes, she herself—for an attack upon her father was an attack upon her—was reviled and made the subject of profane jest and vituperation on the lips of an outlaw! Let Bel consider it in this point of view, and how could she possibly find fault with him?"

"Yes. Let Bel consider it in this point of view!" said Harvey, chiming in with a droll and affected gravity; "I'll go and put the subject to her in this light, this very instant."

"No," said Ned, "you need not be in a hurry. But, in earnest, Harvey, at another time I would like you to do it: it is but justice."

"I'll harrow up," replied Harvey, with a deep tragic voice, "her inmost soul."

"In order that you may have free scope," said Hazard, "it will be better for Mark and me to set off home immediately."

"'Sir Lucius, we won't run,'" said I, laughing. "Do you think there is danger, Ned? shall we make a rapid retreat?"

"'Brush,' exclaimed Harvey, 'the sooner you are off, the better!' I will meet you anon, and report to you at Swallow Barn."

Without taking leave of the family we commenced our retreat; and during the ride Ned displayed the same alternations of feeling that were manifested in our interview with Harvey. These emotions resolved themselves, at last, into one abiding and permanent determination, and that, considering the character and temper of Hazard, was sufficiently comic, namely,—that in his future intercourse with Bel, he would invariably observe the most scrupulous regard to all the high-flown and overstrained elegancies and proprieties of conduct which she so pretended to idolize. His humor was that of dogged submission to her most capricious whims. Never did spaniel seem so humbled.

" I know I shall make a fool of myself," said he, " but that is her look-out, not mine. I'll give her enough of her super-subtle, unimaginable, diabolical dignity !—I will be the very essence of dulness, and the quintessence of decorum !—I will turn myself into an ass of the first water, until I make her so sick of pedantry and sentiment, that a good fellow shall go free with her all the rest of her life !"

CHAPTER XL.

As soon as we had left The Brakes Harvey sought an opportunity to communicate to Bel all that he had learned from us in regard to the cause and circumstances of the quarrel between Ned and Rutherford; presenting to her, in the strongest point of view he was able, the signal injustice she had done to so faithful and devoted a lover. " I should not have regarded the matter a rush," said Harvey, " if it were not that Ned, as I have often told you, is one of the most sensitive creatures alive, and so much inclined to melancholy that there is no knowing what effect such an incident may have upon his temper." Bel smiled incredulously, and seemed as if she did not know whether to take Harvey in jest or earnest.

" You may treat this lightly," continued Harvey, " but I am sure you will feel some unpleasant misgivings when you come to reflect on it." She smiled again.

" It is not a just return for that admirable constancy," Harvey proceeded, " which Ned, notwithstanding his upper current of levity, has always shown towards you ; and which, amidst all his waywardness, has always set steadily towards you. If he has been volatile in his pursuits, you cannot deny that he has connected you with the pleasantest passages of his life; if he has been strange in his conduct, now and then, it is very obvious that he has never ceased to feel the desire to make himself agreeable to you; if he has occasionally erred from the straight line of decorum, every transgression may be traced to some ardent endeavor to support your cause, even at the expense of your good opinion. Now, this is what I call faith, honor and gallantry. It shows single-heartedness, homage and modesty. It is in the very best strain of a cavalier devoted to his lady-love; and has more true chivalry in it than all the formal courtesies in the world—"

Bel began to look grave.

" It cuts Ned to the heart to think his mistress ungrateful; and, particularly, that she should listen to a vile strolling tinker, and take his account of a fray as if it were gospel, instead of suspending her opinion until she should have a more authentic relation from himself. This has sunk deeper into his feelings than any act of unkindness that ever befell him. And from you, Bel! —Conceive what anguish Ned must have experienced when your cold looks chided him for one of the most disinterested actions of his life."

" Why didn't he tell us all about this quarrel when he brought the hawk home ?" said Bel. " Why was he silent then, I should like to know ?"

" Was it for him," asked Harvey, " to vaunt his exploits in your ear? A brave man naturally forbears to speak of his achievements; and therein is Ned's true modesty of character conspicuous. He would have concealed this from *you* until he had grown gray, lest you might have been tempted to think he played the braggart with you. I cannot sufficiently admire such forbearance."

" Ah me, cousin !" said Bel, " I do not know what to think. You perplex me. I would not willingly offend the meanest creature that lives. I am sure I have no reason to be unkind to Mr. Hazard. But still it is not my fault that I cannot set the same

value upon his virtues that you and others do.—I almost wish I
had not been so marked in my demeanor to him this morning.
I am sure I am not ungrateful in my temper, cousin Harvey.
Did he speak much of it?"

"Rather in sorrow than in anger," returned Harvey. "But
the thought haunted him all the time he was here. He broke
out once or twice and swore."

"Swore at *me?*" exclaimed Bel.

"No; I was mistaken in saying he swore. He gave vent to
some piteous feelings,—as well he might:—but they were expressed chiefly in sighs."

"I wish I knew whether you were in earnest, Harvey," said
Bel, beseechingly. "Mercy on me! I do not know what to think.
I wish I were in heaven! And still, I won't believe Ned Hazard
cares the thousandth part as much for me as you make out."

This was not true, for Bel was inwardly very much moved
with the whole relation, and began to feel, what she never before
acknowledged, that Ned had a very fair claim to her consideration.

Harvey was making an experiment upon her heart; and, having set her to musing over the affair, left her to settle the case
with her own conscience. He had now satisfied himself that Ned,
if he used even ordinary discretion, might turn the accident to
good account; and he therefore said nothing more to Bel, knowing that the more she thought of what had passed, the graver
would be the impression on her mind.

The next morning he hastened over to Swallow Barn, where,
like a trusty minister, he detailed the sum of his observations in
a solemn council, convoked for that purpose.

Never was any topic more minutely or more ably discussed.
We all agreed that Ned's prospects were brightening; that a
crisis had arrived which it required great judgment to manage

with effect; and that, above all things, he must be very guarded for the future. It was also resolved that he should henceforth be more special and direct in his attentions, and not scruple to assume the posture of an avowed lover; that he should put on as much propriety of manner as might be found requisite to gratify Bel's most visionary requisitions; and that, in particular, he must neither swear in her presence, nor talk lightly before her.

"Oh, as to that," said Ned, who had grown as pliant as a trained hound in our hands, "I have already resolved to show her that I can play the part of the most solemn fool in the world. But, what perplexes me most is to find out some senti- mental subject for conversation. I shall commit myself by some egregious blunder of a joke, if I get to talking at random. Faith, I have a great mind to write down a whole discourse and commit it to memory.

"Talk to her," said Harvey, upon classical matters. Show her your learning. She thinks you don't read; rub up some of your college pedantry : any thing, man ;—give her a little of the heathen mythology !"

"Oh, I'll do it !" cried Ned with exultation. "I'll astonish her with a whole Encyclopedia of nonsense."

"Take care, though," interrupted Harvey, "to season it well with delicate and appropriate allusions to the affair in hand. Let it be congenial and lover-like; no matter how nonsensical. But don't be bombastic, Ned."

"Trust me !" he replied, "I'll suit her to the twentieth part of a scruple."

Here our conclave broke up with a flash of merriment; and we did nothing but jest all the rest of the day.

Harvey dined with us; and when, in the evening, he thought of returning, Carey came into the parlor to make a proposition which had the effect to retain our guest with us all that night. The incident that followed will require a chapter to itself.

CHAPTER XLI.

WHEN Carey came into the parlor he pulled off his hat and made a profound bow; and then advanced to the back of Ned's chair, where, in a low and orderly tone of voice, he made the following grave and interesting disclosure: namely, that the boys—meaning some of the other negroes who belonged to the plantation—had found out what had been disturbing the poultry-yard for some time past: that it was not a mink, as had been given out, but nothing less than a large old *'possum* that had been traced to a gum tree over by the river, about a mile distant: that the boys had *diskivered* him (to use Carey's own term) by some feathers near the tree; and, when they looked into the hollow, they could see his eyes shining "like foxfire." He said they had been trying to screw him out, by thrusting up a long stick, cut with a fork at the end, (an approved method of bringing out squirrels, foxes and rabbits from their holes, and much in practice in the country,) and tangling it in his hair, but that this design was abandoned under the supposition that, perhaps, Master Edward would like to hunt him in the regular way.

Ned professed a suitable concern in the intelligence; but inquired of Carey, whether he, as an old sportsman, thought it lawful to hunt an opossum at midsummer. This interrogatory set the old negro to chuckling, and afterwards, with a wise look, to putting the several cases in which he considered a hunt at the present season altogether consonant with prescriptive usage. He admitted that *'possums* in general were not to be followed till persimmon time, because they were always fattest when that fruit was ripe; but, when they couldn't get persimmons they were " mighty apt" to attack the young fowls and cut their throats : that it was good law to hunt any sort of creature when he was known to be doing mischief to the plantation. But even then, Carey affirmed with a " howsomdever," and " nevertheless," that if they carried young, and especially a " *'possum,*" (which has more young ones than most other beasts,) he thought they ought to be let alone until their appropriate time. This, however, was a large male opossum, that was known to be engaged in nefarious practices; and, moreover, was " shocking fat ;" and therefore, upon the whole, Carey considered him as a lawful subject of chase.

To this sagacious perpending of the question, and to the conclusion which the veteran had arrived at, Ned could oppose no valid objection. He, therefore, replied that he was entirely convinced that he, Carey, had taken a correct view of the subject ; and that if Mr. Riggs and Mr. Littleton could be prevailed upon to lend a hand, nothing would be more agreeable than the proposed enterprise.

We were unanimous on the proposition. Harvey agreed to defer his return to The Brakes until the next morning; and it was arranged that we should be apprised by Carey when the proper hour came to set out on the expedition. Carey then detailed the mode of proceeding : A watch was to be set near the henroost, the dogs were to be kept out of the way, lest they might steal upon the enemy unawares, and destroy him without a chase ; notice was to be given of his approach ; and one or two of those on the watch were to frighten him away ; and after allowing him time enough to get back to the woods, the dogs were to be put upon the trail and to pursue him until he was *treed*.

Having announced this, the old servant bowed again and left the room, saying, that it would be pretty late before we should be called out, because it was natural to these thieving animals to wait until people went to bed ; and that a *'possum* was one of the cunningest things alive.

Midnight arrived without a summons from our leader : the family had long since retired to rest ; and we began to fear that our vigil was to end in disappointment. We had taken posses sion of the settees in the hall, and had almost dropped asleep, when, about half past twelve, Carey came tiptoeing through the back door and told us, in a mysterious whisper, that the depre dator upon the poultry-yard had just been detected in his visit : that big Ben (for so one of the negroes was denominated, to dis tinguish him from little Ben,) had been out and saw the animal skulking close under the fence in the neighborhood of the roost. Upon this intelligence, we rose and followed the old domestic to the designated spot.

Here were assembled six or seven of the negroes, men and boys, who were clustered into a group at a short distance from the poultry-yard. Within a hundred paces the tall figure of big Ben was discerned, in dim outline, proceeding cautiously across a field until he had receded beyond our view. A nocturnal ad venture is always attended with a certain show of mystery : the presence of darkness conjures up in every mind an indefinite sense of fear—faint, but still sufficient to throw an interest around trivial things, to which we are strangers in the daytime. The lit tle assembly of blacks we had just joined were waiting in noiseless reserve for some report from Ben ; and, upon our arrival, were expressing in low and wary whispers, their conjectures as to the course the game had taken, or recounting their separate experience as to the habits of the animal. It was a cloudless night; and the obscure and capacious vault above us showed its thousands of stars, with a brilliancy unusual at this season. A chilling breeze swept through the darkness and fluttered the neighboring foliage with an alternately increasing and falling murmur. Some of the younger negroes stood bareheaded, with no clothing but coarse shirts and trowsers, shivering amongst the crowd, and, every now and then, breaking out into exclamations, in a pitch of voice that called down the reproof of their elders. Ned commanded all to be silent and to seat themselves upon the ground; and while we remained in this position, Ben reappeared and came directly up to the circle. He reported that he had detected the object of our quest near at hand; and had followed him through the weeds and stubble of the adjoining field, until he had seen him take a course which rendered it certain that he had been sufficiently alarmed by the rencounter to induce him to retire into the neighborhood of the gum. It was, therefore, Ben's advice that Ned, Harvey, and myself, should take Carey as a guide, and ct, as fast as we could, to the neighborhood of the tree spoken of, in order that we might be sure to see the capture; and that he would remain behind, where, after a delay long enough to allow us to reach our destination, he would put the dogs, which were now locked up in the stable, upon the trail; and then come on as rapidly as they were able to follow the scent.

Ben had the reputation of being an oracle in matters of woodcraft; and his counsel was, therefore, implicitly adopted. Carey assured us that "there was no mistake in him," and that we might count upon arriving at the appointed place, with the utmost precision, under his piloting. We accordingly set forward. For nearly a mile we had to travel through weeds and bushes; and having safely accomplished this, we penetrated into a piece of swampy woodland that lay upon the bank of the river. Our way was sufficiently perplexed; and, notwithstanding Carey's exorbitant boasting of his thorough knowledge of the ground, we did not reach the term of our march without some awkward mistakes, —such as taking ditches for fallen trees, and blackberry bushes for smooth ground. Although the stars did their best to afford us light, the thickness of the wood into which we had advanced wrapt us, at times, in impenetrable gloom. During this progress we were once stopped by Harvey calling out, from some twenty paces in the rear, that it was quite indispensable to the success of the expedition, so far as he was concerned, that Carey should correct a topographical error, into which he, Mr. Riggs, found himself very unexpectedly plunged; " I have this moment," said he, " been seized by the throat by a most rascally grapevine; and in my sincere desire to get out of its way, I find that another of the same tribe has hooked me below the shoulders. Meantime, my hat has been snatched from my head; and, in these circumstances, gentlemen, perhaps it is not proper for me to budge a foot."

Notwithstanding these embarrassments, we at last reached the gum tree, and " halting in his shade, " if the tree could be said to be proprietor of any part of this universal commodity, patiently awaited the events that were upon the wind. The heavy falling dew had shed a dampness through the air that almost stiffened our limbs with cold. It was necessary that we should remain silent; and, indeed, the momentary expectation of hearing our followers advance upon our footsteps fixed us in a mute and earnest suspense. This feeling absorbed all other emotions for a time; when finding that they were not yet afoot, we began to look round upon the scene, and note the novel impressions it made upon our senses. The wood might be said to be vocal with a thousand unearthly sounds; for, the wakeful beings of midnight, that inhabit every spray and branch of the forest, are endued with voices of the harshest discord. The grove, which in daylight is resonant with melody, is now converted into a sombre theatre of gibbering reptiles, screeching insects, and nightbirds of melancholy and grating cries. The concert is not loud, but incessant, and invades the ear with fiendish notes : it arouses thoughts that make it unpleasant to be alone. Through the trees the murky surface of the river was discernible, by the flickering reflections of the stars, with darkness brooding over the near perspective. In the bosom of this heavy shadow, a lonely taper shot its feeble ray from the cabin window of some craft at anchor; and this was reflected, in a long, sharp line, upon the water below it. The fretful beat of the waves was heard almost at our feet; and the sullen plash of a fish, springing after his prey, occasionally reached us with strange precision. Around us, the frequent crash of rotten boughs, breaking under the stealthy footsteps of the marauder of the wood that now roamed for booty, arrested our attention and deceived us with the thought that the special object of our search was momentarily approaching.

Still, however, no actual sign was yet given us that our huntsmen were on their way. Harvey grew impatient, and took our old guide to task for having mistaken his course ; but Carey persisted that he was right, and that this delay arose only from Ben's wary caution to make sure of his game. At length, a deep-toned and distant howl reached us from the direction of the house.

" Big Ben's awake now," said Carey; " that's Cæsar's voice, and he never speaks without telling truth."

We were all attention; and the *tonguing* of this dog was followed by the quick yelping of four or five others. Ned directed Carey to seat himself at the foot of the gum tree, in order that he might prevent the opossum from retreating into the hollow; and then suggested that we should conceal ourselves under the neighboring bank.

By this time, the cries of the dogs were redoubled, and indicated the certainty of their having fallen upon the track of their prey. Carey took his seat, with his back against the opening of the hollow, and we retired to the bank, under the shelter of some large and crooked roots of a sycamore that spread its bulk above the water. Whilst in this retreat, the halloos of Ben and his assistants, encouraging the dogs, became distinctly audible, and gradually grew stronger upon our hearing. Every moment the animation of the scene increased ; the clamor grew musical as it swelled upon the wind ; and we listened with a pleasure that one would scarce imagine could be felt under such circumstances, instantly expecting the approach of our companions. It was impossible longer to remain inactive ; and, with one impulse, we sprang from our hiding place, and hurried to the spot where we had left old Carey stationed, as a sentinel, at the door of the devoted quadruped's home. At this moment, as if through the influence of a spell, every dog was suddenly hushed into profound silence.

" They have lost their way," said Ned, " or else the animal has taken to the brook and confounded the dogs. Is it not possible, Carey, that he has been driven into a tree nearer home ? "

" Never mind !" replied Carey, " that '*possum*'s down here in some of these bushes watching us. Bless you ! if the dogs had treed him you would hear them almost crazy with howling. These '*possums* never stay to take a chase, because they are the sorriest things in life to get along on level ground ;—they sort of hobble ; and that's the reason they always take off,—as soon as they see a body,—to their own homes. You trust big Ben ; he knows what he's about."

The chase, in an instant, opened afresh ; and it was manifest that the pursuers were making rapidly for the spot on which we stood. Carey begged us to get back to our former concealment ;

but the request was vain.   The excitement kept us on foot, and
it was with difficulty we could be restrained from rushing forward
to meet the advancing pack.   Instead, however, of coming down
to the gum tree, the dogs suddenly took a turn and sped, with
urgent rapidity, in a contrary direction, rending the air with a
clamor that far exceeded any thing we had yet heard.   " We have
lost our chance !" cried Harvey.   " Here have we been shivering
in the cold for an hour to no purpose.   What devil tempted us to
leave Ben ?   Shall we follow ?"

" Pshaw, master Harvey !"   exclaimed the old negro,—"don't
you know better than that?   It's only some *varmint* the dogs
have got up in the woods.   When you hear such a desperate
barking, and such hard running as that, you may depend the dogs
have hit upon a gray-fox, or something of that sort, that can give
them a run.   No *'possum* there !   Big Ben isn't a going to let
Cæsar sarve him that fashion !"

Ben's voice was heard, at this period, calling back the dogs
and reproving them for going astray ; and, having succeeded in a
few minutes in bringing them upon their former scent, the whole
troop were heard breaking through the undergrowth, in a direction leading immediately to the tree.

" Didn't I tell you so, young masters !" exclaimed Carey.

" There he is ! there he is !" shouted Ned.   " Look out, Carey !   Guard the hole !   He has passed.   Well done, old fellow !
I think we have him now."

This quick outcry was occasioned by the actual apparition of
the opossum, almost at the old man's feet.   The little animal had
been lying close at hand ; and, alarmed at the din of the approaching war, had made an effort to secure his retreat.   He came
creeping slyly towards the tree ; but, finding his passage intercepted, had glided noiselessly by, and in a moment the moving and misty object, that we had obscurely discerned speeding with an awk-

ward motion through the grass, was lost to view. A few seconds only elapsed, and the dogs swept past us with the fleetness of the wind. They did not run many paces before they halted at the root of a large chestnut that threw its aged and ponderous branches over an extensive surface, and whose distant extremities almost drooped back to the earth. Here they assembled, an eager

and obstreperous pack, bounding wildly from place to place, and looking up and howling, with that expressive gesture which may be seen in this race of animals when they are said to be baying the moon.

This troop of dogs presented a motley assortment. There were two conspicuous for their size and apparently leaders of the company,—a mixture of hound and mastiff—who poured out their long, deep and bugle-like tones, with a fulness that was echoed back from the farthest shore of the river, and which rang through the forest with a strength that must have awakened the sleepers at the mansion we had left. Several other dogs of inferior proportions, even down to the cross and peevish terrier of the kitchen, yelped, with every variety of note,—sharp, quick and piercing to the ear. This collection was gathered from the negro families of the plantation ; and they were all familiar with the discipline of the wild and disorderly game in which they were engaged. A distinguished actor in this scene was our old friend Wilful, who, true to all his master's pranks, appeared in the crowd with officious self-importance, bounding violently above the rest, barking with an unnecessary zeal, and demeaning himself, in all respects, like a gentlemanly, conceited, pragmatical and good-natured spanial. This canine rabble surrounded the tree, and, with vain efforts, attempted to scale the trunk. or started towards the outer circumference. and jumped upwards, with an earnestness which showed that their sharp sight had detected their fugitive aloft.

In this scene of clamor and spirited assault Ben and our old groom were the very masters of the storm. They were to be seen every where exhorting, cheering and commanding their howling subordinates, and filling up the din with their own no less persevering and unmeasured screams.

" Speak to him, Cæsar !" shouted Carey in a prolonged and hoarse tone—" Speak to him, old fellow !—That's a beauty !"

" Howl, Boson !" roared Ben, to another of the dogs.— " Whoop ! Whoop ! let him have it !—sing out !—keep it up, Flower !"

" Wilful ! you rascal," cried Ned. " Mannerly,—keep quiet, would you jump out of your skin, old dog ?—quiet, until you can do some good."

A rustling noise was heard in some of the higher branches of the tree, and we became advised that our besieged enemy was betaking himself to the most probable place of safety. The moon, in her last quarter, was seen at this moment, just peering above the screen of forest that skirted the eastern horizon ; and a dim ray was beginning to relieve the darkness of the night. This aid came opportunely for our purpose, as it brought the top of the chestnut in distinct relief upon the faintly illuminated sky. The motion of the upper leaves betrayed to Ben the position of the prey ; and, in an instant, he swung himself up to the first bough, and proceeded urgently upward. " I see the *varmint* here in the crotch of one of the tip-top branches !" he exclaimed to us, as he hurried onward. " Look out below !"

The terrified animal, on finding his pursuer about to invade his place of safety, speedily abandoned it ; and we could distinctly hear him making his way to the remote extremity of the limb. As soon as he had gained this point he became visible to us all, clinging like an excrescence that had grown to the slender twigs which sustained him. Ben followed as near as he durst venture with his heavy bulk, and began to whip the bough up and down, with a vehement motion that flung the animal about through the air, like a ball on the end of a supple rod. Still, however, the way-laid freebooter kept his hold with a desperate tenacity.

During this operation the dogs, as if engrossed with the contemplation of the success of the experiment, had ceased their din ; and, at intervals only, whined with impatience.

" He can never stand that," said Harvey, as if involuntarily speaking his thoughts. " Look out ! he is falling. No, he has saved himself again !"

Instead of coming to the ground, the dexterous animal, when forced at last to abandon the limb, only dropped to a lower elevation, where he caught himself again amongst the foliage, in a position apparently more secure than the first. The dogs sprang forward, as if expecting to receive him on the earth ; and, with the motion, uttered one loud and simultaneous cry.—Their disappointment was evinced in an eager and impressive silence. The negroes set up a shout of laughter ; and one of them ejaculated, with an uncontrolled merriment,—

"'Not going to get possum from top of tree at one jump, I know. He come down stairs presently. Terrible *varmint* for grabbing !—his tail as good as his hand,—Oh, oh !"

Ben now called out to know how far he had dropped ; and being informed, was immediately busy in the endeavor to reach the quarter indicated.

A repetition of the same stratagem, that had been employed above, produced the same result; and the badgered outlaw descended still lower, making good his lodgment with a grasp instinctively unerring, but now rendered more sure by the fate that threatened him below. This brought him within fifteen feet of the jaws of his ruthless enemies.

The frantic howl, screech, and halloo that burst from dog, man, and boy, when the object of their pursuit thus became distinctly visible, and their continued reduplications—breaking upon the air with a wild, romantic fury—were echoed through the lonely forest at this unwonted hour, like some diabolical incantation, or mystic rite of fantastic import, as they have been sometimes fancied in the world of fiction, to picture the orgies of a grotesque superstition. The whole pack of dogs was concentrated upon one spot, with heads erect and open mouths, awaiting the inevitable descent of their victim into the midst of their array.

Ben, indefatigable in his aim, had already arrived at the junction of the main branch of the tree with the trunk ; and there united in the general uproar. Hazard now interposed and commanded silence; and then directed the people to secure the dogs, as his object was to take the game alive. This order was obeyed, but not without difficulty; and, after a short delay, every dog was fast in hand. We took time, at this juncture, to pause. At Ned's suggestion, Wilful was lifted up by one of the negroes, with the assistance of Ben, to the first bough, which being stout enough to give the dog, practised in such exploits, a foothold, though not the most secure, he was here encouraged, at this perilous elevation, to renew the assault. Wilful crept warily upon his breast, squatting close to the limb, until he reached that point where it began to arch downward, and from whence it was no longer possible for him to creep farther. During this endeavor he remained mute, as if devoting all his attention to the safe accomplishment of his purpose; but as soon as he gained the point above mentioned, he recommenced barking with unwearied earnestness. The opossum began now to prepare himself for his last desperate effort. An active enemy in his rear had cut off his retreat, and his further advance was impossible, without plunging into the grasp of his assailants. As if unwilling to meet the irrevocable doom, and anxious to make the most of the brief remnant of his minutes,—showing how acceptable is life in its most wretched category,—the devoted quadruped still refused the horrid leap; but, releasing his fore feet, swung downward from the bough, holding fast by his hind legs and tail,— the latter being endued with a strong contractile power and ordinarily used in this action. Here he exhibited the first signs of pugnacity; and now snapped and snarled towards the crowd below, showing his long sharp teeth, with a fierceness that contrasted singularly with the cowering timidity of his previous behavior. In one instant more Wilful, as if no longer able to restrain his impatience, or, perhaps, desirous to signalize himself by a feat of bravery, made one spring forward into the midst of the foliage that hung around his prey, and came to the ground, bringing with him the baffled subject of all this eager pursuit.

Ned seized Wilful in the same moment that he reached the earth; and thus prevented him from inflicting a wound upon his captive. The opossum, instead of essaying a fruitless effort to escape, lay on the turf, to all appearance, dead. One or two of those who stood around struck him with their feet; but, faithful to the wonderful instinct of his nature, he gave no signs of animation; and when Hazard picked him up by the tail, and held him suspended at arm's length with the dogs baying around him, the counterfeit of death was still preserved.

More with a view to exhibit the peculiarities of the animal than to prolong the sport, Hazard flung him upon the ground and directed us to observe his motions. For a few moments he lay as quiet as if his last work had been done; and then slowly and warily turning his head round, as if to watch his captors, he began to creep, at a snail's pace, in a direction of safety; but, no sooner was pursuit threatened, or a cry raised, than he fell back into the same supine and deceitful resemblance of a lifeless body.

He was at length taken up by Ben, who causing him to grasp a short stick with the end of his tail, (according to a common instinct of this animal,) threw him over his shoulders, and prepared to return homeward.

It was now near three o'clock; and we speedily betook ourselves to the mansion, fatigued with the exploits of the night.

"After all," said Harvey Riggs, as he lit a candle in the hall, preparatory to a retreat to his chamber, "we have had a great deal of toil to very little purpose. It is a savage pleasure to torture a little animal with such an array of terrors, merely because he makes his livelihood by hunting. God help us, Ned, if we were to be punished for such pranks!"

" To tell the truth," replied Ned, " I have some such misgivings myself to-night, and that's the reason I determined to take
our captive alive. To-morrow I shall have him set at liberty
again ; and I think it probable he will profit by the lesson he
has had, to avoid molesting the poultry-yard !"

CHAPTER XLII.

ONE ACT OF A FARCE.

THE next morning we fell into a consultation, or rather resolved ourselves into a committe of the whole, on the subject of Ned's affairs; and the result of our deliberation was, that we should forthwith proceed to The Brakes, and there renew our operations as circumstances might favor.

Hazard, it will be remembered, had determined to assume a more sapient bearing in his intercourse with Bel, and to dazzle her with a display of learning and sentiment. "I will come up, Mark," said he, "as near as possible to that model of precision and grace, the ineffable Swansdown,—whom Bel thinks one of the lights of the age."

Ned, accordingly, withdrew to make his toilet; and, in due time, reappeared, decked out in a new suit of clothes, adjusted with a certain air of fashion which he knew very well how to put on. His cravat, especially, was worthy of observation, as it was composed with that elaborate and ingenious skill which, more than the regulation of any other part of the apparel, denotes a familiarity with the usages of the world of dandyism.

"I fancy this will do," said he, eyeing his person, and turning himself round so as to invite our inspection. "I think I have seized upon that secret grace which fascinates the imagination of female beholders."

We agreed that nothing could be better.

" I flatter myself," he continued, pleased with the conceit, " that I shall amaze her to-day. But remember, you are not to laugh, nor make any remaaks upon my conversation. I mean to conduct this thing with a sort of every day ease."

" You may trust us," said Harvey, " if you are careful not to overdo your own play. Don't be too preposterous."

Here ended all that is necessary to be told of the preliminaries to our visit, and we now shift the scene to the moment when our triumvirate arrived at The Brakes, somewhere about eleven o'clock.

We found the ladies preparing to take a morning ride. Their horses were at the door, and Ralph was ready to escort them. Our coming was hailed with pleasure ; and we were immediately enlisted in their service. I thought I could perceive some expression of wonder in Bel's face when her eye fell upon Hazard ; and indeed his appearance could scarcely escape remark from any one intimately acquainted with him. His demeanor corresponded to his dress. Instead of the light, careless, cavalier manner in which he was wont to address the family at The Brakes, there was an unsmiling sobriety in his accost, and a rather awkward gravity. Bel imputed this to the coldness she had shown at their former interview ; and, annoyed by the reflection that she had unjustly dealt with him, she was now almost as awkward as himself in framing her deportment in such wise as might convey her regret for what had passed, without absolutely expressing it in language.

This desire on her part favored our design, and we had therefore little difficulty, when we came to mount our horses, to despatch Bel and Hazard in the van of the party. I immediately took Catharine under my convoy ; and Harvey and Ralph brought up the rear.

For the first fifteen minutes our conversation was all common place ; and Ned frequently looked round with a droll expression of faint-heartedness.   We had chosen a road that wound through the shade of a thick wood, and our horses' feet fell silently upon the sand.   In a short time we arrived at a piece of scenery of very peculiar features.   It was an immense forest of pine, of which the trees, towering to the height of perhaps a hundred feet or more, grew in thick array, shooting up their long and sturdy trunks to nearly their full elevation without a limb,—resembling huge columns of a slaty hue, and uniting their clustered tops in a thick and dark canopy.   No other vegetation diversified the view ; even the soil below exhibited the naked sand, or was sparsely covered with a damp moss, which was seen through the russet vail formed by the fallen and withered foliage of the wood.   This forest extended in every direction as far as the eye could pierce its depths,—an image of desolate sterility ; and the deep and quiet shade which hung over the landscape cast upon it a melancholy obscurity.   Where the road penetrated this mass the trees had been cut away in regular lines, so as to leave, on either side, a perpendicular wall of mathematical precision, made up of vast pillars that furnished a resemblance to a lengthened aisle in some enormous cathedral.

When we entered into this pass, Bel, with her harebrained cavalier, was still in advance ; and the rest of us were riding immediately after them in one platoon.   Ned was evidently daunted, and by no means played off the bold game he had threatened ; but an opportunity now arrived, and as if taking courage from the occasion, he launched out in a style that took us by surprise.

Bel had remarked to him the uncommon character of the scene, and said that, from its novelty, it had always been a favorite spot.   " This place is familiar to you," she added.—

" I know each lane," said he, quoting from Milton, with an emphatic earnestness—

> " And every alley green;
> Dingle and bushy dell, in this wild wood."

" And every bosky bourne," said Harvey, from the rear, drawling it out, like a school-boy reciting verses—

> " From side to side,
> My daily walks and ancient neighborhood."

—" Hold your profane tongue, Harvey!" said Ned. " It is not fit for such as you to mar the thoughts of the divine bard by uttering them in such an irreverent tone."

Bel stared at Ned and then smiled.

" Riggs," continued Hazard, " is the most inveterate jester I ever knew. He spreads the contagion of his levity into all societies. For my part, I think there are scenes in nature, as there are passages in life, which ought to repress merriment in the most thoughtless minds ; and this is one of them. Such a spot as this kindles a sort of absorbing, superstitious emotion in me that makes me grave."

" I observe that you are grave," remarked Bel.

" Since I left college," said Ned, " and particularly since my last return to Swallow Barn, I have devoted a great deal of my time to the study of those sources of poetical thought and association which lurk amongst the majestic landscapes of the country."

" Hear that!" whispered Harvey to me.

" I venerate," proceeded Ned, " old usages; popular errors have a charm for my imagination, and I do not like to see them rudely reformed. ' The superstitious, idleheaded eld,' as the poet calls it, has a volume of delightful lore that I study with rapture. And although, I dare say, you have never observed my secret devotion to such pursuits.—"

" No indeed ! I never suspected you of it," interrupted Bel.

—" I have taken great pains to preserve the race of sprites and witches from the ruin that threatens them. The poetry of this local mythology, Bel, is always rich, and renders the people who possess it not only more picturesque, but more national, and, in many respects, more moral."

" I am delighted to hear you say so," said Bel, innocently, " for I have precisely the same opinion."

" Indeed !" exclaimed Ned. " I did not know there was another human being in Virginia who would venture to acknowledge this."

" Nor I neither," whispered Harvey again ; " we shall hear more anon."

" This belief," continued Ned, " is, to the ignorant, a tangible religion which takes hold of the vulgar imagination with a salutary terror ; while to cultivated minds it furnishes treasures of classical beauty. The ancients "—

" Heaven preserve us !" said Harvey, still in a low voice ; " now for something in the style of parson Chub."

Ned turned round and smiled. " The ancients, Bel—I see Harvey does not believe me—but the ancients stocked such a place as this with tutelar deities : they had their nymphs of the wood and grove, of the plain, of the hill, the valley, the fountain, the river, and the ocean. I think they numbered as many as three thousand. I can hardly tell you their different denominations ; but there were Oreads and Dryads and Hamadryads, Napeæ, Nereids, Naiads, and—the devil knows what all !"

" That was a slip," said Harvey, aside ; " one more and he is a lost man."

Bel opened her eyes with amazement at this volley of learning, and not less at the strange expletive with which he concluded, as if utterly at a loss to understand the meaning of this exhibition.

"Our English ancestors," proceeded Ned, "in the most palmy age of their poetry, had their goblin and elf and ouphe, 'swart fairy of'the mine,' 'blue meagre hag,' and 'stubborn unlaid ghost,' —to say nothing of witch and devil. Our times, more philosophic, have sadly dispeopled these pleasure-grounds of romance."

"Indeed have they!" cried Bel, who was listening in wondering attention.

"You see it every where," added Ned; "they are gradually driving away even the few harmless wanderers that, for a century past, inhabited such spots as this; and in a short time we shall not have the groundwork for a single story worth reading."

"Ned calls that sentiment," said Harvey. "It sounds amazingly like a schoolmaster's lecture."

This remark, although intended only for us in the rear, was overheard by both Ned and Bel; upon which Ned reined up his horse, so as to face us, and burst out a-laughing.

"I'll thank you, Harvey Riggs," said he, "when I am engaged in a confidential discourse, to keep your proper distance. I do not choose to have such an impenetrable, hardened outlaw to all the fascinations of romance and poetry, within hearing."

"Indeed, upon my word, cousin Harvey!" said Bel, "Mr. Hazard has been contributing very much to my edification"

We had now passed the confines of the pine forest, and were following a road that led by a circuit round to The Brakes, so as to approach the house from the quarter opposite to that by which we had left it. By this track it was not long before we concluded our ride and found ourselves assembled in the parlor.

"How did I acquit myself?" inquired Ned of Harvey and myself, when we were left alone.

"You have utterly astonished us both," replied Harvey; "and, what is better, Bel is quite enchanted. Where did you get all that nonsense?"

" 'Gad, I once wrote an essay on popular superstitions !" answered Ned, "and had it all at my finger-ends.   So, I thought I would take the chance of the pine forest to give it to Bel."

" It had a very prosy air," said Harvey.   " However, you are on the right track."

During the day Ned made a great many efforts at sentiment, but they generally ended either in unmeaning words or dull discourses, which came from him with a gravity and an earnestness that attracted universal remark ; and by nightfall, it was admitted by the ladies, that Hazard had a good deal of information on topics to which he was hitherto deemed a total stranger, but that he had certainly lost some of his vivacity.   Catharine said, " she was sure something unpleasant had occurred to him : his manners were strange ;—she should not be surprised if he had some affair of honor on hand,—for, he evidently talked like a man who wanted to conceal his emotions.   It was just the way with gentlemen who were going to fight a duel."

Bel was also perplexed.   She could not account for it, except by supposing that he was more deeply wounded by her conduct than he chose to confess.   It made her unhappy.   In short, Ned's substitution of a new character began already to make him dull, and to disturb the rest of the company.

When we announced our intention to return to Swallow Barn after tea, old Mr. Tracy interposed to prevent it.   He said he had set his heart upon a hand at whist, and that we must remain for his gratification.   Our return was accordingly postponed ; and when, at ten o'clock, the old gentleman retired to rest, we were challenged by Harvey to a game at brag.   The consequence was, that, all unconscious of the flight of the hours, we were found in our seats when the servants came in the morning and threw open the shutters, letting in the daylight upon a group of sallow, bilious and night-worn faces, that were discovered brooding over a disorderly table, in the light of two candles which were flaring in their sockets and expending their substance, in overflowing currents, upon the board.

Alarmed by this disclosure, we broke up the sitting, and were shown by Ralph to our unseasonable beds.

CHAPTER XLIII.

WHETHER it was that Hazard was anxious to conceal from the family his last night's frolic; or that his thoughts were engrossed with the approaching crisis in his affairs; or, perchance, that he was nervous from overwatching during the two previous nights and unable to sleep, he rose early, and met the family at their usual breakfast time. Neither Harvey, Ralph, nor myself, suffered under the same difficulties, and, therefore, it was fully ten, o'clock before we were seen in the parlour.

Ned's mean was truly sad. He had a haggard look, a stagnated, morbid complexion, and blood-shot eyes. His dress, which the day before had been adjusted with such an unwonted precision, afforded now an expressive testimony of the delinquent irregularity of its wearer. Nothing more infallibly indicates the long nocturnal revel than the disordered plight of the dress the next morning: a certain rakish air is sure to linger about its deepened folds, and betray the departure from the sober usages of life.

Hazard's manners corresponded with this unhappy exterior. A certain lassitude attended his movements, and a pitiful dejection sat upon his visage. If he had been master of his own actions, he would never have risked the perilous fortunes of the day in his present shattered condition; but a spell was upon him, and it seemed as if fate had decreed him to abide the chance. He was moody; and conversed with the ladies with a bearing that implied an abstracted mind and an alarmed conscience. Sometimes, it is true, he raised his spirits to a forced gaiety, but it was manifest, in spite of this, that he was disquieted, pensive, and even melancholy. What added to the singularity of these phenomena was, that while Catharine and Bel were yet in the parlour, he got up abruptly, and wandered out upon the lawn, and then took a solitary ramble towards the river, where he was observed, from the windows, walking to and fro, absorbed in contemplation.

None of these symptoms of a perturbed imagination escaped Bel. She was exceedingly puzzled, and revolved in her mind all that had lately passed, to ascertain the cause. At length,—as it usually happens with women in such cases,—when she found herself unable to penetrate the mystery, her heart began to attune itself to pity. She grew to be quite distressed. Harvey read the workings of her thoughts in her face, and took an opportunity to draw her into a private conference.

"My dear Bel, you see how it is," he said, shaking his head mournfully. "Poor fellow! I did'nt expect to see it come to such an extremity as this."

"Cousin! I pray you, what is it?" demanded Bel.—"You alarm me."

"Ah!" returned Harvey, turning up his eyes, and laying his hand upon his breast—"It cannot be concealed. These are the very doleful doings of the little Archer. The young gentleman is cruelly transfixed;—he is spitted with the bolt, and is ready to be geared to a smoke-jack, and turned round and round before the fire that consumes him like a roasting woodcock."

"Let us have a truce to jesting," said Bel.—"And tell me, Harvey,—for indeed I cannot guess it,—what ails Edward Hazard?"

"You would never believe me," replied Harvey, "although I have told you a hundred times, that Ned was a man of deep and secret emotions. Now, you must perceive it; for the fact is becoming too plain to be mistaken. I consider it a misfortune for any man who wishes to stand well with a woman, to have been educated in habits of close intimacy with her. She is certain, in that case, to be the last person to do justice to his merits."

"It would be vanity in me, cousin," said Bel, "to persuade myself that Edward Hazard was so much interested in my regard as to grow ill on that account. What have his merits to do with any supposed attachment to me?"

"He desires to be thought a liege man to his lady, Bel!" answered Harvey. "To tell you the truth, Ned's as full of romance as you are; and I have been looking to see some extravagance that would defy all calculation: some freak that would not fail to convince even *you* that the man was on the verge of madness. And now, here it is! he has gone through five degrees of love."

"Five degrees! Pray, what are they?"

"The first is the *mannerly* degree: it is taken at that interesting epoch when a man first begins to discover that a lady has an air, a voice, and a person more agreeable than others; he grows civil upon this discovery; and if he has any wit in him it is sure to appear. The next is the *poetical* degree; it was in this stage that we surprised Ned upon the bank of the river, when he was singing out your name so musically, for the entertainment of Mark Littleton. The third is the *quixotic* love, and carries a gentleman in pursuit of stray hawks, and sets him to breaking the heads of saucy bullies. The fourth is the *sentimental ;* when out comes all his learning, and he fills his mistress's head with unimaginable conceits. Then comes the *horrible :* you may know this, Bel, by a yellow cheek, a wild eye, a long beard, an unbrushed coat, and a most woe-begone, lackadaisical style of conversation. This sometimes turns into the *furious;* and then, I would not answer for the consequences! It strikes me that Ned looks a little savage this morning."

" Cousin, that is all very well said," interrupted Bel. " But, I see none of your degrees in Edward Hazard."

"Why, he has not slept a wink for two nights past," said Harvey?"

" And pray, what prevented him from sleeping?"

" Thinking of you, Bel! You have been buzzing about in his brain, like a bee in his night-cap. And it stands to reason! neither man nor beast can do without sleep. If he were a rhinoceros he must eventually sink under such privations. There he was, the livelong night, stalking about like a spectre on the banks of Acheron!"

" And you, Harvey," added Bel, laughing, " were one of the principal imps that stalked by his side. You are not aware that I have been made acquainted with your vagaries. I happen to know that you were engaged in the refined and elegant amusement of hunting an opossum all night, with a band of negroes."

" Who was so indiscreet as to tell you that!" asked Harvey. " I am sure the story has been marred in the telling ; and therefore, I will relate to you the plain truth. Ned was uneasy in mind, and could not close his eyes ; so, like the prince in the story-book, he summoned his followers to attend him to the chase in the vain hope that he should find some relief from the thoughts that rankled—"

" Irreclaimable cousin Harvey !"

" Fact, I assure you! Nothing takes off the load from the mind like an opossum hunt."

" And then, last night," resumed Bel, you were up playing cards until daylight. That was to chase away sorrow too, I suppose ?"

" Ned could not sleep last night either," said Harvey. " But Bel, don't say until *daylight.* We broke up at a very reasonable hour."

" I have heard all about it," answered Bel.

" I admit," returned Harvey, " that appearances are a little against us : but, they are only appearances. If you had seen how Ned played, you would have been satisfied that the game had no charms for him; for he sighed,—swore, and flung away his money like a fool. I suppose he must have lost, at least, a hundred dollars."

" And with it, his good looks and peace of mind besides," added Bell. " Gaming, fighting and drinking ! Ah, me !"

" All for love, Bel ! all for love ! It is the most *transmogriphying* passion !" exclaimed Harvey. " Things the most opposite in nature come out of it. Now tell me honestly,—have you not seen a change in Ned that surprises you ?"

" Indeed I have," answered Bel.

" What do you impute it to ?"

" I am sure I do not know."

" Then, to be done with this levity," said Harvey, " it is what I have said. Ned is awkward in his zeal to serve you ; but he is the truest of men. He gets into all manner of difficulties on your account, and suffers your displeasure like a martyr. He talks of you even in his sleep ; and grows tiresome to his friends with the eternal repetition of your praises. It is a theme which, if you do not put an end to it, will grow to be as hacknied as a piece of stale politics. If you could make it consistent, Bel, with your other arrangements, I do really think it your duty to put the youth out of misery : for, he never will be fit company for any rational man until this infection is cured."

"You would not have me marry a man I do not love," said Bel, gravely.

"No, indeed, my dear Bel," returned Harvey. "But I have been all along supposing you did love him."

"You know my objections," said Bel.

"I think they were all removed yesterday," answered Harvey.

"If they were, they have come back again to-day."

"That shows," said Harvey, "what a ticklish thing is this love. May the saints shield me from all such disasters as falling in love!"

"Your prayer has been granted before it was asked," returned Bel, smiling.

Here ensued a pause, during which the lady stood for some moments wrapt in thought, with her foot rapidly beating against the floor.

"I do not think," she said at last, "at least, I am not altogether certain, cousin, that I love him well enough to"—

"Faith, Bel, I think you come pretty near to it," whispered Harvey; the longer you ponder over such a doubt, the clearer it will appear.—Drum it out with your foot; that is the true device:—Love is very much a matter of the nerves after all."

"I will talk no more!" exclaimed Bel, with a lively emotion.

With these words, she retreated into the drawing-room, and sat down to the piano, where she played and sung as if to drown her thoughts.

During all this while, the unconscious subject of this colloquy was pursuing his secret meditations. It is meet that I should tell my reader what was the real cause of the cloud that sat upon his brow. In truth, he was endeavoring to screw his courage up to a deed of startling import. It was his fixed re-

solve, when he crept to his bed at the dawn, to bring matters,
that very day, to some conclusion with his mistress ; and this
fancy took such complete possession of his faculties, that he
found it in vain to attempt repose. His fortitude began to
waver as the hour of meeting Bel drew nigh, and every moment
shook the steadiness of his nerves. He cast a glance at the
reflection of his forlorn figure in the glass, and his heart grew
sick within him. As if ashamed of the tremor that invaded his
frame, he swore a round oath to himself—that come what would,
he would fulfil his purpose. It was in this state of feeling that
he appeared at breakfast. Every instant the enterprise grew
more terrible to his imagination; until it was, at last, arrayed
before his thoughts as something awful. It is a strange thing
that so simple a matter should work such effects ; and stranger
still, that, notwithstanding the painful sensations it excites, there
should lurk at the bottom of the heart a certain remainder of
pleasant emotion, that is sufficient to flavor the whole. Ned
experienced this ; and inwardly fortified his resolution by frequent appeals to his manhood. In such a state of suspense it
was not to be expected that he should be much at ease in conversation. On the contrary, he spoke like a frightened man,
and accompanied almost every thing he said with a muscular
effort at deglutition, which is one of the ordinary physical symptoms of fear.

His walk by the river side was designed to reassemble his
scattered forces ; an undertaking that he found impossible in
the face of the enemy. They were a set of militia-spirits that
could not be brought to rally on the field of battle. Having
argued himself into a braver temper, he returned from his
wanderings and stalked into the drawing-room, with an ill-coun-
terfeited composure. By a natural instinct, he marched up
behind Bel's chair, and for some moments seemed to be absorbed

with the music. After a brief delay, during which the color had flown from his cheek, he crossed the room to the window, and, with his hands in his pockets, gazed out upon the landscape. Restless, uncertain and perplexed, he returned again to the chair, and cast a suspicious and rueful glance around him.

Harvey, observing how matters stood, silently tripped out of the room.

Bel executed a lively air, and concluded it with a brisk pounding upon the keys; and then sprang up, as if about to retreat.

"Play on," said Ned, with a husky voice; don't think of stopping yet. I delight in these little melodies. You cannot imagine, Bel, how music exhilarates me."

"I didn't know that you were in the room," returned Bel. "What shall I play for you?"

"You can hardly go amiss. Give me one of those lively strains that make the heart dance," said he, with a dolorous accent. "But you have some exquisite ballads too; and I think you throw so much soul into them that they are irresistible. I will have a ballad."

Whilst he was wavering in his choice she struck up a waltz. Ned, during this performance, sauntered to the farther end of the drawing-room; and, having planted himself opposite a picture that hung against the wall, stood minutely surveying it, with his lips, at the same time, gathered up to an inarticulate and thoughtful whistle. The cessation of the music recalled him to the piano with a start; and he hastened to say to Bel,—that there was something unspeakably pathetic in these simple and natural expressions of sentiment; that it belonged to the ballad to strike more directly upon the heart than any other kind of song; and that, for his part, he never listened to one of those expressive little compositions without an emotion almost amounting to melancholy.

What is he talking about?—thought Bel. She paused in profound astonishment: and then asked him, if he knew what it was she had been playing?

" The tune is familiar to me," stammered Ned. " But, I have a wretched memory for names."

" You have heard it a thousand times," said she. " It is the waltz in the Freyschutz."

" Oh, true!" exclaimed Ned. " It is a pensive thing; it has several touching turns in it. Most waltzes have something of that in them. Don't you think so?"

" Most waltzes," replied Bel, laughing, " have a great many turns in them: but, as to the pensiveness of the music, I never observed that."

" Indeed!" exclaimed Ned, confounded past all hope of relief; " It depends very much upon the frame of mind you are in. There are moods—and they come on me sometimes like shadows— which predispose the heart to extract plaintive thoughts from the liveliest strains.—If there be one desponding cord in the strings of the soul,—that one will begin to vibrate—with a single sym- pathetic note—that may be hurried across it in the rush of the gayest melody.—I mean,—that there is something in all music that arouses mournful emotions,—when the mind is predisposed to—melancholy."

As a man who takes his seat in a surgeon-dentist's chair, to have his teeth filed, having made up his mind to endure the operation, bears the first application of the tool with composure, but, feeling a sense of uneasiness creeping upon him with every new passage of the file across the bone, is hurried on rapidly to higher degrees of pain with every succeeding jar— until at last it seems to him as if his powers of sufferance could be wound up to no higher pitch, and he therefore meditates an abrupt leap from the hands of the operator—so did Ned find himself, as he plunged successively from one stage to the other of the above-recited exquisite piece of nonsense.

When he had finished, his face (to use the phrase of a novel writer) ' was bathed in blushes ;' and Bel had turned her chair half round, so as to enable her to catch the expression of his countenance; for, she began to feel some misgiving as to tho soundness of his intellect.

Of all the ordinary vexations of life it is certainly the most distressing, for a man of sense to catch himself unseasonably talking like a fool, upon any momentous occasion wherein he should especially desire to raise an opinion of his wisdom ; such as in the case of a member of congress making his first speech, or of an old lawyer before a strange tribunal, or, worse than all, of a trembling lover before a superfastidious mistress. The big drops of perspiration gathered on Ned's brow : he felt like a thief taken in the mainor : he was caught in the degree of *back berinde and bloody hand,* known to the Saxon Forest laws, with his folly on his back. He could have jumped out of the window ; but, as it was, he only ordered a servant to bring him a glass of water, and coughed with a short dry cough, and swallowed the cool element at a draught.

As motion conduces to restore the equilibrium of the nerves, Ned now paced up and down the apartment, with stately and measured strides.

" Courage !" said he, mentally. " I'll not be frightened !" So, he made another convulsive motion of· the œsophagus,—such as I have seen a mischievous, truant boy make, when on his trial before the pedagogue—and marched up directly behind Bel.

All this time she sat silent ; and taking the infection of fear from her lover, began to cower like a terrified partridge.

" Miss Tracy," said Ned, after a long pause, with a feeble, tremulous utterance, accompanied by a heavy suspiration.

" Sir—"

" Miss Tracy,"—here Ned put his hands upon the back of Bel's chair, and leaned a little over her;—" You,—you—play very well,—would you favor me with another song,—if you please ?"

" I havn't sung a song for you," replied Bel.

" Then, you can do it, if you would try."

" No. It would be impossible. I am out of voice."

" So am I," returned Ned, with comic perturbation. " It is strange that we should both have lost our voices at the very time when we wanted them most."

" I am sure I don't see," said Bel, blushing, " any thing extraordinary in my not being able to sing."

" Well,—I think it very extraordinary," said Ned, with a dry laugh and an affected, janty air, as he took a turn into the middle of the room,—" that the fountains of speech should be sealed up, when I had something of the greatest importance in the world to communicate to you."

" What is that ?" inquired Bel.

" That I am the most particularly wretched and miserable coxcomb in the whole state of Virginia," said he, rising into a more courageous tone.

" Your speech serves to little purpose," muttered Bel, " if it be to utter nothing better than that."

" I am a boy,—a drivelling fool," continued Ned, very little like a man who had lost his power of articulation—" I am vexed with myself, and do not deserve to be permitted to approach you."

Bel was covered with confusion ; and an awkward silence now intervened, during which she employed herself in turning over the leaves of a music-book.

" Do you relent, Bel?" said Ned, in a soft and beseeching

accent. "Have you thought better of the proposition I made you a year ago? Do you think you could overcome your scruples?"

Bel, somewhat startled by these tender tones, withdrew her eyes from the music-book, and slowly turned her head round to the direction of the voice. There, to her utter amazement, was her preposterous lover on one knee, gazing pitifully in her face.

It is necessary that I should stop at this interesting moment, to explain this singular phenomenon; for, doubtless, my reader concludes Ned to be the veriest mountebank of a lover that ever tampered with the beautiful passion.

It is common to all men, and, indeed, to all animals, when sore perplexed with difficulties, to resort for protection to the strongest instincts nature has given them. Now, Ned's predominating instinct was to retreat behind a jest, whenever he found that circumstances galled him. For some moments past he had been brightening up, so that he had almost got into a laugh,— not at all dreaming that such a state of feeling would be unpropitious to his suit; and when he arrived at the identical point of his wooing above described, he was sadly at a loss to know what step to take next. His instinct came to his aid, and produced the comic result I have recorded. It seemed to strike him with that deep sense of the ridiculous, that is apt to take possession of a man who seriously makes love; and the incorrigible wight, therefore, reckless of consequences, dropped upon his knee,—one-tenth part in jest, and nine-tenths in earnest. It was well nigh blowing him sky high!

"Is this another prank, Mr. Hazard?" said Bel.—"Am I to be for ever tortured with your untimely mirth? How,—how can you sport with my feelings in this way!" Here she burst into tears; and, putting her hand across her eyes, the drops were seen trickling through her fingers.

Ned suddenly turned as pale as ashes. "By all that is ho
nest in man !" he exclaimed—and then ran on with a list of lover-
like abjurations, vowing and protesting, in the most passionate
terms—according to the vulgar phrase, "by all that was black and
blue,"—that he was devoted to his mistress, body and soul. Never did there rush from an opened flood-gate a more impetuous
torrent than now flowed from his heart through the channel of
his lips. He was hyperbolically oratorical ; and told her, amongst
other things, that she "was the bright luminary that gilded his
happiest dreams."

"I have not deserved this from you," said Bel, whose emotions
were too violent to permit her to hear one word of this vehement declaration. "At such a moment as this, you might have
spared me an unnecessary and cruel jest."

She arose from her seat and was about to retire ; but Ned,
springing upon his feet at the same time, took her by the hand
and detained her in the room.

"For heaven's sake, Bel !" he ejaculated, "what have I done?
Why do you speak of a jest? Never in my life have my feelings
been uttered with more painful earnestness !"

"I cannot answer you now," returned Bell, in a tone of affliction ; "leave me to myself."

"Isabel Tracy !" said Ned, dropping her hand, as he assumed
a firm and calm voice, "you discard me now for ever. You fling
me back upon the world the most wretched scapegrace that ever
hid himself in its crowds."

"I neither promise nor reject," said Bel, beginning to tremble
at Ned's almost frenzied earnestness. "If I have mistaken
your temper or your purpose, you have yourself to blame. It is
not easy to overcome the impressions which a long intercourse
has left upon my mind. You have seemed to me, heretofore,
indifferent to the desire to please. You have taught me to

think lightly of myself, by the little value you appeared to place upon my regards. You have jested when you should have been serious, and have been neglectful when I had a right to expect attention. You have offended my prejudices on those points that I have been accustomed to consider indispensable to the man I should love. You will not wonder, therefore, that I should misconceive your conduct. I must have a better knowledge of you and of my own feelings, before I can commit myself by a promise. Pray, permit me to retire."

This was uttered with a sedate and womanly composure that forbade a reply, and Bel left the room.

Hazard was thrown, by this scene, into a new train of sensations. For the first time in his life, he was brought to comprehend the exact relation he held to his mistress. He had no further purpose in remaining at The Brakes ; and he and I, accordingly, very soon afterwards set out for Swallow Barn.

We discussed fully the events of the morning as we rode along; and, upon the whole, we considered this important love-affair to have passed through its crisis, and to rest upon auspicious grounds. This conclusion arose upon Ned's mind in a thousand shapes :

—" I have got a mountain off my shoulders," said he ; " I am unpacked ; and feel like a man who has safely led a forlorn hope I would fight fifty Waterloos, rather than go through such a thing again ! Egad ! I can sing and laugh once more. Bel's a woman of fine sense, Littleton. She is not to be trifled with. Faith, I stand pretty fairly with her, too ! It is certainly no refusal : ' Faint heart never won fair lady.' A lover to thrive must come up boldly to the charge. But, after all, I was considerably fluttered—not to say most unspeakably alarmed."

These, and many more such fragments of a boasting, doubtful and self-gratulating spirit, burst from him in succession; and were, now and then, accompanied with lively gesticulations on horseback, which if a stranger could have seen, they would have persuaded him that the performer was either an unhappy mortal, on his way to the madhouse, or a happy lover on the way from his mistress.

CHAPTER XLIV.

ORATORY.

As some adventurous schoolboy, who, having but lately learned to swim, has gone, upon a fair summer evening, to the river hard by, to disport himself in the cool and limpid wave, so did I first sit down to write this book. And as that same urchin, all diffident of his powers, has never risked himself beyond the reach of some old, stranded hulk, not far from shore; but now, enchanted by the fragrance of the season, by the golden and purple-painted clouds, and by the beauty of the wild-flowers that cluster at the base of the shady headland on the farther side of a narrow cove; and incited by the jollity of his boyhood, and seduced by the easy, practick eloquence of a heedless, good-natured playfellow, he has thoughtlessly essayed to reach the pleasant promontory which he has gained in safety, albeit, faint-hearted and out of breath:—so have I waywardly ventured on the tide of Ned's courtship; but, having reached such a sheltered head land, do, in imitation of my daunted schoolboy, here break up my voyage; like him, thinking it safest to get back by trudging round the pebbly margin of the cove.

In other words, I esteem myself lucky in having followed Ned's love-affair into a convenient resting-place, where I am willing, at least for the present, to leave it; and shall indeed be thankful if no future event, during my sojourn at Swallow Barn, shall impose upon me the duty of tracing out the sequel of this tortuous and difficult history. For wisely has it been said, " that the current of true love never did run smooth ;"—to me it seems that its path is like that of the serpent over the rock. And that chronicler shall have reason to count himself sadly tasked, whose lot it may be to follow the lead of a capricious maiden wheresoever it shall please her fickleness to decoy her charmed and fretful lover. Little did I dream, when I came to the Old Dominion and undertook to write down the simple scenes that are acted in ʾꞱ gentleman's hall, I should, in scarce a month gone by, find myself tangled up in a web of intricate love-plots which should so overmatch my slender powers ! But I have borne me like a patient and trusty historian, through the labyrinth of my story ; and now, right gladly, escape to other matters more german to my hand.

To say nothing, then, of the manner in which Ned Hazard bore his present doubtful fortune, nor what resolves he took in this emergency ; nor even dwelling upon his frequently repeated visits to The Brakes, during which, I rejoice to think, nothing especially worthy of note occurred, I pass over some days, in order that I may introduce a new scene.

Meriwether, one night when we were about to retire to rest, suggested to Ned and myself,—and the suggestion was made half in the tone of a request, implying that he would be pleased if we adopted it,—that we might have an agreeable jaunt if we would consent to accompany him, the next morning, in his ride to the Quarter. Now, this Quarter is the name by which is familiarly known that part of the plantation where the principal negro population is established.

" You, doubtless, Mr. Littleton," said he, " take some interest in agricultural concerns. The process of our husbandry,—slovenly to be sure,—may, nevertheless, be worthy of your observation. But I can add to your amusement by showing you my blooded colts, which, it is not vanity to affirm, are of the finest breed in Virginia ; and when I say that,—it is equivalent to telling you that there is nothing better in the world."

Here Meriwether paused for a moment, with that thoughtful expression of countenance which indicates the gathering up of one's ideas ; then changing the tone of his voice to a lower key, he continued,—

"The improvement of the stock of horses,—notwithstanding this matter is undervalued in some portions of our country,—I regard as one of the gravest concerns to which a landed proprietor can devote his attention. The development of the animal perfections of this noble quadruped, by a judicious system of breeding, requires both the science and the talent of an accomplished naturalist. We gain by it symmetry, strength of muscle, soundness of wind, ease of action, speed, durability, power of sustaining fatigue, and fitness for the multiform uses to which this admirable beast is subservient. What, sir, can be more worthy of some portion of the care of a patriotic citizen ? But look, my dear sir, at the relation which the horse holds to man. We have no record in history of an age wherein he has not been intimately connected with the political and social prosperity of the most powerful and civilized nations. He has always assisted to fight our battles, to bear our burthens, to lighten our fatigues, and to furnish our subsistence. He has given us bread by tillage and meat by the chase. He has even lodged in the same homestead with his master man, frequently under the same roof. He has been accustomed to receive his food from our hands, and to be caressed by our kindness. We nurse him in sickness, and guard him in health. He has been, from one age to another, the companion of the warrior at home, his trusty friend in travel, and his sure auxiliary and defence in battle. What more beautiful than the sympathy between them? when the cockles of his master's heart rise up at the sound of distant war, he neighs at the voice of the trumpet, and shakes his mane in his eagerness to share the glory of the combat."

Frank had now got to striding backward and forward through the room; and, at this last flourish, came up to the table, where he stood erect; then, in that attitude, went on.

" And yet,—however martial his temper,—he will amble gently under the weight of the daintest dame, and yield obedience to her tender hand and silken rein. I have horses in my stable now, that, in the field upon a chase, will champ their bits, and bound with an ardor which requires my arm to check; whilst the same animals, at home here, are as passive to Lucretia's command as a lady's pony."

" You say so," interrupted my cousin Lucretia, " but, indeed, Mr. Meriwether, 1 do not like to ride these blooded horses!"

Meriwether continued, without heeding the interruption:

—" The horse has a family instinct, and knows every member of the household: he recognizes his master's children when they come to his stall, and is pleased to be fondled by them. Then, see how faithfully he drudges in the field, and wears away his life in quiet and indispensable services. I venerate the steady sobriety of the robust, broad-chested, massive-limbed wagon-horse, that toils without repining, through the summer heats and winter snows. I contemplate, with a peculiar interest, the unremitting labor of the stage-horse, as he performs his daily task with unrelaxed speed, from one year's end to another: and,—you may smile at it,—but I have a warm side of my heart for the thoughtful and unobtrusive hack that our little negroes creep along with to mill. But, above all, where do you find such a picture of patience, considerateness, discretion, long-suffering, amiable obedience, (here Frank began to smile,) as in the faithful brute that bears his master,—say a country doctor, for example, or a deputy sheriff, or one of your weather-beaten, old, tippling,—(at each of these epithets the orator laughed) gossipping, night-wandering——"

" *Noctua bundus,*" said Mr. Chub, who was sitting all the time at one of the windows.—

—" Right !" replied Meriwether, turning towards the parson and waving his hand,—" night-wandering politicians ? I say, where is there a finer type of resignation, christian resignation, than in the trusty horse that bears such a master, through all seasons, no matter how inclement,—fast, without refusing, and slow, without impatience,—for hours together ; and then stands, perhaps,—as I have often seen him,—with his rein fastened to a post or to a fence corner, without food or drink ; and, as likely as not, (for he is subject to all discomforts,) facing a drifting snow or a pelting hail-storm, for the livelong day ; or through the dreary watches of the night, solitary, silent, unamused, without one note of discontent ; without one objurgatory winnow to his neglectful master ? And then, at last, when the time arrives when he is to measure his homeward way, with what a modest and grateful undertone he expresses his thanks ! The contemplation of these moral virtues in the horse, is enough to win the esteem of any man for the whole species. Besides, what is a nation without this excellent beast ? What machinery or labor-saving inventions of man could ever compensate him for the deprivation of this faithful ally ?"—

I do not know how long Meriwether would have continued this laudatory oration, for he was every moment growing more eloquent, both in manner and matter, and, no doubt, would very soon have struck out into some episodes that would have carried him along, like a vessel caught up in the trade winds, had not my

cousin Lucretia warned him that it was growing too late for so
promising a discourse; which having the effect to bring him to a
stop, I availed myself of the opportunity to say, that I should be
highly gratified with the proposed ride. So did Ned.

"Then," said he, "remember I ride at sunrise: Lucretia will
give us a cup of coffee before we set out. Be up, therefore, at the
crowing of the cock!"

CHAPTER XLV.

ALMOST with the first appearance of light, Meriwether came and knocked at our chamber doors, so earnestly that the whole household must have been roused by the noise. Our horses could be heard pawing the gravel at the front door, impatient of delay. The sun was scarcely above the horizon before we were all mounted and briskly pursuing our road, followed by Carey, who seemed, on the present occasion, to be peculiarly charged with professional importance.

The season was now advanced into the first week of August: a time when, in this low country, the morning air begins to grow sharp, and to require something more than the ordinary summer clothing. The dews had grown heavier; and the evaporation produced that chilling cold which almost indicated frost. There was, however, no trace of this abroad; but every blade of grass, and every spray was thickly begemmed with dewdrops. The tall and beautiful mullen, which suggested one of the forms of the stately candelebra—almost the first plant that puts forth in the spring, and amongst the first to wither—was now to be seen marshalled in groups over the fallows, with its erect and half-dried spire hung round with that matchless jewelry, which the magic hand of night scatters over the progeny of earth. The fantastic

spider-webs hung like fairy tissues over every bush, and decked
with their drapery every bank; whilst their filaments, strung with
watery beads, and glittering in the level beams of the sun, rendered them no longer snares for the unwary insects for which they
were spread. Our road through the woods was occasionally way-
laid by an obtrusive pine-branch that, upon the slightest touch,
shook its load of vapor upon our shoulders, as we stooped beneath
it. The lowing of cows and the bleating of sheep struck upon
our ear from distant folds ; and all the glad birds of summer were
twittering over the woodland and open plain. The rabbit leaped
timidly along the sandy road before us, and squatted upon his
seat, as if loth to wet his coat amongst the low whortleberry and
wild-indigo that covered the contiguous soil.

Emerging from the forest, a gate introduced us to a broad
stubble-field, across whose level surface, at the distance of a mile,
we could discern the uprising of several thin lines of smoke, that
formed a light cloud which almost rested on the earth ; and, under this, a cluster of huts was dimly visible. Near these, an extensive farm-yard surrounded a capacious barn together with some
fodder-houses and stacks of grain, upon which were busily employed a number of laborers, who, we could see, were building up
the pile from a loaded wagon that stood close by.

As we advanced, a range of meadows opened to our view, and
stretched into the dim perspective, until the eye could no longer
distinguish their boundary. Over this district, detached herds
of horses were observable, whisking their long tails as they graz-
ed upon the pasture, or curvetting over the spaces that separated
them from each other.

"There !" said Meriwether, kindling up at the sight of this
plain, " there is the reward I promised you for your ride. I
have nothing better to show you at Swallow Barn. You see, on
yonder meadow, some of the most unquestioned nobility of

Virginia. Not a hoof stays on that pasture, that is not warmed by as pure blood as belongs to any potentate in the world."

Carey rode up to us, at this speech, to observe, as I suppose, the effect which his master's communication might have upon me ; for he put on a delighted grin, and said somewhat officiously—

" I call them my children, master Littleton."

" Truly then, Carey, you have a large family," said I.

" They are almost all on 'em, sir," replied Carey, " straight down from old Diomed, that old master Hoomes had *fotch* out from England, across the water more than twenty years ago. Sir Archy, master Littleton, was a son of Old Diomed, and I can't tell you how many of his colts I've got. But, sir, you may depend upon it, he was a great horse ! And *thar* was Duroc, master ! You've hearn on him?—I've got a heap of colts of Duroc's.—Bless your heart ! he was another of old Diomed's."

" Carey is a true herald," said Mèriwether. " Nearly all that you see have sprung from the Diomed stock. It is upwards of forty years since Diomed won the Derby in England. He was brought to this country in his old age ; and is as famous amongst us, almost, as Christopher Columbus ; for, he may be said to have founded a new empire here. Besides that stock, I have some of the Oscar breed ; one of the best of them is the gelding I ride. You may know them, wherever you see them, by their carriage and indomitable spirit."

" I know nothing about it," said I,—" but I have heard a great deal said of the Godolphin Arabian."

" I can show you some of that breed, too," replied Meriwether,—" Wildair, who I believe was a grandson of the Arabian."

" *Old* Wildair—mark you, master !" interrupted Carey, very sagely,—" not Col. Symmes' Wildair."

" Old Wildair, I mean," rejoined Frank.—" He was imported

into Maryland, and taken back to England before the Revolution :—but I have some of his descendants."

"And *thar's* Regulus's breed," said Carey. "They tell me he was genuine Arabian too. "

"I am not sure, returned Meriwether, "that I have any of that breed.—Carey affects to say that there are some of them here."

"Bless your soul! master Frank," interrupted the old groom, —"didn't I carry the Ace of Diamonds, over here to the Bowling Green, that next summer coming after the war, to—"

"Ride on and open the gate for us," said Frank.—"Set that old negro to talking of pedigrees, and his tongue goes like a mill !"

We now entered upon the meadow, and soon came up with several of the beautiful animals whose ancestry had been the subject of this discussion. They were generally in the wild and unshorn condition of beasts that had never been subjected to the dominion of man. It was apparent that the proprietor of the stock kept them more for their nobleness of blood than for any purpose of service. Some few of the older steeds showed the care of the groom; but even these were far from being in that sleek state of nurture which we are apt to associate with the idea of beauty in the horse. One, skilled in the points of symmetry, would, doubtless, have found much to challenge his admiration in their forms; but this excellence was, for the most part, lost upon me. Still, however, unpractised as I was, there was, in the movements of these quadrupeds, a charm that I could not fail to recognize. No sooner were we descried upon the field, than the different troops, in the distance, were set in motion, as if by some signal to which they were accustomed; and they hurried tumultuously to the spot where we stood, exerting their utmost speed, and presenting a wonderfully animated spectacle. The swift career of the horse, upon an open plain, is always an interesting sight; but as we saw it now, exhibited in squadrons, pursuing an unrestrained and irregular flight, accompanied with wild and expressive neighs, and enlivened with all the frolicksome antics that belong to high-mettled coursers,—it was a scene of singularly gay and picturesque beauty. The ludicrous earnest ness, too, with which they crowded upon us !—there was in it the natural grace of youth, united with the muscular vigor of maturity. One reared playfully, as he thrust himself into the compact assembly ; another advanced at a long, swinging trot, striking the ground at every step with a robust and echoing stroke, and then, halted suddenly, as if transfigured into a statue. Some kicked at their comrades, and seized them with their teeth in the wantonness of sport : others leaped in quick bounds, and made short circuits, at high speed, around the mass, with heads and tails erect, displaying the flexibility of their bodies in caracols of curious nimbleness. The younger colts impertinently claimed to be familiar with the horses we rode ; and were apt to receive, in return, a severe blow for the intrusion. Altogether, it was a scene of boisterous horse-play, well befitting the arrogant nature of such a licentious, high-blooded, far-descended and riotous young nobility.

It may be imagined that this was a sight of engrossing interest to Meriwether. Both he and Carey had dismounted, and were busy in their survey of the group.—all the while descanting upon the numberless perfections of form that occurred to their view ; and occasionally interlarding their commendations with the technical lore of genealogy, which, so far as I was concerned, might as profitably have been delivered in Greek.

The occasion of this rapid concentration of our cavalry was soon explained. Meriwether was in the habit of administering a weekly ration of salt to these wandering hordes at this spot

and they, therefore, were wont to betake themselves to the ren-
dezvous, with all the eagerness we had witnessed, whenever any
sign was offered them that the customary distribution was to be
made. Care was now taken that they should not be disappointed
in their reasonable expectations; and Carey was, accordingly,
dispatched to the stable for the necessary supplies.

Having gratified our curiosity in this region, we now visited
the farm-yard. Within this inclosure, a party of negroes were
employed in treading out grain. About a dozen horses were
kept at full trot around a circle of some ten or fifteen paces
diameter, which was strewed with the wheat in sheaf. These
were managed by some five or six little blacks, who rode like
monkey caricaturists of the games of the circus, and who mingled with the labors of the place that comic air of deviltry which
communicated to the whole employment something of the complexion of a pastime. Whilst we remained here, as spectators of
this stirring and busy occupation, a dialogue took place, which, as
it made some important veterinary disclosures, I will record for
the benefit of all those who take an interest in adding to the
treasures of pharmacy.

One of the horses had received an injury in a fore-leg, a
day or two before; and was now confined in the stable under
the regimen of the overseer. The animal was brought out for
inspection, and the bandages, which had been bound round the
limb, were removed in our presence. To a question as to the
cause of this injury, Carey replied—

"The mischeevous young devil wa'nt content with the paster,
but she must be loping over the fence into the cornfield! It
was a marcy she wa'nt foundered outright, on the green corn;
but she sprained her pasten-joint, any how;—which she deserved
for being so obstropolous."

A consultation was now held upon the case, at which divers

of the elder negroes assisted. But, in general, every attempt by any of these to give an opinion was frowned down by the author-itative and self-sufficient Carey, who was somewhat tyrannical in the assertion of his prerogative.

Frank Meriwether ventured to suggest that the injured part should be bathed frequently with ice-water; to which prescrip-tion our ancient groom pointedly objected,—saying all the *cretur* wanted, was to have her leg dressed, every night and morning, with a wash that he could make, of vinegar and dockweed, and half a dozen other ingredients, which, he affirmed, would pro-duce a cure, " in almost no time."

A conspicuous and, till now, somewhat restive member of the council, was a broad-shouldered, dwarfish old negro, known by the name of uncle Jeff, who had manifested several decided symp·toms of a design to make a speech; and now, in despite of Carey's cross looks, gave his advice in the following terms—

" One of the stonishingst things for a sprain that I knows on, is this—" said he, stepping into the ring and laying the fingers of his right hand upon the palm of his left—" Bless your soul, Mas Frank! I have tried it, often and often, on people, but, in pertickler, upon horses: oil of spike—" he continued, striking his palm, at the enumeration of each ingredient;—" oil of spike, campfire, a little castile soap, and the best of whiskey, all put into a bottle and boiled half away—It's mazing how it will cure a sprain! My old 'oman was sick abed all last winter, with a sprain on her knee; and she tried Doctor Stubbs, and the leech doctor, and all the tother larned folks—but no use, tell she tuck some my intment! She said herself—if you believe me—thar was none on 'em no touch to my intment. It's mazing, Mas Frank! Oh, oh!—"

" Sho !" ejaculated Carey, in a short, surely growl, after hear-ing this wise morsel of experience to the end, and looking as angry as a vexed bull-dog; "Sho! Jeff, you tell me! Think I never seed a hos with a sprained foot, all the way up to my time of life? Stan off, man! I knows what I am about!"

Meriwether turned to me, with a look of jocular resignation, and said, laughing—

"You see how it is! This old magnifico will allow no man to have an opinion but himself. Rather than disturb the peace, I must submit to his authority. Well, Jeffry, my old fellow, as we can't convince Mr. Carey, I suppose we had better not make him angry. You know what an obstinate, cross-grained, old bully, he is? I am afraid he will take us both in hand, if we contradict him: so I'm for letting him alone."

"Consarn his picture!" said Jeff, in a low tone of voice, accompanied by a laugh, in which all the other negroes joined, as we broke up the consultation and walked away.

CHAPTER XLVI

THE QUARTER

HAVING despatched these important matters at the stable, we
left our horses in charge of the servants, and walked towards the
cabins, which were not more than a few hundred paces distant.
These hovels, with their appurtenances, formed an exceedingly
picturesque landscape. They were scattered, without order, over
the slope of a gentle hill; and many of them were embowered
under old and majestic trees. The rudeness of their construction rather enhanced the attractiveness of the scene. Some few
were built after the fashion of the better sort of cottages; but age
had stamped its heavy traces upon their exterior: the green moss
had gathered upon the roofs, and the course weatherboarding had
broken, here and there, into chinks. But the more lowly of these
structures, and the most numerous, were nothing more than plain
log-cabins, compacted pretty much on the model by which boys
build partridge-traps; being composed of the trunks of trees, still
clothed with their bark, and knit together at the corners with so
little regard to neatness that the timbers, being of unequal lengths,
jutted beyond each other, sometimes to the length of a foot.
Perhaps, none of these latter sort were more than twelve feet
square, and not above seven in height. A door swung upon wood-
en hinges, and a small window of two narrow panes of glass were,

in general, the only openings in the front. The intervals between
the logs were filled with clay; and the roof, which was constructed of smaller timbers, laid lengthwise along it and projecting two
or three feet beyond the side or gable walls, heightened, in a very
marked degree, the rustic effect. The chimneys communicated
even a droll expression to these habitations. They were, oddly
enough, built of billets of wood, having a broad foundation of
stone, and growing narrower as they rose, each receding gradually
from the house to which it was attached, until it reached the
height of the roof. These combustible materials were saved from
the access of the fire by a thick coating of mud; and the whole
structure, from its tapering form, might be said to bear some resemblance to the spout of a tea kettle; indeed, this domestic implement would furnish no unapt type of the complete cabin.

From this description, which may serve to illustrate a whole
species of habitations very common in Virginia, it will be seen,
that on the score of accommodation, the inmates of these dwellings were furnished according to a very primitive notion of comfort. Still, however, there were little garden-patches attached to
each, where cymblings, cucumbers, sweet potatoes, water-melons
and cabbages flourished in unrestrained luxuriance. Add to this,
that there were abundance of poultry domesticated about the
premises, and it may be perceived that, whatever might be the
inconveniences of shelter, there was no want of what, in all countries, would be considered a reasonable supply of luxuries.

Nothing more attracted my observation than the swarms of
little negroes that basked on the sunny sides of these cabins, and
congregated to gaze at us as we surveyed their haunts. They
were nearly all in that costume of the golden age which I have
heretofore described; and showed their slim shanks and long
heels in all varieties of their grotesque natures. Their predominant love of sunshine, and their lazy, listless postures, and ap-

parent content to be silently looking abroad, might well afford a comparison to a set of terrapins luxuriating in the genial warmth of summer, on the logs of a mill-pond.

And there, too, were the prolific mothers of this redundant brood,—a number of stout negro-women who thronged the doors of the huts, full of idle curiosity to see us. And, when to these are added a few reverend, wrinkled, decrepit old men, with faces shortened as if with drawing-strings, noses that seemed to have run all to nostril, and with feet of the configuration of a mattock, my reader will have a tolerably correct idea of this negro-quarter, its population, buildings, external appearance, situation and extent.

Meriwether, I have said before, is a kind and considerate master. It is his custom frequently to visit his slaves, in order to inspect their condition, and, where it may be necessary, to add to their comforts or relieve their wants. His coming amongst them, therefore, is always hailed with pleasure. He has constituted himself into a high court of appeal, and makes it a rule to give all their petitions a patient hearing, and to do justice in the premises. This, he tells me, he considers as indispensably necessary;—he says, that no overseer is entirely to be trusted : that there are few men who have the temper to administer wholesome laws to any population, however small, without some omissions or irregularities; and that this is more emphatically true of those who administer them entirely at their own will. On the present occasion, in almost every house where Frank entered, there was some boon to be asked; and I observed, that in every case, the petitioner was either gratified or refused in such a tone as left no occasion or disposition to murmur. Most of the women had some bargains to offer, of fowls or eggs or other commodities of household use, and Meriwether generally referred them to his wife, who, I found, relied almost entirely on this resource, for the

supply of such commodities; the negroes being regularly paid
for whatever was offered in this way.

One old fellow had a special favour to ask,—a little money to
get a new padding for his saddle, which, he said, "galled his cretur's back." Frank, after a few jocular passages with the veteran,
gave him what he desired, and sent him off rejoicing.

"That, sir," said Meriwether, "is no less a personage than
Jupiter. He is an old bachelor, and has his cabin here on the
hill. He is now near seventy, and is a kind of King of the Quarter.
He has a horse, which he extorted from me last Christmas; and
I seldom come here without finding myself involved in some new
demand, as a consequence of my donation. Now he wants a pair
of spurs which, I suppose, I must give him. He is a preposterous
coxcomb, and Ned has administered to his vanity by a present of
a *chapeau de bras*—a relic of my military era, which he wears on
Sundays with a conceit that has brought upon him as much envy
as admiration—the usual condition of greatness."

The air of contentment and good humor and kind family attachment, which was apparent throughout this little community,
and the familiar relations existing between them and the proprietor struck me very pleasantly. I came here a stranger, in great
degree, to the negro character, knowing but little of the domestic
history of these people, their duties, habits or temper, and somewhat disposed, indeed, from prepossessions, to look upon them as
severely dealt with, and expecting to have my sympathies excited
towards them as objects of commiseration. I have had, therefore,
rather a special interest in observing them. The contrast between
my preconceptions of their condition and the reality which I have
witnessed, has brought me a most agreeable surprise. I will not
say that, in a high state of cultivation and of such self-dependence
as they might possibly attain in a separate national existence,
they might not become a more respectable people; but I am quite

sure they never could become a happier people than I find them here. Perhaps they are destined, ultimately, to that national existence, in the clime from which they derive their origin—that this is a transition state in which we see them in Virginia. If it be so, no tribe of people have ever passed from barbarism to civilization whose middle stage of progress has been more secure from harm, more genial to their character, or better supplied with mild and beneficent guardianship, adapted to the actual state of their intellectual feebleness, than the negroes of Swallow Barn. And, from what I can gather, it is pretty much the same on the other estates in this region. I hear of an unpleasant exception to this remark now and then; but under such conditions as warrant the opinion that the unfavorable case is not more common than that which may be found in a survey of any other department of society. The oppression of apprentices, of seamen, of soldiers, of subordinates, indeed, in every relation, may furnish elements for a bead-roll of social grievances quite as striking, if they were diligently noted and brought to view.

What the negro is finally capable of, in the way of civilization, I am not philosopher enough to determine. In the present stage of his existence, he presents himself to my mind as essentially parasitical in his nature. I mean that he is, in his moral constitution, a dependant upon the white race; dependant for guidance and direction even to the procurement of his most indispensable necessaries. Apart from this protection he has the helplessness of a child,—without foresight, without faculty of contrivance, without thrift of any kind. We have instances, in the neighborhood of this estate, of individuals of the tribe falling into the most deplorable destitution from the want of that constant supervision which the race seems to require. This helplessness may be the due and natural impression which two centuries of servitude have stamped upon the tribe. But it is not the less a present and in-

surmountable impediment to that most cruel of all projects—the
direct, broad emancipation of these people ;—an act of legislation
in comparison with which the revocation of the edict of Nantes
would be entitled to be ranked among political benefactions. Taking instruction from history, all organized slavery is inevitably
but a temporary phase of human condition. Interest, necessity
and instinct, all work to give progression to the relations of mankind, and finally to elevate each tribe or race to its maximum of
refinement and power. We have no reason to suppose that the
negro will be an exception to this law.

At present, I have said, he is parasitical. He grows upward,
only as the vine to which nature has supplied the sturdy tree as
a support. He is extravagantly imitative. The older negroes
here have—with some spice of comic mixture in it—that formal,
grave and ostentatious style of manners, which belonged to the
gentlemen of former days; they are profuse of bows and compliments, and very aristocratic in their way. The younger ones are
equally to be remarked for aping the style of the present time,
and especially for such tags of dandyism in dress as come within
their reach. Their fondness for music and dancing is a predominant passion. I never meet a negro man—unless he is quite old
—that he is not whistling ; and the women sing from morning till
night. And as to dancing, the hardest day's work does not restrain their desire to indulge in such pastime. During the har-
vest, when their toil is pushed to its utmost—the time being one
of recognized privileges—they dance almost the whole night.
They are great sportsmen, too. They angle and haul the seine,
and hunt and tend their traps, with a zest that never grows weary.
Their gayety of heart is constitutional and perennial, and when
they are together they are as voluble and noisy as so many blackbirds. In short, I think them the most good-natured, careless,
light-hearted, and happily-constructed human beings I have ever

seen. Having but few and simple wants, they seem to me to be provided with every comfort which falls within the ordinary compass of their wishes ; and, I might say, that they find even more enjoyment,—as that word may be applied to express positive pleasures scattered through the course of daily occupation—than any other laboring people I am acquainted with.

I took occasion to express these opinions to Meriwether, and to tell him how much I was struck by the mild and kindly aspect of this society at the Quarter.

This, as I expected, brought him into a discourse.

"The world," said he, "has begun very seriously to discuss the evils of slavery, and the debate has sometimes, unfortunately, been levelled to the comprehension of our negroes, and pains have even been taken that it should reach them. I believe there are but few men who may not be persuaded that they suffer some wrong in the organization of society—for society has many wrongs, both accidental and contrived, in its structure. Extreme poverty is, perhaps, always a wrong done to the individual upon whom it is cast. Society can have no honest excuse for starving a human being. I dare say you can follow out that train of thought and find numerous evils to complain of. Ingenious men, some of them not very honest, have found in these topics themes for agitation and popular appeal in all ages. How likely are they to find, in this question of slavery, a theme for the highest excitement ; and, especially, how easy is it to inflame the passions of these untutored and unreckoning people, our black population, with this subject! For slavery, as an original question, is wholly without justification or defence. It is theoretically and morally wrong— and fanatical and one-sided thinkers will call its continuance, even for a day, a wrong, under any modification of it. But, surely, if these people are consigned to our care by the accident, or, what is worse, the premeditated policy which has put them upon our commonwealth, the great duty that is left to us is, to shape our conduct, in reference to them, by a wise and beneficent consideration of the case as it exists, and to administer wholesome laws for their government, making their servitude as tolerable to them as we can consistently with our own safety and their ultimate good. We should not be justified in taking the hazard of internal convulsions to get rid of them; nor have we a right, in the desire to free ourselves, to whelm them in greater evils than their present bondage. A violent removal of them, or a general emancipation, would assuredly produce one or the other of these calamities. Has any sensible man, who takes a different view of this subject, ever reflected upon the consequences of committing two or three millions of persons, born and bred in a state so completely dependent as that of slavery—so unfurnished, so unintellectual, so utterly helpless, I may say—to all the responsibilities, cares and labors of a state of freedom? Must he not acknowledge, that the utmost we could give them would be but a nominal freedom, in doing which we should be guilty of a cruel desertion of our trust—inevitably leading them to progressive debasement, penury, oppression, and finally to extermination? I would not argue with that man whose bigotry to a sentiment was so blind and so fatal as to insist on this expedient. When the time comes, as I apprehend it will come,—and all the sooner, if it be not delayed by these efforts to arouse something like a vindictive feeling between the disputants on both sides—in which the roots of slavery will begin to lose their hold in our soil; and when we shall have the means for providing these people a proper asylum, I shall be glad to see the State devote her thoughts to that enterprise, and, if I am alive, will cheerfully and gratefully assist in it. In the mean time, we owe it to justice and humanity to treat these people with the most considerate kindness. As to what are ordinarily imagined to be the evils or sufferings of their condition, I do not believe in them. The evil is generally felt on the side of the master. Less work is exacted of them than voluntary laborers choose to perform : they have as many privileges as are compatible with the nature of their occupations : they are subsisted, in general, as comfortably—nay, in their estimation of comforts, more comfortably, than the rural population of other countries. And as to the severities that are alleged to be practised upon them, there is much more malice or invention than truth in the accusation. The slaveholders in this region are, in the main, men of kind and humane tempers—as pliant to the touch of compassion, and as sensible of its duties, as the best men in any community, and as little disposed to inflict injury upon their dependents. Indeed, the owner of slaves is less apt to be harsh in his requisitions of labor than those who toil much themselves. I suspect it is invariably characteristic of those who are in the habit of severely tasking themselves, that they are inclined to regulate their demands upon others by their own standard. Our slaves are punished for misdemeanors, pretty much as disorderly persons are punished in all societies ; and I am quite of opinion that our statistics of crime and punishment will compare favorably with those of any other population. But the punishment, on our side, is remarked as the personal act of the master; whilst, elsewhere, it goes free of ill-natured comment, because it is set down to the course of justice. We, therefore, suffer a reproach which other polities escape, and the conclusion is made an item of complaint against slavery.

" It has not escaped the attention of our legislation to provide against the ill-treatment of our negro population. I heartily concur in all effective laws to punish cruelty in masters. Public opinion on that subject, however, is even stronger than law, and no man can hold up his head in this community who is chargeable with mal-treatment of his slaves.

" One thing I desire you specially to note : the question

of emancipation is exclusively our own, and every intermed-
dling with it from abroad will but mar its chance of success.
We cannot but regard such interference as an unwarrantable and
mischievous design to do us injury, and, therefore, we resent
it—sometimes, I am sorry to say, even to the point of involving
the innocent negro in the rigor which it provokes. We think,
and, indeed, we know, that we alone are able to deal properly with
the subject; all others are misled by the feeling which the natural sentiment against slavery, in the abstract, excites. They act
under imperfect knowledge and impulsive prejudices which are
totally incompatible with wise action on any subject. We, on the
contrary, have every motive to calm and prudent counsel. Our
lives, fortunes, families—our commonwealth itself, are put at the
hazard of this resolve. You gentlemen of the North greatly misapprehend us, if you suppose that we are in love with this slave
institution—or that, for the most part, we even deem it profitable
to us. There are amongst us, it is true, some persons who are
inclined to be fanatical on this side of the question, and who bring
themselves to adopt some bold dogmas tending to these extreme
views—and it is not out of the course of events that the violence of
the agitations against us may lead ultimately to a wide adoption
of these dogmas amongst the slaveholding States. It is in the
nature of men to recalcitrate against continual assault, and,
through the zeal of such opposition, to run into ultraisms which
cannot be defended. But at present, I am sure the Southern
sentiment on this question is temperate and wise, and that we
neither regard slavery as a good, nor account it, except in some favorable conditions, as profitable. The most we can say of it is that,
as matters stand, it is the best auxiliary within our reach.

  "Without troubling you with further reflections upon a dull
subject, my conclusion is that the real friends of humanity
should conspire to allay the ferments on this question, and, even

at some cost, to endeavor to encourage the natural contentment of the slave himself, by arguments to reconcile him to a present destiny, which is, in fact, more free from sorrow and want than that of almost any other class of men occupying the same field of labor."

Meriwether was about to finish his discourse at this point, when a new vein of thought struck him:

" It has sometimes occurred to me," he continued, " that we might elevate our slave population, very advantageously to them and to us, by some reforms in our code. I think we are justly liable to reproach, for the neglect or omission of our laws to recognize and regulate marriages, and the relation of family amongst the negroes. We owe it to humanity and to the sacred obligation of Christian ordinances, to respect and secure the bonds of husband and wife, and parent and child. I am ashamed to acknowledge that I have no answer to make, in the way of justification of this neglect. We have no right to put man and wife asunder. The law should declare this, and forbid the separation under any contingency, except of crime. It should be equally peremptory in forbidding the coercive separation of children from the mother—at least during that period when the one requires the care of the other. A disregard of these attachments has brought more odium upon the conditions of servitude than all the rest of its imputed hardships; and a suitable provision for them would tend greatly to gratify the feelings of benevolent and conscientious slaveholders, whilst it would disarm all considerate and fairminded men, of what they deem the strongest objection to the existing relations of master and slave.

" I have also another reform to propose," said Meriwether, smiling. " It is, to establish by law, an upper or privileged class of slaves—selecting them from the most deserving, above the age of forty-five years. These I would endue with something of a

feudal character. They should be entitled to hold small tracts
of land under their masters, rendering for it a certain rent, paya-
ble either in personal service or money. They should be elevated
into this class through some order of court, founded on certificates
of good conduct, and showing the assent of the master. And I
think I would create legal jurisdictions, giving the masters or
stewards civil and criminal judicial authority. I have some dream
of a project of this kind in my head," he continued, " which I have
not fully matured as yet. You will think, Mr. Littleton, that I
am a man of schemes, if I go on much longer—but there is something in this notion which may be improved to advantage, and I
should like, myself, to begin the experiment. Jupiter, here, shall
be my first feudatory—my tenant in socage—my old villain!"

"I suspect," said I, "Jupiter considers that his dignity is not
to be enhanced by any enlargement of privilege, as long as he is
allowed to walk about in his military hat as King of the Quarter."

" Perhaps not," replied Meriwether, laughing; " then I shall
be forced to make my commencement upon Carey."

" Carey," interrupted Hazard, "would think it small promo-
tion to be allowed to hold land under you!"

" Faith! I shall be without a feudatory to begin with," said
Meriwether. " But come with me ; I have a visit to make to the
cabin of old Lucy."

CHAPTER XLVII.

Lucy's cottage was removed from the rest of the cabins, and seemed to sleep in the shade of a wood upon the skirts of which it was situated. In full view from it was a narrow creek, or navigable inlet from the river which was seen glittering in the sunshine through the screen of cedars and shrubbery that grew upon its banks. A garden occupied the little space in front of the habitation; and here, with some evidence of a taste for embellishment which I had not seen elsewhere in this negro hamlet, flowers were planted in order along the line of the inclosure, and shot up with a gay luxuriance. A draw-well was placed in the middle of this garden, and some few fruit-trees were clustered about it These improvements had their origin in past years, and owed their present preservation to the thrifty care of the daughter of the aged inhabitant, a spruce, decent and orderly woman, who had been nurtured among the family servants at Swallow Barn, and now resided in the cabin, the sole attendant upon her mother.

When we arrived at this little dwelling, Lucy was alone, her daughter having, a little while before, left her to make a visit to the family mansion. The old woman's form showed the double havoc of age and disease. She was bent forward, and sat near her hearth, with her elbows resting on her knees; and her hands (in which she grasped a faded and tattered handkerchief) supported her chin. She was smoking a short and dingy pipe; and, in the weak and childish musing of age, was beating one foot upon the floor with a regular and rapid stroke, such as is common to nurses when lulling a child to sleep. Her gray hairs were covered with a cap; and her attire generally exhibited an attention to cleanliness, which showed the concern of her daughter for her personal comfort.

The lowly furniture of the room corresponded with the appearance of its inmate. It was tidy and convenient, and there were even some manifestations of the ambitious vanity of a female in the fragments of looking-glass, and the small framed prints that hung against the walls. A pensive partner in the quiet comfort of this little apartment, was a large cat, that sat perched upon the sill of the open window, and looked demurely out upon the garden,—as if soberly rebuking the tawdry and gairish bevy of sunflowers that erected their tall, spinster-like figures so near that they almost thrust their heads into the room.

For the first few moments after our arrival, the old woman seemed to be unconscious of our presence. Meriwether spoke to her without receiving an answer; and, at last, after repeating his salutation two or three times, she raised her feeble eyes towards him, and made only a slight recognition by a bow. Whether it was that his voice became more familiar to her ear, or that her memory was suddenly resuscitated, after her master had addressed some questions to her, she all at once brightened up into a lively conviction of the person of her visitor; and, as a smile played across her features, she exclaimed,—

"God bless the young master! I didn't know him. He has come to see poor old mammy Lucy!"

"And how is the old woman?" asked Meriwether, stooping to speak, almost in her ear.

"She hasn't got far to go," replied Lucy. "They are a-coming for her:—they tell me every night that they are a-coming to take her away."

"Who are coming?" inquired Frank.

"They that told the old woman," she returned, looking up wildly and speaking in a louder voice, "that they buried his body in the sands of the sea.—"

Saying these words, she began to open out the ragged handkerchief which, until now, she had held in her clenched hand.— "They brought me this in the night," she continued,—"and then, I knew it was true."

In the pause that followed, the old negro remained in profound silence, during which the tears ran down her cheeks. After some minutes she seemed suddenly to check her feelings and said, with energy,—

"I told them it was a lie: and so it was!—The old woman knew better than them all. Master Frank didn't know it, and Miss Lucretia didn't know it, but mammy Lucy, if she is old, knew it well!—Five years last February!—How many years, honey, do you think a ship may keep going steady on without stopping?—It is a right long time,—isn't it, honey?

This exhibition of drivelling dotage was attended with many other incoherent expressions that I have not thought it worth while to notice; and I would not have troubled my reader with these seemingly unmeaning effusions of a mind in the last stages of senility, if they had not some reference to the circumstances I am about to relate. The scene grew painful to us as we prolonged our visit; and therefore, after some kind words to the old woman, we took our departure. As we returned to Swallow Barn, Frank Meriwether gave me the particulars of old Lucy's pathetic history, which I have woven, with as much fidelity as my memory allows, into the following simple and somewhat melancholy narrative.

DURING the latter years of the war of the revolution my uncle Walter Hazard, as I have before informed my reader, commanded a troop of volunteer cavalry, consisting principally of the yeomanry in the neighborhood of Swallow Barn; and, at the time of the southern invasion by Lord Cornwallis, this little band was brought into active service, and shared, as freely as any other corps of the army, the perils of that desultory warfare which was waged upon the borders of North Carolina and Virginia. The gentlemen of the country, at that time, marshalled their neighbors into companies; and, seldom acting in line, were encouraged to harass the enemy wherever opportunity offered. The credit as well as the responsibility of these partisan operations fell to the individual leaders who had respectively signalized themselves by their zeal in the cause.

This kind of irregular army gave great occasion for the display of personal prowess; and there were many gentlemen whose bold adventures, during the period alluded to, furnished the subject of popular anecdotes of highly attractive interest. Such exploits, of course, were attended with their usual marvels; and there was scarcely any leader of note who could not recount some passages in his adventures, where he was indebted for his safety to the attachment and bravery of his followers,—often to that of his personal servants.

Captain Hazard was a good deal distinguished in this war, and took great pleasure in acknowledging his indebtedness, on one occasion, for his escape from imminent peril, to the address and gallantry of an humble retainer,—a faithful negro, by the name of Luke,—whom he had selected from the number of his slaves to attend him as a body-servant through the adventures of the war.

It furnishes the best answer that can be made to all the exaggerated opinions of the misery of the domestic slavery of this

region, that, in the stormiest period of the history of the United
States, and when the whole disposable force of the country was
engrossed in the conduct of a fearful conflict, the slaves of Virginia were not only passive to the pressure of a yoke which the
philosophy of this age affects to consider as the most intolerable
of burthens, but they also, in a multitude of instances, were found
in the ranks, by the side of their masters, sharing with them the
most formidable dangers, and manifesting their attachment by
heroic gallantry.

After the close of the war Captain Hazard was not unmindful
of his trusty servant. Luke had grown into a familiar but respectful intimacy with his master, and occupied a station about
his person of the most confidential nature. My uncle scarcely
ever rode out without him, and was in the habit of consulting
him upon many lesser matters relating to the estate, with a
seriousness that showed the value he set upon Luke's judgment.
He offered Luke his freedom; but the domestic desired no
greater liberty than he then enjoyed, and would not entertain the
idea of any possible separation from the family. Instead, therefore, of an unavailing, formal grant of manumission, my uncle
gave Luke a few acres of ground, in the neighborhood of the
Quarter, and provided him a comfortable cabin. Before the war
had terminated, Luke had married Lucy, a slave who had been
reared in the family, as a lady's maid, and, occasionally, as a
nurse to the children at Swallow Barn. Things went on very
smoothly with them, for many years. But, at length, Luke
waxed old, and began to grow rheumatic; and, by degrees, retired from his customary duties, which were rendered lighter as
his infirmities increased. Lucy, from the spry and saucy-eyed
waiting-woman, was fast changing into a short, fat and plethoric
old dame. Her locks accumulated the frost of each successive
winter; and she, too, fell back upon the reserve of comfort laid

up for their old age by their master,—who himself, by a like process, had faded away, from the buxom, swashing madcap of the
revolutionary day, into a thin, leather-cheeked old campaigner,
who sometimes told hugely long stories, and sent for Luke to
put his name on the back of them. In short, five and thirty
years, had wrought their ordinary miracles ; and first, the veteran Luke disappeared from this mortal stage; and then his master : and old Lucy was left a hale and querulous widow, with
eight or nine children, and her full dower interest in the cabin
and its curtilage.

The youngest, but one, of her children was named Abraham
—universally called Abe. All before Abe had arrived at manhood, and had been successively dismissed from Lucy s cabin, as
they reached the age fit to render them serviceable, with that
satisfied unconcern that belongs to a negro mother who trusts to
the kindness of her master. This family was remarkable for its
intelligence; and those who had already left the maternal nest
had, with perhaps one or two exceptions, been selected for the
mechanical employments upon the estate :—they were shoe-
makers, weavers, or carpenters; and were held in esteem for
their industry and good character. Abe, however, was an exception to the general respectability of Luke's descendants. He
was, at the period to which my story refers, an athletic and singularly active lad, rapidly approaching to manhood; with a frame
not remarkable for size, but well knit, and of uncommonly sym-
metrical proportions for the race to which he belonged. He had
nothing of the flat nose and broad lip of his tribe,—but his face
was rather moulded with the prevailing characteristics of the negroes of the West Indies. There was an expression of courage
in his eye that answered to the complexion of his mind : he was
noted for his spirit, and his occasional bursts of passion, which,
even in his boyhood, rendered him an object of fear to his older

associates. This disposition was coupled with singular shrewdness of intellect, and an aptitude for almost every species of
handicraft. He had been trained to the work of a blacksmith,
and was, when he chose to be so, a useful auxiliary at the anvil.
But a habit of associating with the most profligate menials belonging to the extensive community of Swallow Barn, and the
neighboring estates, had corrupted his character, and, at the time
of life which he had now reached, had rendered him offensive to
the whole plantation.

Walter Hazard could never bear the idea of disposing of any
of his negroes ; and when Meriwether came to the estate, he was
even more strongly imbued with the same repugnance. Abe
was, therefore, for a long time, permitted to take his own way,—
the attachment of the family for his mother procuring for him
an amnesty for many transgressions. Lucy, as is usual in almost
all such cases, entertained an affection for this outcast, surpassing
that which she felt for all the rest of her offspring. There was
never a more exemplary domestic than the mother : nor was she
without a painful sense of the failings of her son ; but this only
mortified her pride without abating her fondness—a common
effect of strong animal impulses, not merely in ignorant minds.
Abe had always lived in her cabin, and the instinct of long association predominated over her weak reason ; so that although she
was continually tormented with his misdeeds, and did not fail to
reprove him even with habitual harshness, still her heart yearned
secretly towards him. Time fled by, confirming this motherly
attachment, and, in the same degree, hardening Abe into the most
irreclaimable of culprits. He molested the peace of the neighborhood by continual broils ; was frequently detected in acts of
depredation upon the adjoining farms ; and had once brought
himself into extreme jeopardy by joining a band of out-lying negroes, who had secured themselves, for some weeks, in the fast-

nesses of the low-country swamps, from whence they annoyed the vicinity by nocturnal incursions of the most lawless character. Nothing but the interference of Meriwether, at the earnest implorings of Lucy, saved Abe, on this occasion, from public justice. Abe was obliged in consequence to be removed altogether from the estate, and consigned to another sphere of action.

Meriwether revolved this matter with great deliberation; and, at length, determined to put his refractory bondsman in the charge of one of the pilots of the Chesapeake, to whom, it was supposed, he might become a valuable acquisition;—his active, intelligent and intrepid character being well suited to the perilous nature of that service. The arrangements for this purpose were speedily made, and the day of his removal drew nigh.

It was a curious speculation, on the part of the family, and an unpleasant one, to see how Lucy would bear this separation. The negroes, like all other dependants, are marked by an abundant spirit of assentation. They generally agree to whatever is proposed to their minds, by their superiors, with an acquiescence that has the show of conviction. But, it is very hard to convince the mind of a mother, of the justice of the sentence that deprives her of her child,—especially a poor, unlearned, negro mother. Lucy heard all the arguments to justify the necessity of sending Abe abroad; assented to all; bowed her head, as if entirely convinced;—and thought it—very hard. She was told that it was the only expedient to save him from prison; she admitted it; but still said—that it was a very cruel thing to sever mother and son. It was a source of unutterable anguish to her, which no kindness on the part of the family could mitigate. Forgetting Abe's growth to manhood, his delinquencies, the torments he had incessantly inflicted upon her peace, and unmindful of the numerous children that, with their descendants, were still around her, she seemed to be engrossed by her affection for this worthless

scion of her stock;—showing how entirely the unreasoning instincts of the animal sway the human mind, in its uneducated condition. All the considerations that proved Abe's banishment a necessary, and, even for himself, a judicious measure, seemed only to afford additional reinforcements to the unquenchable dotings of the mother.

From the time of the discovery of the transgression which brought down upon Abe the sentence that was to remove him from Swallow Barn, until the completion of the preliminary arrangements for his departure, he was left in a state of anxious uncertainty as to his fate. He was afraid to be seen at large, as some risk was hinted to him of seizure by the public authorities; and he, therefore, confined himself, with a sullen and dejected silence, in Lucy's cabin,—seldom venturing beyond the threshold; and, when he did so, it was with the stealthy and suspicious motion which is observable in that class of animals that pursue their prey by night, when induced to stir abroad in daytime.

It is a trait in the dispositions of the negroes on the old plantations, to cling with more than a freeman's interest to the spot of their nativity. They have a strong attachment to the places connected with their earlier associations,—what in phrenology is called inhabitiveness;—and the pride of remaining in one family of masters, and of being transmitted to its posterity with all their own generations, is one of the most remarkable features in these negro clans. Being a people of simple combinations and limited faculty for speculative pleasures, they are a contented race,—not much disturbed by the desire of novelty. Abe was not yet informed whether he was to be sold to a distant owner, given over to public punishment, or condemned to some domestic disgrace. Apparently, he did not much care which :—his natural resoluteness had made him dogged.

It was painful, during this period, to see his mother. In all respects unlike himself, she suffered intensely; and, though hoary with sixty winters, hovered about him, with that busy assiduity which is one of the simplest forms in which anxiety and grief are apt to show themselves. She abandoned her usual employments, and passed almost all her time within her cabin, in a fretful subserviency to his wants ; and, what might seem to be incompatible with this strong emotion of attachment,—though, in fact, it was one of the evidences of its existence,—her tone of addressing him was that of reprimand, seldom substituted by the language of pity or tenderness. I mention this, because it illustrates one point of the negro character. She provided for him, as for a sickly child, what little delicacies her affluence afforded; and, with a furtive industry, plied her needle through the livelong night, in making up, from the scanty materials at her command, such articles of dress as might be found or fancied to be useful to him, in the uncertain changes that awaited him. In these preparations there was even seen a curious attention to matters that might serve only to gratify his vanity ; some fantastical and tawdry personal ornaments were to be found amongst the stock of necessaries which her foresight was thus providing.

I hope I shall not be thought tedious in thus minutely remarking the trifles that were observable in the conduct of the old domestic on this occasion. My purpose is to bring to the view of my reader an exhibition of the natural forms in which the passions are displayed in those lowest and humblest of the departments of human society, and to represent truly a class of people to whom justice has seldom been done, and who possess many points of character well calculated to win them a kind and amiable judgment from the world. They are a neglected race, who seem to have been excluded from the pale of human sympathy, from mistaken opinions of their quality, no less than from the unpretending lowliness of their position. To me, they have always appeared as a people of agreeable peculiarities, and not without much of the picturesque in the development of their habits and feelings.

When it was, at last, announced that Abe was to be disposed of in the manner I have mentioned, the tidings were received by the mother and son variously, according to their respective tempers. Lucy knew no difference between a separation by a hundred or a thousand miles : she counted none of the probabilities of future intercourse ; and the traditionary belief in the danger of the seas, with their unknown monsters, and all the frightful stories of maritime disaster, rose upon her imagination with a terrifying presage of ill to her boy. Abe, on the other hand, received the intelligence with the most callous unconcern. He was not of a frame to blench at peril, or fear misfortune ; and his behavior rather indicated resentment at the authority that was exercised over him, than anxiety for the issue. For a time, he mused over this feeling in sullen silence : but, as the expected change of his condition became the subject of constant allusion among his associates, and as the little community in which he had always lived gathered around him, with some signs of unusual interest, to talk over the nature of his employments, a great deal reached his ears from the older negroes, that opened upon his mind a train of perceptions highly congenial to the latent properties of his character. His imagination was awakened by the attractions of this field of adventure ; by the free roving of the sailor ; and by the tumultuous and spirit-stirring roar of the ocean, as they were pictured to him in story. His person grew erect, his limbs expanded to their natural motion, and he once more walked with the light step and buoyant feelings of his young and wayward nature.

The time of departure arrived. A sloop that had been lying at anchor in the creek, opposite to Lucy's cabin, was just preparing to sail. The main-sail was slowly opening its folds, as it rose along the mast: a boat with two negroes had put off for the beach, and the boatmen landed with a summons to Abe, informing him that he was all they now staid for. Abe was seated on his chest in front of the dwelling; and Lucy sat on a stool beside him, with both of his hands clasped in hers. Not a word passed between them ; and the heavings of the old woman's bosom might have been heard by the standers-by. A bevy of negroes stood around them : the young ones, in ignorant and wondering silence ; and the elders conversing with each other in smothered tones, with an occasional cheering word addressed to mammy Lucy—as they called her. Old uncle Jeff was conspicuous in this scene. He stood in the group, with his corncob pipe, puffing the smoke from his bolster-lips, with lugubriously lengthened visage.

The two boatmen pressed into the crowd to speak to Lucy, but were arrested by the solemn Jeff, who, thrusting out his broad, horny hand, and planting it upon the breast of the fore-most, whispered, in a half audible voice,—" The old woman's taking on !—wait a bit—she'll speak presently !"

With these words, the whole company fell into silence and continued to gaze at the mother. Abe looked up, from the place wnere ne sat, through his eyelashes, at the little circle, with an awkwardly counterfeited smile playing through the tears that filled his eyes.

" It a'most goes to kill her," whispered one of the women to ner neighbor.

" I've seen women," said Jeff, " this here way, afore in my time : they can bear a monstrous sight. But, when they can once speak, then it's done,—you see."

Lucy was now approached by two or three of the old women, who began to urge some feeble topics of consolation in her ear, in that simple phrase which nature supplies, and which had more of encouragement in its tones than in the words: but the only response extracted was a mute shake of the head, and a sorrowful uplifting of the eye, accompanied by a closer grasp of the hands of Abe.

" It's no use," said Jeff, as he poured a volume of smoke from his mouth, and spoke in a deep voice, in the dialect of his people,—" it's no use till nature takes its own way. When the tide over yonder (pointing to the river) comes up, speeches arn't going to send it back: when an old woman's heart is full it's just like the tide."

" The wind is taking hold of the sail," said one of the boat-men, who until now had not interfered in the scene, " and the captain has no time to stay."

Lucy looked up and directed her eye to the sloop, whose can-vas was alternately filling and shaking in the wind, as the boat vacillated in her position. The last moment had come. The mother arose from her seat, at the same instant with her son, and flung herself upon his neck, where she wept aloud.

" Didn't I tell you so !" whispered Jeff to some old crones ; " when it can get out of the bosom by the eyes, it carries a mon-strous load with it."

" To be sure !" exclaimed the beldams, which is a form of interjection amongst the negroes, to express both assent and wonder.

This burst of feeling had its expected effect upon Lucy. She seemed to be suddenly relieved, and was able to address a few short words of parting to Abe : then taking from the plaits of her bosom, a small leather purse containing a scant stock of sil-ver,—the hoard of past years—she put it into the unresisting hand of Abe. The boy looked at the faded bag for a moment, and gathering up something like a smile upon his face, he forced the money back upon his mother, himself replacing it in the bosom

of her dress. " You don't think I am going to take your money
with me!" said he, " I never cared about the best silver my master ever had: no, nor for freedom neither. I thought I was
always going to stay here on the plantation. I would rather have
the handkerchief you wear around your neck, than all the silver
you ever owned."

Lucy took the handkerchief from her shoulders, and put it in
his hand. Abe drew it into a loose knot about his throat, then
turned briskly round, shook hands with the by-standers, and,
shouldering his chest, moved with the boatmen, at a rapid pace,
towards the beach.

In a few moments afterwards, he was seen standing up in the
boat, as it shot out from beneath the bank, and waving his hand
to the dusky group he had just left. He then took his seat, and
was watched by his melancholy tribe until the sloop, falling away
before the wind, disappeared behind the remotest promontory.

Lucy, with a heavy heart, retired within her cabin, and threw
herself upon a bed ; and the comforting gossips who had collected before the door, after lingering about her for a little while,
gradually withdrew, leaving her to the assiduities of her
children.

Some years elapsed ; during which interval frequent reports
had reached Swallow Barn, relating to the conduct and condition
of Abe ; and he himself had, once or twice, revisited the family.
Great changes had been wrought upon him ; he had grown into
a sturdy manhood, invigorated by the hardy discipline of his
calling. The fearless qualities of his mind, no less than the
activity and strength of his body, had been greatly developed to
the advantage of his character ; and, what does not unfrequently
happen, the peculiar adaptation of his new pursuits to the temper and cast of his constitution, had operated favorably upon his
morals. His errant propensities had been gratified ; and the

alternations between the idleness of the calm and the strenuous and exciting bustle of the storm, were pleasing to his unsteady and fitful nature. He had found, in other habits, a vent for inclinations which, when constrained by his former monotonous avocations, had so often broken out into mischievous adventures. In short, Abe was looked upon by his employers as a valuable seaman; and the report of this estimation of him had worked wonders in his favor at Swallow Barn.

From the period of his departure up to this time, poor old Lucy nursed the same extravagant feelings towards him; and these were even kindled into a warmer flame by his increasing good repute. Her passion, it may be called, was a subject of constant notice in the family. It would have been deemed remarkable in an individual of the most delicate nurture; but in the aged and faithful domestic, it was a subject of commiseration on account of its influence upon her happiness, and had almost induced Meriwether to recall Abe to his former occupation; although he was sensible that, by doing so, he might expose him to the risk of relapsing into his earlier errors. But, besides this, Abe had become so well content with his present station that it was extremely likely he would, of his own accord, have sought to return to it. The vagrant, sunshiny, and billowy life of a sailor has a spell in it that works marvellously upon the heedless and irresponsible temperament of a negro. Abe was, therefore, still permitted, like a buoy, to dance upon the waves, and to woo his various destiny between the lowest trough of the sea, and the highest white-cap of the billow.

At the time to which my story has now advanced, an event took place that excited great interest within the little circle of Swallow Barn. It was about the breaking up of the winter—towards the latter end of February—some four years ago, that in the afternoon of a cheerless day, news arrived at Norfolk that

an inward-bound brig had struck upon the shoal of the middle
ground, (a shallow bar that stretches seaward beyond the mouth
of the Chesapeake, between the two capes,) and, from the threatening aspect of the weather, the crew were supposed to be in
great danger. It was a cold, blustering day, such as winter
sometimes puts on when he is about to retreat :—as a squadron,
vexed with watching a politic enemy, finding itself obliged, at last,
to raise the blockade, is apt to break ground with an unusual
show of bravado.   The wind blew in gusts from the northwest ; a
heavy rack of dun and chilly clouds was driven churlishly before the
blast, and spitted out some rare flakes of snow.   These moving
masses were forming a huge, black volume upon the eastern
horizon, towards the ocean, as if there encountering the resistance of an adverse gale.   From the west the sun occasionally
shot forth a lurid ray, that, for the instant, flung upon this dark
pile a sombre, purple hue, and lighted up the foam that gathered
at the top of the waves, far seaward ; thus opening short glimpses
of that dreary ocean over which darkness was brooding.   The
sea-birds soared against the murky vault above them ; and, now
and then, caught upon their white wings the passing beam, that
gave them almost a golden radiance ; whilst, at the same time,
they screamed their harsh and frequent cries of fear or joy.
The surface of the Chesapeake was lashed up into a fretful sea, and
the waves were repressed by the weight of the wind; billow pursuing billow with an angry and rapid flight, and barking, with the
snappish sullenness of the wolf. Across the wide expanse of Hampton Road might have been seen some few bay-craft, apparently
not much larger than the wild-fowl that sailed above them, beating, with a fearful anxiety, against the gale, for such harbors as
were nearest at hand; or scudding before it under close-reefed
sails, with ungovernable speed, towards the anchorages to leeward.
Every moment the wind increased in violence ; the clouds

swept nearer to the waters; the gloom thickened; the birds
sought safety on the land; the little barks were quickly vanishing from view : and, before the hour of sunset, earth, air, and sea
were blended into one mass, in which the eye might vainly endeavor to define the boundaries of each : whilst the fierce howling
of the wind, and the deafening uproar of the ocean gave a desolation to the scene, that made those, who looked upon it from the
shore, devoutly thankful that no ill luck had tempted them upon
the flood.

It was at this time that a pilot-boat was seen moored to a
post at the end of a wooden wharf that formed the principal
landing-place at the little seaport of Hampton. The waves were
dashing, with hollow reverberations, between the timbers of the
wharf, and the boat was rocking with a violence that showed the
extreme agitation of the element upon which it floated. Three
or four sailors—all negroes—clad in rough pea-jackets, with blue
and red woollen caps, were standing upon the wharf or upon the
deck of the boat, apparently making some arrangements for venturing out of the harbor. The principal personage among them,
whose commands were given with a bold and earnest voice, and
promptly obeyed, was our stout friend Abe, now grown into the
full perfection of manhood, with a frame of unsurpassed strength
and agility. At the nearer extremity of this wharf, landward,
were a few other mariners, white men, of a weather-beaten exterior,
who had seemingly just walked from the village to the landing-
place, and were engaged in a grave consultation upon some
question of interest. This group approached the former while
they were yet busy with the tackling of the boat. Abe had
stepped aboard with his companions, and they were about letting
all loose for their departure.

" What do you think of it now, Abe ?" asked one of the older
seamen, as he turned his eyes towards the heavens, with a look of

concern. " Are you still so crazy as to think of venturing out in
this gale ?"

" The storm is like a young wolt," replied Abe. " It gets one
hour older and two worse. But this isn't the hardest blow I
ever saw, Master Crocket."

" It will be so dark to-night," said the other, " that you will
not be able to see your jib ; and, by the time the wind gets round
to the northeast. you will have a drift of snow that will shut

your eyes. It will be a dreadful night outside of the capes ; I
see no good that is to come of your foolhardiness "

" Snow-storm or hail-storm, it's all one to me," answered Abe.
" The little Flying Fish has ridden, summer and winter, over as
heavy seas as ever rolled in the Chesapeake. I knows what she
can do, you see !"

" Why, you couldn't find the brig if you were within a cable's
length of her. such a night as this," said another speaker ; " and

if you were to see her I don't know how you are to get along-side."

"You wouldn't say so, master Wilson," returned Abe, "if you were one of the crew of the brig yourself. We can try, you know; and if no good comes on it, let them that *saunt* me judge of that. I always obeys orders!"

"Well," replied the other, "a negro that is born to be hanged —you know the rest, Abe :—the devil may help you, as he sometimes does."

" There is as good help for a negro as there is for a white man, master Wilson—whether on land or water. And no man is going to die till his time comes. I don't set up for more spirit than other people ; but I never was afeard of the sea."

During this short dialogue, Abe and his comrades were busily reefing the sail, and they had now completed all their preparations. The day had come very near to the hour of sunset. Abe mustered his crew, spoke to them with a brave, encouraging tone, and ordered them to cast off from the wharf. In a moment, all hands were at the halyards ; and the buoyant little Flying Fish sprang from her mooring, under a single sail double-reefed, and bounded along before the wind, like an exulting doe, loosened from thraldom, on her native wastes.

"That's a daring fellow !" said one of the party that stood upon the wharf, as they watched the gallant boat heaving playfully through the foam—" and wouldn't mind going to sea astride a shark, if any one would challenge him to it."

"If any man along the Chesapeake," said the other, "can handle a pilot-boat such weather—Abe can. But it's no use for a man to be tempting Providence in this way. It looks wicked !"

" He is on a good errand," interrupted the first speaker. " And God send him a successful venture ! That negro has a great deal of good and bad both in him—but the good has the upper hand."

The Flying Fish was soon far from the speakers, and now showed her little sail, as she bent it down almost to kiss the water, a spotless vision upon the dark and lowering horizon in the east. At length she was observed close hauled upon the wind, and rapidly skimming behind the headlands of Old Point Comfort; whence, after some interval, she again emerged, lessened to the size of a water-fowl by distance, and holding her course, with a steady and resolute speed, into the palpable obscure of the perspective.

When the last trace of this winged messenger of comfort was lost in the terrific desert of ocean, with its incumbent night, the watchful and anxious spectators on the wharf turned about and directed their steps, with thoughtful forebodings, to the public house at some distance in the village.

From what I have related, the reader will be at no loss to understand the purpose of this perilours adventure. The fact was, that as soon as the intelligence reached Norfolk that the brig had got into the dangerous situation which I have described, some of the good people of that borough took measures to communicate with the crew, and to furnish them such means of relief as the suddenness of the emergency enabled them to command. The most obvious suggestion was adopted of dispatching, forthwith, a small vessel to bring away those on board, if it should be ascertained that there was no hope of saving the brig itself. This scheme, however, was not so easy of accomplishment as it, at first, seemed. Application was made to the most experienced mariners in port to undertake this voyage; but, they either evaded the duty, by suggesting doubts of its utility, or cast their eyes towards the heavens and significantly shook their heads, as they affirmed there would be more certainty of loss to the deliverers than to the people of the stranded vessel. The rising tempest and the unruly season boded disaster to whomsoever should be so rash as to encounter the hazard. Rewards were offered; but these, too, failed of effect, and the good intentions of the citizens of Norfolk were well nigh disappointed, when chance brought the subject to the knowledge of our old acquaintance Abe. This stout-hearted black happened to be in the borough at the time; and was one of a knot of seamen who were discussing the proposition of the chances of affording relief. He heard, attentively, all that was said in disparagement of the projected enterprise; and it was with some emotion of secret pleasure that he learned that several seamen of established reputation had declined to undertake the-venture. The predominant pride of his nature was aroused; and he hastened to say, that whatever terrors this voyage had for others, it had none for him. In order, therefore, that he might vouch the sincerity of his assertion by acts, he went immediately to those who had interested themselves in concerting the measure of relief, and tendered his services for the proposed exploit. As may be supposed, they were eagerly accepted. Abe's conditions were, that he should have the choice of his boat, and the selection of his crew. These terms were readily granted; and he set off, with a busy alacrity, to make his preparations. The Flying Fish was the pilot-boat in which Abe had often sailed, and was considered one of the best of her class in the Chesapeake. This little bark was, accordingly, demanded for the service, and as promptly put at Abe's command. She was, at that time, lying at the pier at Hampton, as I have already described her. The crew, from some such motive of pride as first induced Abe to volunteer in this cause, was selected entirely from the number of negro seamen then in Norfolk. They amounted to four or five of the most daring and robust of Abe's associates, who, lured by the hope of reward, as well as impelled by that spirit of rivalry that belongs to even the lowest classes of human beings, and which is particularly excitable in the breasts of men who are trained to dangerous achievements, readily enlisted in the expedition, and placed themselves under the orders of their gallant and venturous captain.

This tender of service and its acceptance, produced an almost universal reprobation of its rashness, from the sea-faring men of the port.   And while all acknowledged that the enterprise could not have been committed to a more able or skilful mariner than Abe, yet it was declared to be the endeavor of a fool-hardy madman who was rushing on his fate.   The expression of such distrust only operated as an additional stimulant to Abe's resolution, and served to hurry him, the more urgently forward, to the execution of his purpose.   He, therefore, with such dispatch as the nature of his preparations allowed, mustered his intrepid crew in the harbor of Norfolk, and repaired with them to the opposite shore of the James River, to the little sea-port, where my reader has already seen him embarking upon his brave voyage, amidst the disheartening auguries of wise and disciplined veterans of the sea.

I might stop to compare this act of an humble and unknown negro, upon the Chesapeake, with the many similar passages in the lives of heroes whose names have been preserved fresh in the verdure of history, and who have won their immortality upon less noble feats than this; but History is a step-mother, and gives the bauble fame to her own children, with such favoritism as she lists, overlooking many a goodly portion of the family of her husband Time.   Still, it was a gallant thing, and worthy of a better chronicler than I, to see this leader and his little band—the children of a despised stock—swayed by a noble emulation to relieve the distressed; and (what the fashion of the world will deem a higher glory) impelled by that love of daring which the romancers call chivalry—throwing themselves upon the unruly waves of winter, and flying, on the wing of the storm, into the profound, dark abyss of ocean, when all his terrors were gathering in their most hideous forms; when the spirit of ill shrieked in the blast, and thick night, dreary with unusual horrors, was falling close around them; when old mariners grew pale with the thought of the danger, and the wisest counselled the adventurers against the certain doom that hung upon their path:—I say, it was a gallant sight to see such heroism shining out in an humble slave of the Old Dominion!

They·say the night that followed was a night of the wildest horrors. Not a star twinkled in the black heavens: the winds rushed forth, like some pent-up flood suddenly overbearing its barriers, and swept through the air with palpable density: men, who chanced to wander at that time, found it difficult to keep their footing on the land: the steeples of Norfolk groaned with the unwonted pressure; chimneys were blown from their seats; houses were unroofed, and the howling elements terrified those who were gathered around their own hearths, and made them silent with fear: the pious fell upon their knees: nurses could not hush their children to sleep: bold-hearted revellers were dismayed, and broke up their meetings: the crash of trees, fences, out-buildings mingled with the ravings of the tempest: the icicles were swept from the eaves, and from every penthouse, till they fell in the streets like hail: ships were stranded at the wharves, or were lifted, by an unnatural tide, into the streets: the ocean roared with more terrific bass than the mighty wind, and threw its spray into the near heaven, with which it seemed in contact: and, as anxious seamen looked out at intervals during the night, towards the Atlantic, the light-house, that usually shot its ray over the deep, was invisible to their gaze, or seemed only by glimp-ses, like a little star immeasurably remote, wading through foam and darkness.

What became of our argonauts?—The next morning told the tale. One seaman alone of the brig survived to relate the fate of

his companions. In the darkest hour of the night their vessel
went to pieces, and every soul on board perished, except this man.
He had bound himself to a spar, and, by that miraculous fortune
which the frequent history of shipwreck recounts, he was thrown
upon the beach near Cape Henry.   Bruised, chafed. and almost
dead, he was discovered in the morning and carried to a neighboring house, where care and nursing restored him to his strength.
All that this mariner could tell was, that early in the night,—
perhaps about eight o'clock,—and before the storm had risen to
its height, (although, at that hour, it raged with fearful vehemence,)
a light was seen gliding, with the swiftness of a meteor, past the
wreck ; a hailing cry was heard as from a trumpet, but the wind
smothered its tones and rendered them inarticulate ; and, in the
next moment, the spectre of a sail (for no one of the sufferers believed it real) flitted by them, as with a rush of wings, so close
that some affirmed they could have touched it with their hands :
that, about an hour afterwards, the same hideous phantom, with
the same awful salutation, was seen and heard by many on board,
a second time : that the crew, terrified by this warning, made all
preparations to meet their fate ; and when at last, in the highest
exasperation of the storm, the same apparition made its third
visit, the timbers of the brig parted at every joint, and all, except the relator himself, were supposed to have been ingulfed
in the wave, and given to instant death.
    Such, was the sum of this man's story. What was subsequent-
ly known, proved its most horrible conjecture to be fatally true.
    Various speculation was indulged, during the first week after
this disaster. as to the destiny of Abe and his companions.   No
tidings having arrived, some affirmed that nothing more would
ever be heard of them.   Others said that they might have luffed
up close in the wind and ridden out the night, as the Flying Fish
was stanch and true : others, again, held that there was even a

chance, that they had scudded before the gale, and, having good
sea-room, had escaped into the middle of the Atlantic. No vessels appeared upon the coast for several days, and the hope of
receiving news of Abe, was not abandoned.

The next week came and went. There were arrivals, but no
word of the Flying Fish. Anxiety began to give way to the conviction that all were lost. But, when the third week passed over,
and commerce grew frequent, as the spring advanced, all doubts
were abandoned, and the loss of the Flying Fish and her crew,
ceased any longer to furnish topics of discussion.

My reader must now get back to Swallow Barn. The story
of Abe's adventure had reached the plantation, greatly exaggerated
in all the details; none of which were concealed from Lucy. On
the contrary, the wonder-loving women of the Quarter daily reported to her additional particulars, filled with extravagant
marvels, in which, so far from manifesting a desire to soothe the
feelings of the mother and reconcile her to the doom of Abe, all
manner of appalling circumstances were added, as if for the pleasure of giving a higher gust to the tale.

It may appear unaccountable, but it was the fact, that Lucy,
instead of giving herself up to such grief as might have been expected from her attachment to her son, received the intelligence
even with composure. She shed no tears, and scarcely deserted
her customary occupations. She was remarked only to have
become more solitary in her habits, and to evince an urgent and
eager solicitude to hear whatever came from Norfolk, or from the
Chesapeake. Scarcely a stranger visited Swallow Barn, for some
months after the event I have recounted, that the old woman did
not take an occasion to hold some conversation with him ; in which
all her inquiries tended to the tidings which might have existed
of the missing seamen.

As time rolled on, Lucy's anxiety seemed rather to increase ;

and it wrought severely upon her health. She was observed to be falling fast into the weakness and decrepitude of age: her temper grew fretful, and her pursuits still more lonesome. Frequently, she shut herself up in her cabin for a week or a fortnight, during which periods she refused to be seen by any one. And now, tears began to visit her withered cheeks. Meriwether made frequent efforts to reason her out of this painful melancholy; her reply to all his arguments was uniformly the same;—it was simple and affecting—" I cannot give him up, master Frank !"

In this way a year elapsed; but, with its passage, came no confirmation to Lucy's mind of the fate of her son; and so far was time from bringing an assuagement of her grief, that it only cast a more permanent dejection over her mind. She spoke continually upon the subject of Abe's return, whenever she conversed with any one; and her fancy was filled with notions of preternatural warnings, which she had received in dreams, and in her solitary communings with herself. The females of the family at Swallow Barn exercised the most tender assiduities towards the old servant, and directed all their persuasions to impress upon her the positive certainty of the loss of Abe; they endeavored to lift up her perception to the consolations of religion,—but the insuperable difficulty which they found in the way of all attempts to comfort her, was the impossibility of convincing her that the case was, even yet, hopeless. That dreadful suspense of the mind, when it trembles in the balance between a mother's instinctive love for her offspring, on the one side, and the thought of its perdition on the other, was more than the philosophy or resignation of an ignorant old negro woman could overcome. It was to her the sickness of the heart that belongs to hope deferred,—and the more poignant, because the subject of it was incapable of even that moderate and common share of reason that would have intelligently weighed the facts of the case.

Months were now added to the year of unavailing regrets that had been spent. No one ever heard Lucy say wherefore, but all knew that she still reckoned Abe's return amongst expected events. It was now, in the vain thought that the old woman's mind would yield to the certainty implied by the lapse of time and the absence of tidings, that my cousin Lucretia prepared a suit of mourning for her, and sent it, with an exhortation that she would wear it in commemoration of the death of her son. Meriwether laid some stress upon this device; for, he said, grief was a selfish emotion, and had some strange alliance with vanity.—It was a metaphysical conceit of his, which was founded in deep observation; and he looked to see it illustrated in the effect of the mourning present upon Lucy. She took the dress—it was of some fine bombazet,—gazed at it, with a curious and melancholy eye, and then shook her head and said,—it was a mistake:—" I will never put on that dress," she observed, " because it would be bad luck to Abe. What would Abe say if he was to catch mammy Lucy wearing black clothes for him ?"

They left the dress with her, and she was seen to put it carefully away. Some say that she was observed in her cabin, one morning soon after this, through the window, dressed out in this suit; but she was never known to wear it at any other time. About this period, she began to give manifest indications of a decay of reason. This was first exhibited in unusual wanderings, by night, into the neighboring wood; and then, by a growing habit of speaking and singing to herself. With the loss of her mind her frame still wasted away, and she gradually began to lose her erect position.

Amongst the eccentric and painful developments of her increasing aberration of mind, was one which presented the predominating illusion that beset her in an unusually vivid point of view.

One dark and blustering night of winter, the third anniversary of that on which Abe had sailed upon his desperate voyage,—for Lucy had noted the date, although others had not,—near midnight, the inhabitants of the Quarter were roused from their respective cabins by loud knockings in succession at their doors ; and when each was opened, there stood the decrepit figure of old Lucy, who was thus making a circuit to invite her neighbors, as she said, to her house.

"He has come back !" said Lucy to each one, as they loosed their bolts; "he has come back ! I always told you he would come back upon this very night! Come and see him ! Come and see him ! Abe is waiting to see his friends to-night."

Either awed by the superstitious feeling that a maniac inspires in the breasts of the ignorant, or incited by curiosity, most of the old negroes followed Lucy to her cabin. As they approached it, the windows gleamed with a broad light, and it was with some strange sensations of terror that they assembled at her threshold, where she stood upon the step, with her hand upon the latch. Before she opened the door to admit her wondering guests, she applied her mouth to the keyhole, and said in an audible whisper, " Abe, the people are all ready to see you, honey ! Don't be frightened,—there's nobody will do you harm !"

Then, turning towards her companions, she said, bowing her head,—

" Come in, good folks ! There's plenty for you all. Come in and see how he is grown !"

She now threw open the door, and, followed by the rest, entered the room. There was a small table set out, covered with a sheet; and upon it three or four candles were placed in bottles for candlesticks. All the chairs she had were ranged around this table, and a bright fire blazed in the hearth.

" Speak to them, Abe !" said the old woman, with a broad

laugh. " This is uncle Jeff, and here is Dinah, and here is Ben,"
—and in this manner she ran over the names of all present ; then
continued,—

" Sit down, you negroes ! Have you no manners ? Sit down
and eat as much as you choose; there is plenty in the house.
Mammy Lucy knew Abe was coming: and see what a fine feast
she has made for him !"

She now seated herself, and addressing an empty chair beside
her, as if some one occupied it, lavished upon the imaginary Abe
a thousand expressions of solicitude and kindness. At length
she said,—

" The poor boy is tired, for he has not slept these many long
nights. You must leave him now :—he will go to bed. Get you
gone ! get you gone ! you have all eaten enough !"

Dismayed and wrought upon by the unnatural aspect of the
scene, the party of visitors quitted the cabin almost immediately
upon the command ; and the crazed old menial was left alone to
indulge her sad communion with the vision of her fancy.

From that time until the period at which I saw her, she continued occasionally to exhibit the same evidences of insanity.
There were intervals, however, in which she appeared almost
restored to her reason. During one of these, some of the negroes
hoping to remove the illusion that Abe was still alive, brought
her a handkerchief resembling that which she had given to him
on his first departure ; and, in delivering it to her, reported a
fabricated tale, that it had been taken from around the neck of
Abe, by a sailor who had seen the body washed up by the tide
upon the beach of the sea, and had sent this relic to Lucy as a
token of her son's death. She seemed, at last, to believe the
tale ; and took the handkerchief and put it away in her bosom.
This event only gave a more sober tone to her madness. She
now keeps more closely over her hearth, where she generally

passes the livelong day, in the posture in which we found her. Sometimes she is heard muttering to herself,—" They buried his body in the sands of the sea," which she will repeat a hundred times. At others, she falls into a sad but whimsical speculation, the drift of which is implied in the question that she put to Meriwether whilst we remained in her cottage;—" How many years may a ship sail at sea without stopping?"

CHAPTER XLVIII.

CLOUDS.

THE time had now arrived when it was necessary for me to return to New-York. It was almost two months since I had left
home, and I was cautioned by my northern friends not to remain
in the low-country of Virginia longer than until the middle of
August. Hazard endeavored to persuade me that the season had
all the indications of being unusually healthy, and that I might
therefore remain without risk. He had manifestly views of his
own to be improved by my delay, which rendered him rather an
interested adviser; and, in truth, we had grown so intimate by
our late associations, that I felt it somewhat difficult to bring myself to the necessary resolution of taking leave. But go I must
—or inflict upon my good mother and sisters that feminine torture which visits the bosoms of this solicitous sex when once
their apprehensions are excited on any question of health. I
therefore announced my fixed determination on the subject to the
family, and pertinaciously met all the arguments which were
directed to unsettle my resolve, with that hardy denial of assent
which is the only refuge of a man in such a case. My preparations were made, and the day of my departure was named.

Unluckily for my plan, the elements made war against it.
The very day before my allotted time, there came on a soft

drizzling rain, which began soon after breakfast; and when we met at dinner, Hazard came to me, rubbing his hands and smiling with a look of triumph, to tell me that however obstinate I might be in my purpose, here was a flat interdict upon it.

" We generally have," said he, " what we call a long spell in August. The rain has begun; and you may consider yourself fortunate if you get away in a week." I took it as a jest; but the next morning, when I went to my chamber-window, I found that Ned's exultation was not without some reason. It had rained all night, not in hard showers, but in that gentle, noiseless outpouring of the heavens, which showed that they meant to take their own time to disburthen themselves of their vapor. Far as my eye could reach, the firmament was clad in one broad, heavy, gray robe. The light was equally diffused over this mass, so as entirely to conceal the position of the sun; and, somewhat nearer to earth, small detachments of dun clouds floated across the sky in swift transit, as if hastening to find their place in the ranks of the sombre army near the horizon. I came down to breakfast, where the family were assembled at a much later hour than usual. A small fire was burning in the hearth : the ladies were in undress, and something of the complexion of the sky seemed to have settled upon the countenances of all around me; —a quiet, unelastic, sober considerateness, that was not so frequently disturbed as before with outbreaks of merriment. My cousin Lucretia poured out our coffee with a more sedate and careful attention: Prudence looked as if she had overslept herself:—Meriwether hung longer over the newspaper than common, and permitted us to take our seats at table some time before he gave up reading the news. The little girls had a world of care upon their shoulders ;—and Parson Chub dispatched his meal with unwonted expedition, and then, thrusting his hands into his pockets, went into the hall, and walked to and fro thoughtfully.

Hazard was the only one of the party who appeared untouched by the change of the weather; and he kept his spirits up by frequent sallies of felicitation directed to me, on the auspicious prospect I had before me.

After breakfast, we went to the door. The rain pattered industriously from the eaves down upon the rose-bushes. The gravel walk was intersected by little rivers that also ran along its borders; and the grass-plots were filled with lakes. The old willow, saturated with rain, wept profuse tears, down every trickling fibre, upon the ground. The ducks were gathered at the foot of this venerable monument, and rested in profound quiet, with their heads under their wings. Beyond the gate, an old plough-horse spent his holiday from labor in undisturbed idleness—his head downcast, his tail close to his rump and his position motionless, as some inanimate thing, only giving signs of life by an occasional slow lifting up of his head—as if to observe the weather —and a short, horse-like sneeze.

The rain poured on; and now and then some one affirmed that it grew brighter, and that, perhaps, at mid-day it would clear up. But mid-day came, and the same continual dripping fell from leaf, and roof, and fence. There was neither light nor shade : all the picturesque had vanished from the landscape : the foreground was full of falling drops, and the perspective was mist. The dogs crept beneath the porch, or intruded with their shaggy and rain-besprinkled coats, into the hall, leaving their footsteps marked upon the floor wherever they walked. The negro women ran across the yard with their aprons thrown over their heads. The working men moved leisurely along, like sable water-gods, dripping from every point, their hats softened into cloth-like consistence, and their faces beneath them long, sober, and trist. During the day Rip made frequent-excursions out of doors, and returned into the house with shoes covered with mud, much to the annoyance of

Mrs. Winkle, who kept up a quick and galling fire of reproof upon the young scapegrace. As for Hazard and myself, we betook ourselves to the library, whither Meriwether had gone before us, and there rambled through the thousand flowery by-paths of miscellaneous literature ; changing our topics of study every moment, and continually interrupting each other by reading aloud whatever passages occurred to provoke a laugh. This grew tedious in turn; and then we repaired to the drawing-room, where we found the ladies in a similar unquiet mood, making the like experiments upon the piano. We were all nervous.

Thus came and went the day. The next was no better. When I again looked out in the morning, there stood the weeping willow the same vegetable Niobe as before, and there the meditative ducks; there the same horse,—or another like him —looking into the inscrutable recesses of a fence corner; and there the dogs, and the muddy-footed Rip. To vary the scene, we took umbrellas and walked out, holding our way trippingly over the wet path towards the bridge. The pigeons, like ourselves, tired of keeping the house, had ranged themselves upon the top of the stable, or on the perches before the doors of their own domicil, dripping images of disconsolateness. A stray flock of blackbirds sometimes ventured across the welkin ; and the cows, in defiance of the damp earth, had composedly lain down in the mud. The only living thing who seemed to feel no inconvenience from the season was the hog, who pursued his epicurean ramble in despite of the elements.

The rain poured on; and the soaked field and drenched forest had no pleasure in our eyes; so, we returned to the house, and again took refuge in the library. Despairing of the sun, I at length sat down to serious study, and soon found myself occupied in a pursuit that engrossed all my attention.

I have said before that Meriwether had a good collection of

books. These had been brought together without order in the selection, and they presented a mass of curious literature in almost every department of knowledge. My love of the obsolete led me amongst the heavy folios and quartos that lumbered the lower shelves of the library, where I pitched upon a thin, tall folio, which contained the following pithy title-page: " Some account of the Renowned Captayne John Smith, with his travel and adventures in the Foure Quarters of the Earthe ; showing his gallante Portaunce in divers perillous Chaunces, both by Sea and Land : his Feats against the Turke, and his dolefull Captivitie in Tartaria. Also, what befell in his Endeavours towards the Planting of the Colonie of Virginia; and, in especiall, his Marvellous Prouess and Incredible Escapes amongst the Barbarous Salvages. Together with Sundrie other Moving Accidents in his Historie. London. Imprinted for Edward Blackmore, 162—."

This title was set out in many varieties of type, and occupied but a small portion of the page, being encompassed by a broad margin which was richly illuminated with a series of heraldic ornaments, amongst which was conspicuous the shield with three turbaned heads and the motto " vincere est vivere." There were, also, graphic representations of soldiers, savages, and trees, all colored according to nature, and, as the legend at the foot imported, " graven by John Barra."

The date of the work had been partially obliterated,—three numerals of the year being only distinguishable ; but from these it was apparent that this memoir was published somewhere about the end of the first quarter of the seventeenth century—perhaps about 1625, or not later than 1629.

The exploits of Captain Smith had a wonderful charm for that period of my life when the American Nepos supplied the whole amount of my reading; but I have never, since that boy-

ish day, taken the trouble to inquire whether I was indebted for
the captivation of the story to the events it recorded, or to my
own pleasant credulity,—that natural stomach for the marvellous, which, in early youth, will digest agate and steel. This little chronicle, therefore, came most opportunely in my way; and
I gave myself up to the perusal of it with an eager appetite.

I was now on the spot where Smith had achieved some of his
most gallant wonders. The narrative was no longer the mere
fable that delighted my childhood; but here I had it in its most
authentic form, with the identical print, paper and binding in
which the story was first given to the world by its narrator—for
aught that I knew, the Captain himself—perhaps the Captain's
good friend, old Sam Purchas, who had such a laudable thirst for
the wonderful. This was published, too, when thousands were
living to confute the author if he falsified in any point.

And here, on a conspicuous page, was " An Exact Portraic-
tuer of Captayne Iohn Smith, Admiral of all New England,"
taken to the life ; with his lofty brow that imported absolute verity on the face of it, and his piercing eye, and fine phrenological
head, with a beard of the ancient spade cut; arrayed in his proper doublet, with gorget and ruff; one arm a-kimbo, the other
resting on his sword. Below the picture were some fair lines inferring that he " was brass without, and gold within." Throughout the volume, moreover, were sundry cuts showing the Captain
in his most imminent hazards, of a flattering fancy, but in total
disregard of all perspective. And here, in view of the window,
was the broad James River, upon which he and his faithful
Mosco (otherwise called by the more euphonious name of Utta-
santasough), two hundred years gone by, had sailed, in defiance
of twenty kings whose very names I am afraid to write. History is never so charming as under the spell of such associations ;
the narrative avouched by present monuments, and facts suffi-

ciently dim by distance, for the imagination to make what it pleases out of it, without impugning the veracity of the story.

I have sometimes marvelled why our countrymen, and especially those of Virginia, have not taken more pains to exalt the memory of Smith. With the exception of the little summary of the schools, that I have before noticed,—and which is unfortunately falling into disuse,—some general references to his exploits as they are connected with the history of our States, and an almost forgotten memoir by Stith, we have nothing to record the early adventures and chivalric virtues of the good soldier, unless it be some such obsolete and quaint chronicle as this of Swallow Barn, which no one sees. He deserves to be popularly known for his high public spirit, and to have his life illustrated in some well told tale that should travel with Robinson Crusoe and the Almanack—at least through the Old Dominion:—and in the Council Chamber at Richmond, or in the Hall of Delegates, the doughty champion should be exhibited on canvas in some of his most picturesque conjunctures. And then, he should be lifted to that highest of all glorifications,—the truest touchstone of renown,— the signposts.

Smith's character was moulded in the richest fashion of ancient chivalry; and, without losing any thing of romance, was dedicated, in his maturer years, to the useful purposes of life. It was marked by great devotion to his purpose, a generous estimate of the public good, and an utter contempt of danger. In the age in which he lived, nobleness of birth was an essential condition to fame. This, unfortunately for the renown of Smith, he did not possess; otherwise, he would have been as distinguished in history as Bayard, Gaston de Foix, Sir Walter Manny, or any other of the mirrors of knighthood whose exploits have found a historian. Smith, however, was poor, and was obliged to carve his way to fame without the aid of chroniclers; and there is, consequently, a great obscurity resting upon the meagre details which now exist of his wonderful adventures.   These rude records show a perplexing ignorance of geography, which defies all attempts at elucidation.   Muniments, however, of unquestionable authenticity, still exist to confirm the most remarkable prodigies of his story. The patent of knighthood conferred upon him by Sigismund Bathor, in 1603, is of this character.   It recites some of the leading events of his life, and was admitted to record by the Garter King-at-arms of Great Britain, twenty-two years afterwards, when Smith's services in the establishment of the American colonies attracted a share of the public attention.

He possessed many of the points of a true knight.   He was ambitious of honor, yet humble in his own praise,—tempering his valor with modesty, and the reckless gallantry of the cavalier with irreproachable manners.   A simple testimony to this effect, but a sincere one, is given by an old soldier who had followed him through many dangers, and who shared with him the disasters of the defeat at Rothenturn.   It is appended, by the author of it, to Smith's account of New England.   His name was Carlton, and he had served as Smith's ensign in the wars of Transylvania. These lines, addressed to the " honest Captaine," are somewhat crabbed, but they tell pleasantly—

> " Thy words by deeds, so long thou hast approved,
> Of thousands know thee not, thou art beloved.
> And this great Plot will make thee ten times more
> Knowne and beloved than e'er thou wert before.
> I never knew a warrior yet but thee,
> From wine, tobacco, debts, dice, oaths so free.
> *   *   *   *   *   *   *   *   *

He signs himself,

> " Your true friend, sometime your souldier,
>
>   THO. CARLTON "

The uncouthness of the verse accords with the station of the writer, and gives a greater relish to the compliment.

It may be pleasing to the fair portion of my readers, to learn something of his devotion to dames and lady-love, of which we have good proof. He was so courteous and gentle, that he might be taken for a knight sworn to the sex's service. He was a bachelor too, by 'r lady!—and an honor to his calling; mingling the refinement of Sir Walter Raleigh, his prototype, with the noble daring of Essex and Howard. Hear with what suavity and knightly zeal he commends his gratitude to the sex, in recounting his various fortunes " to the illustrious and most noble Princesse, The Lady Francis, Duchesse of Richmond and Lenox;" and with what winning phrase, like a modest cavalier, he consigns his History of Virginia to her protection!—

" I confess my hand, though able to wield a weapon among the Barbarous, yet well may tremble in handliug a pen among so many judicious: especially, when I am so bold as to call so piercing and so glorious an Eye, as your Grace, to view these poore ragged lines. Yet my comfort is, that heretofore, honorable and vertuous Ladies, and comparable but amongst themselves, have offered me rescue and protection in my greatest dangers: even in forraine parts, I have felt relief from that sex. The beauteous Lady Tragabizanda, when I was a slave to the Turkes, did all she could to secure me. When I overcame the Bashaw of Nalbritz in Tartaria, the charitable Lady Callamata supplyed my necessities. In the utmost of many extremities, that blessed Pokahontas, the great King's daughter of Virginia, oft saved my life. When I escaped the cruelties of Pirats and most furious stormes, a long time alone, in a small boat at Sea, and driven ashore in France, the good Lady, Madam Chanoyes, bountifully assisted me.

" And so verily, these adventures have tasted the same influence from your Gratious hand, which hath given birth to the publication of this narration." And, thereupon, he prays that his " poore booke," which had " no helpe but the Shrine of her glorious name to be sheltered from censorious condemnation," might be taken under her protection; and "that she would vouchsafe some glimpse of her honorable aspect to accept his labours," that they might be presented "to the King's Royall Majestie, the most admired Prince Charles, and the Queene of Bohemia."

He tells her that "her sweet Recommendations would make it worthier their good countenances," and concludes by assuring her, "that this page should record to Posteritie that his service should be to pray to God that she might still continue the Renowned of her Sexe, the most honored of Men, and The Highly Blessed of God."

What a fine knightly tone is there in this commendation of the graces of his mistress, and what a world of adventure does it suggest!

After a whole morning of pleasant study I closed the Chronicle and restored it to its shelf, with a renewed admiration of the sturdy and courteous cavalier who is so pre-eminently entitled to be styled the True Knight of the Old Dominion.

The character of Smith, like the extraordinary incidents of his life, strikes me as approaching nearer to the invention of a fiction than that of any other real personage of history. There is in it so much plain sense, mingled with such glory of manhood; so much homely wisdom and dauntless bravery combined—so much chivalrous adventure, set off with so much honesty; so much humility, and yet so much to boast of—if his nature were vainglorious:—these qualities are all so well balanced in his composition that they have an epic consistency, and seem more like an imagination, than a reality. It puts one in mind of Chaucer's Knight, whose description, though often quoted, will bear a repetition here, for its singular application to the history of the founder of Virginia.

> " A knight there was, and that a worthy man,
> That fro the time that he firste began
> To riden out, he loved chevalrie,
> Trouthe and honour, fredom and curtesie.——

At mortal batailes hadde he ben fiftene,
And foughten for our faith at Tramissene
In listes thries, and ay slain his fo.
This ilke worthy knight hadde ben also
Somtime with the lord of Palatie,
Agen another hethen in Turkie :
And evermore he hadde a sovereine pris.
And though that he was worthy he was wise,
And of his port as meke as is a mayde,
He never yet no vilaine ne sayde
In alle his lif, unto no manere wight.
He was a veray parfit, gentil knight."

CHAPTER XLIX.

ANOTHER morning came. The rain had ceased, and nature, after her three days of drab sobriety, appeared once more in her gay and gallant apparel of sunshine and flowers. The air had grown cooler. The verdure of the fields was revived. The birds sang with unwonted vivacity, as if in compensation for long pent-up melodies. The change of weather was like the bursting forth of a new spring. My spirits were attuned to this renovation of earth and air, by the prospect of returning home—for having once set my thoughts in that direction, the pleasure of the return rose above the regrets of parting with friends here, or so mingled with them as to divide the mastery of the contest.

I had determined that my homeward journey should be inland, and my design, therefore, was to take the public stage from Petersburg, thence to Richmond, Fredericksburg, and Washington.

Soon after breakfast, Meriwether's carriage was at the door to transport me as far as the first of the towns mentioned above. I found that my cousin Lucretia had provided me a store of refreshment sufficient to have sustained me all the way to New-York. This was neatly put up in a basket, and placed in the carriage, on the plea that I might be hungry upon my journey;

or, at all events, that I might not find as good fare at the inns as I desired. It was in vain to refuse; " the stages were long, and no one knew the comfort of being well stocked with such necessaries until he was on the road." I submitted with a good grace, resolved to leave what was given me in the carriage, when I arrived at Petersburg.

And now came the moment of leave-taking, the most painful of all the accompaniments of travel. If I had been nurtured in the family from infancy, I could not have called forth more affectionate solicitude; and I was obliged to promise, what already was indeed my secret purpose, to repeat my visit. Meriwether expressed the kindest concern at my leaving him, and engaged, what was quite unusual for him, to write to me frequently after I should arrive at home. The little girls kissed me a dozen times, and the whole household, servants and all, collected at the door to exchange farewells. Ned Hazard now sprang into the carriage with me, and we drove off.

That night I arrived at Petersburg. Hazard and I parted here the next morning, with many vows of friendship.

In due course of time, I was safely seated at Longsides, upon the North River, where I have become famous, at least with my mother and sisters, for my long stories and rapturous commendations of Swallow Barn, and my peremptory way of telling how things are done in the Old Dominion.

POSTSCRIPT.

In the course of the winter that followed my return to Longsides, I received several letters from Hazard, from Meriwether, and, indeed, from most of the family. Harvey Riggs, also, has been a punctual correspondent. A letter from him, dated the tenth of January, 1830, gives me a droll history of the festivities at The Brakes on the first day of the year, when, in pursuance of an arrangement which Ned himself had before communicated to me, Hazard and Bel were joined in the bands of holy wedlock, Bel having, at last, surrendered at discretion. Harvey's comments upon this incident are expressed in the following extract:—

" After you left us, Ned relapsed into all his extravagancies. In truth, I believe Bel grew heartily tired of that incompatible formality of manner which he assumed at our instigation. It sat upon him like an ill-fitted garment, and rendered him the dullest of mortals. Bel took the matter into consideration, and at last begged him to be himself again. Never did a schoolboy enjoy a holiday more than he this freedom; the consequence was, that the wight ran immediately into the opposite extreme, and has carried the prize, notwithstanding he had trespassed against all decorum, and had been voted incorrigible. The stars have had an influence upon this match ! I devoutly believe that it all comes from old Diana's prophecy.

" Meriwether discourses philosophically upon the subject, and says that ' marriage is a matter to be soberly looked at ; for if it be unwisely contrived, it is one of the most irrevocable errors in the world, though not the most unlikely to have its full share of repentance.' "

The revelry had scarcely ceased at the date of this letter ; and it was a part of the family plans that Ned should live, for the present, at The Brakes.

Accounts as late as April inform me, that Philly Wart has just been re-elected to the Legislature, much against his wish, and, indeed, in the face of his protestations that he declined a poll. He is said to have remarked, rather petulantly, at the close of the election, " that it was all nonsense to argue the question of constitutional doctrine,—here was a case in point,—the will of the constituent will bind the representative in spite of all theories !.

The worthy barrister had, a short time before, covered himself with glory by one of his most flowery speeches at the bar, in defending his brother, Toll Hedges, upon an indictment for an assault on one of the justices of the quorum.

It is at a still later date that Ned writes me touching the affairs at The Brakes. Mr. Tracy had not yet become reconciled to the extinction of the lawsuit. Ned accompanied him lately upon his morning ride, and the old gentleman took his course to the Apple-pie. Here, as Ned describes him, he took a stand upon the mound that formed one of the abutments of the dam, and remained silently pondering over the landscape for a full half hour, and, most of the time, tugging at his under lip with his hand. " It was singular," he remarked to Hazard, after this interval, " that Meriwether should have fallen into the error of thinking that he had a claim to this land. I have a mind to give him my ideas on paper. It will be instructive to you, Mr. Hazard."

" Frank stood upon his survey" replied Ned.

" I doubt if there was a survey," rejoined the old gentleman ; " there is no memorandum of it in my notes."

Ned was almost afraid to contradict him ; but at length ventured to say,—

" It was produced, you remember, at the trial, signed by Jeremiah Perkins himself."

Mr. Tracy knitted his brows for a moment, and then said, " It is very strange ! I don't think there was a survey.   There is some mistake.   I wish the thing were to go over again !"

The tenor of all my letters now shows that every thing goes on smoothly on the James River, and that the Old Dominion contains some very happy persons within its bosom.

THE END.